pandemonium

Also by Lauren Oliver

BEFORE I FALL

DELIRIUM

HANA: A DELIRIUM SHORT STORY
(an original eBook)

For younger readers
LIESL & PO

Visit
www.laurenoliverbooks.com www.hodder.co.uk/crossover
for the latest news, competitions
and exclusive material from Lauren Oliver.

pandemonium

LAUREN OLIVER

HODDER &
STOUGHTON

First published in America in 2012 by HarperCollins Children's Books
A division of HarperCollins Publishers
First published in Great Britain in 2012 by Hodder & Stoughton
An Hachette UK company

2

A CIP catalogue record for this title is available from the British Library

Hardback 978 1 444 72292 5
Trade paperback 978 1 444 72293 2
eBook 978 1 444 72294 9

Typeset in Sabon by Palimpsest Book Production Limited, Falkirk, Stirlingshire

Printed and bound by Clays Ltd, St Ives plc

Hodder & Stoughton policy is to use papers that are natural, renewable and recyclable products and made from wood grown in sustainable forests. The logging and manufacturing processes are expected to conform to the environmental regulations of the country of origin.

Hodder & Stoughton Ltd
338 Euston Road
London NW1 3BH

www.hodder.co.uk

To my parents:
Thank you for all the books, phone calls,
free meals, endless patience, and boundless love.

now

Alex and I are lying together on a blanket in the back-yard of 37 Brooks. The trees look larger and darker than usual. The leaves are almost black, knitted so tightly together they blot out the sky.

'It probably wasn't the best day for a picnic,' Alex says, and just then I realize that yes, of course, we haven't eaten any of the food we brought. There's a basket at the foot of the blanket, filled with half-rotten fruit, swarmed by tiny black ants.

'Why not?' I say. We are staring at the web of leaves above us, thick as a wall.

'Because it's snowing.' Alex laughs. And again I realize he's right: it is snowing, thick flakes the colour of ash swirling all around us. It's freezing cold, too. My breath comes in clouds, and I press against him, trying to stay warm.

'Give me your arm,' I say, but Alex doesn't respond. I try to move into the space between his arm and his chest but his body is rigid, unyielding. 'Alex,' I say. 'Come on, I'm cold.'

'I'm cold,' he parrots, from lips that barely move. They are blue, and cracked. He is staring at the leaves without blinking.

'Look at me,' I say, but he doesn't turn his head, doesn't blink, doesn't move at all. A hysterical feeling is building inside me, a shrieking voice saying *wrong, wrong, wrong,* and I sit up and place my hand on Alex's chest, as cold as ice. 'Alex,' I say, and then, a short scream: 'Alex!'

'Lena Morgan Jones!'

I snap into awareness, to a muted chorus of giggles.

Mrs. Fierstein, the twelfth-grade science teacher at Quincy Edwards High School for Girls in Brooklyn, Section 5, District 17, is glaring at me. This is the third time I've fallen asleep in her class this week.

'Since you seem to find the Creation of the Natural Order so exhausting,' she says, 'might I suggest a trip to the principal's office to wake you up?'

'No!' I burst out, louder than I intended to, provoking a new round of giggles from the other girls in my class. I've been enrolled at Edwards since just after winter break – only a little more than two months – and already I've been labelled the Number-One Weirdo. People avoid me like I have a disease – like I have *the* disease.

If only they knew.

'This is your final warning, Miss Jones,' Mrs. Fierstein says. 'Do you understand?'

'It won't happen again,' I say, trying to look obedient and contrite. I'm pushing aside the memory of my nightmare, pushing aside thoughts of Alex, pushing aside thoughts of Hana and my old school, push, push, push, like Raven taught me to do. The old life is dead.

Mrs. Fierstein gives me a final stare – meant to intimidate

me, I guess – and turns back to the board, returning to her lecture on the divine energy of electrons.

The old Lena would have been terrified of a teacher like Mrs. Fierstein. She's old, and mean, and looks like a cross between a frog and a pit bull. She's one of those people who makes the cure seem redundant – it's impossible to imagine that she would ever be capable of loving, even without the procedure.

But the old Lena is dead too.

I buried her.

I left her beyond a fence, behind a wall of smoke and flame.

then

In the beginning, there is fire.

Fire in my legs and lungs; fire tearing through every nerve and cell in my body. That's how I am born again, in pain: I emerge from the suffocating heat and the darkness. I force my way through a black, wet space of strange noises and smells.

I run, and when I can no longer run, I limp, and when I can't do that, I crawl, inch by inch, digging my fingernails into the soil, like a worm sliding across the overgrown surface of this strange new wilderness.

I bleed, too, when I am born.

I'm not sure how far I've travelled into the Wilds, and how long I've been pushing deeper and deeper into the woods, when I realize I've been hit. At least one regulator must have clipped me while I was climbing the fence. A bullet has skimmed me on the side, just below my armpit, and my T-shirt is wet with blood. I'm lucky, though. The wound is shallow, but seeing all the blood, the missing skin, makes everything real:

this new place, this monstrous, massive growth everywhere, what has happened, what I have left.

What has been taken from me.

There is nothing in my stomach, but I throw up anyway. I cough up air and spit bile into the flat, shiny leaves on either side of me. Birds twitter above me. An animal, coming to investigate, scurries quickly back into the tangle of growth.

Think, think. Alex. Think of what Alex would do.

Alex is here, right here. Imagine.

I take off my shirt, rip off the hem, and tie the cleanest bit tightly around my chest so it presses against my wound and helps stanch the bleeding. I have no idea where I am or where I'm going. My only thought is to move, keep going, deeper and deeper, away from the fences and the world of dogs and guns and—

Alex.

No. Alex is here. You have to imagine.

Step by step, fighting thorns, bees, mosquitoes; snapping back thick, broad branches; clouds of gnats, mists hovering in the air. At one point, I reach a river: I am so weak, I am nearly taken under by its current. At night, driving rain, fierce and cold: huddled between the roots of an enormous oak, while around me unseen animals scream and pant and rattle through the darkness. I'm too terrified to sleep; if I sleep, I'll die.

I am not born all at once, the new Lena.

Step by step – and then, inch by inch.

Crawling, insides curled into dust, mouth full of the taste of smoke.

Fingernail by fingernail, like a worm.

That is how she comes into the world, the new Lena.

*   *   *

When I can no longer go forward, even by an inch, I lay my head on the ground and wait to die. I'm too tired to be frightened. Above me is blackness, and all around me is blackness, and the forest sounds are a symphony to sing me out of this world. I am already at my funeral. I am being lowered into a narrow, dark space, and my aunt Carol is there, and Hana, and my mother and sister and even my long-dead father. They are all watching my body descend into the grave, and they are singing.

I am in a black tunnel filled with mist, and I am not afraid.

Alex is waiting for me on the other side; Alex standing, smiling, bathed in sunlight.

Alex reaching out his arms to me, calling—

Hey. Hey.

Wake up.

'Hey. Wake up. Come on, come on, come on.'

The voice pulls me back from the tunnel, and for a moment I'm horribly disappointed when I open my eyes and see not Alex's face, but some other face, sharp and unfamiliar. I can't think; the world is all fractured. Black hair, a pointed nose, bright green eyes – pieces of a puzzle I can't make sense of.

'Come on, that's right, stay with me. Bram, where the hell is that water?'

A hand under my neck, and then, suddenly, salvation. A sensation of ice, and liquid sliding: water filling my mouth, my throat, pouring over my chin, melting away the dust, the taste of fire. First I cough, choke, almost cry. Then I swallow, gulp, suck, while the hand stays under my neck, and the voice keeps whispering encouragement. 'That's right. Have as much as you need. You're all right. You're safe now.'

Black hair, loose, a tent around me: a woman. No, a girl – a girl with a thin, tight mouth, and creases at the corners of her eyes, and hands as rough as willow, as big as baskets. I think, *Thank you.* I think, *Mother.*

'You're safe. It's okay. You're okay.'

That's how babies are born, after all: cradled in someone else's arms, sucking, helpless.

After that, the fever pulls me under again. My waking moments are few, and my impressions disjointed. More hands, and more voices; I am lifted; a kaleidoscope of green above me, and fractal patterns in the sky. Later there is the smell of campfire, and something cold and wet pressed against my skin, smoke and hushed voices, searing pain in my side, then ice, relief. Softness sliding against my legs.

In between are dreams unlike any I've ever had before. They are full of explosions and violence: dreams of skin melting and skeletons charred to black bits.

Alex never comes to me again. He has gone ahead of me and disappeared beyond the tunnel.

Almost every time I wake she is there, the black-haired girl, urging me to drink water, or pressing a cool towel to my forehead. Her hands smell like smoke and cedar.

And beneath it all, beneath the rhythm of the waking and sleeping, the fever and the chills, is the word she repeats, again and again, so it weaves its way into my dreams, begins to push back some of the darkness there, draws me up out of the drowning: *Safe. Safe. Safe. You're safe now.*

The fever breaks, finally, after I don't know how long, and at last I float into consciousness on the back of that word, gently, softly, like riding a single wave all the way into the shore.

* * *

Before I even open my eyes, I'm conscious of plates banging together, the smell of something frying, and the murmur of voices. My first thought is that I'm at home, in Aunt Carol's house, and she's about to call me down for breakfast – a morning like any other.

Then the memories – the flight with Alex, the botched escape, my days and nights alone in the Wilds – come slamming back, and I snap my eyes open, trying to sit up. My body won't obey me, though. I can't do more than lift my head; I feel as though I've been encased in stone.

The black-haired girl, the one who must have found me and brought me here – wherever here is – stands in the corner, next to a large stone sink. She whips around when she hears me shift in my bed.

'Easy,' she says. She brings her hands out of the sink, wet to the elbow. Her face is sharp, extremely alert, like an animal's. Her teeth are small, too small for her mouth, and slightly crooked. She crosses the room, squats next to the bed. 'You've been out for a whole day.'

'Where am I?' I croak. My voice is a rasp, barely recognizable as my own.

'Home base,' she says. She is watching me closely. 'That's what we call it, anyway.'

'No, I mean—' I'm struggling to piece together what happened after I climbed the fence. All I can think of is Alex. 'I mean, is this the Wilds?'

An expression – of suspicion, possibly – passes quickly over her face. 'We're in a free zone, yes,' she says carefully, then stands and without another word moves away from the bed, disappearing through a darkened doorway. From deeper inside the building I can hear voices indistinctly. I feel a brief pang of fear, wonder if I've been wrong to mention the Wilds, wonder if these people are safe. I've never heard anyone call unregulated land a 'free zone' before.

But no. Whoever they are, they must be on my side; they saved me, have had me completely at their mercy for days.

I manage to haul myself into a half-seated position, propping my head up against the hard stone wall behind me. The whole room is stone: rough stone floors, stone walls on which, in places, a thin film of black mould is growing, an old-fashioned stone basin fitted with a rusted faucet that clearly hasn't functioned in years. I'm lying on a hard, narrow cot, covered with ratty quilts. This, in addition to a few tin buckets in the corner underneath the defunct sink, and a single wooden chair, is the room's only furniture. There are no windows in my room, and no lights, either – just two emergency lanterns, battery-operated, which fill the room with a weak bluish light.

On one wall is tacked a small wooden cross with the figure of a man suspended in its middle. I recognize the symbol – it's a cross from one of the old religions, from the time before the cure, although I can't remember which one now.

I have a sudden flashback to junior-year American history and Mrs. Dernler glaring at us from behind her enormous glasses, jabbing the open textbook with her finger, saying, 'You see? You see? These old religions, stained everywhere with love. They reeked of *deliria*; they bled it.' And of course at the time it seemed terrible, and true.

Love, the deadliest of all deadly things.

Love, it kills you.

Alex.

Both when you have it . . .

Alex.

And when you don't.

Alex.

'You were half dead when we found you,' the black-haired girl says matter-of-factly as she re-enters the room. She's holding an earthenware bowl with both hands, carefully. 'More than half. We didn't think you were going to make it. I thought we should at least try.'

She gives me a doubtful look, as though she's not sure I've been worth the effort, and for a moment I think of my cousin Jenny, the way she used to stand with her hands on her hips, scrutinizing me, and I have to close my eyes quickly to keep all of it from rushing back – the flood of images, memories, from a life that is now dead.

'Thank you,' I say.

She shrugs, but says, 'You're welcome,' and seems to mean it. She draws the wooden chair to the side of the bed and sits. Her hair is long and knotted above her left ear. Behind it, she has the mark of the procedure – a three-pronged scar – just like Alex did. But she cannot be cured; she is here, on the other side of the fence: an Invalid.

I try to sit up all the way but have to lean back after only a few seconds of struggle, exhausted. I feel like a puppet halfway come to life. There's a searing pain behind my eyes, too, and when I look down I see my skin is still criss-crossed with a web of cuts and scrapes and scratches, insect bites and scabs.

The bowl the girl is holding is full of mostly clear broth, tinged with just a bit of green. She starts to pass it to me, then hesitates. 'Can you hold it?'

'Of course I can hold it,' I say, more sharply than I'd meant to. The bowl is heavier than I thought it would be. I have trouble lifting it to my mouth, but I do, finally. My throat feels as raw as sandpaper and the broth is heaven against it, and even though it has a weird mossy aftertaste, I find myself gulping and slurping down the whole bowl.

'Slowly,' the girl says, but I can't stop. Suddenly hunger yawns open inside me, black and endless and all-consuming. As soon as the broth is gone I'm desperate for more, even though my stomach starts cramping right away. 'You'll make yourself sick,' the girl says, shaking her head, and takes the empty bowl from me.

'Is there any more?' I croak.

'In a little while,' she says.

'Please.' The hunger is a snake; it is lashing at the pit of my stomach, eating me from the inside out.

She sighs, stands, and disappears through the darkened doorway. I think I hear a crescendo in the hallway voices, a swelling of sound. Then, abruptly, silence. The black-haired girl returns with a second bowl of broth. I take it from her and she sits again, drawing her knees up to her chest, like a kid would. Her knees are bony and brown.

'So,' she says, 'where did you cross from?' When I hesitate, she says, 'That's okay. You don't have to talk about it if you don't want to.'

'No, no. It's fine.' I sip from this bowl of broth more slowly, savouring its strange, earthy quality: as though it has been stewed with stones. For all I know, it has been. Alex told me once that Invalids – the people who live in the Wilds – have learned to make do with only the barest provisions. 'I came over from Portland.' Too soon the bowl is empty again, even though the snake in my stomach is still lashing. 'Where are we now?'

'A few miles east of Rochester,' she says.

'Rochester, New Hampshire?' I ask.

She smirks. 'Yup. You must have been hoofing it. How long were you out on your own?'

'I don't know.' I rest my head against the wall. Rochester, New Hampshire. I must have looped around the northern border when I was lost in the Wilds: I've ended up sixty miles southwest of Portland. I'm exhausted again, even though I've been sleeping for days. 'I lost track of time.'

'Pretty ballsy of you,' she says. I'm not really sure what 'ballsy' means, but I can guess. 'How did you cross?'

'It wasn't – it wasn't just me,' I say, and the snake lashes, seizes up. 'I mean, it wasn't supposed to be just me.'

'You were with somebody else?' She's staring at me penetratingly again, her eyes almost as dark as her hair. 'A friend?'

I don't know how to correct her. My best friend. My boyfriend. My love. I'm still not totally comfortable with that word, and it seems almost sacrilegious, so instead I just nod.

'What happened?' she asks, a little more softly.

'He – he didn't make it.' Her eyes flash with understanding when I say 'he': If we were coming from Portland together, from a place of segregation, we must have been more than just friends. Thankfully she doesn't push it. 'We made it all the way to the border fence. But then the regulators and the guards . . .' The pain in my stomach intensifies. 'There were too many of them.'

She stands abruptly and retrieves one of the water-spotted tin buckets from the corner, places it next to the bed, and sits again.

'We heard rumours,' she says shortly. 'Stories of a big escape in Portland, lots of police involvement, a big cover-up.'

'So you know about it?' I try once again to sit up all the way, but the cramping doubles me back against the wall. 'Are they saying what happened to . . . to my friend?'

I ask the question even though I know. Of course I know.

I saw him standing there, covered in blood, as they descended on him, swarmed him, like the black ants in my dream.

The girl doesn't answer, just folds her mouth into a tight line and shakes her head. She doesn't have to say anything else – her meaning is clear. It's written in the pity on her face.

The snake uncoils fully and begins thrashing. I close my eyes. Alex, Alex, Alex: my reason for everything, my new life, the promise of something better – gone, blown away into ash. Nothing will ever be okay again. 'I was hoping . . .' I let out a little gasp as that terrible, lashing thing in my stomach comes riding toward my throat on a surge of sickness.

She sighs again and I hear her stand up, scrape the chair away from the bed.

'I think—' I can barely force the words out; I'm trying to swallow back the nausea. 'I think I'm going to—'

And then I'm tipping over the bed, throwing up into the bucket she has placed beside me, my body gripped by waves of sickness.

'I knew you would make yourself sick,' the girl says, shaking her head. Then she disappears into the dark hallway. A second later, she pops her head back into the room. 'I'm Raven, by the way.'

'Lena,' I say, and the word brings with it a new round of vomiting.

'Lena,' she repeats. She raps on the wall once with her knuckles. 'Welcome to the Wilds.'

Then she disappears, and I am left with the bucket.

* * *

Later in the afternoon, Raven reappears, and I again try the broth. This time I sip slowly and manage to keep it down. I'm still so weak I can barely lift the bowl to my lips, and Raven has to help me. I should be embarrassed, but I can't feel anything: Once the nausea subsides it is replaced by a numbness so complete it is like sinking under ice water.

'Good,' Raven says approvingly after I've made it through half the broth. She takes the bowl and disappears again.

Now that I'm awake, and conscious, all I want is to sleep again. At least when I'm sleeping I can dream myself back to Alex, can dream myself into a different world. Here, in this world, I have nothing: no family, no home, no place to go. Alex is gone. By now even my identity will have been Invalidated.

I can't even cry. My insides have been turned to dust. I think over and over of that final moment, when I turned and saw him standing behind that wall of smoke. In my head I try and reach back, through the fence, past the smoke; I try and grab his hand and pull.

Alex, come back.

There is nothing to do but sink. The hours close around me, encase me completely.

A bit later I hear scuffling footsteps, and then echoes of laughter and conversation. This, at least, gives me something to focus on. I try to differentiate the voices, take a guess at how many speakers there are, but the best I can do is separate out a few low tones (men, boys) and some high-pitched giggling, the occasional burst of laughter. Once I hear Raven cry out, 'All right, all right,' but for the most part, the voices are waves of sound, tones only, like a distant song.

Of course it makes sense that girls and boys would be sharing a house in the Wilds – that's the whole point, after all: freedom to choose, freedom to be around one another, freedom to look and touch and love one another – but the idea is very different from the reality, and I can't help but start to panic a little.

Alex is the only boy I've ever known or really spoken to. I don't like to think of all those male strangers, just on the other side of the stone wall, with their baritone voices and their snorts of laughter. Before I met Alex, I lived almost eighteen years believing fully in the system, believing 100 percent that love was a disease, that we must protect ourselves, that girls and boys must stay rigorously separate to prevent contagion. Looks, glances, touches, hugs – all of it carried the risk of contamination. And even though being with Alex changed me, you don't shake loose the fear all at once. You can't.

I close my eyes, breathe deeply, again try and force myself down through layers of consciousness, to let myself be carried away by sleep.

'All right, Blue. Out of here. Bedtime.'

I snap my eyes open. A girl, probably six or seven, has been standing in the doorway, watching me. She's thin and very tan, wearing dirty jean shorts and a cotton sweater about fourteen sizes too big for her – so big it is slipping off her shoulders, showing shoulder blades as peaked as bird wings. Her hair is dirty blonde, falling almost all the way to her waist, and she isn't wearing any shoes. Raven is trying to manoeuver around her, carrying a plate.

'I'm not tired,' the girl says, keeping her eyes locked on me. She hops around from foot to foot but won't come any farther into the room. Her eyes are a startling shade of blue, a vivid sky colour.

'No arguing,' Raven says, bumping Blue playfully with her hip as she passes. 'Out.'

'But—'

'What's rule number one, Blue?' Raven's voice turns sterner.

Blue brings her thumb to her mouth, rips at her thumbnail. 'Listen to Raven,' she mumbles.

'*Always* listen to Raven. And Raven says bedtime. Now. Go.'

Blue shoots me a last, regretful look and then scurries away. Raven sighs, rolls her eyes, and pulls the chair up to the bed. 'Sorry,' she says. 'Everyone is dying to see the new girl.'

'Who's everyone?' I say. My throat is dry. I haven't been able to stand and make it over to the basin, and it's clear that the pipes don't work anyway. There wouldn't be any plumbing in the Wilds. All those networks – the water, the electricity – were bombed out years ago, during the blitz. 'I mean, how many of you are there?'

Raven shrugs. 'Oh, you know, it changes. People go in and out, pass between homesteads. Probably twenty or so, right now, but in June we've had as many as forty floaters, and in the winter we close up this homestead completely.'

I nod, even though her talk of homesteads and floaters confuses me. Alex told me the barest little bit about the Wilds, and of course we crossed once together successfully: the first and only time I'd ever been in unregulated land before our big escape.

Before my big escape.

I dig my fingernails into my palms.

'Are you okay?' Raven's peering at me closely.

'I could use some water,' I say.

'Here,' she says. 'Take this.' She passes me the plate she's been holding: two small round patties, like pancakes but darker and grainier, are sitting at its centre. She removes a dented tin soup can from a shelf in the corner, uses it as a ladle to scoop a bit of water from one of the buckets under the sink, and carries it back to me. I can only hope that bucket doesn't do double duty as a vomit basin.

'Hard to find glass around here,' she says when I raise my eyebrows at the soup can, and then adds, 'Bombs.' She says it as though she's in a grocery store and saying *Grapefruit*, as though it's the most everyday thing in the world. She sits again, braiding a bit of hair between her long brown fingers absentmindedly.

I lift the soup can to my lips. Its edges are jagged, and I have to sip carefully.

'You learn to make do out here,' Raven says with a kind of pride. 'We can build out of nothing – out of scraps and trash and bones. You'll see.'

I stare at the plate in my lap. I'm hungry, but the words *trash* and *bones* make me nervous about eating.

Raven must understand what I'm thinking, because she laughs. 'Don't worry,' she says. 'It's nothing gross. Some nuts, a bit of flour, some oil. It's not the best thing you'll ever eat in your life, but it will keep your strength up. We're running low on supplies; we haven't had a delivery in a week. The escape really screwed us, you know.'

'My escape?'

She nods. 'They've had the borders running live in all the cities for a hundred miles for the past week, doubled security at the fences.' I open my mouth to apologize, but she cuts me off. 'It's all right. They do this every time there's a breach. They always get worried there'll be some mass uprising and people will rush the Wilds. In a few days they'll get lazy again, and then we'll get our supplies. And in the meantime . . .' She jerks her chin toward the plate. 'Nuts.'

I take a nibble of the pancake. It's not bad, actually: toasty and crunchy and just a little bit greasy, leaving a sheen of oil on my fingertips. It's a lot better than the broth, and I say so to Raven.

She beams at me. 'Yeah, Roach is the resident cook. He can make a good meal out of anything. Well, he can make an edible meal out of anything.'

'Roach? Is that his real name?'

Raven finishes a braid, flicks it over her shoulder, starts on another one. 'As real as any name,' she says. 'Roach has been in the Wilds his whole life. Originally comes from one of the homesteads farther south, close to Delaware. Someone down there must have named him. By the time he got up here, he was Roach.'

'What about Blue?' I ask. I make it through the whole first pancake without feeling queasy, then set the plate on the floor next to the bed. I don't want to push my luck.

Raven hesitates for just a fraction of a second. 'She was born right here, at the homestead.'

'So you named her for her eyes,' I say.

Raven stands abruptly, and turns away before saying, 'Uh-huh.' She goes to the shelves by the sink and clicks off one of the battery-operated lanterns, so the room sinks even further into darkness.

'How about you?' I ask her.

She points to her hair. 'Raven.' She smiles. 'Not the most original.'

'No, I mean – were you born here? In the Wilds?'

The smile disappears just like that, like a candle being snuffed out. For a second she looks almost angry. 'No,' she says shortly. 'I came here when I was fifteen.'

I know I shouldn't, but I can't stop myself from pressing. 'By yourself?'

'Yes.' She picks up the second lantern, which is still emitting a pale bluish light, and moves toward the door.

'So what was your name before?' I say, and she freezes, her back to me. 'Before you came to the Wilds, I mean.'

For a moment she stands there. Then she turns around. She is holding the lantern low so her face is in darkness. Her eyes are two bare reflections, glittering, like black stones in the moonlight.

'You might as well get used to it now,' she says with quiet intensity. 'Everything you were, the life you had, the people you knew . . . dust.' She shakes her head and says, a little more firmly, 'There is no before. There is only now, and what comes next.'

Then she heads into the hallway with her lantern, leaving me in total darkness, my heart beating very fast.

The next morning, I wake up starving. The plate is still there with the second pancake, and I half tumble out of bed reaching for it, banging onto my knees on the cold stone floor. A beetle is exploring the surface of the pancake – normally, before, this would have grossed me out, but now I'm too hungry to care. I flick the insect away, watch it scurry into a corner, and eat the pancake greedily with both hands, sucking on my fingers. It saws off only the barest corner of my hunger.

I climb slowly to my feet, leaning on the bed for support. It's the first time I've stood in days, the first time I've done more than crawl to a metal basin in the corner – placed there by Raven – when I've had to use the bathroom. Crouching in the dark, head down, thighs shaking, I am an animal, not even human anymore.

I'm so weak I've hardly made it to the doorway before I have to take a break, leaning against the doorjamb. I feel like one of the grey herons – with their swollen beaks and bellies, and tiny spindly legs – I used to see sometimes at the cove in Portland, totally out of proportion, lopsided.

My room opens into a long, dark hallway, also windowless, also stone. I can hear people talking and laughing, the sounds of chairs scraping and water sloshing: kitchen sounds. Food sounds. The hallway is narrow, and I run my hands along the walls as I move forward, getting a sense of my legs and body again. A doorway on my left, missing its door, opens into a large room, stacked, on one side, with medical and cleaning supplies – gauze, tubes and tubes of bacitracin, hundreds of boxes of soap, bandages – and, on the other, with four narrow mattresses laid directly on the floor, heaped with an assortment of clothes and blankets. A little farther I see another room that must be used entirely for sleeping: this one has mattresses laid from wall to wall, covering almost every inch of the floor, so the room looks like an enormous patchwork quilt.

I feel a pang of guilt. I've obviously been given the nicest bed, and the nicest room. It still amazes me to think how wrong I was all those years, when I trusted in rumours and lies. I thought the Invalids were beasts; I thought they would rip me apart. But these people saved me, and gave me the softest place to sleep, and nursed me back to health, and haven't asked for anything in return.

The animals are on the other side of the fence: monsters wearing uniforms. They speak softly, and tell lies, and smile as they're slitting your throat.

The hallway takes a sharp left and the voices swell. I can smell meat cooking now, and my stomach growls loudly. I pass more rooms, some for sleeping, one mostly empty and lined with shelves: a half-dozen cans of beans, a half-used bag of flour, and, weirdly, a dusty coffeemaker are piled in one corner; in another corner, buckets, tins of coffee, a mop.

Another right and the hallway ends abruptly in a large room, much brighter than the others. A stone basin, similar to the one in my room, runs along one whole wall. Above it, a long shelf holds a half-dozen battery-operated lanterns, which fill the space with a warm light. In the centre of the room are two large, narrow wooden tables, packed with people.

As I enter, the conversation stops abruptly: dozens of eyes sweep upward in my direction, and I'm suddenly aware that I am wearing nothing more than a large, dirty T-shirt that reaches just to mid-thigh.

There are men in the room too, sitting elbow-to-elbow with women – people of all ages, everyone uncured – and it is so strange and upside down, it nearly takes my breath away. I'm petrified. I open my mouth to speak, but nothing emerges. I feel the weight of silence, the heavy burn of all those eyes.

Raven comes to my rescue.

'You must be hungry,' she says, standing and gesturing to a boy sitting at the end of the table. He's probably thirteen or fourteen – thin, wiry, with a smattering of pimples on his skin.

'Squirrel,' she says sharply. Another crazy nickname. 'You finished eating?'

He stares dolefully at his empty plate as though he could telepathically force more food to materialize there.

'Yeah,' he says slowly, looking from the empty plate to me and back again. I hug my arms around my waist.

'Then get up. Lena needs a place to sit.'

'But—,' Squirrel starts to protest, and Raven glares at him.

'Up, Squirrel. Make yourself useful. Go check the nests for messages.'

Squirrel shoots me a sullen look, but he stands up and brings his plate to the sink. He releases it clatteringly onto the stone – which makes Raven, who has sat down again, call out, 'You break, you buy, Squirrel,' and provokes a few titters – then stomps dramatically up the stone steps at the far end of the room.

'Sarah, get Lena something to eat.' Raven has returned to her own food: a pile of greyish mush lumped in the centre of her plate.

A girl pops up eagerly, like a jack-in-the-box. She has enormous eyes, and a body as tight as a wire. Everyone in the room is skinny, actually – all I see are elbows and shoulders everywhere, edges and angles.

'Come on, Lena.' She seems to relish saying my name, as though it's a special privilege. 'I'll fix you a plate.' She points to the corner: an enormous dented iron pot and a warped covered pan are set over an old-fashioned wood-burning stove. Next to it, mismatched plates and platters – and some cutting boards – are stacked haphazardly.

This means actually entering the room, walking past both tables. If my legs felt unsteady before, now I'm worried they'll actually buckle at any second. Strangely, I can feel the texture of the men's eyes differently. The women's eyes are sharp, evaluating; the men's eyes are hotter, stifling, like a touch. I'm having trouble breathing.

I go haltingly toward the stove, where Sarah is standing, nodding at me encouragingly, as though I'm a baby – even though she can't be more than twelve herself. I stay as close as possible to the sink – just in case I do stumble, I want to be able to reach out and steady myself quickly.

The faces in the room are mostly a blur, a wash of colour, but a few stand out: I see Blue watching me, wide-eyed; a boy, probably my age, with a crazy thatch of blond hair, who looks like he might start laughing any second; another boy, a little older, scowling; a woman with long auburn hair hanging loose down her back. For a moment our eyes meet and my heart stutters: I think, *Mom*. It hasn't occurred to me until now that my mother could be here – that she must be here, somewhere, in the Wilds, in one of the homesteads or camps or whatever they're called. Then the woman shifts slightly and I see her face and realize that no, of course it's not her. She's far too young, probably the age of my mother when I last saw her twelve years ago. I'm not sure I'd even recognize my mother if I saw her again; my memories of her are so fuzzy, distorted through layers of time and dream.

'Slop,' Sarah says as soon as I make it to the stove. I'm exhausted from the walk across the room. I can't believe that this is the same body that used to do six-mile runs on an easy day, sprint up and down Munjoy Hill like it was nothing.

'What?'

'Slop.' She lifts the cover off the tin pot. 'That's what we call it. It's what we eat when supplies run low. Oatmeal, rice, sometimes some bread – whatever grains we have left. Boil the shit out of it, and there you go. Slop.'

It startles me to hear a curse word come from her mouth.

Sarah takes a plastic plate – with ghostly silhouettes of animals still faintly visible on its surface, a kid's plate – and piles a big serving of slop at its centre. Behind me, at the tables, people have started talking again. The room fills with the low buzz of conversation, and I start to feel slightly better; at least that means some of the attention is off me.

'The good news,' Sarah continues cheerfully, 'is that Roach brought home a present last night.'

'What do you mean?' I'm struggling to absorb the lingo, the pattern of speech. 'He got supplies?'

'Better.' She grins at me, slides the top off the second covered pan. Inside is golden-brown meat, seared, crispy: a smell that almost brings me to tears. 'Rabbit.'

I've never eaten rabbit before – never thought of it as something you could eat, especially not for breakfast – but I gratefully accept the plate from her, and can hardly stop myself from ripping into the meat right there, standing. I'd prefer to stand, actually. Anything would be better than having to sit down among all those strangers.

Sarah must sense my anxiety. 'Come on,' she says. 'You can sit next to me.' She reaches out and takes my elbow, steering me toward the table. This, too, is surprising. In Portland, in bordered communities, everyone is very careful about touching. Even Hana and I hardly ever hugged or put our arms around each other, and she was my best friend.

A cramp runs through me, and I double over, almost dropping my plate.

'Easy.' Across the table is the blond-haired boy, the one who looked as though he could hardly contain his laughter earlier. He raises his eyebrows; they're the same pale blond as his hair, practically invisible. I notice that he, like Raven, has a procedural mark behind his left ear, and like hers, it must be fake. Only uncureds live in the Wilds; only people who have chosen, or been forced, to flee the bordered cities. 'You okay?'

I don't answer. I can't. A whole lifetime of fears and warnings beat through me, and words flash rapidly in my mind: *illegal, wrong, sympathizer, disease.* I take a deep breath, try to ignore the bad feeling. Those are Portland words, old words; they, like the old me, have been left behind the fence.

'She's fine,' Sarah jumps in. 'She's just hungry.'

'I'm fine,' I echo about fifteen seconds too late. The boy smirks again.

Sarah slides onto the bench and pats the empty space next to her, which Squirrel has just vacated. At least we're at the very end of the table, and I don't have to worry about being sandwiched next to someone else. I sit down, keeping my eyes on my plate. I can feel everyone watching me again. At least the conversation continues, a comforting blanket of noise.

'Go ahead.' Sarah looks at me encouragingly.

'I don't have a fork,' I say quietly. The blond guy does laugh then, loud and long. So does Sarah.

'No forks,' she says. 'No spoons. No nothing. Just eat.'

I risk glancing up and see that the people around me are watching, smiling, apparently amused. One of them, a grizzled, grey-haired man who must be at least seventy, nods at me, and I drop my eyes quickly. My whole body is hot with embarrassment. Of course they wouldn't care about silverware and things like that in the Wilds.

I take the piece of rabbit with my hands, tear a tiny bit of flesh from the bone. And then I think I really might cry: never in my whole life has anything tasted this good.

'Good, huh?' Sarah says, but I can't do anything but nod. Suddenly I forget about the roomful of strangers and all the people watching me. I tear at the rabbit like an animal. I shovel up a bit of slop with my fingers, suck them into my mouth.

Even that tastes good to me. Aunt Carol would absolutely flip if she could see me. When I was little, I wouldn't even eat my peas if they were touching my chicken; I used to make neat compartments on my plate.

All too soon the plate is clean, except for a few bones. I drag the back of my hand across my mouth. I feel a surge of nausea and I close my eyes, willing it away.

'All right,' Raven says, standing abruptly. 'Time for rounds.'

There's a flurry of activity: people scraping away from their benches, bursts of conversations I can't follow ('Laid traps yesterday,' 'Your turn to check Grandma'), and people are passing behind me, releasing their plates noisily into the basin, then stomping up the stairs to my left, just past the stove. I can feel their bodies, and smell them, too: a flow, a warm, human river. I keep my eyes closed, and as the room empties, the nausea subsides somewhat.

'How are you feeling?'

I open my eyes and Raven is standing across from me, leaning both hands on the table. Sarah is still sitting next to me. She has brought one leg to her chest, on the bench, and is hugging her knee. In this pose, she actually looks her age.

'Better,' I say, which is true.

'You can help Sarah with the dishes,' she says, 'if you're feeling up to it.'

'Okay,' I say, and she nods.

'Good. And afterward, Sarah, you can take her up. You might as well get a feel for the homestead, Lena. But don't push it, either. I don't want to have to drag your ass out of the woods again.'

'Okay,' I repeat, and she smiles, satisfied. She's obviously used to giving orders. I wonder how old she is. She speaks with such easy command, even though she must be younger than half the Invalids here. I think, *Hana would like her*, and the pain returns, knifing just below my ribs.

'And Sarah' – Raven is heading for the stairs – 'get Lena some pants from the store, okay? So she doesn't have to prance around half naked.'

I feel myself going red again, and reflexively start fiddling with the hem of my shirt, tugging it lower down my thighs. Raven catches me and laughs.

'Don't worry,' she says, 'it's nothing we haven't seen before.' Then she takes the stairs two at a time, and is gone.

I used to be on dish duty every night at Aunt Carol's house, and I got used to it. But washing dishes in the Wilds is another story. First there's the water. Sarah leads me back through the hall, to one of the rooms I passed on my way to the kitchen.

'This is the supply room,' she says, and for a moment frowns at all the empty shelves and the mostly used bag of flour. 'We're running a little low,' she explains, as though I can't see that for myself. I feel a twist of anxiety – for her, for Blue, for everyone here, all that bone and thinness.

'Over here is where we keep the water. We pull it in the mornings – not me, I'm too small still.' She's over in the corner by the buckets, which now I see are full. She hefts one up by its handle with both hands, grunting. It's oversized, nearly as big as her torso. 'One more should do it,' she says. 'A small one should be okay.' She toddles out of the room, straining, with the bucket in front of her.

I find, to my embarrassment, that I can barely lift one of the smallest buckets. Its metal handle digs painfully into the palms of my hands – which are still covered in scabs and blisters from my time alone in the Wilds – and before I've even reached the hallway I have to set the bucket down and lean against the wall.

'You okay?' Sarah calls back.

'Fine!' I say, a little too sharply. There's no way I'm going to let her come to my rescue. I heave the bucket in the air again, advance forward a few halting steps, place it on the ground, rest. Heave, shuffle, ground, rest. Heave, shuffle, ground, rest. By the time I reach the kitchen, I'm out of breath and sweating; salt stings my eyes. Fortunately, Sarah doesn't notice. She's squatting at the stove, poking around at the fire with the charred end of a wooden stick, coaxing it higher.

'We boil the water in the mornings,' she says, 'to sanitize it. We have to, or we'll be shitting a river from breakfast to dinner.' In her last words, I recognize Raven's voice; this must be one of her mantras.

'Where does the water come from?' I ask, grateful that she has her back to me so that I can rest, momentarily, on one of the nearest benches.

'Cocheco River,' she says. 'It's not too far. A mile, a mile and a half, tops.'

Impossible: I can't imagine carrying those buckets, full, for a mile.

'The river's where we get our supplies, too,' Sarah rattles on. 'Friends on the inside float them down to us. The Cocheco crosses into Rochester and then out again.' She giggles. 'Raven says that someday they'll make it fill out a Purpose of Travel form.'

Sarah feeds the stove wood from a pile stacked in the corner. Then she stands up, nodding once. 'We'll just warm the water a little bit. It cleans better when it's hot.'

On one of the high shelves above the sink is an enormous tin stockpot, big enough for a child to bathe in comfortably. Before I can offer to help, Sarah hefts herself onto the basin – balancing carefully on its rim, like a gymnast – and stands, removing the pot from the shelf. Then she hops off the sink, landing soundlessly. 'Okay.' She brushes hair out of her face; it has come loose from its ponytail. 'Now the water goes into the pot, and the pot goes on the stove.'

Everything in the Wilds is process, slow steps, shuffling forward. Everything takes time. While we wait for the water in the pot to heat, Sarah lists the people in the homestead, a blur of names I won't remember: Grandpa, the oldest; Lu, short for Lucky, who lost a finger to a bad infection but managed to keep her life, and the rest of her limbs, intact; Bram, short for Bramble, who appeared miraculously in the Wilds one day, in the middle of a tangle of brambles and thorns, as though deposited there by wolves. There's a story for almost everyone's name, even Sarah's. When she first came to the Wilds seven years ago with her older sister, she begged the homesteaders to give her a cool new name. She pulls a face, remembering – she wanted something tough, like Blade, or Iron – but Raven had only laughed, put a hand on her head, and said, 'You look just like a Sarah to me.' And so Sarah she remained.

'Which one is your sister?' I ask. I think briefly of my sister, Rachel – not the Rachel I left behind, the cured one, all blank and curtained off, but the Rachel I can still remember from my childhood – and then let the image skitter away.

'Not here anymore. She left the homestead earlier in the summer; joined the R. She's going to come back for me as soon as I'm old enough to help.' There's a note of pride in her voice, so I nod encouragingly, even though I have no idea what the 'R' is.

More names: Hunter, the blond boy who was sitting across from me at the table ('That's his before name,' Sarah says, pronouncing the word *before* in a kind of hush, like a curse word – 'He can't actually hunt for nothing'); Tack, who came from up north a few years ago.

'Everyone says he has a bad attitude,' she says, and again I hear the echo of Raven's voice in her words. She is worrying the fabric of her T-shirt, which is worn so thin it is practically translucent. 'But I don't think so. He's always been nice to me.'

From her description, I've matched Tack with the black-haired guy who was scowling at me when I came into the kitchen. If that's his normal look, I can see why people think he has a bad attitude.

'Why's he called Tack?' I ask.

She giggles. 'Sharp as,' she says. 'Grandpa named him.'

I decide to stay away from Tack, if I remain at the homestead at all. I can't see that I have much of a choice, but I can feel that I don't belong here, and a part of me wishes that Raven had left me where she found me. I was closer to Alex then. He was just on the other side of that long, black tunnel. I could have walked through its blackness; I could have found him again.

'Water's ready,' Sarah announces finally.

Process, agonizingly slow: we fill up one of the basins with the hot water, and Sarah measures soap into the sink slowly, not wasting a drop. That's another thing I can see about the Wilds: everything gets used, reused, rationed, measured.

'So what about Raven?' I ask as I submerge my arms in the hot water.

'What about her?' Sarah's face brightens. She loves Raven, I can tell.

'What's her story? Where did she come from before?' I don't know why I'm pushing the issue. I'm just curious, I guess, curious to know how you become someone like that: confident, fierce, a leader.

Sarah's face clouds over. 'There is no before,' she says shortly, then falls silent for the first time in an hour. We wash the dishes without speaking.

Sarah turns talkative again when the dishes are done and it's time to outfit me with clothes.

She leads me to a small room I mistook for one of the bedrooms before. There are clothes strewn everywhere, masses of them, all over the floor and shelves. 'This is the store,' she says, giggling a little and gesturing grandly with one hand.

'Where did all the clothes come from?' I move carefully into the room, stepping on shirts and balled-up socks as I do. Every inch of floor space is covered in fabric.

'We find them,' Sarah says vaguely. And then, turning suddenly fierce, 'The blitz didn't work like they said, you know. The zombies lied, just like they lie about everything else.'

'Zombies?'

Sarah grins. 'That's what we call the cureds, after they've had the procedure. Raven says they might as well be zombies. She says the cure turns people stupid.'

'That's not true,' I say instinctively, and nearly correct her: it's the passions that turn us stupid, animal-like. Free from love is close to God. That's an old adage from *The Book of Shhh*. The cure was supposed to free us from extreme emotions, bring us clarity of thought and feeling.

But when I think about Aunt Carol's glassy eyes, and my sister's expressionless face, I think that the term *zombies* is actually pretty accurate. And it's true that all the history books, and all our teachers, lied about the blitz; the Wilds were supposed to have been wiped absolutely clean during the bombing campaign. Invalids – or homesteaders – aren't even supposed to exist.

Sarah shrugs. 'If you're smart, you care. And if you care, you love.'

'Did Raven tell you that, too?'

She smiles again. 'Raven's super smart.'

It takes me a little bit of digging, but I finally find a pair of army-green pants and a long-sleeved cotton T-shirt. It feels too weird to wear someone else's old underwear, so I keep on the pair I've been wearing. Sarah wants me to model my new outfit – she's enjoying this, and keeps begging me to try on different things, acting like a normal kid for the first time – and when I ask her to turn around so I can change, she stares at me like I'm crazy. I guess there isn't much privacy in the Wilds. But finally she shrugs and swivels to face the wall.

It feels good to get out of the long T-shirt, which I've been wearing for days. I know I smell bad, and I'm desperate for a shower, but for now I'm just grateful for some relatively clean clothes. The pants fit well, low on my hips, and they don't even drag too badly after I roll them at the waist a few times. The T-shirt is soft and comfortable.

'Not bad,' Sarah says when she turns around to face me again. 'You look almost human.'

'Thanks.'

'I said almost.' She giggles again.

'Well, then, almost thanks.'

Shoes are harder. Most people in the Wilds go without during the summer, and Sarah proudly shows me the bottoms of her feet, which are brown and hardened with calluses. But finally we find a pair of running shoes that are just a tiny bit too big; with thick socks, they'll be fine.

When I kneel down to lace up the sneakers, another pang goes through me. I've done this so many times – before cross-country meets, in the locker rooms, sitting next to Hana, surrounded by a blur of bodies, joking with each other about who's a better runner – and yet somehow I always took it for granted.

For the first time the thought comes to me – *I wish I hadn't crossed* – and I push it away instantly, try to bury it. It's done now, and Alex died for it. There's no point in looking back. I can't look back.

'Are you ready to see the rest of the homestead?' Sarah asks.

Even the act of undressing and redressing has exhausted me. But I'm desperate for air, and space.

'Show me,' I say.

We go back through the kitchen and up the narrow stone stairs beyond the stove. Sarah darts ahead of me, disappearing as the stairs make a sharp turn. 'Almost there!' she calls back.

A final serpentine twist, and suddenly the stairs are no more: I step into a blazing brightness, and soft ground underneath my shoes. I stumble, confused and temporarily blinded. For a second I feel as though I've walked into a dream and I stand, blinking, struggling to make sense of this otherworld.

Sarah is standing a few feet away from me, laughing. She lifts her arms, which are bathed in sunshine. 'Welcome to the homestead,' she says, and performs a little skipping dance in the grass.

The place where I've been sleeping is underground – that I could have guessed from the lack of windows and the quality of dampness – and the stairs have led upward, aboveground, and then released us abruptly. Where there should be a house, an over-structure, there is just a large expanse of grass covered in charred wood and enormous fragments of stone.

I was not prepared for the feeling of the sunshine, or the smell of growth and life. All around us are enormous trees, leaves just tinged with yellow as though they are catching fire slowly from the outside, patterning the ground with alternating spots of light and shadow. For a second something deep and old rises inside me and I could fall on the ground and weep for joy, or open up my arms and spin. After being enclosed for so long, I want to drink in all the space, all the bright, empty air stretching around me on all sides.

Sarah explains, 'This used to be a church.' She points behind me, to the splintered stones and the blackened wood. 'The bombs didn't reach the cellar, though. There are plenty of underground places in the Wilds where the bombs didn't touch. You'll see.'

'A church?' This surprises me. In Portland, our churches are made of steel and glass and clean white plaster walls. They are sanitized spaces, places where the miracle of life, and God's science, is celebrated and demonstrated with microscopes and centrifuges.

'One of the old churches,' Sarah says. 'There are lots of those, too. On the west side of Rochester there's a whole one, still standing. I'll show you someday, if you want.' Then she reaches forward and grabs the bottom of my T-shirt, tugging at me. 'Come on. Lots to see.'

The only other time I've been to the Wilds was with Alex.

We snuck across the border once so that he could show me where he lived. That settlement, like this one, was situated in a large clearing, a place once inhabited, an area the trees and growth had not yet reclaimed. But this clearing is massive, and filled with half-tumbled-down stone archways and walls that are partially standing, and – in one place – a series of concrete stairs that spiral up from the ground and end in nothing. On the last step, several different birds have made their nests.

I can barely breathe as Sarah and I make our way slowly through the grass, which is damp and almost knee-high in places. It is a ruined-world, a nonsense-place. Doors that open nowhere; a rusted truck, wheel-less, sitting in the middle of a stretch of pale green grass, with a tree growing straight through its centre; bits of glittering, twisted metal everywhere, melted and bent into unrecognizable shapes.

Sarah walks next to me, practically skipping, excitement bubbling out of her now that we're outside. She easily dodges the stones and the metal detritus littering the grass, while I have to keep my eyes constantly on the ground. It is slow-going, and tiring.

'This used to be a town,' Sarah says. 'This was probably the main street. The trees are still young in a lot of places around here, but there aren't hardly any buildings left at all. That's how you know where the houses were. Wood burns a lot easier. Obviously.' She drops her voice to a hush, eyes growing wide. 'It wasn't even the bombs that did the worst damage, you know. It was the fires that came after.'

I manage to nod.

'This was a school.' She gestures to another enormous area of low growth, roughly the shape of a rectangle. The trees around its perimeter are marked from the fire: seared white, and practically leafless, they remind me of tall, spindly ghosts. 'Some of the lockers were just sitting there, hanging open. Some of them had clothes in them and stuff.' She looks momentarily guilty, and then it hits me – the clothing in the storage room, the pants and shirt I am wearing – all of those clothes must have come from somewhere, must have been scavenged.

'Stop for a second.' I'm feeling out of breath, and so we stand for a moment in front of the old school while I rest. We're in a patch of sunshine, and I'm grateful for the warmth. Birds twitter and zip overhead, small, quick shadows against the sky. Distantly I can make out sounds of good-natured shouting and laughter, Invalids tromping through the woods. The air is full of whirling, floating golden-green leaves.

A squirrel sits back on its haunches, working a nut quickly between its paws, on the top step of what must have been an entrance to the school. Now the stairs run aground, into soft earth and a covering of wildflowers. I think of all the feet that must have stepped right there, where the squirrel is. I think of all the small, warm hands spinning out locker combinations, all the voices, the rush and patter of movement. I think of what it must have been like during the blitz – the panic, the screaming, the running, the fire.

In school we always learned that the blitz, the cleansing, was quick. We saw footage of pilots waving from their cockpits as bombs dropped on a distant carpet of green, trees so small they looked like toys, narrow plumes of smoke rising, featherlike, from the growth. No mess, no pain, no sounds of screaming. Just a whole population – the people who had resisted and stayed, who refused to move into the approved and bordered places, the nonbelievers and the contaminated – deleted all at once, quick as the stroke of a keyboard, turned into a dream.

But of course it wouldn't really have been like that. It couldn't have been. The lockers were still full: of course. The children wouldn't have had time to do anything but fight and claw for the exits.

Some of them – very few – may have escaped and made their home in the Wilds, but most of them died. Our teachers told us the truth, at least, about that. I close my eyes, feel myself swaying on my feet.

'Are you okay?' Sarah asks. She puts her hand on my back. 'We can turn around.'

'I'm okay.' I open my eyes. We've only gone a few hundred feet. Most of the old main street still stretches in front of us, and I'm determined to see all of it.

We walk even slower now, as Sarah points out the empty spaces and broken foundations where buildings must once have existed: a restaurant ('a pizza restaurant – that's where we got the stove'); a deli ('you can still see the sign – see? Kind of buried over there? "Sandwiches made to order"'); a grocery store.

The grocery store seems to depress Sarah. Here the ground is churned up, the grass even newer than everywhere else; the site of years and years of digging. 'For a long time we kept finding things to eat, buried all around here. Cans of food, you know, and even some packaged stuff that made it through the fires.' She sighs, looks wistful. 'It's all gone now, though.'

We walk on. Another restaurant, marked by an enormous metal counter, and two metal-backed chairs sitting side by side in a solid square of sunlight; a hardware store ('saved our lives plenty of times'). Next to the hardware store is an old bank:

here, too, there are stairs that disappear into the earth, a yawning mouth cut into the ground. The dark-haired boy – the glarer – is just emerging into the sunshine. He has a rifle slung casually over one shoulder.

'Hey, Tack,' Sarah says shyly.

He ruffles her hair as he passes. 'Boys only,' he says. 'You know that.'

'I know, I know.' She rolls her eyes. 'I'm just showing Lena around. That's where the boys sleep,' Sarah explains to me.

So even the Invalids have not entirely done away with segregation. This small piece of normalcy – of familiarity – is a relief.

Tack's eyes click to me, and he frowns.

'Hi.' My voice comes out as a squeak. I try, unsuccessfully, to smile. He's very tall and, like everyone else in the Wilds, thin; but his forearms are roped with muscle, and his jaw is square and strong. He, too, has a procedural mark, a three-pronged scar behind his left ear. I wonder if it is a fake, like Alex's was; or whether, perhaps, the cure didn't work on him.

'Just stay out of the vaults.' The words are directed at Sarah, but he keeps his eyes locked on me. They are cold, appraising.

'We will,' Sarah says. As he stalks away, she whispers to me, 'He's like that with everyone.'

'I can see what Raven means about the attitude problem.'

'Don't feel bad, though. I mean, you can't take it personally.'

'I won't,' I say, but the truth is that the brief encounter has shaken me. Everything is wrong here, upside down and inverted: the door frames that open into air, invisible structures – buildings, signposts, streets, still casting the shadow of the past over everything. I can feel them, can hear the rush of hundreds of feet, can hear old laughter running underneath the birdsong: a place built of memory and echo.

I am suddenly exhausted. We have made it only halfway down the old street, but my earlier resolution to walk the whole area now seems absurd. The brightness of the sun, the air and space around me – all of it feels disorienting. I turn around – too quickly, clumsily – and trip over a slab of limestone spattered in bird shit; for one second I am in free fall and then I'm landing, hard, face down in the dirt.

'Lena!' Sarah is next to me in a second, helping to pull me to my feet. I've bitten down on my tongue and my mouth tastes like metal. 'Are you okay?'

'Just give me a second,' I say, gasping a little. I sit back on the limestone. Something occurs to me: I don't even know what day it is, what month. 'What's today's date?' I ask Sarah.

'August twenty-seventh,' she answers, still looking at me with her face all creased up, worried. But she's keeping her distance.

August 27. I left Portland on August 21. I've lost almost a week in the Wilds, in this upside-down place.

This is not my world. My world is unfolding miles away: a world of doors that lead to rooms, and clean white walls, and the quiet hum of refrigerators; a world of carefully plotted streets, and pavement that is not full of fissures. Another pang shoots through me. In less than a month, Hana will have her procedure.

Alex was the one who understood things here. He could have built up this collapsed street for me, turned it into a place of sense and order. He was going to lead me through the wilderness. With him, I would have been okay.

'Can I get you anything?' Sarah's voice is uncertain.

'I'll be all right.' I can barely force the words out, past the pain. 'It's just the food. Not used to it.'

I'm going to be sick again. I duck my head between my knees, coughing to force down the sob that shudders through me.

Sarah must know, though, because she says, in the quietest voice, 'You get used to it after a while.' I get the sense she's talking about more than the breakfast.

After that there is nothing to do but make our way back: down the bombed-out road, through the shards, metal glittering in the high grass like snakes lying in wait.

Grief is like sinking, like being buried. I am in water the tawny colour of kicked-up dirt. Every breath is full of choking. There is nothing to hold on to, no sides, no way to claw myself up. There is nothing to do but let go.

Let go. Feel the weight all around you, feel the squeezing of your lungs, the slow, low pressure. Let yourself go deeper. There is nothing but bottom. There is nothing but the taste of metal, and the echoes of old things, and days that look like darkness.

now

That is the girl I was then: stumbling, sinking, lost in brightness and space. My past had been wiped clean, bleached a stark and spotless white.

But you can build a future out of anything. A scrap, a flicker. The desire to go forward, slowly, one foot at a time. You can build an airy city out of ruins.

This is the girl I am right now: knees pressed together, hands on my thighs. Silk blouse pulling tight against my neck, skirt with a woollen waistband, standard issue, bearing the Quincy Edwards High School crest. It's itchy; I wish I could scratch, but I won't. She would take that as a sign of nerves, and I am not nervous, will never be nervous again in my life.

She blinks. I don't. She is Mrs. Tulle, the principal, with a face like a fish pressed to glass; eyes so large they appear distorted.

'Is everything okay at home, Magdalena?'

It's strange to hear her use my full name. Everyone has always called me Lena.

'Fine,' I say.

She shuffles the papers on her desk. Everything in her office is ordered, all the edges lined up correctly. Even the water glass on her desk is centreed perfectly on its coaster. The cureds have always liked order: straightening, aligning, making adjustments. *Cleanliness Is Next to Godliness, and Order Is Ascension.* It gives them something to do, I guess – tasks to fill those long, empty hours.

'You live with your sister and her husband, is that correct?'

I nod, repeat the story of my new life: 'My mother and father were killed in one of the Incidents.'

This, at least, is not so much of a lie. The old Lena, too, was an orphan; as good as one, anyway.

I do not have to clarify the reference to the Incidents. Everyone has heard about them by now: last fall, the resistance coordinated its first major, violent, visible strikes. In a handful of cities, members of the resistance – helped by sympathizers, and in some cases, young uncureds – caused simultaneous explosions in important municipal buildings.

In Portland, the resistance chose to explode a portion of the Crypts. In the ensuing chaos, two dozen civilians were killed. The police and regulators were able to restore order, but not before several hundred prisoners had escaped.

It's ironic. My mother spent ten years tunnelling her way out of that place, when she might have just waited another few months and strolled free.

Mrs. Tulle winces.

'Yes, I saw that in your records.' Behind her, a humidifier whirs quietly. Still, the air is dry. Her office smells like paper and, faintly, of hairspray. A trickle of sweat rolls down my back. The skirt is hot.

'We're concerned that you seem to be having trouble

adjusting,' she says, watching me with those fish eyes. 'You've been eating lunch by yourself.' It's an accusation.

Even this new Lena feels slightly embarrassed; the only thing worse than having no friends is being pitied for having no friends. 'To be honest, I'm having some trouble with the girls,' new Lena says. 'I'm finding them a little bit . . . immature.' As I speak, I angle my head away slightly, so she can see the triangular scar just behind my left ear: the mark of the procedure, the mark of being cured.

Instantly, her expression softens. 'Well, yes, of course. Many of them are younger than you, after all. Not yet eighteen, uncured.'

I spread my hands as if to say, *Of course*.

But Mrs. Tulle isn't done with me, although her voice has lost its edge. 'Mrs. Fierstein says you fell asleep in class again. We're worried, Lena. Do you feel the workload is too much for you? Are you having trouble sleeping at night?'

'I have been a little stressed,' I admit. 'It's all this DFA stuff.'

Mrs. Tulle raises her eyebrows. 'I didn't realize you were in the DFA.'

'Division A,' I say. 'We're having a big rally next Friday. Actually, there's a planning meeting this afternoon in Manhattan. I don't want to be late.'

'Of course, of course. I know all about the rally.' Mrs. Tulle lifts her papers, jogs them against the desk to make sure their edges are aligned, and slides them into a drawer. I can tell I'm off the hook. The DFA is the magic word: *Deliria*-Free America. Open sesame. She is all kindness now. 'It's very impressive that you're trying to balance your extracurricular involvements with your schoolwork, Lena. And we support the work the DFA is doing. Just be sure you can find a balance. I don't want your board scores to suffer because of your social work, however important it is.'

'I understand.' I duck my head and look penitent. The new Lena is a good actress.

Mrs. Tulle smiles at me. 'Now go on. We don't want you to be late to your meeting.'

I stand up, shoulder my tote bag. 'Thanks.'

She inclines her head toward the door, a signal that I can leave.

I walk through the scrubbed linoleum halls: more white walls, more quiet. All the other students have gone home by now.

Then it's out through the double doors, into the dazzling white landscape: an unexpected March snow, hard, bright light, trees encased in thick black sheaths of ice. I pull my jacket tighter and stomp my way out of the iron gates, onto Eighth Avenue.

This is the girl I am now. My future is here, in this city, full of icicles dangling like daggers getting ready to drop.

There's more traffic in the sister cities than I've ever seen in my life. Hardly anyone had working cars in Portland; in New York, people are richer and can afford the gas. When I first came to Brooklyn, I used to go to Times Square just to watch them, sometimes a dozen at a time, one right after the other.

My bus gets stuck on 31st Street behind a garbage truck that has backed into a soot-coloured snowbank, and by the time I get to the Javits Centre, the DFA meeting has already begun. The steps are empty, as is the enormous entrance hall, and I can hear the distant, booming feed from a microphone, applause that sounds like a roar. I hurry to the metal detector and unload my bag, then stand with arms and legs splayed while a man sweeps impassively with the wand over my breasts and between my legs. I have long since outgrown being embarrassed by these procedures. Then it's over to the folding table set just in front of two enormous double doors; behind them, I can hear another smattering of applause, and more microphone-voice, amplified, thunderous, passionate. The words are inaudible.

'Identity card, please,' drones the woman behind the table, a volunteer. I wait while she scans my ID; then she waves me on with a jerk of her head.

The auditorium is enormous. It must fit at least two thousand people and is, as always, almost entirely full. There are a few empty seats off to the very left, close to the stage, and I skirt the periphery of the room, trying to slip into a chair as inconspicuously as possible. I don't have to worry. Everyone in the room is transfixed by the man behind the podium. The air is charged; I have the sense of thousands and thousands of droplets, suspended, waiting to fall.

'. . . is not sufficient to ensure our safety,' the man is saying. His voice booms through the room. Under the high fluorescent lights, his hair shines a brilliant black, like a helmet. This is Thomas Fineman, the founder of the DFA. 'They talk to us of risk and harm, damages and side effects. But what risk will there be to us as a people, as a society, if we do not act? If we do not insist on protecting the whole, what good is the health of a mere portion?'

A smattering of applause. Thomas adjusts his cuffs, leans closer to the microphone. 'This must be our single, unified purpose. This is the point of our demonstration. We ask that our government, our scientists, our agencies, protect us. We ask that they keep faith with their people, keep faith with God and his Order. Did God himself not reject, over thousands of years, millions of species that were faulty or flawed in some way, on his way to a perfect creation? Do we not learn that it is sometimes necessary to purge the weak, and the diseased, in order to evolve to a better society?'

The applause swells, cresting. I clap as well. Lena Morgan Jones claps.

This is my mission, the job that I have been given by Raven: Watch the DFA. Observe. Blend.

They have told me nothing else.

'Finally, we ask the government to stand behind the promise of *The Book of Shhh*: to ensure the Safety, Health, and Happiness of our cities and our people.'

I observe:

Rows of high lights.

Rows of half-moon faces, pale, bloated, fearful, and grateful – the faces of the cured.

Grey carpet, rubbed bare by the pressure of so many feet.

A fat man to my right, wheezing, pants belted high over his paunch.

A small area cordoned off next to the stage, three chairs, only one of them occupied.

A boy.

Of all the things I see, the boy is the most interesting. The other things – the carpet, the faces – are the same at every meeting of the DFA. Even the fat man. Sometimes he is fat, sometimes he is thin, sometimes it is a woman instead. But it is all the same – they are always all the same.

The boy's eyes are dark blue, a stormy colour. His hair is caramel blond and wavy, and hangs to his mid-jawline. He is wearing a collared red polo shirt, short-sleeved despite the weather, and pressed dark jeans. His loafers are new, and he also wears a shiny silver watch around one wrist. Everything about him says rich. His hands are folded in his lap. Everything about him says right, too. Even his unblinking expression as he watches his father onstage is perfection and practice, the embodiment of a cured's controlled detachment.

Of course he isn't cured, not yet. This is Julian Fineman, Thomas Fineman's son, and although he is eighteen, he has not yet had the procedure. The scientists have so far refused to treat him. Next Friday, the same day as the big planned DFA rally in Times Square, that will change. He will have his procedure, and he will be cured.

Possibly. It is also possible he will die, or that his mental functioning will be so severely damaged, he might as well be dead. But he will still have the procedure. His father insists on it. Julian insists on it.

I have never seen him in person before, although I have seen his face on posters and in the back of pamphlets. Julian is famous. He is a martyr to the cause, a hero to the DFA, and president of the organization's youth division.

He is taller than I expected. And better-looking, too. The photos have not done justice to the angle of his jaw, or the broadness of his shoulders: a swimmer's build.

Onstage, Thomas Fineman is wrapping up his portion of the speech. 'We do not deny the dangers of insisting that the cure be administered earlier,' he is saying, 'but we assert that the dangers of delaying the cure are even worse. We are willing to accept the consequences. We are brave enough to sacrifice a few for the good of the whole.' He pauses while again the auditorium is filled with applause, tilting his head appreciatively until the roar fades away. The light winks off his watch: he and his son have identical models.

'Now, I'd like to introduce you to an individual who

embodies all the values of the DFA. This young man understands better than anyone the importance of insisting on a
cure, even for those who are young, even for those who might
be endangered by its administration. He understands that in
order for the United States to prosper, in order for all of us to
live happily and in safety, it is necessary to occasionally sacrifice the needs of the individual. Sacrifice is safety, and health
is only in the whole. Members of the DFA, please welcome to
the stage my son, Julian Fineman.'

Clap, clap, clap goes Lena, along with the rest of the crowd.
Thomas leaves the stage as Julian takes it. They pass each other
on the stairs, give each other a brief nod. They do not touch.

Julian has brought notes, which he sets on the podium in
front of him. For a moment, the auditorium is filled with the
amplified sounds of rustling paper. Julian's eyes scan the crowd,
and for a second they land on me. He half opens his mouth
and my heart stops: it is as though he has just recognized me.
Then his eyes continue to sweep, and my heart comes
hammering back against my ribs. I'm just being paranoid.

Julian fumbles with the microphone to adjust it to his height.
He is even taller than his father. It's funny that they look so
different: Thomas, tall and dark and fierce-looking, a hawk;
his son, tall and broad and fair, with those improbably blue
eyes. Only the hard angle of their jaws is the same.

He runs a hand through his hair, and I wonder whether he
is nervous. But when he begins speaking, his voice is full and
steady.

'I was nine when I was told I was dying,' he says plainly,
and again I feel that expectation hanging in the air, shimmering
droplets, as though everyone has just leaned forward a fraction
of an inch. 'That's when the seizures began. The first one was

so bad I nearly bit off my tongue; during the second seizure, I cracked my head against the fireplace. My parents were concerned.'

Something wrenches in my stomach – deep inside, underneath the layers I've built over the past six months, past the fake Lena with her shell and her ID cards and the three-pointed scar behind her ear. This is the world we live in, a world of safety and happiness and order, a world without love.

A world where children crack their heads on stone fireplaces and nearly gnaw off their tongues and the parents are concerned. Not heartbroken, frantic, desperate. Concerned, as they are when you fail mathematics, as they are when they are late to pay their taxes.

'The doctors told me a tumour was growing in my brain and causing the seizures. The operation to remove it would be life-threatening. They doubted I would make it. But if they did not operate – if they let the tumour grow and expand – I had no chance at all.'

Julian pauses, and I think I see him shoot a momentary glance in his father's direction. Thomas Fineman has taken the seat his son vacated, and is sitting, legs crossed, face expressionless.

'No chance at all,' Julian repeats. 'And so the sick thing, the growth, had to be excised. It had to be lifted away from the clean tissue. Otherwise, it would only spread, turning the remaining healthy tissue sick.'

Julian shuffles his notes and keeps his eyes locked to the pages in front of him as he reads out, 'The first operation was a success, and for a while, the seizures stopped. Then, when I was twelve, they returned. The cancer was back, this time pressing at the base of my brain stem.'

His hands tighten on the sides of the podium and release.

For a moment, there is silence. Someone in the audience coughs. Droplets, droplets: we are all identical drips and drops of people, hovering, waiting to be tipped, waiting for someone to show us the way, to pour us down a path.

Julian looks up. There is a screen behind him on which his image is projected, blowing up his face by a power of fifteen. His eyes are a swirl of blue and green and gold, like the surface of the ocean on a sunny day, and behind the flatness, the practiced calm, I think I see something flashing there – an expression that is gone before I can find a name for it.

'I've had three operations since the first one,' he says. 'They have removed the tumour four times, and three times it has regrown, as sicknesses will, unless they are removed swiftly and completely.' He pauses to let the significance of the statement sink in. 'I have now been cancer free for two years.' There is a smattering of applause. Julian holds up a hand and the room once again goes silent.

Julian smiles, and the enormous Julian behind him smiles also: a pixelated version, a blur. 'The doctors have told me that further surgeries may endanger my life. Too much tissue has been removed already, too many excisions performed; if I am cured, I might lose the ability to regulate my emotions at all. I might lose the ability to speak, to see, to move.' He shifts at the podium. 'It is possible that my brain will shut down entirely.'

I can't help it; I am holding my breath too, along with everybody else. Only Thomas Fineman looks relaxed; I wonder how often he has heard this speech.

Julian leans forward another inch toward the microphone, and suddenly it is like he is addressing each and every one of us individually: his voice is low and urgent, a secret whispered in our ears.

'They have refused to cure me for this reason. For more than a year we have been fighting for a procedure date, and finally we have arranged one. On March twenty-third, the day of our rally, I will be cured.'

Another smattering of applause, but Julian pushes through it. He is not done yet.

'It will be a historic day, even though it may prove to be my last. Don't think I don't understand the risks, because I do.' He straightens up, and his voice becomes louder, thunderous. The eyes on the screen are flashing now, dazzling, full of light. 'But there is no choice, just as there wasn't when I was nine. We must excise the sickness. We must cut it out, no matter what the risks. Otherwise it will only grow. It will spread like the very worst cancer and put all of us – every single person born into this vast and wonderful country – at risk. So I say to you: We will – we must – cut away the sickness, wherever it is. Thank you.'

There; that's it. He has done it. He has tipped us over, all of us in our teetering expectancy, and now we are pouring toward him, coursing on a wave of sound, of roaring shouts and applause. Lena claps along with everybody else until her palms burn; she keeps clapping until they go numb. Half the audience stands, cheering. Someone starts a chant of 'DFA! DFA!' and soon we are all chanting: it is earsplitting, a deafening roar. At a certain point Thomas joins his son onstage again and they stand solemnly, side by side – one fair, one dark, like the two sides of the moon – watching over us as we keep clapping, keep chanting, keep roaring our approval. They are the moon; we are a tide, their tide, and under their direction we will wipe clean all the sickness and blight from the world.

then

Someone is always sick in the Wilds. As soon as I am strong enough to move out of the sickroom and onto a mattress on the floor, Squirrel has to move in; and after Squirrel's turn, it is Grandpa's. At night, the homestead echoes with the sounds of coughing, heaving, feverish chatter: noises of disease, which run through the walls and fill us all with dread. The problem is the space and the closeness. We live on top of one another, breathe and sneeze on one another, share everything. And nothing and no one is ever really clean.

Hunger gnaws at us, makes tempers run short. After my first exploration of the homestead, I retreated underground, like an animal scrabbling back into the safety of its lair. One day passes, then two. The supplies have yet to come. Each morning different people go out to check for messages; I gather that they have found some way to communicate with the sympathizers and resisters on the other side. That is all there is for me to do: listen, watch, stay quiet.

In the afternoons I sleep, and when I can't sleep, I close

my eyes and imagine being back in the abandoned house at 37 Brooks with Alex lying next to me. I try to feel my way through the curtain; I imagine if I can somehow pull apart the days that have passed since the escape, can mend the tear in time, I can have him back.

But whenever I open my eyes I am still here, on a mattress on the floor, and still hungry.

After another four days, everyone is moving slowly, as though we're all underwater. The pots are impossible for me to lift. When I try to stand too quickly I get dizzy. I have to spend more time in bed, and when I'm not in bed I think that everyone is glaring at me, can feel the Invalids' resentment, hard-edged, like a wall. Maybe I'm just imagining it, but this is, after all, my fault.

The catch, too, has been poor. Roach traps a few rabbits and there is general excitement; but the meat is tough and full of gristle, and when everything is dished up there is barely enough to go around.

Then one day I am in the storeroom, sweeping – Raven insists we go through the motions, insists on keeping everything clean – when I hear shouts from aboveground, laughter and running. Feet pound down the stairs. Hunter comes swinging into the kitchen, followed by an older woman, Miyako. I have not seen them – or anyone – so energetic in days.

'Where's Raven?' Hunter demands breathlessly.

I shrug. 'I don't know.'

Miyako lets out an exasperated sound, and both she and Hunter spin around, prepared to dart up the stairs again.

'What's going on?' I ask.

'We got a message from the other side,' Hunter says. That's what people here call the bordered communities: the other side, when they're feeling generous; Zombieland, when they aren't. 'Supplies are coming in today. We need help taking delivery.'

'Can you help?' Miyako asks, sizing me up. She is broad through the shoulders, and very tall – if she had enough to eat, she would be an Amazon. As it is she is all muscle and sinew.

I shake my head. 'I – I'm not strong enough.'

Hunter and Miyako exchange a look.

'The others will help,' Hunter says in a low voice. Then they pound up the stairs again, leaving me alone.

Later that afternoon they come back, ten of them, bearing heavy-duty garbage bags. The bags have been placed in half-full wooden crates in the Cocheco River at the border, and the crates have floated down to us. Even Raven can't maintain order, or control her excitement. Everyone rips the bags to shreds, shouting and whooping as supplies tumble onto the floor: cans of beans, tuna, chicken, soup; bags of rice, flour, lentils, and more beans; dried jerky, sacks of nuts and cereal; hard-boiled eggs, nestled in a bin of towels; Band-Aids, Vaseline, tubes of ChapStick, medical supplies; even a new pack of underwear, a bundle of clothes, bottles of soap and shampoo. Sarah hugs the jerky to her chest, and Raven puts her nose in a package of soap, inhaling. It's like a birthday party but better: ours to share, and just for that moment I feel a rush of happiness. Just for that moment, I feel as though I belong here.

Our luck has turned. A few hours later, Tack takes down a deer.

That night we have our first proper meal since I've arrived. We dish up enormous plates of brown rice, topped with meat braised and softened with crushed tomatoes and dried herbs.

It's so good I could cry, and Sarah actually does cry, sitting and sobbing in front of her plate. Miyako puts her arm around her and murmurs into Sarah's hair. The gesture makes me think of my mother; a few days ago I asked Raven about her, with no luck.

What does she look like? Raven had asked, and I had to confess I didn't know. When I was younger she had long, soft auburn hair, and a full-moon face. But after over ten years in Portland's prison, the Crypts – where she had been my whole life, while I believed her dead – I doubt she resembles the woman from my hazy childhood memories.

Her name is Annabel, I told her, but Raven was already shaking her head.

'Eat, eat,' Miyako urges Sarah, and she does. We all do, ravenously: scooping up rice with our hands, lifting our plates to lick them clean. Someone from the other side has even thought to include a bottle of whiskey, wrapped carefully in a sweatshirt, and everyone cheers when that makes the rounds as well. I had alcohol only once or twice when I lived in Portland, and never understood its appeal, but I take a sip from the bottle when it makes its way to me. It burns hard going down, and I start coughing. Hunter grins and claps me on the back. Tack nearly tears the bottle out of my hands and says, curtly, 'Don't drink it if you're just going to spit it up.'

'You get used to it,' Hunter leans in to whisper, almost an identical refrain to Sarah's remark a week ago. I'm not sure whether he's talking about the whiskey or Tack's attitude. But already there's a warm glow spreading through my stomach. When the bottle comes around again I take a slightly larger sip, and another, and the warmth spreads to my head.

Later: I'm seeing everything in pieces and fractions, like a series of photographs shuffled randomly together. Miyako and Lu in the corner, arms interlinked, dancing, while everyone claps; Blue sleeping curled up on a bench, and then borne out of the room, still asleep, by Squirrel; Raven standing on one of the benches, making a speech about freedom. She is laughing, too, her dark hair a shimmering curtain, and then Tack is helping her down: brown hands around her waist, a moment of suspension when she pauses, airborne, in his arms. I think of birds and flying away. I think of Alex.

One day Raven turns to me and says abruptly, 'If you want to stay, you have to work.'

'I work,' I say.

'You clean,' she counters. 'You boil the water. The rest of us haul water, look for food, scout for messages. Even Grandma hauls water – a mile and a half, with heavy buckets. And she's sixty years old.'

'I—' Of course she's right, and I know it. The guilt has been with me every day, as heavy as the thickness of the air. I heard Tack say to Raven that I'm a waste of a good bed. I had to squat in the storeroom for almost half an hour afterward with my arms wrapped around my knees until I stopped shaking. Hunter's the only one of the homesteaders who's nice to me, and he's nice to everybody.

'I'm not ready. I'm not strong enough.'

She watches me for a second, and lets the silence stretch uncomfortably between us so I can feel the absurdity of the words. If I'm not strong by now, that's my fault too. 'We're moving soon. Relocation starts in a few weeks. We'll need all the help we can get.'

'Moving?' I repeat.

'Going south.' She turns away, starts retreating down the hallway. 'Shutting up the homestead for the winter. And if you want to come, you're going to help.'

Then she pauses. 'You're welcome to stay here, of course,' she says, turning around and raising an eyebrow. 'Although winters are deadly. When the river freezes, we can't get any supplies. But maybe that's what you want?'

I don't say anything.

'You have until tomorrow to choose,' she says.

The next morning, Raven shakes me awake from a nightmare. I sit up, gasping. I remember a fall through the air, and a mass of black birds. All the other girls are still sleeping, and the room is full of their rhythmic breathing. There must be a candle burning out in the hall, casting a tiny bit of light into the room. I can just make out Raven's shape, squatting in front of me, and register the fact that she is already dressed.

'What did you choose?' she whispers.

'I want to work,' I whisper back, because it's the only thing I can say. My heart is still beating, hard, in my chest.

I can't see her smile, but I think I hear it: her lips cracking, a small exhalation that could be a laugh. 'Good for you.' She holds up a dented bucket. 'It's water time.'

Raven withdraws, and I fumble for my clothes in the dark. When I first arrived at the homestead, the sleeping room looked like a mess, an explosion of fabric and clothing and miscellaneous belongings. Over time I've realized it isn't actually so disorganized. Everyone has a little area, a space circumscribed for their things. We've drawn invisible circles around our little beds, or blankets, or mattresses, and people guard those spaces fiercely, like dogs marking out their territory.

You must keep everything you own and need inside your little circle. Once it leaves, it is no longer yours. The clothes I've picked out from the store are folded at the very bottom of my blanket.

I fumble out of the room and feel my way down the hall. I find Raven by the kitchen, surrounded by empty buckets, coaxing last night's fire up with the blunt, charred end of a large stick. She hasn't turned on the lanterns here, either. It would be a waste of battery power. The smell of smoking wood, the low, flickering shadows, Raven's shoulders touched by an orange glow: it makes me feel as though I haven't yet woken from my dream.

'Ready?' She straightens up when she hears me, loops a bucket over each arm.

I nod, and she jerks her head toward the remaining buckets.

We wind our way upstairs and then get coughed out into the outside world: the release from inside, from the air and the closeness, is just as startling and abrupt as it was the time I explored the rest of the homestead with Sarah. The first thing that strikes me is the cold. The wind is icy and drives right through my T-shirt, and I let out a gasp without meaning to.

'What's the matter?' Raven asks, speaking at a normal volume now that we're outside.

'Cold,' I reply. The air smells like winter already, though I can see that the trees still have their leaves. At the very edge of the horizon, over the ragged and frayed skyline of the trees, there is a bare, golden glow where the sun is edging upward. The world is all greys and purples. The animals and birds are just beginning to stir.

'Less than a week until October,' Raven says, shrugging, and then, as I trip over a piece of twisted metal siding half embedded in the ground, she says, 'Watch your step.'

That's when it really hits me: I've been following the rhythm of the days, keeping mental track of the date. But really I've been pretending that while I stayed buried underground, the rest of the world stayed motionless as well.

'Let me know if I'm walking too fast,' Raven says.

'Okay,' I say. My voice sounds strange in the empty, thin air of this autumn world.

We pick our way down the old main street. Raven walks easily, avoiding the torn-up bits of concrete and the twisted metal litter almost instinctively, the way that Sarah did. At the entrance to the old bank vault, where the boys sleep, Bram is waiting for us. Bram has dark hair and mocha-coloured skin. He's one of the quieter boys, one of the few who doesn't scare me. He and Hunter are always together; in Zombieland, we would have called them Unnaturals, but here their relationship seems normal, effortless. Seeing them reminds me of pictures of Hana and me: one dark, one light. Raven passes him several buckets wordlessly, and he falls in next to us in silence. But he smiles at me, and I'm grateful for it.

Even though the air is cold, soon I'm sweating and my heart pushes painfully against my ribs. It has been more than a month since I've walked more than sixty feet at a time. My muscles are weak, and carrying even the empty buckets makes my shoulders ache after a few minutes. I keep shifting the handles in my palms; I refuse to complain or ask Raven to help, even though she must see that I'm having trouble keeping up. I don't even want to think about how long and slow the way back will be, once the buckets are full.

We've left the homestead and the old main street behind, and veered off into the trees. All around us, the leaves are different shades of gold, orange, red, and brown. It is as though the whole forest is burning, a beautiful slow smoulder. I can feel the space all around me, unbounded and unwalled, bright open air. Animals move, unseen, to our left and right, rustling through the dry leaves.

'Almost there,' Raven calls back. 'You're doing good, Lena.'

'Thanks,' I puff out. Sweat is dripping into my eyes, and I can't believe I was ever cold. I don't even bother to elbow or swat the stray branches out of my way. As Bram pushes through them ahead of me, they rebound and thwack me hard on my arms and legs, leaving tiny stinging lashes all over my skin. I'm too tired to care. I feel as though we've been walking for hours, but that's impossible. Sarah said the river was a little over a mile away. Besides, the sun has only just risen.

A little bit farther and we hear it, over the twittering of the birds and the rush of the wind in the trees: the low, babbling sound of moving water. Then the trees break apart, and the ground turns rocky, and we're standing at the edge of a wide, flat stream. Sunlight glints off the water, giving the impression of coins laid underneath its surface. Fifty feet to our left is a miniature waterfall, where the stream comes churning over a series of small, black, lichen-spotted rocks. All of a sudden I have to fight the desire to cry. This place has always existed: while cities were bombed and fell into ruins, while walls went up – the stream was here, running over the rocks, full of its own secret laughter.

We are such small, stupid things. For most of my life I thought of nature as the stupid thing: blind, animal, destructive. We, the humans, were clean and smart and in control; we had wrestled the rest of the world into submission, battered it down, pinned it to a glass slide and the pages of *The Book of Shhh*.

Raven and Bram are already wading into the stream, holding their buckets, crouching to fill them.

'Come on,' Raven says shortly. 'The others will be waking up.'

They have both come barefoot; I crouch down to untie my shoes. My fingers are swollen from the cold, even though I can no longer feel it. Heat drums through my body. I have a hard time with the laces, and by the time I edge close to the water, Raven and Bram have their buckets full, lined up on the bank. Pieces of grass and dead insects swirl over their surface; we will pick them out later, and boil the water to sterilize it.

My first step into the stream nearly takes me off my feet. Even this close to the bank, the current is much stronger than it looks. I pinwheel my arms wildly, trying to stay upright, and drop one of the buckets. Bram, who is waiting on the bank, starts to laugh. His laugh is high and surprisingly sweet.

'All right.' Raven gives him a push. 'That's enough of a show. We'll see you at the homestead.'

He touches two fingers obediently to his temple. 'See you later, Lena,' he says, and I realize it's the first time somebody other than Raven, Sarah, or Hunter has spoken to me in a week.

'See you,' I say.

The streambed is coated in tiny pebbles, slick and hard on the underside of my feet. I retrieve the fallen bucket and crouch low, as Raven and Bram did, letting it fill. Lugging it back to the bank is harder. My arms are weak, and the metal handles dig painfully into my palms.

'One more to go,' Raven says. She is watching me, arms crossed.

The next one is slightly larger than the first, and more difficult to manoeuvre once it's full. I have to carry it with both hands, half bent over, letting the bucket bang against my shins. I wade out of the stream and set it down with a sigh of relief. I have no idea how I'll make it back to the homestead carrying both buckets at once. It's impossible. It will take me hours.

'Ready to go?' Raven asks.

'Just give me a second,' I say, resting my hands on my knees. My arms are already trembling a little. I want to stay here for as long as possible, with the sun breaking through the trees, and the stream speaking its own, old language, and the birds zipping back and forth, dark shadows. *Alex would love it here*, I think without meaning to. I've been trying so hard not to think his name, not to even breathe the idea of him.

On the far side of the bank there is a small bird with ink-blue feathers, preening at the edge of the water; and suddenly I have never wanted anything more than to strip down and swim, wash off all the layers of dirt and sweat and grime that I have not been able to scrub away at the homestead.

'Will you turn around?' I ask Raven. She rolls her eyes, looking amused, but she does.

I wiggle out of my pants and underwear, strip off my tank top and drop it on the grass. Wading back into the water is equal parts pain and pleasure – a cutting cold, a pure feeling that drives through my whole body. As I move toward the centre of the stream, the stones underneath my feet get larger and flatter, and the current pushes at my legs more strongly. Even though the stream isn't very wide, just beyond the miniature waterfall there's a dark space where the streambed bottoms out, a natural swimming hole. I stand shivering with the water rushing around my knees, and at the last second can't quite bring myself to do it. It's so cold: the water looks so dark, and black, and deep.

'I won't wait for you forever,' Raven calls out, with her back to me.

'Five minutes,' I call, and I spread my arms and dive forward into the deepness of the water. I am slammed – the cold is a wall, frigid and impenetrable, and tears at every nerve in my body – there's a ringing in my ears, and a rushing, rushing all around me. The breath goes out of me and I come up gasping, breaking the surface, as above me the sun rises higher and the sky deepens, becomes solid, to hold it.

And just as suddenly the cold is gone. I put my head under again, treading water, and let the stream push and pull at me. With my head underwater I can almost understand its accents, the babbling, gurgling sound. With my head under-water I hear it say the name I've tried so hard not to think – *Alex, Alex, Alex* – and hear it, too, carrying the name away. I come out of the stream shivering and laughing, and dress with my teeth chattering, my fingernails edged with blue.

'I've never heard you laugh before,' Raven says, after I've pulled on my clothes. She's right. I haven't laughed since coming to the Wilds. It feels stupidly good. 'Ready?'

'Ready,' I say.

That first day, I have to carry one bucket at a time, lugging with both hands, sloshing water as I go, sweating and cursing. A slow shuffle; set one bucket down, go back and get the other bucket. Forward a few feet. Then pause, rest, panting.

Raven goes ahead of me. Every so often she stops, puts down her buckets, and strips willow bark from the trees, scattering it across the path so that I can find my way, even after I've lost sight of her. She comes back after half an hour, bringing a metal cup full of water, sanitized, for me to drink, and a small cotton cloth filled with almonds and dried raisins for me to eat. The sun is high and bright now, light cutting like blades between the trees.

Raven stays with me, although she never offers to help and I don't ask her to. She watches impassively, arms crossed, as I make my slow, agonizing way through the forest.

Final tally: two hours. Three blisters on my palms, one the size of a cherry. Arms that shake so badly I can barely bring them to my face when I try to wash off the sweat. A raw, red cut in the flesh of one hand, where the metal handle of one of the buckets has worn away the skin.

At dinner, Tack gives me the biggest serving of rice and beans, and although I can barely hold my fork because of the blisters, and Squirrel accidentally charred the rice so that it's brown and crispy on its underside, I think it is the best meal I have had since I came to the Wilds.

I'm so tired after dinner I fall asleep with my clothes on, almost as soon as my head hits the pillow, and so I forget to ask God, in my prayers, to keep me from waking up.

It's not until the following morning that I realize what day it is: September 26.

Hana was cured yesterday.

Hana is gone.

I have not cried since Alex died.

Alex is alive.

That becomes my mantra, the story I tell myself every day, as I emerge into the inky dawn and the mist and begin, slowly, painstakingly, to train again.

If I can run all the way to the old bank – lungs exploding, thighs shaking – then Alex will be alive.

First it's forty feet, then sixty, then two minutes straight, then four.

If I can make it to that tree, Alex will come back.

Alex is standing just beyond that hill; if I can make it to the top without stopping, he'll be there.

At first I trip and nearly twist my ankle about half a dozen times. I'm not used to the landscape of litter, can hardly see in the low, murky dawn light. But my eyes get better, or my feet learn the way, and after a few weeks my body gets used to the planes and angles of the ground, and the geometry of all those broken streets and buildings, and then I can run the whole length of the old main street without watching my feet.

Then it's farther, and faster.

Alex is alive. Just one more push, just a final sprint, and you'll see.

When Hana and I were on the track team together, we used to play little mental games like this to keep ourselves motivated. Running is a mental sport, more than anything else. You're only as good as your training, and your training is only as good as your thinking. If you make the whole eight miles without walking, you'll get 100 percent on your history boards. That's the kind of thing we used to say together. Sometimes it worked, sometimes it didn't. Sometimes we'd give up, laughing, at mile seven, saying, *Oops! There goes our history score.*

That's the thing: we didn't really care. A world without love is also a world without stakes.

Alex is alive. Push, push, push. I run until my feet are swollen, until my toes bleed and blister. Raven screams at me even as she is preparing buckets of cold water for my feet, tells me to be careful, warns me about the dangers of infection. Antibiotics are not easy to come by here.

The next morning I wrap my toes in cloth, stuff my feet into my shoes, and run again. If you can . . . just a little bit farther . . . just a little bit faster . . . you'll see, you'll see, you'll see. Alex is alive.

I'm not crazy. I know he isn't, not really. As soon as my runs are done and I'm hobbling back to the church basement, it hits me like a wall: the stupidity of it all, the pointlessness. Alex is gone, and no amount of running or pushing or bleeding will bring him back.

I know it. But here's the thing: when I'm running, there's always this split second when the pain is ripping through me and I can hardly breathe and all I see is colour and blur – and in that split second, right as the pain crests, and becomes too much, and there's a whiteness going through me, I see something to my left, a flicker of colour (auburn hair, burning, a crown of leaves) – and I know then, too, that if I only turn my head he'll be there, laughing, watching me, holding out his arms.

I don't ever turn my head to look, of course. But one day I will. One day I will, and he'll be back, and everything will be okay.

And until then: I run.

now

After the DFA meeting, I follow the crowd streaming out into the watery, early spring light. The energy is still there, pulsing through us all, but in the sunshine and the cold it feels meaner, harder-edged: an impulse to destroy.

Several buses are waiting at the curb, and already the lines to board zigzag back up the stairs of the Javits Centre. I've been waiting for half an hour, and have already seen three different rotations of buses, when I realize I've left one of my gloves inside the auditorium. I stop myself from cursing. I am packed among the cured, surrounded by them, and don't want to raise any alarms.

I'm only twenty people from the front of the line now, and for a moment I consider leaving the glove. But the past six months have taught me too much about wanting: in the Wilds it is practically a sin to waste, and it is definitely bad luck. Waste today, want tomorrow – another of Raven's favourite mantras.

I slip out of line, attracting puzzled looks and frowns, and head back up the stairs to the polished glass doors. The regulator who was manning the metal detector is gone, though he has left a portable radio on, and a half-drunk cup of coffee, lid off, sitting next to it. The woman who checked my ID has also disappeared, and the folding table has been cleared of DFA leaflets. The overhead lights have been turned off, and the room feels even vaster than usual.

Swinging open the auditorium doors, I am momentarily disoriented. I am staring, suddenly, at the enormous peak of a snow-capped mountain as though falling toward it from above. The picture is projected, huge, on the screen where Julian Fineman's face was enlarged earlier. But the room is otherwise dark, and the image is sharp and vivid. I can make out the dense ring of trees, like a black fur, at its base, and the sharp, bladelike peaks at its summit, crowned with lacy white caps. My breath catches a little. It's beautiful.

Then the picture changes. This time I am looking at a pale, sandy beach, and a swirling blue-green ocean. I take several steps into the room, suppressing a cry. I haven't seen the ocean since leaving Portland.

The picture changes again. Now the screen is full of huge trees, shooting up toward the sky, which is just visible through the canopy of thick branches. Sunlight slants at steep angles across the reddish trunks and the undergrowth of curling green ferns and flowers. I move forward again – entranced, compelled – and bump against one of the metal folding chairs. Instantly a person jumps from the front row, and a shadow silhouette floats onto the screen, obscuring a portion of the forest. Then the screen goes blank and the lights go on, and the silhouette is Julian Fineman. He is holding a remote control.

'What are you doing here?' he demands. I've clearly caught him off guard. Without waiting for me to reply, he says, 'The meeting's over.'

Beneath the aggression, I sense something else: embarrassment. And I am positive, then, that this is Julian Fineman's secret: he sits in the dark, he imagines himself into other places. He looks at beautiful pictures.

I'm so surprised I can barely stammer out a reply. 'I – I lost my glove.'

Julian looks away from me. I see his fingers tighten on the remote control. But when his eyes slide back to mine, he has regained his composure, his politeness. 'Where were you sitting?' he asks me. 'I can help you look for it.'

'No,' I burst out too loudly. I'm still in shock. The air between us still feels charged and unstable, like it did during the meeting. Something deep inside of me is aching – those pictures, that ocean, blown up on the enormous screen, made me feel as though I could fall through space and into the forest, could lick the snow off the mountaintop like whipped cream from a spoon. I wish I could ask him to turn off the lights, to show me again.

But he is Julian Fineman, and he is everything I hate, and I will not ask him for anything.

I move quickly back up to where I was sitting. Julian watches me the whole time, although he doesn't move – he stands there, perfectly still, in front of the now-blank screen. Only his eyes are mobile, alive. I can feel them on my neck, on my back, tangled in my hair. I find my glove easily and scoop it off the ground, holding it up for Julian's inspection.

'Found it,' I say, deliberately avoiding his eyes. I start walking quickly to the exit. He stops me with a question.

'How long were you standing there?'

'What?' I turn around again to look at him. His face is now expressionless, unreadable.

'How long were you there? How many pictures did you see?'

I hesitate, wondering whether this is some kind of test. 'I saw the mountain,' I say finally.

He looks down at his feet, then meets my gaze again. Even from a distance, I am startled by the clarity of his eyes. 'We're looking for strongholds,' he says, lifting his chin, as though expecting me to contradict him. 'Invalid camps. We're using all kinds of surveillance techniques.'

So, another fact: Julian Fineman is a liar.

At the same time, it's a mark of progress that someone like Julian would even use the word. A year ago, Invalids weren't even supposed to exist. We were supposed to have been exterminated during the blitz. We were the stuff of myth, like unicorns and werewolves.

That was before the Incidents, before the resistance started asserting itself more forcefully and we became impossible to ignore.

I force myself to smile. 'I hope you find them,' I say. 'I hope you find every last one.'

Julian nods.

As I turn around, I add, 'Before they find you.'

His voice rings out sharply. 'What did you say?'

I shoot him a look over my shoulder. 'Before they find us,' I say, and push through the doors, letting them swing shut behind me.

By the time I make it back to Brooklyn, the sun has set. The apartment is cold. The shades are drawn, and a single light burns in the foyer. The sideboard just inside the hall is stacked with a slender pile of mail.

NO ONE IS SAFE UNTIL EVERYONE IS CURED, reads the writing on the first envelope, printed neatly above our address. Then, beneath it: PLEASE SUPPORT THE DFA.

Next to the mail is a small silver tray for our identification papers. Two IDs are lined up next to each other: Rebecca Ann Sherman and Thomas Clive Sherman, both unsmiling in their official portraits, staring straight ahead. Rebecca has coal-black hair, perfectly parted, and wide brown eyes. Thomas's hair is clipped so short it's difficult to judge what colour it might be. His eyes are hooded, as though he's close to sleep.

Beneath their IDs are their documents, clipped together neatly. If you were to page through the packet, you would learn all the relevant facts about Rebecca and Thomas: dates and places of birth, parents and grandparents, salaries, school grades, incidents of disobedience, evaluation and board scores, the date and place of their wedding ceremony, all previous addresses.

Of course, Rebecca and Thomas don't really exist, any more than Lena Morgan Jones exists: a thin-faced girl, also unsmiling in her official ID. My ID goes next to Rebecca's. You never know when there might be a raid, or a census. It's better if you don't have to go digging for your documents. It's best, actually, if nobody ever goes digging around here.

It wasn't until I moved to New York City that I understood Raven's obsession with order in the Wilds: the surfaces must look right. They must be smooth. There must never be any crumbs.

That way there is never any trail to follow.

The curtains are closed in the living room. This keeps the heat in and also the eyes – of the neighbours, of the regulators, of passing patrols – out. In Zombieland, someone is always watching. There is nothing else for people to do. They do not think. They feel no passion, no hatred, no sadness; they feel nothing but fear, and a desire for control. So they watch, and poke, and pry.

At the back of the apartment is the kitchen. Hanging on the wall above the table is a photograph of Thomas Fineman, and another of Cormac T. Holmes, the scientist credited with performing the first-ever successful cure.

Past the stove is a little alcove pantry. It is lined with narrow shelves and absolutely packed with food. The memory of a long hunger is difficult to shake, and all of us – the ones who know – are secret hoarders now. We pack granola bars in our bags and stuff our pockets with sugar packets.

You never know when the hunger will be back.

One of the pantry's three walls is, in fact, a hidden door. I ease it open to reveal a set of rough wooden stairs. A light glows dimly in the basement, and I hear the staccato rhythm of voices. Raven and Tack are fighting – nothing new there – and I hear Tack, sounding pained, say, 'I just don't understand why we can't be honest with each other. We're supposed to be on the same side.'

Raven responds sharply, 'You know that's unrealistic, Tack. It's for the best. You have to trust me.'

'You're the one who isn't trusting—'

His voice cuts off sharply as I shut the door behind me, a little louder than I normally would, so they'll know I'm there. I hate listening to Tack and Raven fight – I'd never heard any adults fight until I escaped to the Wilds – though over time I've grown more used to it. I've had to. It seems like they're always bickering about something.

I go down the stairs. As I do, Tack turns away, passing a hand over his eyes. Raven says shortly, 'You're late. The meeting ended hours ago. What happened?'

'I missed the first round of buses.' Before Raven can start lecturing, I quickly add, 'I left a glove and had to go back for it. I spoke to Julian Fineman.'

'You what?' Raven bursts out, and Tack sighs and rubs his forehead.

'Only for, like, a minute.' I almost tell them about the pictures and decide, at the last minute, that I won't. 'It's cool. Nothing happened.'

'It's not cool, Lena,' Tack says. 'What did we tell you? It's all about staying under the radar.'

Sometimes it feels as though Tack and Raven take their roles as Thomas and Rachel – strict guardians – a little bit too seriously, and I have to fight the urge to roll my eyes.

'It was no big deal,' I insist.

'Everything's a big deal. Don't you get it? We—'

Raven cuts him off. 'She gets it. She's heard it a thousand times. Give her a break, okay?'

Tack stares at her mutely for a second, his mouth a thin white line. Raven meets his gaze steadily. I know they're angry about other things – that it's not just me – but I feel a hot rush of guilt anyway. I'm making things worse.

'You're unbelievable,' Tack says. I don't think he means for me to hear.

Then he brushes past me and pounds up the stairs.

'Where are you going?' Raven demands, and for a moment something flares in her eyes – some need, or fear. But it's gone before I can identify it.

'Out,' Tack says without stopping. 'There's no air down here.

I can hardly breathe.' Then he's pushing into the pantry and the door closes at the top of the stairwell, and Raven and I are left alone.

For a second we stand in silence. Then Raven barks a laugh. 'Don't mind him,' she says. 'You know Tack.'

'Yeah,' I say, feeling awkward. The fight has soured the air; Tack was right. The basement feels heavy, clotted. Normally it's my favourite place in the house, this secret space – Tack and Raven's, too. It's the only place where we can shed the false skins, fake names, fake pasts.

At least this room feels inhabited. The upstairs looks like a normal house, and smells like a normal house, and is full of normal-house things; but it's off somehow, as though it were tipped just a few inches on its foundations.

In contrast to the rest of the apartment, the basement is a wreck. Raven can't clean and straighten as fast as Tack can accumulate and unravel. Books – real books, banned books, old books – are piled everywhere. Tack collects them. No, more than that. He hoards them, the way the rest of us hoard food. I tried to read a few of them, just to find out what it was like before the cure, and before all the fences, but it made my chest ache to imagine it: all that freedom, all that feeling and life. It's better, much better, not to think about it too much.

Alex loved books. He was the one who first introduced me to poetry. That's another reason I can't read anymore.

Raven sighs and starts shuffling some papers piled hap-hazardly on a rickety wooden table in the centre of the room. 'It's this goddamn rally,' she says. 'It's got everybody all twitchy.'

'What's the problem?' I ask.

She waves away the question. 'Same as always. Rumours

about a riot. The underground is saying the Scavengers will show, try to pull something major. But nothing's confirmed.'

Raven's voice takes on a hard edge. I don't even like to say the word *Scavengers*. It leaves a bad taste in my mouth, of things rotting, of ash. All of us – the Invalids, the resistance – hate the Scavengers. They give us a bad name. Everyone agrees that they'll ruin, have already ruined, so much of what we are working to achieve. The Scavengers are Invalids, like us, but they don't stand for anything. We want to take down the walls and get rid of the cure. The Scavengers want to take down everything – burn everything to dust, steal and slaughter and set the world to flame.

I've only run into a group of Scavengers once, but I still have nightmares about them.

'They won't be able to pull it off,' I say, trying to sound confident. 'They're not organized.'

Raven shrugs. 'I hope not.' She stacks books on top of one another, making sure their corners are aligned. For a second I feel a rush of sadness for her: standing in the middle of so much mess, stacking books as though it means something, as though it will help.

'Is there anything I can do?'

'Don't worry about it.' Raven gives me a tight smile. 'That's my job, okay?'

That is another one of Raven's catchphrases. Like her insistence that the past is dead, it has become a kind of mantra. *I worry; you do what I say.* We all need mantras, I guess – stories we tell ourselves to keep us going.

'Okay.' For a moment we stand there. It's strange. In some ways Raven does feel like family – she's the closest thing I have to it, anyway – but at other times it occurs to me I don't really know her any better than I did in August, when she first found me. I still don't know much about the person she was before coming to the Wilds. She has closed that part of herself down, folded it back to some deep, unreachable place.

'Go on,' she says, jerking her head toward the stairs. 'It's late. You should eat something.'

As I head up the stairs I brush my fingers, once, against the metal license plate we've tacked onto the wall. We found it in the Wilds, half buried in the mud and slush, during the relocation; we were all close to dead at that point, exhausted and starving, sick and freezing. Bram was the one who spotted it; and as he lifted it out of the ground, the sun had burst through the cloud cover, and the metal had flared a sudden white, almost blinding me so I could barely read the words printed underneath the number.

Old words; words that nearly brought me to my knees.

Live free or die.

Four words. Thirteen letters. Ridges, bumps, swirls under my fingertips.

Another story. We cling tightly to it, and our belief turns it to truth.

then

It gets colder by the day. In the morning, the grass is coated in frost. The air stings my lungs when I run; the edges of the river are coated thinly with ice, which breaks apart around our ankles as we wade into the water with our buckets. The sun is sluggish, collapsing behind the horizon earlier and earlier, after a weak, watery swim across the sky.

I am growing stronger. I am a stone being excavated by the slow passage of water; I am wood charred by a fire. My muscles are ropes, my legs are wooden. My palms are calloused – the bottoms of my feet, too, are as thick and blunt as stone. I never miss a run. I volunteer to cart the water every day, even though we're supposed to rotate. Soon I can carry two buckets by myself the whole way back to camp without once pausing or stopping.

Alex passes next to me, weaving in and out of the shadows, threading between the crimson-and-yellow trees. In the summer he was fuller: I could see his eyes, his hair, a flash of his elbow. As the leaves begin to whirl to the ground and more and more trees are denuded, he is a stark black shadow, flickering in my peripheral vision.

I am learning, too. Hunter shows me how the messages are passed to us: how the sympathizers on the other side alert us to an arriving shipment.

'Come on,' he says to me one morning after breakfast. Blue and I are in the kitchen, scrubbing dishes. Blue has never quite opened up to me. She answers my questions with simple nods or shakes of her head. Her smallness, her shyness, the thinness of her bones: when I'm with Blue, I can't help but think of Grace.

That's why I avoid her as much as possible.

'Come on where?' I ask Hunter.

He grins. 'You a good climber?'

The question takes me by surprise. 'I'm okay,' I say, and have a sudden memory of scaling the border fence with Alex. I replace it quickly with another image: I am climbing into the leafy branches of one of the big maples in Deering Oaks Park. Hana's blonde hair flashes underneath the layers of green; she is circling the trunk, laughing, calling up for me to go higher.

But then I must take her out of the memory. I've learned to do that here, in the Wilds. In my head I trim her away – her voice, the flashing crown of her head – and leave only the sense of height, the swaying leaves, the green grass below me.

'It's time to show you the nests, then,' Hunter says.

I'm not looking forward to being outside. It was bitterly cold last night. The wind shrieked through the trees, tore down the stairs, probed all the cracks and crevices of the burrow with long, icy fingers. I came in half frozen from my run this morning, my fingers numb and blunt and useless. But I'm curious about the nests – I've heard the other homesteaders use the word – and I'm anxious to get away from Blue.

'Can you finish up here?' I ask Blue, and she nods, chewing on her lower lip. Grace used to do that too, when she was nervous. I feel a sharp pang of guilt. It's not Blue's fault that she reminds me of Grace.

It's not Blue's fault I left Grace behind.

'Thanks, Blue,' I say, and lay one hand on her shoulder. I can feel her trembling slightly beneath my fingers.

The cold is a wall, a physical force. I've managed to find an old wind breaker in the collection of clothes, but it's far too big and doesn't stop the wind from biting at my neck and fingers, slipping beneath the collar and freezing my heart in my chest. The ground is frozen and the frost-coated grass crunches under our feet. We walk quickly, to stay warm; our breath comes in clouds.

'How come you don't like Blue?' Hunter asks abruptly.

'I do,' I say quickly. 'I mean, she doesn't really talk to me, but . . .' I trail off. 'Is it that obvious?'

He laughs. 'So you don't like her.'

'She just reminds me of someone, that's all,' I say shortly, and Hunter turns serious.

'From before?' he asks.

I nod, and he reaches out and touches me once, lightly, on the elbow, to show me he understands. Hunter and I talk about everything except before. Of all the homesteaders, he is the one I feel closest to. We sit next to each other at dinner; and sometimes we stay up afterward, talking until the room is smudgy with smoke from the dying fire.

Hunter makes me laugh, even though for a long time I thought I would never laugh again.

It wasn't easy to feel comfortable around him. It was hard to shake all the lessons I learned on the other side, in Portland, warnings drilled into me by everyone I admired and trusted. The disease, they taught me, grew in the space between men and women, boys and girls; it was passed between them in looks and smiles and touches, and would take root inside of them like mould that rots a tree from the inside out. Then I found out that Hunter was an Unnatural, a thing I'd always been taught to revile.

Now Hunter is Hunter, and a friend, and nothing more.

We head north, away from the homestead. It's early, and the woods are quiet except for the crunch of our shoes on the thick layering of dead leaves. It hasn't rained in several weeks. The woods are starved for water. It's funny how I've learned to feel the woods, to understand them: their moods and tantrums, their explosions of joy and colour. It's so different from the parks and the carefully tended natural spaces in Portland. Those places were like animals at the zoo: caged in and also flattened, somehow. The Wilds are alive, and temperamental, and beautiful. Despite the hardships here, I am growing to love them.

'Almost there,' Hunter says. He nods to our left. Beyond the denuded branches I can see a crown of razor wire, looped at the top of a fence, and I feel a flash of fear, hot and sudden. I didn't realize we'd come so close to the border. We must be skirting the edge of Rochester. 'Don't worry.' Hunter reaches out and squeezes my shoulder. 'This side of the border isn't patrolled.'

I've been in the Wilds for a month and a half now, and in that time I've almost forgotten about the fences. It's amazing how close I have been, all this time, to my old life. And yet the distance that divides me from it is vast.

We veer away from the fence again. Soon we come to an area of enormous trees, bare branches grey and gnarled like arthritic fingers. It may have been years since they've bloomed at all; the trees seem to have been dead a long time. But when I say so to Hunter, he just laughs and shakes his head.

'Not dead.' He raps one with his knuckles as we pass. 'Just biding their time. Storing up energy. They tuck all their life away deep inside, for winter. When it gets warm, they'll bloom again. You'll see.'

I'm comforted by his words. *You'll see* means *We're coming back here*. It means *You're one of us now*. I run my fingers along a tree, feel the bark flake dryly under my fingertips. It's impossible to imagine anything alive under all that hardness, anything flowing or moving.

Hunter stops so abruptly I almost run into him. 'Here we are,' he says, grinning. 'The nests.'

He points upward. High in the branches of the trees are massive tangles of birds' nests: curls and spray, bits of moss and hanging creepers, all woven together so that it looks as though the trees are crowned with hair.

But even stranger: the branches are painted.

Drips of green and yellow paint stain the bark; delicate forked footprints, also coloured, dance along the nests.

'What . . . ?' I see a large bird, about the size of a crow, wing toward a nest directly above our heads. It pauses, watching us. Everything about the bird is black, except for its feet, which are painted a vivid shade of bright green. It is carrying something in its mouth. After a moment it flaps into the nest, and a chorus of chirping begins.

'Green,' Hunter says, looking satisfied. 'That's a good sign. Supplies will be coming today.'

'I don't understand.' I'm pacing underneath the network of nests. There must be hundreds of them. Some of the nests are actually strung up between the branches of different trees, forming a dense canopy. It is even colder here; the sun barely penetrates.

'Come on,' Hunter says. 'I'll show you.'

He hoists himself up into the nearest tree, swinging easily up the trunk, using the many branches and protrusions as hand- and footholds.

I follow Hunter clumsily, imitating the placement of his hands and feet. It has been a long time since I've climbed a tree, and I remember it from childhood as effortless: swinging up into the branches without thought, unconsciously finding the nooks and cricks in the tree. Now it is painful and difficult.

I finally make it to one of the thicker, low-hanging branches. Hunter is straddling it, waiting for me. I crouch behind him. My legs are shaking a little, and he reaches back and loops his hands around my ankles, steadying me.

The nests are full of birds: piles of sleek black feathers, and winking black eyes. They are hopping and picking among heaps of tiny brown seeds, stockpiled for the winter. Several of them, disturbed by our arrival, go shrieking and cawing toward the sky.

The nests are coated with the same vivid green paint, a network of thatched claw prints as the birds flutter between nests.

'I still don't understand,' I say. 'Where does the colour come from?'

'From the other side,' Hunter says, and I can hear the pride in his voice. 'From Zombieland. In the summer, there are blueberry bushes that grow on the other side of the fence. The birds scavenge for food there. Over the years, the insiders started feeding them pellets and seeds, keeping them fat through winter. They line up different-coloured troughs when they need to get us messages: half seeds, half paint. The birds eat and then they fly back here, to store up seeds for later. The nests get coloured, and we get our messages. Green, yellow, or red. Green if everything's fine, if we can expect a shipment. Yellow if there's a problem or delay.'

'Don't the colours get all mixed up?' I say.

Hunter swivels around to look at me, eyes shining. 'That's the brilliant thing,' he says, and tips his head back toward the nests. 'The birds don't like the colour. It attracts predators. So they're constantly reforming the nests. It's like a blank palette every day.'

And even as I'm watching, the bird in the nest closest to us is selecting the green-tinged twigs, wrestling them away from the nests with her beak: pruning, snipping, cleaning, like a woman fussing over weeds in a garden. The nest is being transformed in front of my eyes, remade into something dull and brown and normal-coloured.

'It's amazing,' I say.

'It's nature.' Hunter's voice turns serious. 'Birds feed; then they nest. Paint them any colour you want, send them halfway around the world, but they'll always find a way back. And eventually they'll show their true colours again. That's what animals do.'

As he speaks, I think of the raids last summer: when the regulators in their stiff uniforms stormed an illegal party, swinging baseball bats and police batons, letting loose the foaming, snapping bull mastiffs on the crowd. I think of the swinging arc of blood on a wall; the sounds of skulls cracking underneath heavy wood. Underneath their badges and their blank gazes, the cureds are full of a hatred that's colder and also more frightening. They are detached from passion, but also from sympathy.

Underneath their colours, they are animals, too. I could not have stayed there; I will never go back. I will not become one of the walking dead.

It's not until we're on the ground again and headed back to the homestead that I'm struck by something else Hunter said.

'What does red mean?' I ask.

He looks at me, startled. We've been silent for a while, both lost in thought. 'What?'

'Green is for supplies. Yellow when there's been a delay. So what does red mean?'

For a moment I see fear flashing in Hunter's eyes, and suddenly I am cold again.

'Red means run,' he says.

The relocation will soon begin in earnest. We will move everyone, the whole homestead, south. It is an enormous undertaking, and Raven and Tack spend hours planning, debating, arguing. It is not the first time they have orchestrated a relocation, but I gather that the moves have been hard and dangerous, and Raven considers them both failures.

But spending the winters up north has been even harder, and proved even more fatal, and so we will go. Raven insists that this time there will be no mortalities. Everyone who leaves the homestead will arrive safely at our destination.

'You can't guarantee that,' I hear Tack say to her one night. It's late, and I've been startled awake by the sounds of retching from the sickroom. It's Lu's turn.

I've slipped out of bed and started toward the kitchen for water when I realize Tack and Raven are still there, illuminated by the low, smouldering glow from the fire. The kitchen is murky, filled with wood smoke.

I pause in the hallway.

'Everyone stays alive,' Raven says stubbornly, and her voice trembles a little.

Tack sighs. He sounds tired – and something else, too. Gentle. Concerned. I've come to think of Tack as a dog: all bite and snarl. No softness to him at all.

'You can't save everybody, Rae,' he says.

'I can try,' she says.

I go back to my room without the water, drawing my blankets all the way up to my chin. The air is full of shadows, shifting shapes I can't identify.

There will be two main issues once we leave the homestead: food and shelter. There are other camps, other groups of Invalids, farther south, but settlements are few and separated by large expanses of open land. The northern Wilds are unforgiving in the fall and winter: hard and brittle and barren, full of hungry animals.

Over the years, travelling Invalids have mapped out a route: they have marked the trees with a system of gouges and slashes, to indicate the easiest path south.

Next week, groups of homesteaders – scouts – will leave on preliminary expeditions. Six will trek to our next big camp, which is eighty miles south, carting food and supplies in back-packs strapped to their bodies. When they reach camp, they will bury half the food in the ground, so it will not be consumed by animals, and mark the place of burial with a group of stones. Two will return to the homestead; the other four will go on another sixty miles, where they will bury half of what remains. Two of the four will then return to the homestead.

The fifth scout will wait there while the last scout pushes a final forty miles, equipped with the remaining portion of food. They will return to the homestead together, trapping and foraging what they can. By then we will have made all the arrangements and finished packing up.

When I ask Raven why the camps get closer and closer together as they wind southward, she barely glances up from what she's doing.

'You'll see,' she says shortly. Her hair is plaited into dozens of small braids – Blue's work – and Raven has fixed golden leaves and dried red baneberries, which are poisonous, at their ends.

'Isn't it better to go as far as we can every day?' I press. Even the third camp is a hundred miles from our final destination, although as we move south we'll find other homesteads, better trapping, and people to share their food and shelter with us.

Raven sighs. 'We'll be weak by then,' she says, finally straightening up to look at me. 'Cold. Hungry. It will probably be snowing. The Wilds suck the life out of you, I'm telling you. It's not like going on one of your little morning runs. You can't just keep pushing. I've seen—' She breaks off, shaking her head, as though to dislodge a memory. 'We have to be very careful,' she finishes.

I'm so offended I can't speak for a moment. Raven called my runs 'little', as though they're some kind of game. But I've left bits of myself out there – skin, blood, sweat, and vomit – bits of Lena Haloway, flaking off in pieces, scattered in the dark.

Raven senses she's upset me. 'Help me with these, will you?' she asks. She's making small emergency pouches, one for every homesteader, filled with Advil, Band-Aids, antibacterial wipes. She piles the supplies in the centre of squares of fabric, cut from old sheets, then twists them into pouches and ties them off with wire. 'My fingers are so fat I keep getting everything all tangled.'

It's not true: Raven's fingers are thin, just like the rest of her, and I know she's trying to make me feel better. But I say, 'Yeah, sure.' Raven hardly ever asks for help; when she does, you give it.

The scouts will be exhausted. Even though they will be weighed down by food, it is for storing, not for eating, and they have room to carry only a tiny bit for themselves. The last scout, the one who goes all one hundred and eighty miles, has to be the strongest. Without conferring or discussing it, everyone knows it will be Tack.

One night, I work up the courage to approach him. He is in a rare good mood. Bram brought four rabbits from the traps today, and for once we have all eaten until we were completely full.

After dinner, Tack sits next to the fire, rolling a cigarette. He doesn't look up as I approach.

'What?' he asks, abrupt as ever, but his voice has none of its usual edge.

I suck in a deep breath and blurt out, 'I want to be one of the scouts.' I've been agonizing all week about what to say to Tack – I've written whole speeches in my head – but at the last second these eight words are all that come.

'No,' Tack says shortly. And just like that, all my worrying and planning and strategizing have come to nothing.

I'm torn between disappointment and anger. 'I'm fast,' I say. 'I'm strong.'

'Not strong enough.'

'I want to help,' I press, conscious of the whine that is creeping into my voice, conscious of the fact that I sound like Blue when she is throwing one of her rare tantrums.

Tack runs his tongue along the rolling paper and then twists the cigarette closed with a few expert turns of his fingers. He looks up at me then, and in that second I realize Tack hardly ever looks at me. His eyes are shrewd, appraising, filled with messages I don't understand.

'Later,' he says, and with that, he stands and pushes his way past me and up the stairs.

now

The morning of the rally is unseasonably warm. What little snow has remained on the ground and the roofs runs in rivulets through the gutters, and drips from streetlamps and tree branches. It is dazzlingly sunny. The puddles in the street look like polished metal, perfectly reflective.

Raven and Tack are joining me at the demonstration, although they've informed me that they won't actually stay with me. My job is to keep close to the stage. I'm to watch Julian before he heads uptown to Columbia Memorial, where he will be cured.

'Don't take your eyes off him, no matter what,' Raven has instructed me. 'No matter what, okay?'

'Why?' I ask, knowing my question will go unanswered. Despite the fact that I am officially part of the resistance, I know hardly anything about how it works, and what we're supposed to be doing.

'Because,' she says, 'I said so.'

I mouth the last part along with her, keeping my back turned so she won't see.

Uncharacteristically, there are long lines at the bus stops. Two different regulators are distributing numbers to the waiting passengers; Raven, Tack, and I will be on bus 5, whenever that arrives. The city has quadrupled the quantity of buses and drivers today. Twenty-five thousand people are expected to show up at the demonstration; about five thousand members of the DFA, and thousands of spectators and onlookers.

Many of the groups that oppose the DFA, and the idea of early procedure, will also be there. This includes much of the scientific community. The procedure is just not yet safe for children, they say, and will lead to tremendous social defects: a nation of idiots and freaks. The DFA claims the opposition is overly cautious. The benefits, they say, far outweigh the risks.

And if need be, we will just make our prisons larger, and stick the damaged ones there, out of sight.

'Move up, move up.' The regulator at the front of the line directs us onto the bus. We shuffle forward, showing our identity cards and swiping them, again, as we board, and I am reminded of a bunch of herd animals, heads down, trundling ahead.

Raven and Tack have not been speaking; they must be fighting again. I can sense it between them, a tight electricity, and it's not helping my anxiety. Raven finds an empty two-seater in the back, but Tack, surprisingly, slides in next to me.

'What are you doing?' Raven demands, leaning forward. She has to be careful to keep her voice down. Cureds don't really fight. That is one of the benefits of the procedure.

'I want to make sure Lena's okay,' Tack mutters back. He reaches out and grabs my hand, a quick pulse. A woman seated across the aisle looks at us curiously. 'Are you all right?'

'I'm fine,' I say, but my voice sounds strangled. I wasn't

nervous at all earlier in the morning. Tack and Raven have made me jumpy. They're obviously worried about something, and I think I know what it is: they must believe the rumours of the Scavengers are true. They must believe the Scavengers are going to stage an upset, try to disturb the demonstration in some way.

Even crossing the Brooklyn Bridge doesn't have its usual calming effect. The bridge is, for the first time ever, clogged with traffic: private cars, and buses transporting people to the demonstration.

As we approach Times Square, my anxiety increases. I've never seen so many people in my life. We have to get out at 34th Street because buses cannot progress any farther. The streets are swarming with people: a massive blur of faces, a river of colours. There are regulators, too – volunteer and official – wearing spotless uniforms; then there are members of the armed guard, standing stiffly in rows, staring fixedly straight ahead, like toy soldiers lined up, about to march. Except these soldiers, these real ones, carry enormous guns, barrels gleaming in the sunlight.

As soon as I descend into the crowd I'm pushed and jostled from all sides, and even though Raven and Tack are behind me, I manage to lose sight of them a few times as people flow between us. Now I see why they've given me my instructions early. There's no way I'll be able to keep sight of them.

It is shatteringly loud. The regulators are blowing their whistles, directing foot traffic, and in the distance I can hear drumbeats and chanting. The demonstration doesn't officially start for another two hours, but even now I think I can make out the rhythm of the DFA's chant: *In numbers there is safety and for nothing let us want . . .*

We move north slowly, penned in on all sides, in the endless, deep chasms between the buildings. People have gathered on some of the balconies to watch. I see hundreds and hundreds of waving white banners, signs of support for the DFA – and just a few emerald-coloured ones, signs of opposition.

'Lena!' I turn around. Tack shoves his way through the mass of people, presses an umbrella into my hand. 'It's supposed to rain later.'

The sky is a perfect pale blue and streaked with the thinnest clouds, like bare white tendrils of hair. 'I don't think—,' I start to say, but he interrupts me.

'Just take it,' he says. 'Trust me.'

'Thanks.' I try to sound grateful. It's rare for Tack to be this thoughtful.

He hesitates, chewing on the corner of his lip. I've seen him do that when he's working on a puzzle at the apartment and can't quite get all the pieces aligned. I think he's about to say something else – give me advice – but at the last second he just says, 'I need to catch up with Rebecca.' He stutters, just barely, over Raven's official name.

'Okay.' We've already lost sight of her. I go to wrestle the umbrella into my backpack – getting dirty looks from the people around me, since there's barely room to breathe, much less manoeuvre the bag from my back – when it suddenly occurs to me that we haven't made a plan for after the demonstration. I don't know where I'm supposed to meet Raven and Tack.

'Hey—' I look up, but Tack has already gone. All the faces around me are unfamiliar; I'm entirely surrounded by strangers. I turn a full circle and feel a sharp jab in the ribs. A regulator has reached out and is prodding me forward with his nightstick.

'You're holding everybody up,' he says flatly. 'Move it.'

My chest is full of butterflies. I tell myself to breathe. There's nothing to worry about. It's just like going to a DFA meeting, but bigger.

At 38th Street we pass the barricades, where we have to wait in line and get patted down and searched by police officers carrying wands. They check our necks, too – the uncureds will be in their own special segregated section of the demonstration – and scan our IDs, though fortunately, they don't call everything into SVS, the Secure Validation System. Even so, it takes me an hour to make it through. Beyond the security barricades, volunteers are distributing antibacterial wipes: small white packages printed with the DFA's logo.

CLEANLINESS IS NEXT TO GODLINESS. SECURITY IS IN THE DETAILS. HAPPINESS IS IN THE METHOD.

I allow a silver-haired woman to press a package into my hand.

And then, finally, I've arrived. The drums are furiously loud here, and the chanting a rolling constant, like the sound of waves crashing on the shore.

Once I saw a photo of Times Square: before the cure, before all the borders were closed off. Tack found it near Salvage, a homestead in New Jersey, just across the river from New York. We took refuge there while we were waiting for our forged papers to arrive. One day Tack found a whole photo album, perfectly intact, buried under a pile of limestone and charred timber. In the evenings, I would flip through it and pretend that these photographs – this life of friends and boyfriends and squinting, laughing sunshine shots – were mine.

Times Square looks very different now than it did then. As I move forward in the crowd, my breath catches in my throat.

A towering raised platform, a dais, has been built at one end of the enormous open plaza, underneath a billboard larger than any I have seen in my life. It is plastered all over with signs for the DFA: red and white squares, fluttering lightly in the wind.

The Unified Church of Religion and Science has colonized one billboard and marked it huge with its primary symbol: a giant hand cupping a molecule of hydrogen. The other signs – and there are dozens of them, gigantic, bleached-white walls – are all faded to illegibility, so it's impossible to tell what they once advertised. On one of them I think I can make out the ghostly imprint of a smile.

And of course, all the lights are dead.

The photograph I saw of Times Square was taken at night, but it could have been high noon: I've never seen so many lights in my life, could never even have imagined them. Lights blazing, glittering, lit up in crazy colours that made me think of those spots that float across your vision after you've accidentally looked directly at the sun.

The lightbulbs are still here, but they're dark. On many of them, pigeons are perching, roosting between the blacked-out bulbs. New York and its sister cities have mandatory controls on electricity, just like Portland did – and although there are a greater number of cars and buses, the blackouts are stricter and more frequent. There are just too many people, and not enough juice for all of them.

The dais is wired with microphones and equipped with chairs; behind it is an enormous video screen, like the kind the DFA uses at its meetings. Uniformed men are making last-minute adjustments to the setup. That's where Julian will be; somehow, I'll have to get closer.

I start to push my way slowly, painstakingly, through the

crowd. I have to fight and elbow and say 'Excuse me' every time I try to squeeze by someone. Even being five foot two isn't helping. There simply isn't enough space between bodies – there are no cracks to slip through.

That's when I start to panic again. If the Scavengers do come – or if anything goes wrong – there will be no place to run. We'll be caught here like animals in a pen. People will trample one another trying to get out. A stampede.

But the Scavengers won't come. They wouldn't dare. It's too dangerous. There are too many police, too many regulators, too many guns.

I squeeze my way past a series of bleachers, all roped off, where members of the DFA Youth Guard are sitting: girls and boys on separate bleachers, of course, all of them careful not to look at one another.

At last I make it to the foot of the dais. The platform must be ten or twelve feet in the air. A series of steep wooden steps gives the speakers access from the ground. At the foot of the stairs, a group of people has gathered. I make out Thomas and Julian Fineman behind a blur of bodyguards and police officers.

Julian and his father are dressed identically. Julian's hair is slicked back, and curls just behind his ears. He's shifting from foot to foot, obviously trying to conceal his nervousness.

I wonder what's so important about him – why Tack and Raven told me to keep an eye on him. He has become symbolic of the DFA, of course – sacrifice in the name of public safety – but I wonder whether he presents some kind of additional danger.

I think back to what he said at the rally: *I was nine when I was told I was dying.*

I wonder what it feels like to die slowly.

I wonder what it feels like to die quickly.

I squeeze my nails into my palms, to keep the memories back.

The drumming is coming from behind the dais, a part of the square that's blocked from view. There must be a marching band there. The chanting swells, and now everyone is joining in, the whole crowd unconsciously swaying along to the rhythm. Distantly, I make out some other rhythm, a disjointed staccato: *DFA is dangerous for all . . . The cure should protect, not harm . . .*

The dissenters. They must be sequestered somewhere else, far away from the dais.

Louder, louder, louder. The DFA's chants soon drown out all other sound. I join in, let my body find the rhythm, feel the hum of all those thousands of people buzz up through my feet and into my chest. And even though I don't believe in any of it – the words, the cause, the people around me – it amazes me, still, the surge I get from being in a crowd, the electricity, the sense of power.

Dangerous.

Just as the chanting reaches a crescendo, Thomas Fineman breaks away from the bodyguards and takes the steps up to the top of the dais, two at a time. The rhythm breaks apart into waves of shouting and clapping. White banners and flags appear from everywhere, unfurling, fluttering in the wind. Some of them are DFA-issue. Other people have simply cut up long strips of cloth. Times Square is full of slender white tentacles.

'Thank you,' Thomas Fineman says into the microphone. His voice booms out over all of us; then a sharp screeching sound as the feed lets out a whine. Fineman winces, cups his hand over the microphone, and leans back to mutter instructions to someone. The angle of his neck shows off his procedural mark perfectly. The three-pronged scar is amplified by the video screen.

I turn my eyes to Julian. He is standing with his arms crossed, watching his father, behind the wall of bodyguards. He must be cold; he's only wearing a suit jacket.

'Thank you,' Thomas Fineman tries again, and, when no feed kicks back, adds, 'Much better. My friends—'

That's when it happens.

Pop. Pop. Pop.

Three miniature explosions, like the firecrackers we used to set off at Eastern Prom on the Fourth of July.

One scream, high and desperate.

And then: everything is noise.

Figures in black appear from nowhere, from everywhere. They're climbing up out of the sewers, materializing from the ground, taking shape behind the foul-smelling steam. They swarm down the sides of the buildings like spiders, rappelling on long black ropes. They're scything through the crowd with glittering, sharp blades, grabbing purses and ripping necklaces from around people's necks, slicing rings from their fingers. *Thwack. Thwack.*

Scavengers. My insides turn to liquid. My breath stops in my throat.

People are pushing and shoving, desperately trying to find a way out. The Scavengers have us surrounded.

'Down, down, down!'

Now the air is filled with gunshots. The police have opened fire. One Scavenger has made it halfway down a building toward the ground. A bullet explodes in his back and he jerks once, quickly, and then hangs limp from the end of his rope, swaying lightly in the wind. Somehow one of the DFA banners has become entangled in his equipment; I see the stain of blood spreading slowly across the white fabric.

I am in a nightmare. I am in the past. This isn't happening.

Someone shoves me from behind and I go sprawling to the pavement. The bite of the concrete snaps me into awareness. People are running, stampeding, and I quickly roll out of the way of a pair of heavy boots.

I have to get back on my feet.

I try to stand and get knocked down again. This time the air goes out of me, and I feel someone's weight on the middle of my back. And suddenly the fear turns me sharp and focused. I need to get up.

One of the police barricades has already been broken, and a piece of splintered wood is lying in front of me. I grab it and jab behind me, into the crushing weight of people, of panic, and feel the wood connecting with legs, with muscle and skin. For a brief second I feel the weight shift, a slight release. I jump to my feet and sprint toward the dais.

Julian is gone. I'm supposed to be watching Julian. No matter what happens.

Piercing screams. The smell of fire.

Then I spot him off to my left. He is being hustled toward one of the old subway entrances, which is, like all the other entrances, covered with plywood. But as he approaches, one of the bodyguards steps forward and pushes the plywood inward.

Not a barrier. A door.

Then they are gone, and the sheet of wood swings closed again.

More gunshots. A massive surge in the screaming. A Scavenger has been shot just as he was beginning his descent. He is knocked clear off the balcony and tumbles down into the crowd below. The people are a wave: heads, arms, contorted faces.

I run toward the subway entrance where Julian disappeared. Above it I can see an old series of letters and numbers, faded bare outlines: N, R, Q, 1, 2, 3, 7. And in the middle of all that panic and screaming, there is something comforting about it: an old-world code, a sign from another life. I wonder whether the old world could have possibly been worse than this – that time of dazzling lights and sizzling electricity and people who loved in the open – whether they also screamed and trampled one another to death and turned their guns on their neighbours.

Then the air is knocked out of me again and I'm thrown backward. I land on my left elbow, hear it crack. Pain splinters through me.

A Scavenger looms over me. Impossible to say whether it's a man or a woman. The Scavenger is dressed all in black and has a ski mask pulled low, covering the neck.

'Give me the bag,' the Scavenger growls. But the voice doesn't fool me. It's a girl. She's trying to make her voice sound lower, but you can hear the melody running underneath it.

For some reason, this makes me even angrier. *How dare you?* I feel like spitting at her. *You've screwed everything for everyone.* But I sit up, inching the backpack off my shoulders, feeling little explosions of pain radiating all the way from my elbow to my shoulder.

'Come on, come on. Hurry up.' She's dancing from foot to foot, and as she does she fingers the long, sharp knife she has looped through her belt.

I mentally weigh all the things I have in the bag: a tin water bottle, empty. Tack's umbrella. Two granola bars. Keys. A hardcover edition of *The Book of Shhh*. Tack insisted I bring it, and now I'm glad I did. It's nearly six hundred pages.

Should be heavy enough. I take the shoulder straps in my right hand, tightening my grip.

'I said move.'

The Scavenger, impatient, bends down to grab the bag, and as she does, I swing upward with all my strength, moving through the pain. The bag catches her in the side of the head with enough momentum to knock her off balance – she tumbles to one side, landing hard on the ground. I launch to my feet. She grabs for my ankles, and I kick her hard, twice, in the ribs.

The priests and the scientists are right about one thing: at our heart, at our base, we are no better than animals.

The Scavenger moans, doubling up, and I jump over her, dodging all the police barricades, which are lying in a tumbled, broken ruin. The screaming is still a crest of sound around me: it has turned into one tremendous wail, like a gigantic, amplified siren.

I make it to the old subway entrance. For just a second I hesitate with my hand on the wooden plank. Its texture is comforting – weather-beaten, warmed by the sun – a bit of normalcy in the middle of all this madness.

Another rifle shot: I hear a body thud to the ground behind me. More screaming.

I lean forward and push. The door swings open a few feet, revealing murky darkness and a pungent, musty smell.

I don't look back.

I push the door shut again and stand for a moment, letting my eyes adjust to the dimness, listening for the sound of voices or footsteps. Nothing. The smell is sharper in here; it is the smell of old death, animal bones and rotting things. I bring my jacket cuff to my nose and inhale. There's a steady dripping off to my left. Other than that, it's quiet.

There are stairs in front of me, covered in bits of crumpled newspaper, mashed-up Styrofoam cups, cigarette butts, all dully illuminated by an electric lantern, like the kind we used in the Wilds. Someone must have planted it here earlier.

I move toward the stairs, on high alert. Julian's bodyguards might have heard me shoving open the door. They might be lying in wait, ready to jump me. Mentally I curse the metal detectors and all the body scans. I would give anything to have a knife, a screwdriver, something.

Then I remember my keys. I once again ease my backpack off my shoulders. When I bend my elbow, the pain makes me suck in my breath. I'm thankful I landed on my left arm – with my right arm immobilized, I'd be pretty much useless.

I find my keys at the bottom of my bag, moving agonizingly slowly so I don't make too much noise. I thread the keys through my fingers, like Tack showed me how to do. It's not much of a weapon, but it's better than nothing. Then I go down the stairs, scanning the shadows for anything mobile, any sudden shapes rising through the darkness.

Nothing. Everything is perfectly still, and very quiet.

At the bottom of the stairs, there is a dingy glass booth, still smudgy with fingerprints. Beyond it, rusted turnstiles line the tunnel, a dozen of them, like miniature windmills that have been stilled. I ease myself over one of them and land softly on the other side. From here, various tunnels branch out into the darkness, each marked with different signs, more letters and numbers. Julian might have gone down any one of them. And all of them are swallowed in shadow: the lantern doesn't penetrate this far. I consider going back to retrieve it, but that would only give me away.

Again, I stop and listen. At first there is nothing. Then, I think I hear a muffled thud from the tunnel on my left. As soon as I start toward the sound, however, there is silence once again. Now I'm sure I only imagined the noise, and I hesitate, frustrated, unsure about what to do next. I've failed in my mission, that's obvious – my first real mission of the movement. At the same time, Raven and Tack can't blame me for losing Julian when the Scavengers attacked. I couldn't have predicted or prepared for that chaos. No one could have.

I figure my best bet is to wait down here for a few hours, at least until the police have restored order, which I have no doubt they will. If necessary, I'll camp out for the night. Tomorrow I'll deal with getting back to Brooklyn.

Suddenly, a darting shadow from my left. I whirl around, fist extended, and connect with nothing but air. A giant rat scurries in front of me, a bare inch from my sneaker. I exhale, watching the rat darting off down another tunnel, its long tail dragging in the filth. I've always hated rats.

That's when I hear it, distinct and unmistakable: two thuds, and a low groan, a voice moaning out, 'Please . . .'

Julian's voice.

My body goes prickly all over. Now the fear draws my insides hard and taut. The voice came from somewhere farther down the tunnel.

I ease back against one wall, pressing myself flat, feeling moss and slick tile under my fingers as I move forward slowly, careful not to make any noise when I step, careful not to breathe too loudly. After every few paces I stop and listen, hoping for another sound, hoping Julian will say something again. But the only thing I hear is a steady *drip, drip, drip*. There must be a pipe leaking somewhere.

Then I see it.

The man is strung from a grate in the ceiling, a belt looped tightly around his bulging neck. Above him, water condenses on a metal pipe, dripping onto the tunnel floor. *Drip, drip, drip*.

It's so dark I can't make out the man's face – the grate permits only a trickle of grey light from above – but I recognize him from the heaviness of his shoulders as one of Julian's body-guards. At his feet, another bodyguard is lying curled up in the fetal position. There is a long-handled blade protruding from his back.

I stumble backward, forgetting to be quiet. Then I hear Julian's voice again, fainter: 'Please . . .'

I'm terrified. I don't know which direction the voice is coming from, can't think of anything but getting out, out, out. I'd rather face the Scavengers in the open than trapped here, like a rat, in the dark. I will not die underground.

I run blindly, keeping my arms in front of me, collide first with a wall before groping my way into the centre of the tunnel. Panic has made me clumsy.

Drip, drip, drip.

Please. Please get me out of here. My heart will explode; I can't take a breath.

Two black shapes unfold all at once from either side of me, and in my terror they look like enormous dark birds, reaching out their wings to enfold me.

'Not so fast,' one of them says. He grabs my wrist. The keys are knocked from my hand. Then searing pain, a flash of white.

I sink into the dark.

then

Miyako, who should have been one of the scouts, is instead the last one to enter the sickroom.

'She'll be back on her feet tomorrow,' Raven says. 'You'll see. She's as solid as a rock.'

But the next day, her cough is so bad we can hear it reverberating through the walls. Her breathing sounds thick and watery. She sweats through her blankets even as she cries that she is cold, cold, freezing cold.

She begins coughing up blood. When it's my turn to look after her, I can see it caked in the corners of her mouth. I dab at it with a washcloth, but she is still strong enough to fight me off. The fever makes her see shapes and shadows in the air; she swats at them, muttering.

She can no longer stand, even when Raven and I try to lift her together. She cries out in pain, and eventually we give up. Instead we change the sheets when Miyako pisses them. I think we should burn them, but Raven insists we can't; I see her that night, furiously scrubbing them in the basin, while steam rises from the scalding water. Her forearms are the shiny red of raw meat.

And then one night I wake up and the silence is perfect, a cool, dark pool. For one second, still emerging from the fog of my dreams, I think that Miyako must have gotten better. Tomorrow she will be squatting in the kitchen, tending the fire. Tomorrow we will make rounds together, and I will watch her braiding traps with her long, slender fingers. When she catches me staring, she will smile.

But it is too quiet. I get up, a knot of dread tightening inside my chest. The floor is freezing.

Raven is sitting at the foot of Miyako's bed, staring at nothing. Her hair is loose, and the flickering shadows from the candle next to her make her eyes look like two hollow pits.

Miyako's eyes are closed, and I can tell right away she is dead.

The desire to laugh – hysterical and inappropriate – wells in my throat. To quash it, I say, 'Is she—?'

'Yes,' Raven says shortly.

'When?'

'I'm not sure. I fell asleep for a while.' She passes a hand over her eyes. 'When I woke up, she wasn't breathing.'

My body flashes completely hot and then completely cold. I don't know what to say, so I just stand there for a while, trying not to look at Miyako's body: a statue, a shadow, her face thinned by sickness, whittled down to bone. All I can think about are her hands, which only a few days ago moved so expertly against the kitchen table as she beat out a soft rhythm so that Sarah could sing. They were a blur, like hummingbird wings – full of life.

I feel like something has caught in the back of my throat. 'I – I'm sorry.'

Raven doesn't say anything for a minute. Then: 'I shouldn't have made her carry water. She said she wasn't feeling well. I should have let her rest.'

'You can't blame yourself,' I say quickly.

'Why not?' Raven looks up at me then. In that moment she looks very young – defiant, stubborn, the way that my cousin Jenny used to look when Aunt Carol told her it was time for homework. I have to remind myself that Raven *is* young: twenty-one, only a few years older than me. The Wilds will age you.

I wonder how long I'll last out here.

'Because it's not your fault.' The fact that I can't see her eyes makes me nervous. 'You can't – you can't feel bad.'

Raven stands up then, cupping the candle in one hand.

'We're on the other side of the fence now, Lena,' she says, tiredly, as she passes. 'Don't you get it? You can't tell me what to feel.'

The next day it snows. At breakfast, Sarah cries silently while spooning up oatmeal. She was close to Miyako.

The scouts left the homestead five days ago – Tack, Hunter, Roach, Buck, Lu, and Squirrel – and have taken the shovel with them, for burying supplies. We collect pieces of metal and wood, whatever will serve us for digging instead.

The snow is light, thankfully; by midmorning, a bare half inch is on the ground. But it's very cold, and the ground is frozen solid. After digging and hacking for a half hour, we've only made the barest indentation in the earth, and Raven, Bram, and I are sweating. Sarah, Blue, and a few others are huddled a few feet away from us, shivering.

'This isn't working,' Raven pants out. She throws down a

twisted piece of metal she has been using as a shovel, sends it skittering across the ground with a kick. Then she turns and starts stalking back toward the burrow. 'We'll have to burn her.'

'Burn her?' The words explode out of me before I can stop them. 'We can't burn her. That's—'

Raven whirls around, eyes blazing. 'Yeah? Well what do you want to do? Huh? You want to leave her in the sickroom?'

Normally I back down when Raven raises her voice, but this time I hold my ground. 'She deserves a burial,' I say, wishing my voice wouldn't shake.

Raven covers the ground between us in two long strides.

'It's a waste of our energy,' she hisses, and then I can tell how full of fury and desperation she is. I remember what I heard her tell Tack: everyone stays alive. 'We don't have any to spare.'

She turns her back to me again and announces loudly, so the others can hear, 'We have to burn her.'

We wrap her body in the sheets Raven scrubbed clean. Maybe all along she knew they would be used for this purpose. I keep thinking I'm going to be sick.

'Lena,' Raven barks at me sharply. 'Take her feet.'

I do. Her body is heavier than seems possible. In death, she has become a weight of iron. I'm furious with Raven, so furious I could spit. This is what we are reduced to here. This is what we have become in the Wilds: we starve, we die, we wrap our friends in old and tattered sheets, we burn them in the open. I know it's not Raven's fault – it's the people on the other side of the fence, it's Them, the zombies, my former people – but the anger refuses to dissolve. It burns a hole in my throat.

A quarter mile from the homestead there is a gully where at

one point a stream must have flowed. We place her there, and Raven splashes her with gasoline: just a little, as there isn't much to spare. The snow is falling harder now. At first she won't light. Blue begins to cry, loudly, and Grandma pulls her sharply away from the fire, saying, 'Quiet, Blue. You're not helping.' Blue turns her face into Grandma's overlarge corduroy jacket so the sound of her sobbing is muffled. Sarah is silent, white-faced, trembling.

Raven douses the body with more gasoline and finally gets it lit. The air is filled right away with a choking smoke, the smell of burning hair; the noise is terrible too, a crackling that makes you think of meat falling away from bones. Raven can't even speak the whole eulogy before she starts to gag. I turn away, tears stinging my eyes – from the smoke or from anger, I can't tell.

Suddenly I have the wild urge to dig, to bury, to hack up the earth. I move blindly, numbly, back to the burrow. It takes me a little while to locate the cotton shorts and the old, tattered shirt I was wearing when I came to the Wilds. We've been using the shirt as a dishrag. These are the only items left from before: the remnants of my old life.

The others have now gathered in the kitchen. Bram is stoking the fire, coaxing it to life. Raven is boiling water in a pot: for coffee, no doubt. Sarah is shuffling a pack of water-warped and dog-eared cards. Everyone else is sitting in silence.

'Hey, Lena,' Sarah says as I stalk past her. I've stuffed the shorts and the T-shirt under my jacket and am keeping my arms tightly crossed over my stomach; for some reason, I don't want anyone to know what I'm doing, especially Raven. 'You want to play Spit?'

'Not now,' I growl at her. The Wilds turn us mean, too. Mean and hard, all edges.

'We could play something else,' she says. 'We could play—'

'I said no.' Then I'm running up the stairs before I can see I've hurt her feelings.

The air is thick: a white blur. For a moment the cold stuns me and I stand, blinking, confused. Everything is sprouting a layer of snow, a fuzzy growth. I can still smell Miyako's body burning. And I imagine that with the snow there is ash blowing over us. I fantasize that it will cover us in our sleep, seal us into the burrow, and suffocate us there, underground.

There is a juniper bush at the edge of the homestead, where I start and end my runs. Underneath it the snow has not accumulated. There is a bare dusting on the ground, which I sweep away with the cuff of my jacket.

Then I dig.

I claw at the earth with my fingers. The anger and the grief is still throbbing behind my eyes, narrowing my vision to a tunnel. I can't even feel the cold or the pain in my hands. Dirt and blood are caking my fingernails, but I don't care. I bury those last, tattered parts of me there, under the juniper, in the snow.

Two days after we burn Miyako, the snow has still not stopped. Every day Raven scans the skies anxiously, cursing under her breath. It is time to move. Lu and Squirrel, the first of the scouts, have returned. The homestead is mostly packed up, although we are still gathering food and supplies from the river, and trying to trap and hunt what we can. But the snow makes it hard. The animals stay underground.

As soon as the rest of the scouts return, we will leave. They'll be here any day now – that's what we all tell Raven, to ease her anxiety. The snow falls slowly, steadily, turning the world to white drift.

I've started checking the nests for messages twice a day. The trees, encased in ice, are harder to climb. Afterward, when I come back to the burrow, my fingers throb painfully as the feeling returns to them. For weeks the supplies have been floating to us regularly, although sometimes we've found them caught upriver, in the shallows, which freeze more easily. We have to break them out with broom handles. Roach and Buck make it back to the homestead, exhausted but triumphant. The snow finally stops. Now we are just waiting on Hunter and Tack.

Then one day, the nests are yellow. And again the next day: yellow.

On the third day of yellow, Raven pulls me aside.

'I'm worried,' she says. 'Something must be wrong on the inside.'

'Maybe they're patrolling again,' I say. 'Maybe they've turned on the fence.'

She bites her lip, shakes her head. 'Whatever it is, it must be major. Everyone knows it's time for us to move. We need all the supplies we can get.'

'I'm sure it's temporary,' I say. 'I'm sure tomorrow we'll get a shipment.'

Raven shakes her head again. 'We can't afford to wait much longer,' she says, and her voice is strangled. I know she isn't thinking only of the supplies. She's thinking of Hunter and Tack, too.

The next day, the sky is a pale blue, the sun high and amazingly warm, breaking through the trees and turning the ice to rivulets of flowing water. The snow brought silence with it, but now the woods are alive again, full of dripping and twittering and cracking. It is as though the Wilds have been released from a muzzle.

We are all in a good mood – everyone but Raven, who does her daily scan of the sky and only mutters, 'It won't last.'

On my way to the nests, stamping through the snow, I'm so warm I have to take off my jacket and tie it around my waist. The nests will be green today, I can sense it. They'll be green, and the supplies will come, and the scouts will return, and we'll all flow south together. The light is dazzling, bouncing off the glittering branches, filling my vision with spots of colour, flashes of red and green.

When I get to the nests, I untie my jacket and loop it over one of the lower branches. I've gotten good at the climb – my body finds its way up easily, and I feel a kind of joy in my chest I haven't felt for a long time. From far away I hear a vague humming, a low vibration that reminds me of crickets singing in the summertime.

There is a vast world for us, a boundless space beyond and between the fences and the rules. We will travel it freely. We will be okay.

I have almost reached the nests. I adjust my weight, seek better purchase for my feet, and pull myself upward, toward the final branch.

Just then a shadow zooms past me – so sudden and startling I nearly slip backward. For a moment I feel the terror of free fall – the tipping, the cold air behind me – but at the last second I manage to right myself. My heart is pounding, though, and I can't shake that momentary impression of falling.

And then I see that it wasn't a shadow that startled me.

It was a bird. A bird struggling through stickiness: a bird coated in paint, floundering in its nest, splashing colour everywhere.

Red. Red. Red.

Dozens of them: black feathers coated thickly with crimson-coloured paint, fluttering among the branches.

Red means run.

I don't know how I get down from the tree. I am slipping and sliding, all the grace and ease driven out of my limbs by the panic. Red means run. I drop the last four feet and land tumbling in the snow. Cold seeps through my jeans and sweater. I snatch my jacket and run, just like Hunter told me to do, through the dazzling, melting world of ice, while blackness eats at the edges of my vision. Every step is an agony, and I feel like I'm in one of those nightmares where you're trying to escape but you can't move at all.

Now the humming I heard earlier is louder – not like crickets at all. Like hornets.

Like motors.

My lungs are burning and my chest is aching and tears are stinging my eyes as I flounder toward the homestead. I want to scream. I want to sprout wings and fly. And for a second I think, *Maybe it was all a mistake. Maybe nothing bad will happen.*

That is when the humming turns into a roar, and above the trees I see the first plane tearing across the sky, screaming.

But no. I'm the one screaming.

I am screaming as I run. I am screaming when the first bomb falls, and the Wilds turn to fire around me.

now

I open my eyes into pain. For a second everything is swirling colour, and I have a moment of total panic – *Where am I? What happened?* – but then shapes and boundaries assert themselves. I am in a windowless stone room, lying on a cot. In my confusion I think that perhaps I've made it back to the burrow, and found myself in the sickroom.

But no. This room is smaller and dingier. There are no sinks, and only one bucket in the corner, and the mattress I'm lying on is stained and thin and without sheets.

Memories return: the rally in New York; the subway entrance, the horrible vision of the bodyguards. I remember the rasping voice in my ear: *Not so fast.*

I try to sit up and instantly have to lay back again, over-whelmed by the surge behind my eyes, like the pressure of a knife.

'Water helps.'

This time I do sit up, whipping around despite the pain. Julian Fineman is sitting on a narrow cot behind me, leaning his head against the wall, watching me through heavy-lidded eyes. He is holding a tin cup, which he extends toward me.

'They brought it earlier,' he says. There is a long, thin gash that runs from his eyebrow to his jaw, caked with dried blood, and a bruise on the left side of his forehead, just beneath his hairline. The room is outfitted with a small bulb, set high in the ceiling, and in its white glow, his hair is the colour of new straw.

My eyes go immediately to the door behind him, and he shakes his head. 'Locked from the outside.'

So. Prisoners.

'Who's they?' I ask, even though I know. It must be Scavengers who brought us here. I think of that hellish vision in the tunnels, a guard strung up, another knifed in his back . . . no one but the Scavengers could have done that.

Julian shakes his head. I see, too, that he has bruises around his neck. They must have choked him. His jacket is gone and his shirt is ripped; there's more blood ringing his nostrils, and some of it has dripped onto his shirt. But he seems surprisingly calm. The hand holding the cup is steady.

Only his eyes are electric, restless – that vivid, improbable blue, alert and watchful.

I reach out to take the cup from him, but at the last second he draws it away a fraction of an inch.

'I recognize you,' he says, 'from the meeting.' Something flickers in his eyes. 'You lost your glove.'

'Yeah.' I reach again for the cup.

The water tastes mossy, but it feels amazing on my throat. As soon as I have a sip, I realize I've never been so thirsty in my life. There isn't enough to take more than a bare edge off the feeling; I gulp most of it down in one go before realizing, guiltily, that Julian might want some. There's a half inch of water left, which I try to return to him.

'You can finish it,' he says, and I don't argue. As I drink, I can feel his eyes on me again, and when I look at him, I see that he has been staring at the three-pronged scar on my neck. It seems to reassure him.

Amazingly, I still have my backpack. For some reason, the Scavengers have let me keep it. This gives me hope. They may be vicious, but they're obviously not very practiced at kidnapping people. I remove a granola bar from my bag, then reconsider. I'm not starving yet, and I have no idea how long I'm going to be trapped in this rat hole. I learned in the Wilds: it's better to wait when you still can. Eventually, you'll be too desperate to have self-control.

The rest of the things I've brought – *The Book of Shhh*, Tack's stupid umbrella, the water bottle, which I drank dry on the bus ride into Manhattan, and a tube of mascara, probably Raven's, nestled at the very bottom of the bag – are useless. Now I know why they didn't bother confiscating the backpack. Still, I take everything out, lay it carefully on my bed, and overturn the backpack – shaking it hard, as though a knife or a lock pick or some other kind of salvation might suddenly materialize.

Nothing. Still, there's got to be a way out of here.

I stand up and go to the door, bending my left arm. The pain in my elbow has faded to a dull throb. It isn't broken, then: another good sign.

I try the door: locked, like he said, and made of heavy iron. Impossible to break down. There's a smaller door – about the size of a cat flap – fitted into the larger one. I squat down and examine it. The way its hinges are fitted allows it to be opened from their side, but not from ours.

'That's where they put the water through,' Julian says. 'Food, too.'

'Food?' This surprises me. 'They gave you food?'

'A little bit of bread. Some nuts, too. I ate it all. I didn't know how long you'd be out.' He looks away.

'That's all right.' I straighten up, and scan the walls for cracks or fissures, a hidden door, or a weak place we might be able to push through. 'I would have done the same thing.'

Food, water, an underground cell: those are the facts. I can tell we're underground because of the pattern of mould at the top of the walls – it's a particular kind that we used to get all the time in the burrow. It comes from the dirt all around us.

It means, essentially, that we're buried.

But if they'd wanted us dead, we'd have been dead already. That is a fact also.

Still, it is not particularly comforting. If the Scavengers have kept us alive so far, it can only be because they're planning something far worse for us than death.

'What do you remember?' I ask Julian.

'What?'

'What do you remember? About the attack? Noises, smells, order of events?' When I look directly at Julian, he clicks his eyes away from mine. Of course, he has had years of training – segregation, principles of avoidance, the Protective Three: Distance, Detachment, Dispassion. I'm tempted to remind him that it isn't illegal to make eye contact with a cured. But it seems absurd to have a conversation about right and wrong here.

He must be in denial. That's why he's staying so calm.

He sighs, runs a hand through his hair. 'I don't remember anything.'

'Try.'

He shakes his head, as though trying to dislodge the memory, leans back again, and stares at the ceiling. 'When the Invalids came during the rally . . .'

I wince unconsciously as he pronounces the word. I have to bite my lip to keep from correcting him: Scavengers. Not Invalids. We're not all the same.

'Go on,' I prompt him. I'm moving down the walls now, running my hands along the concrete. I don't know what I'm hoping to find. We're trapped, pure and simple. But it seems to make it easier for Julian to speak when I'm not looking at him.

'Bill and Tony – those are my dad's bodyguards – grabbed me and dragged me toward the emergency exit. We'd planned it earlier, in case something went wrong; we were supposed to go into the tunnels and reconvene, wait for my father.' His voice catches the slightest bit on the word *father*, and he coughs. 'The tunnels were dark. Tony went looking for the flashlights. He'd stashed them earlier. Then we heard – then we heard a shout, and a cracking noise. Like a nut.'

Julian swallows hard. For a moment I feel bad for him. He has seen a lot, and quickly.

But I remind myself that he and his father are the reason that the Scavengers exist – the reason they're forced to exist. The DFA and organizations like it have pushed and squeezed and elbowed out all the feeling in the world. They have clamped their fists around a geyser to keep it from exploding.

But the pressure eventually builds, and the explosion will always come.

'Then Bill went ahead, to make sure Tony was okay. He

told me not to move. I waited there. And then – I felt someone squeezing my throat from behind. I couldn't breathe. Everything went blurry. I saw someone approaching but couldn't make out any features. Then he hit me.' He gestures to his nose and shirt. 'I passed out. When I woke up, I was in here. With you.'

I've finished my tour of our makeshift cell. But I'm filled with nervous energy and can't bring myself to sit down. I continue pacing, back and forth, keeping my eyes trained on the ground.

'And you don't remember anything else? No other noises or smells?'

'No.'

'And nobody spoke? Nobody said anything to you?'

There's a pause before he says, 'No.' I'm not sure whether he's lying or not. But I don't push it. A feeling of complete exhaustion overwhelms me. The pain comes slamming back into my skull, exploding little points of colour behind my eyelids. I thump down hard on the ground, draw my knees up to my chest.

'So what now?' Julian says. There's a small note of desperation in his voice. I realize that he isn't in denial. He isn't calm, either. He's scared, and fighting it.

I lean my head back against the wall and close my eyes. 'Now we wait.'

It is impossible to know what time it is, and whether it is night or day. The electric bulb fitted high in the wall casts a flat white light over everything. Hours pass. At least Julian knows how to be quiet. He stays on his cot, and whenever I am not looking at him, I can feel him watching me. This is, in all probability, the first time he has ever been alone with a girl his age for an extended period of time, and his eyes travel over my hair, and legs, and arms, as though I am a strange species of animal at the zoo. It makes me want to put on my jacket again, to cover up, but I don't. It's hot.

'When did you have your procedure?' he asks me at a certain point.

'November,' I answer automatically. My mind is turning the same questions over and over again. Why bring us here? Why keep us alive? Julian, I can understand. He's worth something. They must be after a ransom.

But I'm not worth anything. And that makes me very, very nervous.

'Did it hurt?' he asks.

I look up at him. I'm once again startled by the clarity of his eyes: now a clear river colour, threaded with purple and navy shadows.

'Not too bad,' I lie.

'I hate hospitals,' he says, looking away. 'Labs, scientists, doctors. All that.'

A few beats of silence stretch between us. 'Aren't you kind of used to it by now?' I say, because I can't help it.

The left corner of his mouth twitches upward: a tiny smile. He looks at me sideways.

'I guess there are some things you never get used to,' he says, and for no reason at all, I think of Alex and feel a tightening in my stomach.

'I guess so,' I say.

Later on there is a change, a shift in the silence. I have been lying on the cot, preserving my strength, but now I sit up.

'What is it?' Julian says, and I hold up my hand to quiet him.

Footsteps on the other side of the door, coming closer. Then a grinding sound, as the hinges on the small metal cat flap squeak open.

Instantly I dive to the ground, trying to catch a glimpse of our captors. I land hard on my right shoulder just as a tray clatters through the opening and the metal door bangs shut again.

'Damn.' I sit up, kneading my shoulder. The plate holds two thick chunks of bread and several ropes of beef jerky. They've given us a metal bottle filled with water as well. Not bad, considering some of the stuff I used to eat in the Wilds.

'See anything?' Julian asks.

I shake my head.

'It wouldn't help us much, I guess.' He hesitates for a second and then slides off the bed, joining me on the ground.

'Information always helps,' I say, a little too sharply. That's something else I learned from Raven. Of course Julian wouldn't understand. People like Julian don't want to know, or think, or choose anymore; that is part of the point.

We both reach for the water, and our hands collide over the tray. Julian jerks back as though he has been burned.

'Go ahead,' I say.

'You first,' he says.

I take the water and begin sipping, watching Julian the whole time. He tears the bread into pieces. I can tell he's trying to make it last; he must be starving.

'Have my bread,' I say. I'm not sure why I offer it to him. It isn't smart. I'll need my strength to break out of here.

He stares at me. Strangely, despite the rest of his

colouring – caramel-and-wheat-blond hair, blue eyes – his lashes are thick and black. 'Are you sure?'

'Take it,' I say, and almost add, *Before I change my mind.*

The second piece he eats greedily, with both hands. When he's finished, I pass him the water bottle, and he hesitates before bringing it to his mouth.

'You can't catch it from me, you know,' I tell him.

'What?' He starts a little, as though I've interrupted a long period of silence.

'The disease. *Amor deliria nervosa.* You can't catch it from me. I'm safe.' Alex told me that very same thing, once. I push the memories of him away, willing them deep into the darkness. 'And besides, you can't catch it from sharing water and food, anyway. That's a myth.'

'You can get it from kissing,' Julian says, after a pause. He hesitates before he says the word *kissing*. It's not a word that gets used very much anymore, except in private.

'That's different.'

'Anyway, I'm not worried about that,' Julian says forcefully, and takes a big slug of water as if to prove it.

'What are you worried about, then?' I take my rope of jerky, lean back against the wall, and start working it with my teeth.

He won't meet my eyes. 'I just haven't spent that much time with—'

'Girls?'

He shakes his head. 'Anyone,' he says. 'Anyone my own age.'

We make eye contact for a second then, and a little jolt goes through me. His eyes have changed: now the crystal waters have deepened and expanded, become an ocean of swirling colour – greens and golds and purples.

Julian seems to feel he has said too much. He stands up,

walks to the door, and returns. This is the first sign of agitation I've seen from him. All day he has been remarkably still.

'Why do you think they're keeping us here?' he asks.

'Ransom, probably.' It's the only thing that makes sense.

Julian fingers the cut on his lip, considering this. 'My father will pay,' he says after a beat. 'I'm valuable to the movement.'

I don't say anything. In a world without love, this is what people are to each other: values, benefits, and liabilities, numbers and data. We weigh, we quantify, we measure, and the soul is ground to dust.

'He won't like dealing with the Invalids, though,' he adds.

'You don't know they're responsible for this,' I say quickly, and then regret it. Even here, Lena Morgan Jones must act the way she is supposed to.

Julian frowns at me. 'You saw them at the demonstration, didn't you?' When I don't answer, he goes on, 'I don't know. Maybe what happened is a good thing. Maybe now people will understand what the DFA is trying to do. They'll understand why it's so necessary.' Julian is using his public voice, as though he's addressing a large crowd. I wonder how many times he has had the same words, the same ideas, drilled into his head. I wonder whether he ever doubts.

I'm suddenly disgusted with him, and his calm certainty about the world, as though all of life can be dissected and neatly labelled, just like a specimen in a laboratory.

But I don't say any of this. Lena Morgan Jones keeps her mask on. 'I hope so,' I say fervently, and then I go to my cot, curling up toward the wall so he'll know I'm done talking to him. For revenge I mouth words, silently, into the concrete – old, forbidden words Raven taught me, from one of the old religions.

The Lord is my shepherd; I shall not want.
He makes me to lie down in green pastures: he leads me beside the
still waters.
He restores my soul: he leads me in the paths of righteousness for
his name's sake.
Yes, though I walk through the valley of the shadow of death, I will
fear no evil . . .

At a certain point, I drift off to sleep. I open my eyes into blackness, suppressing a cry. The electric light has been switched off, leaving us in perfect darkness. I feel hot and sick, and push the woollen blanket all the way to the foot of the cot, enjoying the cool air on my skin.

'Can't sleep?'

Julian's voice startles me. He is not in his cot. I can barely see him. He is a large black shape against the darkness.

'I was sleeping,' I say. 'What about you?'

'No,' he answers. His voice sounds softer now, less precise – as though the darkness has somehow melted its edges. 'It's stupid, but . . .'

'But what?' Dream images are still fluttering through my head, skirting the edges of consciousness. I was dreaming of the Wilds. Raven was there; Hunter was too.

'I have bad dreams. Nightmares.' Julian speaks the words in a rush, obviously embarrassed. 'I always have.'

For a split second I feel a little hitch in my chest, like something hard there has loosened. I will the feeling down and away. We are on opposite sides, Julian and I. There can never be any sympathy between us.

'They say it will get better after the procedure,' he says, almost like an apology, and I wonder if he is thinking the obvious: *If I even make it through.*

I don't say anything, and Julian coughs, then clears his throat.

'What about you?' he asks. 'Did you ever have nightmares? Before you were cured, I mean.'

I think of hundreds of thousands of cureds, sleeping dream-lessly in their marital beds, their heads enveloped in fog, a sweet and empty smoke.

'Never,' I say, and roll over, drawing the covers over my legs again, and pretend to sleep.

then

There is no time to leave the way we planned. We grab what we can and we run, while the Wilds behind us turn to roaring fire and smoke. We stay close to the river, hoping the water will offer us protection if the fire spreads.

Raven holds Blue, stiff-white and terrified, in her arms. I lead Sarah by the hand. She cries soundlessly, wrapped in Lu's enormous jacket. Sarah had no time to grab her own. Lu does without. When the frostbite starts to set in, Raven and I take turns giving Lu our coats. The cold reaches in, squeezes our guts, makes our eyes water.

And behind us is the inferno.

Fifteen of us made it safely away from the homestead; Squirrel and Grandma are missing. No one can remember seeing them, in our rush to leave the burrow. One of the bombs exploded a wall of the sickroom and sent a shower of rock and dirt and insects rocketing into the hall. After that, everything was screaming chaos.

Once the planes withdraw, the helicopters come. For hours they circle above us, and the air is spliced into fragments, beaten to shreds by the endless whirring. They mist the Wilds with chemicals. It burns our throats, stings our eyes, makes us choke. We wrap T-shirts and dish towels around our necks and mouths, move through the haze.

Finally it is too dark for the attacks to continue. The night sky is smudgy with smoke. The woods are full of distant crashing and cracking as so many trees succumb to the flames, but at least we have moved far enough downstream to be safe from the fire. At last Raven thinks it safe to pause and rest, and take stock of what we have.

We have only a quarter of the food we'd been storing, and none of the medical supplies.

Bram thinks we should go back for the food. 'We'll never make it south with what we've got,' he argues, and I can see Raven trembling as she struggles to get a fire lit. She can barely strike a match. Her hands must be freezing. Mine have been numb for hours.

'Don't you get it?' she says. 'The homestead is done. We can't go back. They meant to wipe us out today, all of us. If Lena hadn't warned us, we'd all be dead.'

'What about Tack and Hunter?' Bram says stubbornly. 'What'll they do when they come back for us?'

'Damn it, Bram.' Raven's voice rises a little, hysterical, and Blue, who has fallen asleep finally, curled up among the blankets, stirs fitfully. Raven straightens up. She has managed to get a fire started. She takes a step back and stares at the first twisting flames, blue and green and red.

'They'll have to take care of themselves,' she says more quietly, and even though she has regained her self-control I can hear the pain running under her words, a ribbon of fear and grief. 'We'll have to go on without them.'

'That's fucked,' Bram says, but halfheartedly. He knows she's right.

Raven stands there for a long time, as some of the others move quietly along the banks of the river, setting up camp: piling the backpacks together to form a shelter from the wind, unpacking and repacking the food, figuring out new rations. I go to Raven and stand next to her for a while. I want to put my arms around her, but I can't. You don't do that kind of thing with Raven. And in a weird way, I understand that she needs her hardness now more than ever.

Still, I want to comfort her somehow. So I say, low so that nobody else can hear me, 'Tack will be okay. If anybody can survive out here, no matter what, it's Tack.'

'Oh, I know,' she says. 'I'm not worried. He'll make it just fine.'

But when she looks at me I can see a deadness in her eyes, like she has closed a door somewhere deep inside of her – and I know that even she does not believe it.

The morning dawns grey and cold. It has begun to snow again. I've never been so cold in my life. It takes forever to stamp the feeling back into my feet. We have all slept out in the open. Raven worried that the tents would be too conspicuous, making us easy targets should the helicopters or planes return. But the skies are empty and the woods are still. Bits of ash intermingle with the snow, carrying the faint smell of smoke.

We head for the first encampment, the one Roach and Buck prepared for our arrival: a distance of eighty miles. At first we all walk quietly, occasionally scanning the skies, but after a few hours we start to loosen up. The snow continues to fall, softening the landscape, purifying the air, until the lingering smells of smoke have all been whited out.

Then we talk a little more freely. How did they find us? Why the attack? Why now?

For years, the Invalids have been able to count on one critical fact: they are not supposed to exist. The government has for decades denied that anyone inhabits the Wilds, and thus the Invalids have remained relatively safe. Any large-scale physical attack from the government would be tantamount to an admission of error.

But it seems that has changed.

Much later, we will find out why: the resistance has stepped up its game. They grew tired of waiting, of minor pranks and protests.

And so, the Incidents: explosives planted in prisons, and city halls, and government offices across the country.

Sarah, who has been running ahead, loops back around to me. 'What do you think happened to Tack and Hunter?' she says. 'Do you think they'll be okay? Do you think they'll find us?'

'Shhh.' I hush her sharply. Raven is walking ahead of us, and I glance up to see whether she has heard. 'Don't worry about that. Tack and Hunter can take care of themselves.'

'But what about Squirrel and Grandma? Do you think they got out okay?'

I think about that giant convulsive shudder – stone and dirt blasting inward – all the shouting and the smoke. There was so much noise, so much flame. I try to reach for a memory of Squirrel and Grandma, some vision of them running into the woods, but all I have are silhouettes, screaming and shouted orders, people turning to smoke.

'You ask too many questions,' I tell her. 'You should be saving your strength.'

She has been trotting like a dog. Now she slows down to a walk. 'Are we going to die?' she asks solemnly.

'Don't be stupid. You've relocated before.'

'But the people on the inside of the fence . . .' She bites her lip. 'They want to kill us, don't they?'

I feel something tighten inside of me, a spasm of deep hatred. I reach out and put a hand on her head. 'They haven't killed us yet,' I say, and I imagine that one day I will fly a plane over Portland, over Rochester, over every fenced-in city in the whole country, and I will bomb and bomb and bomb, and watch all their buildings smouldering to dust, and all those people melting and bleeding into flame, and I will see how they like it.

If you take, we will take back. Steal from us, and we will rob you blind. When you squeeze, we will hit.

This is the way the world is made now.

We reach the first encampment just before midnight on the third day, after a last-minute confusion about heading east or west at the large overturned tree lying gutted, roots exposed to the sky, which Roach had marked with a red bandanna. We waste an hour going the wrong way and have to double back, but as soon as we spot the small pyramid of stones Roach and Buck piled together to mark the place where the food is buried, there is general celebration. We run, shouting, the last fifty feet to the small clearing, full of renewed energy.

The plan was to stay here for a day, two tops, but Raven thinks we should camp out longer, and try to trap what we can. It is getting colder and will be increasingly difficult to find small game, and we do not have enough food to make it all the way south.

Now it is safe to set up our tents. For a while it is possible to forget we're on the run, forget we've lost members of our group, forget about all the supplies we left back at the homestead. We light a fire; we sit in its glow, warm our hands, and tell one another stories to distract ourselves from the cold and the hunger, from the air, which smells like coming snow.

now

'Tell me a story.'

'What?' Julian's voice startles me. He's been sitting in silence for hours. I've been pacing again, thinking about Raven and Tack. Did they escape the demonstration? Will they think I've been hurt, or killed? Will they come looking for me?

'I said, tell me a story.' He's sitting on his cot, legs crossed. I've noticed he can sit like that for hours, eyes half closed, like he's meditating. His calm has started to irritate me. 'It'll make the time go faster,' he adds.

Another day, more dragging hours. The light is on again, and breakfast (more bread, more jerky, more water) came again this morning. This time I pressed myself close to the floor and caught a glimpse of dark trousers and heavy boots. A barking male voice directed me to pass the old tray through the flap door, which I did.

'I don't know any stories,' I say. Julian is comfortable looking at me now – too comfortable, actually. I can feel his eyes on me as I walk, like a light touch on my shoulder.

'Tell me about your life, then,' Julian says. 'It doesn't have to be a good story.'

I sigh, running through the life Raven helped me construct for Lena Morgan Jones. 'I was born in Queens. I attended Unity through fifth grade, then transferred to Our Lady of the Doctrine. Last year I came to Brooklyn and enrolled at Quincy Edwards for my final year.' Julian is still watching me, as though he expects more. I make a quick, impatient gesture with my hand and add, 'I was cured in November. I'll take my evaluation later on this semester, though, with everyone else. I don't have a match yet.' I run out of things to say. Lena Morgan Jones, like all cureds, is pretty boring.

'Those are facts,' Julian says. 'That's not a story.'

'Fine.' I go and sit on my cot, bringing my legs underneath me, and turn to him. 'If you're such an expert, why don't you tell me a story?'

I'm expecting him to be flustered, but he just tilts his head back, thinking, blowing air out of his cheeks. The cut on his lip looks even worse today, bruised and swollen. Shades of yellow and green have begun to spread across his jawline. He hasn't complained, though, either about that or the ragged cut on his cheek.

He says finally, 'One time, when I was really little, I saw two people kissing in public.'

'You mean, like, at a marriage ceremony? To seal it?'

He shakes his head. 'No. On the street. They were protesters, you know? It was right in front of the DFA. I don't know if they weren't cured or the procedure didn't take or what. I was only, like, six. They were—' At the last second Julian falters.

'What?'

'They were using their tongues.' He looks at me for just a second, then clicks his eyes away. Tongue-kissing is even worse than illegal nowadays. It's considered dirty, disgusting, a symptom of disease taken root.

'What did you do?' I lean forward in spite of myself. I'm amazed, both by the story and by the fact that Julian is sharing it with me.

Julian cracks a smile. 'Want to hear something funny? At first I thought he was eating her.'

I can't help it: I let out a short bark of laughter. And once I start laughing I can't stop. All the tension from the past forty-eight hours breaks in my chest, and I laugh so hard I start to tear up. The whole world has been turned inside out and upside down. We are living in a funhouse.

Julian starts to laugh too, then winces, touching his bruised lip. 'Ow,' he says, and this makes me laugh even harder, which makes him laugh, which makes him say 'Ow' again. Pretty soon we're both cracking up. Julian has a surprisingly nice laugh, low and musical.

'Okay, your turn,' he finally gasps, as the laughter runs out.

I'm still struggling for breath. 'Wait – wait. What happened after that?'

Julian looks at me, still smiling. He has a dimple in his right cheek; a line has appeared between his eyebrows. 'What do you mean?'

'What happened to the couple? The ones who were kissing?'

The line between his eyebrows deepens, and he shakes his head confusedly. 'The police came,' he says, like it should be obvious. 'They were taken into quarantine at Rikers. For all I know, they're still there.'

And just like that, the remaining laughter is driven out of

me, like a sharp blow to the chest. I remember that Julian is one of Them; the zombies, the enemies. The people who took Alex from me.

Suddenly I feel sick. I have just been laughing with him. We've shared something. He's looking at me like we're friends, like we're the same.

I could throw up.

'So,' he says. 'Now you go.'

'I don't have any stories,' I say. My voice comes out harshly, a bark.

'Everyone has—,' Julian starts to say.

I cut him off. 'Not me,' I say, and climb off the cot again. My body is full of itching; I try to walk it out.

We go the rest of the day without exchanging a word. A few times, Julian seems about to speak, and so eventually I go to the cot and stretch out, closing my eyes and pretending to sleep. But I do not sleep.

The same words are whirling again and again in my mind: *There must be a way out. There must be a way out.*

Real sleep does not come until much later, after the electric light once again clicks off. Real sleep is like sinking slowly, like drowning in a mist. All too soon I am awake again. I sit up, heart pounding.

Julian is shouting in his sleep on the cot next to me, muttering gibberish words. The only one I can make out is *no*.

I wait for a bit, to see whether he will wake himself up. He kicks out, thrashing. The metal bed frame rattles.

'Hey,' I say. His urgent mutterings continue, and I sit up and say a little louder, 'Hey, Julian.'

Still no response. I reach over, fumbling for his arm in

the dark. His chest is damp with sweat. I find his shoulder and shake him gently.

'Wake up, Julian.'

Finally he wakes, gasping, and jerks away from my touch. He sits up. I can hear the rustle of the mattress as his weight shifts, and I can just make out his shape, a heavy blackness, the curve of his spine. For a moment we sit in silence. He is breathing hard. A rasping sound comes from his throat. I lie down again and listen to his breathing in the dark, waiting for it to slow.

'More nightmares?' I ask.

'Yes,' he says after a beat.

I hesitate. Part of me is inclined to roll over and go to sleep. But I'm awake now too, and the darkness is oppressive.

'Want to talk about it?' I say.

There's a long minute of silence. Then Julian begins speaking in a rush.

'I was in a lab complex,' he says. 'And outside there was this big fence. But there were all these . . . I can't really explain it, but it wasn't a real fence. It was made of bodies. Corpses. The air was black with flies.'

'Go on,' I say in a whisper, when Julian pauses again.

He swallows hard. 'When it was time for my procedure, they strapped me down to a table and asked me to open my mouth. Two scientists wrenched open my jaw, and my dad – he was there too – picked up this huge vat of concrete, and I knew that he was going to pour it down my throat. And I was screaming and trying to fight him off, and he kept saying it would feel fine, it would all be better, and then the concrete started filling my mouth and I couldn't breathe . . .'

Julian trails off. There's a squeezing in my chest. For one

wild second I feel like hugging him – but that would be horrible, and wrong on about a thousand levels. Julian must feel better too, after relating the dream to me, because he lies down again.

'I have nightmares too,' I say, and then quickly correct myself. 'Used to, I mean.'

Even in the dark, I can feel Julian staring at me.

'Want to talk about it?' He echoes my words back to me.

I think of the nightmares I used to have about my mother: dreams in which I would watch, helpless, as she walked off a cliff. I have never told anyone about them. Not even Alex. The dreams stopped after I found out she'd been alive, in the Crypts, for all the years I thought she was dead. But now my night-mares have taken new shape. Now they are full of burning, and Alex, and thorns that become chains and drag me into the earth.

'I used to have nightmares about my mom,' I say. I choke a little on the word *mom*, and hope he doesn't notice. 'She died when I was six.' This may as well be true. I will never see her again.

There is rustling from Julian's cot, and when he speaks I can tell he has turned toward me. 'Tell me about her,' he says softly.

I stare up into the darkness, which seems to be full of swirling patterns. 'She liked to experiment in the kitchen,' I say slowly. I can't tell him too much. I can't say anything that will make him suspicious. This is no longer the story of Lena Morgan Jones. But speaking into the darkness feels like a relief, so I let myself go on: 'I used to sit on the counter and watch her messing around. Most of what she made went in the trash. But it was always funny, and it made me laugh.'

I pause. 'I remember one time she made hot pepper pancakes. Those weren't bad.'

Julian is quiet. The rhythm of his breathing has grown steady.

'She used to play games with me too,' I say.

'She did?' Julian's voice has a touch of awe in it.

'Yeah. Real games, too, not just the development stuff they advocate in *The Book of Shhh*. She used to pretend . . .' I stop, biting my lip, worried I've gone too far.

'Pretend what?'

There's a crazy pressure building in my chest, and now all of it is coming back, my real life, my old life – the rickety house in Portland and the sound of the water and the smell of the bay; the blackened walls of the Crypts and the emerald-green diamond patterns of the sun slanting through the trees in the Wilds; all these other selves, stacked one on top of another and buried, so that no one will ever find them. And suddenly I feel I have to keep talking; if I don't, I will explode. 'She had a key she pretended would unlock doors to other worlds. It was just a regular key – I don't know where she got it, some garage sale, probably – but she kept it in a red box and only brought it out on special occasions. And when she did, we would pretend to go travelling through all these different dimensions. In one world, animals kept humans as pets; in another, we could go riding on the tails of shooting stars. There was an underwater world, and one where people slept all day and danced all night. My sister played too.'

'What was her name?'

'Grace,' I say. My throat is squeezing up, and now I'm combining selves and places, combining lives. My mom disappeared before Grace was even born; besides, Grace was my cousin. But strangely, I can picture it: my mother lifting Grace, swooping her around in an enormous circle while music piped from the fuzzy speakers; the three of us galloping down the long wooden hallways, pretending to be catching a star. I open my mouth to say more, but find I can't. I am on the verge of crying, and have to swallow back the feeling, hard, while my throat spasms.

Julian is quiet for a minute. Then he says, 'I used to pretend things too.'

'Yeah?' I turn my face into my pillow so the trembling in my voice will be muffled.

'Yeah. In the hospitals, mostly, and the labs.' Another beat. 'I used to pretend that I was back at home. I'd change the noises into other things, you know? Like the beeping of the heart monitors – that was actually just the "beep-beep-beep" of the coffee machine. And when I heard footsteps I would pretend they were my parents', even though they never were; and I would pretend the smell – you know how hospitals always smell like bleach, and just a little bit like flowers? – was because my mother was washing the sheets.'

The clenching in my throat has subsided, and I can breathe more easily now. I'm grateful to Julian; for not saying that my mother's behaviour seems unregulated, for not being suspicious or asking too many questions. 'Funerals smell like that too,' I say. 'Like bleach. Like flowers, too.'

'I don't like that smell,' Julian says quietly. If he were less well trained, and less careful, he would say *hate*. But he can't say it; it is too close to passion, and passion is too close to love, and love is *amor deliria nervosa*, the deadliest of all deadly things: it is the reason for the games of pretend, for the secret selves, for the spasms in the throat. He says, 'I used to pretend to be an explorer, too. I used to think about what it would be like to go to . . . other places.'

I think of finding him after the DFA meeting: sitting alone in the dark, staring up at those dizzying images of mountains and woods.

'Like where?' I ask, my heart speeding up a bit.

He hesitates. 'Just around,' he says finally. 'Like to other cities in the USA.'

Something tells me he's lying again; I wonder if he was really talking about the Wilds, or other places in the world – the unbordered places, where love still exists, where it was supposed to have consumed everyone by now.

Maybe Julian senses that I don't believe him, because he rushes on. 'It was just kid stuff. The kind of stuff I did on overnights to the labs, when I had tests and procedures and things like that. So I wouldn't be scared.'

In the silence, I can feel the weight of the earth above our heads: layers and layers of it, airless and heavy. I try to fight off the feeling that comes to me: we will be buried here forever. 'Are you scared now?' I ask.

He pauses for just a fraction of a second. 'I'd be more scared if I were alone,' he says.

'Me too,' I say. Again, I feel a rush of sympathy for him. 'Julian?'

'Yeah?'

'Reach out your hand.' I'm not sure what makes me say it – maybe it's the fact that I can't see him. It feels easier with him in the dark.

'For what?'

'Just do it,' I say, and I can hear him shifting; he is already moving, stretching his hand across the space between our cots.

I reach out and find his hand, which is cool and large and dry, and he jerks a bit as our skin comes into contact.

'Do you think we're safe?' he asks. His voice is hoarse.

I'm not sure whether he is referring to the *deliria*, or whether he is asking about the fact that we are trapped here, but he lets me lace my fingers through his. He has never held hands with someone before, I can tell. It takes him a moment of fumbling to understand how to do it.

'We'll be okay,' I say. I don't know whether I believe it or not. He gives my hand a quick squeeze, surprising me – there are some things, I guess, that come naturally, even if you've never done them before. We hold hands across the dark, and after a while I hear his breathing slow and deepen, and I close my eyes and think of waves pulling slowly on a shore. After a little while I am asleep too, and dream of being on a carousel with Grace, and watching, laughing, as all the wooden horses slowly break from their positions and begin galloping up into the air.

then

For three days, the weather holds. The woods are a symphony of cracking and snapping, as the trees and the river slough off their ice. Fat, jewel-coloured droplets of water rain down on our heads as we move through the woods, looking for berries, animal burrows, and good places to hunt. There is a great feeling of release and celebration, almost as if spring has really come, even though we know this is only a temporary reprieve. Raven is the only one who seems no happier.

We must be on constant lookout for food now. On the third morning, Raven nominates me to check the traps with her. Every time we find one empty, Raven curses a little under her breath. The animals have mostly gone underground.

We hear the animal before we get to the last trap, and Raven quickens her pace. There is a frantic sound of scrabbling against the brittle leaves that carpet the forest floor, and a panicked chittering, too. A large rabbit has its hind leg caught in the metal teeth of the trap. Its fur is stained with spots of dark blood. Panicked, the rabbit tries to pull itself forward; then falls back, panting, on its side.

Raven squats and removes a long-handled knife from her bag. It is sharp but spotted with rust and, I imagine, old blood. If we leave the rabbit here, I know it will twist and turn and writhe until it bleeds out from the leg – or, more likely, it will eventually give up and die slowly of starvation. Raven will be doing it a favour by killing it quickly. Still, I can't watch. I've never been on trap duty. I don't have the stomach for it.

Raven hesitates. Then, suddenly, she shoves the knife into my hand.

'Here,' she says. 'You do it.' I know it's not squeamishness on her part; she hunts all the time. This is another one of her tests.

The knife feels surprisingly heavy. I look at the rabbit, scrabbling and sputtering on the ground. 'I – I can't. I've never killed anything before.'

Raven's eyes are hard. 'Well, it's time to learn.' She puts two hands on the squirming rabbit – one on its head, one on its belly, stilling it. The rabbit must think she's trying to help. It stops squirming. Even so, I can see the rapid, desperate pattern of its breathing.

'Don't make me,' I say, both ashamed because I have to plead with her and angry for being made to.

Raven stands up again. 'You still don't get it, do you?' she says. 'This isn't a game, Lena. And it doesn't end here, or when we go south, or ever. What happened at the homestead . . .' She breaks off, shaking her head. 'There is no room for us anywhere. Not unless things change. We'll be hunted. Our homesteads will be bombed and burned. The borders will grow, and cities will expand, and there will be no Wilds left, and nobody to fight, and nothing to fight for. Do you understand?'

I say nothing. Heat is creeping up the back of my neck, making me feel light-headed.

'I won't always be around to help you,' she says, and kneels again, one knee in the dirt. This time she parts the rabbit's fur with her fingers, exposing a pink, fleshy bit of neck, a throbbing artery. 'Here,' she says. 'Do it.'

It strikes me then that the animal under her hands is just like us: trapped, driven out of its home, desperately fighting for breath, for a few more inches of space. And suddenly I am blindingly angry at Raven – for her lectures, and her stubbornness, and for thinking that the way that you help people is by driving them against a wall, by beating them down until they fight back.

'I don't think it's a game,' I say, and I can't keep the anger out of my voice.

'What?'

'You think you're the only one who knows anything.' I'm clenching my fists, one against my thigh, one around the handle of the knife. 'You think you're the only one who knows about loss, or being angry. You think you're the only one who knows about running.' I'm thinking of Alex, and I hate her for that, too; for bringing that back to me. The grief and anger is swelling, a black wave.

'I don't think I'm the only one,' Raven says. 'We've all lost something. That's the rule now, isn't it? Even in Zombieland. They lose more than most, maybe.' She raises her eyes to mine. For some reason I can't stop shaking.

Raven speaks with quiet intensity. 'Here's something else you might as well learn now: if you want something, if you take it for your own, you'll always be taking it from someone else. That's a rule too. And something must die so that others can live.'

My breath stops. For a moment the world stops turning, and everything is silence and Raven's eyes.

'But you know all about that, don't you, Lena?' She never raises her voice, but I feel the words physically – my head starts pounding, my chest is full of searing pain. All I can think is *Don't say it, don't say it, don't say it*, and I'm falling into the long dark tunnels of her eyes, back to that terrible dawn at the border, when the sun seeped across the bay like a slow stain.

She says, 'Didn't you try to cross with someone else? We heard the rumours. You were with somebody . . .' And then, as though she's only just remembering, although now I see that she has known – of course she has known – all along, and hatred and fury are welling up so fast and thick I think I will drown. 'His name was Alex, wasn't it?'

I am in midair, lunging at her, before I realize I've moved. The knife is in my hand and I am going to drive it straight into her throat, bleed her and gut her and leave her to be picked apart by the animals.

Just as I land on top of her, she jabs me in the ribs, pushing me off balance. At the same time her left hand clamps around my right wrist and she pulls me down, hard, driving the knife straight into the rabbit's neck, exactly where she had been exposing its artery. I let out a small cry. I am still holding the knife, and she wraps her fingers around my hand to keep it there. The rabbit jerks once under my hand and then goes still. For a moment I imagine that I can still feel its heartbeat skimming under my fingertips, a quick echo. The rabbit's body is warm. A small bit of blood seeps out from around the tip of the knife.

Raven and I are so close I can smell her breath and the sweat on her clothes. I try to jerk away from her, but she just grips me tighter. 'Don't be angry at me,' she says. 'I'm not the one who did it.' For emphasis, she forces my hand down a little farther. The knife goes another half inch into the rabbit, and more blood bubbles up around its tip.

'Fuck you,' I say, and suddenly I'm crying for the first time since I came to the Wilds; for the first time since Alex died. My throat closes up, and I can barely choke the words out. My anger is ebbing away now, replaced with a crazy grief for the stupid, dumb, trusting animal, who was running too fast and didn't look where it was going and still – even after its leg was scissored in the trap – believed it might escape. Stupid, stupid, stupid.

'I'm sorry, Lena. That's the way it is.' And she does look sorry: her eyes have softened now, and I see how tired she is, and must always have been – to live for years and years and years this way, having to rip and shred just for a space to breathe.

Raven releases me, finally, and quickly and expertly frees the dead rabbit from the trap. She wrenches the knife from the rabbit's skin, wipes it once against the ground, and slips it into her belt. She loops the rabbit's feet through a metal ring on her backpack, so it dangles, headfirst, toward the ground. When she stands, it sways like a pendulum. She is still watching me.

'And now we live for another day,' she says, and turns and walks away.

* * *

I read once about a kind of fungus that grows in trees. The fungus begins to encroach on the systems that carry water and nutrients up from the roots to the branches. It disables them one by one – it crowds them out. Soon, the fungus – and only the fungus – is carrying the water, and the chemicals, and everything else the tree needs to survive. At the same time it is decaying the tree slowly from within, turning it minute by minute to rot.

That is what hatred is. It will feed you and at the same time turn you to rot.

It is hard and deep and angular, a system of blockades. It is everything and total.

Hatred is a high tower. In the Wilds, I start to build, and to climb.

now

I am awakened by a voice barking, 'Tray!' I sit up, and see that Julian has gone to the door. He is crouching on his hands and knees, as I did yesterday, trying to get a look at our captor.

'Bucket!' is the next sharp command, and I feel both relieved and sorry when Julian picks up the tin bucket in the corner, which is making the room stink sharply of urine. Yesterday we took turns with it. Julian made me promise I would keep my back turned and my ears covered and, additionally, hum. When it was my turn I only asked him to turn around – but he covered his ears and sang anyway. He has a terrible voice, totally off-key, but he sang loudly and cheerfully, like he didn't know or didn't care – a song I hadn't heard in forever, one that used to be part of a kids' game.

A new tray comes through, followed by a clean bucket. Then the flap door clangs shut, the footsteps recede, and Julian stands.

'Did you see anything?' I ask, although I know the answer

will be no. My throat is hoarse, and I feel weirdly awkward. I shared too much last night. We both did.

Julian is having trouble looking at me again. 'Nothing,' he says.

We share the meal – this time, a small bowl filled with nuts, and another large piece of bread – in silence. Under the bright light of the ceiling bulb, it feels strange to sit on the floor, so close together, so I eat while pacing the room. There is a tension in the room that did not exist before. Unreasonably, I resent Julian for it. He made me speak last night, and he shouldn't have. At the same time, I was the one who reached for his hand. This seems unimaginable now.

'Are you going to do that all day?' Julian says. His voice is strained, and I can tell he is feeling the tension too.

'If you don't like it, don't watch,' I snap back.

More moments of silence. Then he says, 'My father will get me out of here. He's bound to pay soon.'

Hatred for him blooms again inside of me. He must know that there is no one in the world who will spring me. He must know that when our captors – whoever they are – realize this, I will either be killed or left here to rot.

But I don't say anything. I climb the steep, smooth walls of the tower. I enclose myself deep inside its casements; I build stone between us.

The hours here are flat and round, disks of grey layered one on top of the other. They smell sour and musky, like the breath of someone who is starving. They move slowly, at a grind, until it seems as though they are not moving at all. They are just pressing down, endlessly down.

And then, without warning, the light clicks off and plunges

us once again into darkness. I feel a sense of relief so strong it borders on joy: I've made it through another day. With the darkness, some of my unease begins to dissipate. In the daylight Julian and I are edges, set awkwardly and at odds with each other. But in the dark, I'm happy when I hear him settle on his cot, and know that we're separated by only a few feet of space. There's comfort in his presence.

Even the silence feels different now – more forgiving.

After a while, Julian says, 'Are you asleep?'

'Not yet.'

I hear him roll over to face me. 'You want to hear another story?' he asks.

I nod, even though he can't see me, and he takes my silence for assent.

'There once was a really bad tornado.' Julian pauses. 'This is a made-up story, by the way.'

'I got it,' I say, and close my eyes. I think of being back in the Wilds, my eyes stinging from campfire smoke, and Raven's voice coming through the haze.

'And there was this girl, Dorothy, and she fell asleep in her house. And the whole house was lifted off the ground by the tornado and went spinning into the sky. And when she woke up, she was in a strange land filled with little people, and her house had landed on this evil witch. Flattened her. So all the little people – the Munchkins – were really grateful, and they gave Dorothy a pair of magical slippers.' He lapses into silence.

'So?' I say. 'What comes next?'

'I don't know,' he says.

'What do you mean, you don't know?' I say.

Rustling, as he shifts on his cot. 'That's as far as I got,' he says. 'I never read the rest.'

I suddenly feel very alert. 'You didn't make it up, then?'

He hesitates for a second. Then: 'No.'

I keep my voice calm. 'I've never heard that story before,' I say. 'I don't remember it from the curriculum.' Very few stories get approved for Use and Propagation; at most two to three per year, and sometimes none. If I haven't heard it, chances are that's because it was never approved.

Julian coughs. 'It wasn't. On the curriculum, I mean.' He pauses. 'It was forbidden.'

My skin gets a prickly feeling. 'Where did you find a forbidden story?'

'My father knows a lot of important people in the DFA. Government people, priests, and scientists. So he has access to things . . . confidential documents and things that date from the time before. The days of sickness.'

I stay quiet. I can hear him swallow before he goes on.

'When I was little, my dad had this study – he had two studies, actually. A normal study, where he did most of his work for the DFA. My brother and I would sit and help him fold pamphlets all night long. It's funny. To this day, midnight always smells like paper to me.'

I'm startled by the reference to a brother; I've never heard one mentioned before, never seen his image on DFA materials or in the *Word*, the country's newspaper. But I don't want to interrupt him.

'His other study was always locked. No one was allowed inside, and my father kept the key hidden. Except . . .' More rustling. 'Except one day I saw where he put it. It was late. I was supposed to be asleep. I came out of my room for a glass of water, and I saw him from the landing. He went to a book-case in the hallway. On the uppermost shelf he kept a little porcelain statue of a rooster. I watched him lift the neck away from the body and put the key inside.

'The next day I pretended to be sick so I wouldn't have to go to school. And after my mom and dad had left for work and my brother had gone to get the bus, I snuck downstairs, got the key, and unlocked my dad's second study.' He gives a short laugh. 'I don't think I've ever been so scared in my life. My hands were shaking so bad I dropped the key three times before I could even fit it in the lock. I had no idea what I would find inside. I don't know what I was imagining – dead bodies, maybe, or locked-up Invalids.'

I stiffen, as always, when I hear the word, then relax, let it skate by me.

He laughs again. 'I was pissed when I finally got the door open and saw all those books. What a letdown. But then I saw they weren't regular books. They weren't anything like the books we saw in school and read in church. That's when I realized it was – they must be forbidden.'

I can't help it: a memory blooms now, long buried; stepping into Alex's trailer for the first time and seeing dozens and dozens of strange titles, mouldering spines glowing in the candle-light, learning the word *poetry* for the first time. In approved places, every story serves a purpose. But forbidden books are so much more. Some of them are webs; you can feel your way along their threads, but just barely, into strange and dark corners. Some of them are balloons bobbing up through the sky: totally self-contained, and unreachable, but beautiful to watch.

And some of them – the best ones – are doors.

'After that I used to sneak down to the study every time I was home alone. I knew it was wrong, but I couldn't stop.

There was music, too, totally different from the approved stuff on LAMM. You wouldn't believe it, Lena. Full of bad words, all about the *deliria* . . . but not all of them bad or hopeless at all. Everyone was supposed to be unhappy in the time before, right? Everyone was supposed to be sick. But some of the music . . .' He breaks off and sings, quietly, 'All you need is love . . .'

A shiver runs through me. It's strange to hear that word pronounced out loud. Julian falls into silence for a bit. Then he continues, even more quietly, 'Can you believe it? All you need . . .' His voice withdraws, as though he has realized how close we were lying and has moved away. In the dark he is barely an outline. 'Anyway, my dad caught me eventually. I was just a little ways into that story I was telling you about – *The Wonderful Wizard of Oz*, it was called. I've never seen him so angry in my life. He's pretty calm most of the time, you know, thanks to the cure. But that day he dragged me into the living room and beat me so hard I blacked out.' Julian tells me this flatly, without feeling, and my stomach tightens with hatred toward his father, toward everyone like his father. They preach solidarity and sanctity, and in their homes and in their hearts they pound, and pound, and pound.

'He said that would teach me what forbidden books could do,' Julian says, and then, almost musingly, 'The next day I had my first seizure.'

'I'm sorry,' I whisper.

'I don't blame him or anything,' Julian says quickly. 'The doctors said the seizure might have saved my life, actually. That's how they discovered the tumour. Besides, he was only trying to help me. Keep me safe, you know.'

My heart breaks for him in that second, and rather than be

carried away on the tide of it, I think of those smooth walls of hatred, and I think of climbing a set of stairs and taking aim at Julian's father from my tower, and watching him burn.

After a while Julian says, 'Do you think I'm a bad person?'

'No,' I say, squeezing the word past the rock in my throat.

For a few minutes we breathe together, in tandem. I wonder if Julian notices.

'I never figured out why the book was banned,' Julian says after a bit. 'That part must have come later, after the witch, and the shoes. I've been wondering about it ever since. Funny how certain things stay with you.'

'Do you remember any of the other stories you read?' I ask.

'No. None of the songs, either. Just that one line . . . "All you need is love."' He sings the notes again.

We lie in silence for a bit, and I begin to float in and out of consciousness. I am walking the shimmering silver ribbon of a river winding through the forest, wearing shoes that sparkle in the sun as though they are made out of coins . . .

I am passing under a branch and there is a tangle of leaves in my hair. I reach up and feel a warm hand – fingers . . .

I startle into awareness again. Julian's hand is hovering an inch above my head. He has rolled over to the very edge of his cot. I can feel the warmth from his body.

'What are you doing?' My heart is beating very fast. I can feel his hand trembling ever so slightly by my right ear.

'I'm sorry,' he whispers, but doesn't move his hand. 'I . . .' I can't see his face. He is a long, curved shadow, frozen, like something made of polished wood. 'You have nice hair,' he says finally.

My chest feels like it is being squeezed. The room seems hotter than ever.

'Can I?' he asks, so quietly I barely hear him, and I nod because I can't speak. My throat, too, is being squeezed.

Softly, gently, he lowers his hand that final inch. For a moment he leaves it there and again I hear that quick exhale, a release of some kind, and everything in my whole body goes still and white and hot, a starburst, a silent explosion. Then he runs his fingers through my hair and I relax, and the squeezing goes away, and I'm breathing and alive and it's all fine and everything will be okay. Julian keeps running his hand through my hair – twisting it around his fingers, curling it up and over his wrist and letting it drop onto the pillow again – and this time when I close my eyes and see the shining silver river I walk straight into it, and let it carry me down and away.

In the morning I wake up to blue: Julian's eyes, staring at me. He turns away quickly but not quickly enough. He has been watching me sleep. I feel embarrassed and angry and flattered at the same time. I wonder if I've said anything. I used to call Alex's name sometimes, and I'm pretty sure he was in my dreams last night. I don't remember any of them, but I woke up with that Alex-feeling, like a hollow carved in the centre of my chest.

'How long have you been awake?' I ask. In the light every-thing feels tense and awkward again. I can almost believe last night was a dream. Julian put his fingers in my hair. Julian touched me. I let him touch me.

I liked it.

'A while,' he says. 'I couldn't sleep.'

'Nightmares?' I ask. The air in the room is stifling. Each word is an effort.

'No,' he says. I expect him to say something else, but the silence stretches long between us.

I sit up. The room is hot, and it smells. I feel nauseous. I'm reaching for something to say, something to bleed out the tension in the room.

And then Julian says, 'Do you think they're going to kill us?' and the swollenness deflates at once. We're on the same side today.

'No,' I say, with more confidence than I feel. As each day has passed I've grown more and more uncertain. If they – the Scavengers – were planning to ransom Julian, surely they would have done it by now. I think about Thomas Fineman, and the polished metal of his cuff links, and his hard, shiny smile. I think of him beating his nine-year-old son into unconsciousness.

He might have decided not to pay. The thought is there, a needling doubt, and I try to ignore it.

Thinking of Thomas Fineman reminds me: 'How old is your brother now?' I ask.

'What?' Julian sits up so his back is toward me. He must have heard me, but I repeat the question anyway. I watch his spine stiffen: a tiny contraction, barely noticeable.

'He's dead,' he says abruptly.

'How – how did he die?' I ask gently.

Again, Julian nearly spits the word out. 'Accident.'

Even though I can tell Julian's uncomfortable talking about it, I just don't want to let it drop. 'What kind of accident?'

'It was a long time ago,' he says shortly, and then, suddenly whirling on me, 'Why do you care, anyway? Why are you so curious? I don't know shit about you. And I don't pry. I don't bother you about it.'

I'm so startled by his outburst, I nearly snap back. But I've been slipping too much; and so instead I take refuge in the smoothness, the roundness, of Lena Morgan Jones's calm: the calm of the walking dead; the calm of the cured.

I say smoothly, 'I was just curious. You don't have to tell me anything.'

For a second I think I see panic on Julian's face; it flashes there like a warning. Then it's gone, replaced by a sternness I have seen in his father. He nods once, curtly, and stands, begins pacing the room. I take a perverse pleasure in his agitation. He was so calm at first. It's gratifying to see him lose it just a little: down here the protection and certainty offered by the DFA mean nothing.

Just like that we are on opposite sides again. There's comfort in the morning's stony silence. It is how things should be. It is right.

I should never have let him touch me. I shouldn't have even let him get close. In my head, I repeat an apology: *I'm sorry. I'll be careful. No more slipping.* I'm not sure whether I'm speaking to Raven or Alex or both.

The water never comes; neither does the food. And then, midmorning, a subtle change in the air: echoes different from the sounds of dripping water and the hollow flow of underground air. For the first time in hours, Julian looks at me.

'Do you hear—,' he starts to say, and I shush him.

Voices in the hall, and heavy boot steps – more than one person is approaching. My heart speeds up, and I look around instinctively for a weapon. Other than the bucket, there isn't much. I've already tried to unscrew the metal bedposts from the cots, with no success. My backpack is on the other side of the room, and just as I'm thinking of making a dive for it – any weapon is better than no weapon at all – locks scrape open and the door swings inward and two Scavengers step into the room. Both of them are carrying guns.

'You.' The Scavenger in front, middle-aged, with the whitest skin I've ever seen, points to Julian with the butt of his rifle. 'Come on.'

'Where are we going?' Julian asks, although he must know they won't answer. He is standing, keeping his arms pressed to his sides. His voice is steady.

'We'll be asking the questions,' the pale man says, and smiles. He has dark-spotted gums, and yellow teeth. He is wearing heavy military-style pants and an old military jacket, but he is a Scavenger beyond a shadow of a doubt. On his left hand I see a faint pattern of a blue tattoo, and as he steps farther into the room, circling Julian like a jackal looping around its prey, my blood goes cold. He has a procedural scar, too, but his is terribly botched: three slashes on his neck, red like gaping wounds. He has tattooed a black triangle between them. Decades ago the procedure was much riskier than it is now, and growing up we heard stories about the people who weren't cured at all, but turned crazy, or brain-dead, or totally and utterly ruthless – incapable of feeling anything for anyone else, ever.

I try to fight the panic that's building in my chest, sending my heart into a skittering, erratic rhythm. The second Scavenger, a girl who might be Raven's age, is leaning in the door frame, blocking my exit. She's taller than I am but thinner, too. Her face is heavily pierced – I count five rings in each eyebrow, and gems studded into her chin and forehead – as well as what looks like a wedding ring looped through her septum. I don't want to think about where she got it. She has a handgun strapped to a belt hanging low on her hips. I try to estimate how quickly she could have it out and pointed at my head.

Her eyes flick to mine. She must interpret the expression on my face because she says, 'Don't even think about it.'

Her voice is strange and slurry, and when she opens her mouth to yawn I see it is because her tongue is glinting with metal. Metal studs, metal rings, metal wires: all of it looping on and around her tongue, making her look like she has swallowed barbed wire.

Julian hesitates for only a moment more. He jerks forward – a sudden, wrenching movement – and then recovers. As he passes through the door, flanked on one side by the pierced girl and on the other by the albino, he goes gracefully, as though he's strolling to a picnic.

He does not look at me, not even once. Then the door grates shut again, and the locks click into place, and I am left alone.

The waiting is an agony. My body feels like it's on fire. And although I'm hungry, and thirsty, and weak, I can't stop pacing. I try not to think about what they've done with Julian. Maybe he has been ransomed and released after all. But I didn't like the way the albino smiled and said, *We'll be asking the questions.*

In the Wilds, Raven taught me to look for patterns everywhere: the orientation of the moss on the trees; the level of undergrowth; the colour of the soil. She taught me, too, to look for the inconsistencies – an area of sudden growth might mean water. A sudden stillness usually means a large predator is nearby. More animals than usual? More food.

The appearance of the Scavengers is inconsistent, and I don't like it.

To keep myself busy I unpack and repack my backpack.

Then I unpack it again and lay its contents on the ground, as though the sad collection of items is a hieroglyph that might suddenly yield new meaning. Two granola bar wrappers. A tube of mascara. One empty water bottle. *The Book of Shhh.* One umbrella. I get up, turn a circle, and sit down again.

Through the walls, I think I hear a muffled shout. I tell myself it's just my imagination.

I pull *The Book of Shhh* onto my lap and flip through the pages. Even though the psalms and prayers are still familiar, the words look strange and their meanings are indecipherable: it's like returning somewhere you haven't been since you were a child, and finding everything smaller and disappointing. It reminds me of the time Hana unearthed a dress she had worn every day in first grade. We were in her room, bored, messing around, and she and I laughed and laughed, and she kept repeating, *I can't believe I was ever that small.*

My chest begins to ache. It seems impossibly, unbelievably long ago – when I could sit in a room with carpet, when we could spend days messing around, doing nothing in each other's company. I didn't realize then what a privilege that was: to be bored with your best friend; to have time to waste.

Halfway through *The Book of Shhh* a page has been dog-eared. I stop, and see several words in one paragraph have been emphatically underlined. The excerpt comes from Chapter 22: Social History.

When you consider how society may persist in ignorance, you must also consider how long it will persist in delusion; all stupidity is changed to inevitability, and all ills are made into values (choice turned to freedom, and love to happiness), so there is no possibility of escape.

Three words have been forcefully underscored: *You. Must. Escape.*

I flip forward another few chapters and find another dog-eared page where words have been circled, seemingly sloppily and at random. The full passage reads:

The tools of a healthy society are obedience, commitment, and agreement. Responsibility lies both with the government and with its citizens. Responsibility lies with you.

Someone – Tack? Raven? – has circled various words in the paragraph: *The tools are with you.*

Now I'm checking every page. Somehow, they knew this would happen; they knew I might be – or would be – taken. No wonder Tack insisted I bring *The Book of Shhh*; he left clues for me in it. A feeling of pure joy wells up inside of me. They didn't forget about me, and they haven't abandoned me. Until now, I haven't realized how terrified I've been – without Tack and Raven, I have no one. Over the past year, they have become everything to me: friends, parents, siblings, mentors.

There is only one other page that has been marked up. A large star has been drawn next to Psalm 37.

Through wind, and tempest, storm, and rain;
The calm shall be buried inside of me;
A warm stone, heavy and dry;
The root, the source, a weapon against pain.

I read through the psalm several times as disappointment comes thudding back. I was hoping for some kind of encoded message, but no deeper meaning is immediately apparent.

Maybe Tack only meant for me to stay calm. Or maybe the star was penned in earlier, and is unrelated; or maybe I've misunderstood and the markings are random, a fluke.

But no. Tack gave me the book because he knew I might need it. Tack and Raven are meticulous. They don't do things randomly or without purpose. When you are living on a razor's edge, there is no room at all for fumbling.

Through wind, and tempest, storm, and rain . . .

Rain.

Tack's umbrella – the one he pushed into my hands, and insisted I bring, on a cloudless day.

My hands are shaking as I pull the umbrella onto my lap and begin to examine it more closely. Almost immediately, I spot a tiny fissure – imperceptible, had I not been looking for it – that runs the length of the handle. I slide my fingernail into the miniscule crack and try to pry the handle apart, but it won't budge.

'Shit,' I say out loud, which makes me feel a little better. 'Shit, shit, shit.' Each time I say it, I try to pull and twist the umbrella apart, but the wood handle stays cleanly intact, polished and pretty.

'Shit!' Something inside me snaps – it's the frustration, the waiting, the heavy silence. I throw the umbrella, hard, against the wall. It hits with a crack. As it lands, the halves of the handle come neatly apart, and from between them a knife clatters to the ground. When I pull it from its leather sheath, I recognize it as one of Tack's. It has a carved bone handle and a viciously sharp blade. I once saw Tack gut an entire deer with it, cleanly, from throat to tail. Now the blade is polished so brightly that I can see my reflection in it.

Suddenly there is noise from the hallway: clomping footsteps, and a heavy grating sound, too, as though something is being dragged toward the cell. I tense up, gripping the knife, still in a crouch – I could make a run for it when the door opens; I could lunge at the Scavengers, swipe, swipe, take out an eye or get in at least one cut, make a run for it – but before I have time to plan or choose, the door is swinging open and it's Julian who comes toppling through, half conscious, so bruised and bleeding I recognize him only by his shirt, and then the door slams shut again.

'Oh my God.'

Julian looks as though he has been mauled by a wild animal. His clothes are stained with blood, and for one terrifying second I am jettisoned back in time, back to the fence, watching red seep across Alex's shirt, knowing he will die. Then the vision retreats and it's Julian again, on his hands and knees, coughing and spitting blood onto the floor.

'What happened?' I slip the knife quickly under my mattress and kneel down next to him. 'What did they do to you?'

A gurgling sound emerges from the back of his throat, followed by another round of coughing. Julian thuds onto his elbows, and my chest is full of a winging fear. *He's going to die,* I think, and the certainty is carried on a wave of panic.

No. This is different. I can fix this.

'Forget it. Don't try to talk,' I say. He has now slid onto the ground, almost in a fetal position. His left eyelid flutters, and I'm not sure how much he hears or understands. I slide his head onto my lap gently and help him roll over onto his back, biting back the cry that rises to my lips when I see his face: undifferentiated flesh, a beaten, bloody thing. His right eye is swollen completely shut, and blood is flowing rapidly from a deep cut above his right eyebrow.

'Shit,' I say. I've seen bad injuries before, but I've always been able to get some kind of medical supplies, however rudimentary. Here, I've got nothing. And Julian's body is making strange, twitchy motions. I'm worried he might have an attack.

'Stick with me,' I say, trying to keep my voice low and calm, just in case he's conscious and listening. 'I need to get you out of your shirt, okay? Stay as still as you can. I'm going to make you a compress. It will help with the bleeding.'

I unbutton Julian's filthy shirt. At least his chest is unmarked, apart from a few large and mean-looking bruises. All of the blood must be from his face. The Scavengers have worked him over, but they haven't tried to do serious harm. When I ease his arms out of the sleeves he moans, but I manage to get the shirt off. I press it tightly to the wound on his forehead, wishing I had a clean cloth. He moans again.

'Shhh,' I say. My heart is pounding. Waves of heat are radiating from his skin. 'You're okay. Just breathe, all right? Everything's going to be fine.'

There's a little bit of water left in the bottom of the cup they brought for us yesterday. Julian and I were making it last. I dampen Julian's shirt and blot his face with it; then I remember the antibacterial wipes the DFA was distributing at the rally. For the first time, I'm grateful to the DFA for their obsession with cleanliness. I still have the wipe folded into one of my back jeans pockets; as I unwrap it, the astringent smell of alcohol makes me wince, and I know it's going to hurt. But if Julian gets an infection, there's no way we'll make it out of here.

'This is going to sting a little bit,' I say, and bring the wipe into contact with Julian's skin.

Instantly he lets out a roar. His eyes fly open – as much as they can, anyway – and he jerks upright. I have to wrestle him by his shoulders to the ground again.

'Hurts,' he mutters, but at least he's awake now, and alert. My heart leaps in my chest. I realize I've barely been breathing.

'Don't be a baby,' I say, and continue cleaning his face while he tenses his whole body and grits his teeth. Once I've cleaned most of the blood away, I get a better sense of the damage they've done. The cut on his lip has opened up again, and he must have been hit repeatedly in the face, probably with a fist or a blunt object. The cut on his forehead is the most troublesome. It's still bubbling blood. But all in all, it could be much worse. He'll live.

'Here,' I say, and lift the tin cup to his lips, supporting his head on my knees. There's a half inch of water left. 'Drink this.'

When he's finished with the water, he closes his eyes again. But his breathing is regular now, and his tremors have stopped. I take the shirt and rip off a long strip of fabric, trying to will away the memories that are pressing and resurging: I learned this from Alex. At one point, in another lifetime, he saved me when I was hurt. He wrapped and bandaged my leg. He helped me escape from the regulators.

I fold the memory carefully inside of me. I bury it down deep.

'Lift your head a little,' I say, and Julian does, this time soundlessly, so I can work the fabric around it. I tie the length of shirt low on his forehead, knotting it tightly close to the gash, so it forms a kind of tourniquet. Then I lower his head back onto my thighs. 'Can you talk?' I ask, and Julian nods. 'Can you tell me what happened?'

The right corner of his lip is so swollen that his voice sounds distorted, like he's having to squeeze the words past a pillow. 'Wanted to know things,' he says, then sucks in a deep breath and tries again. 'Asked me questions.'

'What kind of questions?'

'My family's apartment. Charles Street. Security codes. Guards – how many and when.'

I don't say anything. I'm not sure Julian realizes what this means, and how bad it is. The Scavengers have grown desperate. They're trying to launch an attack on his house now, use him to find a way in. Maybe they're planning to kill Thomas Fineman; maybe they're just looking for the typical goods: jewellery, electronics that might be bartered on the black market, money, and, of course, weapons. They are always amassing weapons.

This can only mean one thing: their plan to ransom Julian has failed. Mr. Fineman didn't bite.

'Wouldn't tell them anything,' Julian huffs out. 'They said . . . a few more days . . . more sessions . . . I'd talk.'

There's no longer any doubt. We have to get out as soon as possible. Whenever Julian decides to talk – which he will, eventually – neither he nor I will serve any purpose to the Scavengers. And they are not known for their policy of catch-and-release.

'All right, listen.' I try to keep my voice low, hoping he won't read the urgency there. 'We're getting out of here, okay?'

He shakes his head, a tiny gesture of disbelief. 'How?' he croaks out.

'I've got a plan,' I say. This isn't true, but I figure I *will* have a plan. I've got to. Raven and Tack are counting on me. Thinking of the messages they left me, and the knife, fills me once again with warmth. I am not alone.

'Armed.' Julian swallows, then tries again. 'They're armed.'

'We're armed too.' My brain is skipping ahead now, into the hallway: footsteps come down, they go back up, one at a time. One guard only at mealtime. That's a good thing. If we can somehow get him to unlock the door . . . I'm so consumed with the planning, I don't even pay attention to the words coming out of my mouth.

'Look, I've been in bad situations before. You've got to trust me. This one time in Massachusetts—'

Julian interrupts me. 'When . . . you . . . Massachusetts?'

That's when I realize I've screwed up. Lena Morgan Jones has never been to Massachusetts, and Julian knows it. For a moment I debate telling another lie, and in that pause Julian struggles onto his elbows, swiveling around and scooting backward to face me, grimacing the whole time.

'Be careful,' I say. 'Don't push it.'

'When were you in Massachusetts?' he repeats painstakingly slowly, so that each word is clear.

Maybe it's the way that Julian looks, with the blood-spotted strip of shirt knotted around his forehead and his eyes swollen practically shut: the look of a bruised animal. Or maybe it's because I realize, now, that the Scavengers are going to kill us – if not tomorrow, then the next day or the day after that.

Or maybe I'm just hungry, and tired, and sick of pretending.

In a flash, I decide to tell him the truth. 'Listen,' I say, 'I'm not who you think I am.'

Julian gets very still. I'm reminded again of an animal – one time we found a baby raccoon, foundering in a mud pit that had opened up in the ground after a thaw. Bram went to help it, and as he approached, the raccoon went still just like that – an electric stillness, more alert and energetic than any kind of struggle.

'All that stuff I told you – about growing up in Queens and getting held back – none of that was true.'

Once I was on the other side, in Julian's position. I stood, battered between currents, as Alex told me the same thing. *I'm not who you think I am.* I still remember the swim back to shore; the longest and most exhausting of my life.

'You don't need to know who I am, okay? You don't need to know where I really come from. But Lena Morgan Jones is a made-up story. Even this' – I touch my fingers to my neck, running them over the three-pronged scar – 'this was made-up too.'

Julian still doesn't say anything, although he has inched backward even farther and used the wall to pull himself into a seated position. He keeps his knees bent, hands and feet flat on the floor, as though if he could, he would spring forward and run.

'I know you don't have a lot of reason to trust me right now,' I say. 'But I'm asking you to trust me anyway. If we stay here, we'll be killed. I can get us out. But I'm going to need your help.'

There is a question in my words, and I stop, waiting for Julian's answer.

For a long time there is silence. At last he croaks out, 'You.'

The venom in his voice surprises me. 'What?'

'You,' he repeats. And then, 'You did this. To me.'

My heart starts beating hard against my chest, painfully. For a second I think – I almost hope – that he's having some kind of attack, a hallucination or fantasy. 'What are you talking about?'

'Your people,' he says, and then I get a sick taste in my mouth and I know that he's perfectly lucid. I know exactly what he means, and what he thinks. 'Your people did this.'

'No,' I say, and then repeat it a little more emphatically. 'No. We had nothing to do with—'

'You're an Invalid. That's what you're telling me, right? You're infected.' Julian's fingers are trembling lightly against the ground, with a noise like the patter of rain. He's furious, I realize, and probably scared, too. 'You're sick.' He nearly spits out the word.

'Those aren't my people out there,' I say, and now I have to stop the anger from coming and dragging me under: it is a black force, a current tugging at the edges of my mind. 'Those people aren't . . .' I almost say, *They aren't human.* 'They're not Invalids.'

'Liar,' Julian snarls. There it is. Just like the raccoon when Bram finally went to lift it from the mud and it leapt, snapping, and sank its teeth into the flesh of his right hand.

The sick taste in my throat comes all the way from my stomach. I stand up, hoping Julian won't see that I, too, am shaking. 'You don't know what you're talking about,' I say. 'You don't know anything about us, and you don't know anything about me.'

'Tell me,' Julian says, still with that undercurrent of rage and coldness. Each word sounds hard-edged and cutting. 'When did you catch it?'

I laugh, even though none of it is funny. The world is upside down and everything is shit and my life has been cleaved and there are two different Lenas running parallel to each other, the old and the new, and they will never, ever be whole again. And I know Julian won't help me now. I was an idiot to think that he would. He's a zombie, just like Raven has always said. And zombies do what they were built to do: they trundle forward, blindly obedient, until they rot away for good.

Well, not me. I fish the knife out from under the mattress and sit on the cot, then begin running the blade quickly along the metal bedpost, sharpening it, taking pleasure in the way it catches the light.

'It doesn't matter,' I say to Julian. 'None of it matters.'

'How?' he persists. 'Who was it?'

The black space inside me gives a tiny shudder, widens another inch. 'Go to hell,' I say to Julian, but calmly now, and I keep my eyes on the knife, flashing, flashing, flashing, like a sign pointing the way out of the dark.

then

We stay four days at the first encampment. On the night before we are supposed to set out again, Raven takes me aside.

'It's time,' she says.

I'm still angry at her for what she said to me at the traps, although the rage has been replaced by a dull, thudding resentment. All this time, she has known everything about me. I feel as though she has reached into me, to a deep place, and broken something.

'Time for what?' I say.

Behind me, the campfire is burning low. Blue and Sarah and some of the others have fallen asleep outside, a tangle of blankets and hair and legs. They have begun to sleep this way a lot, like a human patchwork: it keeps them warm. Lu and Grandpa are conversing in low voices. Grandpa is chewing some of his last tobacco, working it in and out of his mouth, spitting occasionally into the fire and causing a burst of green flame. The others must have gone into the tents.

Raven gives me the barest trace of a smile. 'Time for your cure.'

My heart jumps in my chest. The night is sharply cold, and it hurts my lungs to breathe deeply. Raven leads me away from the camp, one hundred feet down along the stream, to a broad, flat stretch of bank. This is where we've broken through the thick layer of ice every morning to pull water.

Bram is already there. He has built another fire. This one is burning high and hot, and my eyes sting with ash and smoke when we're still five feet away. The wood is arranged in a teepee formation, and at its crown, blue and white flames are licking up toward the sky. The smoke is an eraser, blurring the stars above us.

'Ready?' Raven asks.

'Just about,' Bram says. 'Five minutes.' He is squatting next to a warped wooden bucket, which is nestled between pieces of wood on the periphery of the fire. He will have soaked it with water so it doesn't catch and burn. The proximity of the fire will eventually cause the water in the bucket to boil. I see him remove a small, thin instrument from a bag at his feet. It looks like a screwdriver, with a thin, round shaft, a sharp and glittering tip. He drops it into the bucket, handle down, and then stands up, watching as the tip of the plastic handle makes slow revolutions in the simmering water.

I feel sick. I look to Raven, but she is staring at the fire, her face unreadable.

'Here.' Bram steps away from the fire and presses a bottle of whiskey into my hands. 'You'll want to drink some of this.'

I hate the taste of whiskey, but I uncap the bottle anyway, close my eyes, and take a big swig. The alcohol sears my throat going down, and I have to fight back the urge to gag. But five seconds later, a warmth radiates up from my stomach, numbing my throat and mouth and coating my tongue, making it easier to take a second sip, and a third.

By the time Bram says, 'We're ready,' I've polished off a quarter of the bottle and above me, through the smoke, the stars make slow revolutions, all of them glittering like pointed metal tips. My head feels detached from my body. I sit down heavily.

'Easy,' Bram says. His white teeth flash in the dark. 'How you feeling, Lena?'

'Okay,' I say. The word is harder to get out than usual.

'She's ready,' Bram says, and then, 'Raven, grab the blanket, will you?' Raven moves behind me, and then Bram tells me to lie back, which I do, gratefully. It helps the woozy, spinning feeling in my head.

'You take her left arm,' Raven says, kneeling next to me. Her earrings – a feather and a silver charm, both threaded through one ear – sway together like a pendulum. 'I'll take her right.'

Their hands grip me tightly from both sides. Then I start to get scared.

'Hey.' I struggle to sit up. 'You're hurting me.'

'It's important that you stay very still,' Raven says. Then she pauses. 'It's going to hurt for a bit, Lena. But it will be over quickly, okay? Just trust us.'

The fear is causing a new fire in my chest. Bram is holding the metal tool, newly sterilized, and its blade seems to catch all the light from the fire behind him, and glow hot and white and terrible. I'm too frightened to try and struggle, and I know it wouldn't do any good. Raven and Bram are too strong.

'Bite on this,' Bram says, and suddenly there is a strip of leather going into my mouth. It smells like Grandpa's tobacco.

'Wait—,' I try to say, but I can't choke the word out past the leather. Then Bram places one hand on my forehead, angling my chin up to the sky, hard, and he's bending over me, blade in hand, and I can feel its tip just pressing into the space behind my left ear, and I want to cry out but I can't, and I want to run but I can't do that, either.

'Welcome to the resistance, Lena,' he whispers to me. 'I'll try to make this quick.'

The first cut goes deep. I am filled with burning. And then I find my voice, and scream.

now

'Lena.'

My name pulls me out of sleep. I sit up, heart careening in my chest.

Julian has moved his cot toward the door, pressed it against the wall, as far away from me as possible. Sweat is beading on my upper lip. It has been days since I've showered, and the room is full of a close, animal smell.

'Is that even your real name?' Julian asks, after a pause. His voice is still cold, although it has lost some of its edge.

'That's my name,' I say. I squeeze my eyes closed, tight, until little bursts of colour appear behind my eyelids. I was having a nightmare. I was in the Wilds. Raven and Alex were there, and there was an animal, too, something enormous we had killed.

'You were calling for Alex,' Julian says, and I feel a small spasm of pain in my stomach. More silence, then: 'It was him, wasn't it? He's the one who got you sick.'

'What does it matter?' I say. I lie down again.

'So what happened to him?' Julian asks.

'He died,' I say shortly, because that is what Julian wants to hear. I picture a tall tower, smooth-sided, stretching all the way to the sky. There are stairs cut in the side of the tower, winding up and up. I take the first step into the coolness and shade.

'How?' Julian asks. 'Because of the *deliria*?' I know if I say yes he'll feel good. *See*, he'll think. *We're right. We've been right all this time. Let people die so that we can be right.*

'You,' I say. 'Your people.'

Julian sucks in a quick breath. When he speaks again, his voice is softer. 'You said you never had nightmares.'

I wall myself up inside. From the tower, the people on the ground are no more than ants, specks, punctuation marks: easily smudged out.

'I'm an Invalid,' I say. 'We lie.'

In the morning my plan has hardened, clarified. Julian is sitting in the corner, watching me the way he did when we were first taken. He is still wearing the rag around his head, but he looks alert now, and the swelling in his face has gone down.

I wrestle the umbrella apart, pulling the nylon shell away from its hinged metal arms. Then I lay the nylon flat and cut it into four long strips. I tie the strips together into a makeshift cord and test its strength. Decent. It won't hold forever, but I don't need longer than a few minutes.

'What are you doing?' Julian asks me, and I can tell he's trying hard not to seem too curious. I don't answer him. I no longer care what he does, or whether he comes with me or remains here to rot forever, as long as he stays out of the way.

It doesn't take me long to remove the hinges from the flap

door, just some wiggling and working with the point of the knife: the hinges are rusted and loose anyway.

Once the hinges are off, I manage to push the door outward, so it falls, clattering into the hall. That will bring someone, and soon. My heart speeds up. It's showtime, as Tack used to say, right before heading out on a hunt. I pull *The Book of Shhh* onto my lap and tear out a page.

'You'll never fit through that space,' Julian says. 'It's too small.'

'Just stay quiet,' I say. 'Can you do that for me? Just don't speak.'

I unscrew the mascara that made its way into my backpack, silently send a message of thanks to Raven – now that she is on the other side, in Zombieland, she can't get enough of its little trinkets and comforts, its well-lit stores stocked with rows and rows of things to buy.

I can feel Julian watching me. I scrawl out a note on the blank side of the page.

The girl is violent. Worried she might kill me. Ready to talk if
you let me out NOW.

I slip the note through the cat-flap door and into the hallway. Then I repack my backpack with *The Book of Shhh*, the empty water bottle, and pieces of the dismantled umbrella. I grip the knife in my hand, stand by the door, and wait, trying to slow my breathing, every so often flipping the knife into my other hand and wiping sweat from my palms onto my pants. Hunter and Bram once took me deer hunting with them, just to watch, and this was the part I couldn't stand: the stillness, the waiting.

Fortunately, I don't wait long. Someone must have heard the flap door fall. Pretty soon I hear another door close – more information; information is good; that means there's another door somewhere, another room underground – and footsteps coming toward me. I hope it's the girl who comes, the one with the wedding ring threaded through her nose.

I hope, above all, it's not the albino.

But the boot steps are heavy, and when they stop just outside the door, it's a man who mutters, 'What the hell?'

My whole body feels wound up, coiled like an electrical wire. I'll have only one shot to get this right.

Now that I've disabled the flap door, I have a solid view of mud-splattered combat boots and baggy green trousers, like the kind lab techs and street sweepers wear. The man grunts, and moves the flap door a few inches with a boot, as though toeing a mouse to see whether it is alive. Then he kneels down and snatches up the note.

I tighten my grip on the knife. Now my heart feels as though it is barely going at all. I am not breathing, and the space between heartbeats is an eternity.

Open the door. Don't call for backup. Open the door now. Come on, come on, come on.

Finally there's a heavy sigh, and the sound of keys jingling; a clicking, too, as I imagine him sliding the safety off his gun.

Everything is sharp and very slow, as though funneled through a microscope. He's going to open the door.

The keys turn in the lock and Julian scrabbles, alarmed, to his feet, letting out a short cry. For a second the guard hesitates. Then the door begins to push inward, inward, toward me – toward where I am standing, pressed up against the wall, invisible.

Just like that the seesaw has swung: the seconds are banging together so fast I can hardly keep track of them. Everything is instinct and blur. Things happen in one collapsed moment: the door swings fully open, just a few inches from my face, as he takes a step into the cell, saying, 'All right, I'm all ears,' and as he does I push against the door with both hands, slamming it toward him, hear a small crack and his short exclamation, a curse and a groan. Julian is saying, 'Holy shit, holy shit.'

I leap out from behind the door – all instinct now, no more thinking – and land on the Scavenger's back. He is staggering on his feet, clutching his head, where the door must have hit him, and my momentum carries him off his feet and onto the ground. I drive a knee into his back and press the knife into his throat.

'Don't move.' I'm shaking. I hope he can't feel it. 'Don't scream. Don't even think about screaming. Just stay where you are, nice and easy, and you won't get hurt.'

Julian watches me, wide-eyed, silent. The Scavenger is good. He stays still. I keep my knee in his back and the tip of my knife at his throat, take one end of the nylon rope in my teeth, and twist his left hand behind his back, and then his right, keeping them both stabilized with my knee.

Julian wrenches away from the wall suddenly and comes over to me.

'What are you doing?' My voice is a snarl, through the nylon and my gritted teeth. I can't take Julian and the Scavenger at once. If he interferes, it's all over.

'Give me the rope,' he says calmly. For a second I don't move, and he says, 'I'm helping you.'

I pass the cord to him wordlessly, and he kneels down behind me. I keep the Scavenger pressed to the ground as Julian binds his hands and feet.

I press my knee harder into the Scavenger's back, holding him still. I picture the spaces between the ribs, the soft skin and layers of fat and flesh – and beneath it all, the heart, squeezing and pumping out life. It would only take one quick jab . . .

'Give me the knife,' Julian says.

I tighten my grip on the handle. 'For what?'

'Just give it to me,' he says.

I hesitate, then pass it back to him. He cuts off the excess nylon cord – he is clumsy with the knife, and it takes him a minute – and then passes both the knife and the strip of nylon back to me.

'You should gag him,' Julian says matter-of-factly. 'So he won't be able to call for help.'

He is amazingly calm. I tip the Scavenger's head up and wrestle the makeshift gag into his mouth. He kicks out with his legs, thrashing like a fish pulled onto land, but I manage to get the fabric knotted behind his head. The bonds are flimsy – he'll get his hands free in ten, fifteen minutes – but that should be enough time.

I climb quickly to my feet and sling my backpack over my shoulders. The door to the cell is still gaping open. Just that – the open door – fills me with a sense of joy so complete I could shout. I imagine Raven and Tack, watching me approvingly.

I won't let you down.

I look back. Julian has gotten to his feet.

'You coming, or what?' I say.

He nods. He still looks like shit, his eyes bare cracks, but his mouth is set tight in a line.

'Let's go, then.' I tuck the knife, sheathed, into the waistband of my pants. I can't worry about whether Julian will slow me down. And he may even be helpful. At least he's another target; if I get pursued or jumped, he'll be a distraction.

We close the cell door carefully behind us, which quiets the sounds of the Scavenger's muffled cries, the scuffing of his shoes against the floor. The hall outside the cell is long, narrow, and well lit: four doors, all of them closed and all of them metal, run along the wall to our left, and at the end of the hall is another steel door. This throws me a bit. I've been assuming our cell was simply annexed off one of the old subway tunnels, and we would emerge into darkness and dankness. But we're obviously in a space that is far more elaborate, an underground complex.

The voices I heard earlier are coming from behind one of the closed doors on our left. I think I recognize the low, flat growl of Albino. I pick up only a few words of conversation: '. . . waiting . . . bad idea from the start.' A staccato response follows: another man's voice. At least I know where the albino is now, although that makes the girl with the piercings unaccounted for. That means at least four Scavengers were involved in our kidnapping. They're obviously getting organized: a very, very bad thing.

As we progress, the voices get louder and clearer. The Scavengers are arguing.

'Stick with the original agreement . . .'

'Don't owe . . . to anyone . . .'

My heart has lodged in my throat, making it difficult to breathe. Just as I'm about to scoot past the door I hear a loud bang from inside the room. I freeze, thinking immediately of gunfire. The door handle rattles. My insides go loose and I think, *This is it, right here.*

Then the voice I don't recognize says loudly, 'Come on, don't be upset. Let's talk about this.'

'I'm tired of talking.' That's Albino: so whatever happened inside, it wasn't a gunshot I heard.

Julian has frozen beside me. We've both instinctively flattened ourselves against the wall – not that it will help us, if the men come bursting out into the hall. Our arms are just touching, and I can feel the light fuzz of blond hair on his forearms. It seems to be conducting a current, small electrical pulses. I inch away from him.

The door handle gives a final rattle and then Albino says, 'All right, I'm listening.' His footsteps retreat back into the room, and the spasm in my chest relaxes. I make a motion to Julian. *Let's go.* He nods. He has been clenching his fists. His knuckles are tiny white half-moons.

All the remaining doors in the hallway are closed, and we hear no more voices, and see no evidence of other Scavengers. I wonder what the rooms contain: maybe, I think, there are prisoners in all of them, lying in twin cots, waiting to be ransomed or killed. The idea makes me sick, but I can't think about it too long. That's another rule of the Wilds: you have to take care of yourself first.

The flip side of freedom is this: when you're completely free, you're also completely on your own.

We reach the door at the end of the hallway. I grab the door handle and pull. Nothing. That's when I see the small keypad fitted just above the door handle, like the kind Hana used to have on her front gate.

The door requires a code.

Julian must notice it at the same time I do, because he mutters, 'Shit. Shit.'

'All right, let's think about this,' I whisper back, trying to sound calm. But my mind has turned to snow: the same idea coming down like a blizzard, freezing my blood. I'm screwed. I'll be trapped here, and when I'm found, I'll have a bruised and bound guard to atone for. They won't be so careless anymore either. No more flap doors for me.

'What do we do?' Julian asks.

'We?' I shoot him a look over my shoulder. The crown of his head is encircled with dried blood, and I look away so I don't start feeling sorry for him. 'We're in this together now?'

'We have to be,' he says. 'We'll need to help each other if we're going to escape.' He puts his hands on my shoulders and moves me gently but firmly out of the way. The touch surprises me. He must really mean what he said about setting our differences aside for now. And if he can do it, so can I.

'You won't be able to pick it,' I say. 'We need a code.'

Julian runs his fingers over the keypad. Then he takes a step back and squints up at the door, runs his hands along the doorjamb as though testing its sturdiness. 'We have a keypad like this on the gate at home,' he says. He's still running his fingers along the doorjamb, tracing cracks in the plaster. 'I can never remember the code. Dad's changed it too many times – too many workers in and out. So we had to develop a system, a series of clues. A code within a code – little signs embedded in and around the gate so whenever the code is changed, I'll know it.'

Suddenly it clicks: the point of his story, and the way out.

'The clock,' I say, and I point to the clock hanging above the door. It's frozen: the small hand hovers slightly above the nine, and the big hand is stuck on the three. 'Nine and three.'

But even as I say it, I'm uncertain. 'But that's only two numbers. Most keypads take four numbers, right?'

Julian punches in 9393, then tries the door. Nothing. 3939 doesn't work, either. Neither does 3399 or 9933, and we're running out of time.

'Shit.' Julian pounds the keypad once with his fist in frustration.

'Okay, okay.' I take a deep breath. I was never good at codes and puzzles; math was always one of my worst subjects. 'Let's think about this.'

At that second, the voices down the hall resurge. A door opens a few inches.

Albino is saying, 'I'm still not convinced. I say if they don't pay, we don't play . . .'

My throat seizes with sudden terror. Albino is coming into the hall. He'll see us at any second.

'Shit,' Julian breathes again, a bare exhale. He's jogging a little on his feet, back and forth, as though he's cold, but I know he must be as scared as I am. Then, suddenly, he freezes. 'Nine fifteen,' he says, as the door opens another couple of inches, and the voices spill into the hall.

'What?' I grip the knife tightly, whipping my head back and forth between Julian and the door: opening, opening.

'Not nine-three. Nine fifteen. Zero-nine-one-five.' He has already bent over the keypad again, punching the numbers in hard. There's a quiet buzz, and a click. Julian leans into the door and it opens, as the voices grow clearer and edged with sharpness, and we slip into the next room just as the door behind us swings open, and the Scavengers take their first steps into the hall.

We're in yet another room, this one large, high-ceilinged,

and well lit. The walls are lined with shelves, and the shelves are crammed so tightly with things that in places the wood has begun to sag and warp under the weight of it all: packages of food, and large jugs of water, and blankets; but also knives, and silverware, and nests of tangled jewellery; leather shoes and jackets; handguns and wooden police batons and cans of pepper spray. Then there are things that have no purpose whatsoever: scattered radio bits lying across the floor, an old wooden wardrobe, leather-topped stools, and a trunk filled with broken plastic toys. At the opposite end of the room is another concrete door, this one painted cherry red.

'Come on.' Julian grabs my elbow roughly, pulling me toward it.

'No.' I wrench away from him. We don't know where we are; we have no idea how long it will be before we escape. 'There's food here. Weapons. We need to stock up.'

Julian opens his mouth to respond when from the hallway comes the stuttered cadence of shouting, and the pounding of feet. The guard must have given the alarm somehow.

'We've got to hide.' Julian pulls me toward the wardrobe. Inside it smells like mouse droppings and mould.

I swing the wardrobe doors closed behind me. The space inside is so small, Julian and I practically have to sit on top of each other. I ease my backpack onto my lap. My back is pressed up against his chest, and I can feel its rise and fall. Despite everything, I'm glad he's with me. I'm not sure I would have made it even this far on my own.

The keypad gives another buzz; the door of the stockroom bursts open, slamming against the wall. I flinch involuntarily, and Julian's hands find my shoulders. He squeezes once, a quick pulse of reassurance.

'Goddammit!' That's Albino; the raspy voice, the anger running through his words, like a live wire. 'How the hell did this happen? How did they—'

'They can't have gone very far. They don't have the code.'

'Well, then, where the hell are they? Two goddamn kids, for shit's sake.'

'They might be hiding in one of the rooms,' the other one, the not-Albino, says.

Another voice – female, this time, probably Piercing – chimes in. 'Briggs is checking on it. The girl jumped Matt, tied him up. She has a knife.'

'Damn it.'

'They're in the tunnels by now,' the girl says. 'Have to be. Matt must have given up the code.'

'Does he say he did?'

'Well, he wouldn't say it, would he?'

'All right, look.' Albino again; he's obviously the one in charge. 'Ring, you search the containment rooms with Briggs. We'll clear out to the tunnels. Nick, take east; I'll get west with Don. Tell Kurt and Forest they're on north, and I'll find someone to cover south.'

I'm tabulating names, numbers: so, we're dealing with at least seven Scavengers. More than I expected.

Albino is saying: 'I want those pieces of shit back here in the next hour. No way I'm losing payday over this, okay? Not because of some eleventh-hour screwup.'

Payday. An idea squirms at the edges of my consciousness; but when I try to fixate on it, it blurs into fog. If it's not about ransom, what kind of pay can the Scavengers be expecting? Maybe they're assuming Julian will roll, give up the security info they'll need to get into his house. But it's an elaborate – and dangerous – procedure for a run-of-the-mill break-in, and it's not standard Scavenger operating procedure, either. They don't plan. They burn, and terrorize, and take.

And I still don't see how I fit in.

Now there's the sound of shuffling, of guns being loaded and straps being snapped into place. That's when the fear comes gunning back: on the other side of a one-inch plywood door are three Scavengers with an army-style arsenal. For a second I think I might faint. It's so hot and close. My shirt is soaked with sweat. We'll never make it out of here alive. There's no way. It's not possible.

I close my eyes and think of Alex, of pressing close to him on the motorcycle and having the same certainty.

Albino says, 'We'll meet back here in an hour. Now go find those little shits and skewer them for me.' Footsteps move toward the opposite corner. So – the red door must lead to the tunnels. The door opens and closes. Then there's quiet.

Julian and I stay frozen. At one point I start to move, and he draws me back. 'Wait,' he whispers. 'Just to be sure.'

Now that there are no voices and no distractions, I'm uncomfortably aware of the heat from his skin, and the tickle of his breath on the back of my neck.

Finally I can't take it anymore. 'It's fine,' I say. 'Let's go.'

We push out of the wardrobe, still moving cautiously, just in case there are any other Scavengers sniffing around.

'What now?' Julian asks me, keeping his voice low. 'They're looking for us in the tunnels.'

'We have to risk it,' I say. 'It's the only way out of here.'

Julian looks away, relenting.

'Let's load up,' I say.

Julian moves to one of the shelves and starts pawing through a heap of clothing. He tosses a T-shirt back to me. 'Here,' he says. 'Looks like it should fit.'

I find a pair of clean jeans, too, a sports bra, and white socks, stripping down quickly behind the wardrobe. Even though I'm still dirty and sweaty, it feels amazing to put on clean clothes. Julian finds a T-shirt and a pair of jeans. They're a little too big, so he holds them up with an electrical wire he uses as a belt. We stuff my backpack with granola bars and water, two flashlights, some packages of nuts, and jerky. I come across a shelf filled with medical supplies, and pack my bag with ointment and bandages and antibacterial wipes. Julian watches me wordlessly. When our eyes meet, I can't tell what he's thinking.

Underneath the medical supplies is a shelf empty but for a single wooden box. Curious, I squat down and swing open its lid. My breath catches in my throat.

ID cards. The box is filled with hundreds and hundreds of ID cards, rubber-banded together. There is a pile of DFA badges too, gleaming brightly under the lights.

'Julian,' I say. 'Look at this.'

He stands next to me, staring wordlessly as I sift past all the laminated cards, a blur of faces, facts, identities.

'Come on,' he says, after a minute. 'We have to hurry.'

I select a half-dozen ID cards quickly, trying to pick girls who look roughly my age, and rubber-band them together, slipping them into a pocket. I take a DFA badge too. It might be useful later.

Finally it's time for the weapons. There are crates of them: old rifles heaped together like a tangle of thick thorns, gathering dust; well-palmed and well-oiled handguns; heavy clubs and boxes of ammunition. I pass Julian a handgun after checking to see that it's loaded. I dump a box of bullets in my backpack.

'I've never shot one before,' Julian says, handling it gingerly, as though he's worried it will explode on its own. 'Have you?'

'A few times,' I say. He sucks his lower lip into his mouth. 'You take it,' he says. I slip the handgun into my backpack, even though I don't like the idea of being weighed down.

Knives, on the other hand, are useful, and not just for hurting people. I find a switchblade and stick it under the strap of the sports bra. Julian takes another switchblade, which he also pockets.

'Ready to go?' he asks me, after I've shouldered my backpack.

That's when it hits me: the shimmering worry at the edge of my thoughts swells and breaks over me. This is wrong – all wrong. This is too organized. There are too many rooms, too many weapons, too much order.

'They must have had help,' I say, as the idea occurs to me for the first time. 'The Scavengers could never have done this on their own.'

'The who?' Julian asks impatiently, casting an anxious look at the door.

I know we have to go, but I can't move; a tingling feeling is working its way from my toes up into my legs. There's another idea flickering in the back of my mind now – a brief impression, something seen or remembered. 'Scavengers. They're uncureds.'

'Invalids,' Julian says flatly. 'Like you.'

'No. Not like me, and not Invalids. Different.' I squeeze my eyes shut and the memory crystallizes: pressing the point of my knife into the flesh below the Scavenger's jaw, just above faint blue markings that looked somehow familiar . . .

'Oh my God.' I open my eyes. My chest feels as though someone is pounding on it.

'Lena, we have to go.' Julian reaches out to grab my arm, but I pull away from him.

'The DFA.' I can barely croak out the words. 'The guy – the guard back there, the one we tied up – he had a tattoo of an eagle and a syringe. That's the DFA crest.'

Julian stiffens. It's as though a current has run through his whole body. 'It must be a coincidence.'

I shake my head. Words, ideas, are tumbling through my head, a stream: everything flows one way. Everything makes sense: talk of payday; all this equipment; the tattoo; the box of badges. The complex, the security – all of it costs money. 'They must be working together. I don't know why, or what for, or—'

'No.' Julian's voice is low and steely. 'You're wrong.'

'Julian—'

He cuts me off. 'You're wrong, do you understand me? It's impossible.'

I force myself not to look away from him, even though there's something strange going on behind his eyes, a roiling and swirling that makes me feel dizzy, as though I'm standing on the edge of a cliff and in danger of falling.

That's how we're standing – frozen like that, a tableau – when the door bangs open and two Scavengers burst into the room.

For a second nobody moves, and I have just enough time to register the basics: one guy (middle-aged), one girl (blue-black hair, taller than I am), both of them unfamiliar. Maybe it's the fear, but I fixate, too, on the strangest details: the way the man's left eyelid droops, as though gravity is pulling on it, and the way the girl stands there, mouth open, so I can see her cherry-red tongue. She must have been sucking on something, I think. A lollipop or candy; my mind flies to Grace.

Then the room unfreezes, and the girl goes for her gun, and there's no thinking anymore.

I lunge at her, knocking the gun from her hand before she has the chance to level it at me. Behind me, Julian shouts something. There's a gunshot. I can't look to see who fired. The girl swings at me, clipping me on the jaw with her fist. I've never been punched before, and it's the shock of it, more than the pain, that stuns me. In that split second she manages to get her knife out, and the next thing I see is the blade whistling toward me. I duck, drive hard into her stomach with my shoulders.

She grunts. The momentum carries us both off our feet, and we tumble backward into a box of old shoes. The cardboard collapses under our weight. We're grappling so close I can taste her hair, her skin in my mouth. First I'm on top, straining, then she is, flipping me down onto my back so my head slams against the concrete, her knees hard in my ribs, thighs gripping me so tight the air is getting squeezed from my lungs. She's wrestling another knife free of her belt. I'm scrabbling on the floor for a weapon – any weapon – but she's on me too hard, is gripping me too tightly, and my fingers are closing on air and concrete.

Julian and the man are locked in a shuffling embrace, both straining for an advantage, heads down, grunting. They swivel hard and hit a low wooden bookshelf filled with pots and pans. It teeters, teeters, and then falls: the pots spill everywhere, a cacophony of ringing and dinging metal. The girl glances backward and just that, that little shift, gives me enough room to move. I rocket my fist up, connecting with the side of her face. It can't hurt too badly, but it sends her sideways and off me, and I'm up and rolling on top of her, ripping the knife out of her grip. My hatred and fear is flowing hard and electric and hot, and without thinking about it I lift the blade and drive it hard down into her chest. She jerks once, lets out a cry, and then goes still. My mind is a loop, an endless refrain: *your-fault-your-fault-your-fault*. There's a mangled sobbing sound coming from somewhere, and it takes me a long time to realize I'm the one crying.

Then everything goes black for a moment – the pain comes a split second after the darkness – as the other Scavenger, the man, catches me on the side of my head with a baton. There's a thunderous crack; I'm tumbling, and everything is a blur of disconnected images: Julian lying face down near the toppled shelf; a grandfather clock in the corner I hadn't noticed before; cracks in the concrete floor, expanding like a web to embrace me. Then a few seconds of nothing. Jump-cut: I'm on my back, the ceiling is revolving above me. I'm dying. Weirdly enough, I think of Julian. He put up a pretty good fight.

The man is on top of me, breathing hot and hard into my face. His breath smells like something spoiling in a closed place. A long, jagged cut runs under his eye – nice one, Julian – and some of his blood drips onto my face. I feel the razor-bite of a knife under my chin, and everything in my body freezes. I go absolutely still.

He's staring at me with such hatred I suddenly feel very calm. I will die. He will kill me. The certainty relaxes me. I am sinking into a white snow. I close my eyes and try to picture Alex the way I used to dream of him, standing at the end of a tunnel. I wait for him to appear, to reach out his hands to me.

I'm fading in and out. I'm hovering above the ground; then I'm on the floor again. There's the taste of swamp in my throat.

'You gave me no choice,' the Scavenger pants out, and I snap my eyes open. There's a note of something there – regret, maybe, or apology – that I didn't anticipate. And with that, the hope comes rushing back, and the terror, too: *Please-please-please-let-me-live.*

But just then he inhales and tenses, and the point of the knife breaks through my skin and it's too late—

Then he jerks, suddenly, on top of me.

The knife clatters out of his hand. His eyes roll up to the ceiling, terrible, a doll's blank gaze. He falls forward slowly, on top of me, knocking the air out of my chest. Julian is standing above him, breathing hard, shaking. The handle of a knife is sticking out of the Scavenger's back.

A dead man is lying on top of me. A hysterical feeling builds in my chest, then breaks, and suddenly I am babbling, 'Get him off of me. Get him off of me!'

Julian shakes his head, dazed. 'I – I didn't mean to.'

'For God's sake, Julian. Get him off of me! We have to go now.'

He starts, blinks, and focuses on me. The Scavenger's weight is crushing.

'Please, Julian.'

Finally Julian moves. He bends down and heaves the body off me, and I scramble to my feet. My heart is racing and my skin is crawling; I have the desperate urge to bathe, to get all that death off me. The two dead Scavengers lie so close to each other they are almost touching. A butterfly pattern of blood spreads across the floor between them. I feel sick.

'I didn't mean to, Lena. I just – I saw him on top of you and I grabbed a knife and I just . . .' Julian shakes his head. 'It was an accident.'

'Julian.' I reach out and put my hands on his shoulders. 'Look. You saved my life.'

He closes his eyes for one second, then opens them again.

'You saved my life,' I repeat. 'Thank you.'

He seems about to say something. Instead he nods and shoulders the backpack. I reach forward impulsively and seize his hand. He doesn't pull away, and I'm glad. I need him to steady me. I need him to help keep me on my feet.

'Time to run,' I say, and together we stumble out of the room and, finally, into the cool mustiness of the old tunnels, into the echoes, and the shadows, and the dark.

then

The temperature drops sharply on the way to the second encampment. Even when I sleep in the tents, I'm freezing. When it's my turn to sleep outside, I often wake up with shards of ice webbed in my hair. Sarah is stoic, silent, and pale-faced.

Blue gets sick. The first day she wakes up sluggish. She has trouble keeping up, and at the end of our day of hiking, she falls asleep even before the fire is built, curling up on the ground like a small animal. Raven moves her into her tent. That night I wake to a muffled shouting. I sit up, startled. The night sky is clear, the stars razor-sharp and glittering. The air smells like snow.

There is rustling from Raven's tent, some whimpering; the sound of whispered reassurances. Blue is having bad dreams.

The next morning, Blue comes down with a fever. There is no choice: she must walk anyway. The snow is coming, and we are still thirty miles from the second camp, and many more miles than that from the winter homestead.

She cries as she walks, stumbling more and more. We take turns carrying her – me, Raven, Hunter, Lu, and Grandpa. She is burning. Her arms around my neck are electric wires, pulsing with heat.

The next day, we reach the second encampment: an area of loose shale set underneath an old, half-tumbled-down brick wall, which forms a kind of barrier and shields us somewhat from the wind. We set to work digging up the food, pitching traps, and scavenging the area, which once must have been a decent-sized town, for canned goods and useful supplies. We'll stay here for two days, possibly three, depending on how much we can find. Beyond the hooting of the owls and the rustling of nighttime creatures, we hear the distant sounds of rumbling trucks. We are less than ten miles from one of the inter-city highways.

It's strange to think how close we have been to the valid places, established cities filled with food, clothing, medical supplies; and yet we may as well be in a different universe. The world is bifurcated now, folded cleanly in half like the pitched steep sides of a tent: the Valids and the Invalids live on different planes, in different dimensions.

Blue's nighttime terrors get worse. Her cries are piercing; she babbles nonsense, a language of gibberish and dream-words. When it is time to start toward the third encampment – the clouds have moved in, heavy-knitted through the sky, and the light is the dull, dark grey of an imminent storm – she is almost unresponsive. Raven carries her that day; she won't let anyone help, even though she, too, is weak, and often falls behind.

We walk in silence. We are weighed down by fear; it blankets us thickly, making it feel as though we are already walking through snow, because all of us know that Blue is going to die. Raven knows it too. She must.

That night Raven builds a fire and places Blue next to it. Even though Blue's skin is burning, she shivers so hard that her teeth knock together. The rest of us move around the fire as quietly as possible; we are shadows in the smoke. I fall asleep outside, next to Raven, who stays awake to rake the fire and make sure Blue stays warm.

In the middle of the night, I wake up to the muffled sounds of crying. Raven is kneeling over Blue. My stomach caves, and I am filled with terror; I have never seen Raven cry before. I'm afraid to speak, to breathe, to move. I know that she must think everyone is asleep. She would never allow herself to cry otherwise.

But I can't stay silent, either. I rustle loudly in my sleeping bag, and just like that the crying stops. I sit up.

'Is she . . . ?' I whisper. I can't say the last word. *Dead.*

Raven shakes her head. 'She's not breathing very well.'

'At least she's breathing,' I say. A long silence stretches between us. I'm desperate to fix this. I know, somehow, that if we lose Blue we lose a piece of Raven, too. And we need Raven, especially now that Tack is gone. 'She'll get better,' I say, to comfort her. 'I'm sure she'll be okay.'

Raven turns to me. The fire catches her eyes, makes them glow like an animal's. 'No,' she says simply. 'No, she won't.'

Her voice is so full of certainty, I can't contradict her. For a moment, Raven doesn't say anything else. Then she says, 'Do you know why I named her Blue?'

The question surprises me. 'I thought you named her for her eyes.'

Raven turns back toward the fire, hugging her knees. 'I lived in Yarmouth, close to a border fence. A poor area. Nobody else wanted to live so close to the Wilds. Bad luck, you know.'

A shiver snakes through me, and I suddenly feel very alert. Raven has never spoken of her life before the Wilds. She has always repeated that there is no such thing. No before.

'I was like everybody else, really. Just accepted what people told me and didn't think too much about it. Only cureds go to heaven. Patrols are for my own protection. The uncured are dirty; they turn into animals. The disease rots you from inside. Stability is godliness and happiness.' She shrugs, as though shaking off the memory of who she was. 'Except that I wasn't happy. I didn't understand why. I didn't understand why I couldn't be like everybody else.'

I think of Hana, spinning around once in her room, arms wide, saying, *You think this is it? This is all there is?*

'The summer I turned fourteen, they started new construction by the fence. They were projects, really, for the poorest families in Yarmouth: the badly matched ones, or families whose reputations had been ruined because of dissent, or even rumours of it – you know what it's like. During the day, I used to play around the construction site. A bunch of us did. Of course, we had to be careful to stay separate, the boys and the girls. There was a line that divided us: everything east of the waterline was ours, everything west of it was theirs.' She laughs softly. 'It seems like a dream now. But at the time it seemed like the most normal thing in the world.'

'There was nothing to compare it to,' I say, and Raven shoots me a quick glance, nodding sharply.

'Then there was a week of rain. Construction came to a standstill, and nobody wanted to explore the site. I didn't mind the rain. I didn't like to be at home very much. My dad was—'

There's a hitch in her voice, and she breaks off. 'He wasn't totally right after the procedure. It didn't work correctly. There was disruption of the mood-regulating temporal lobes. That's what they called it. He was mostly okay, like everybody else. But every so often he flew into rages . . .' For a while she stares at the fire, silent. 'My mom helped us cover the bruises, put on makeup and stuff. We couldn't tell anyone. We didn't want too many people knowing that my dad's cure hadn't worked properly. People get hysterical; he could have been fired. My mom said people would make things difficult. So instead we hid it. Long sleeves in summertime. Lots of sick days. Lots of lies, too – falling down, bumping my head, hitting the door frame.'

I have never imagined Raven as any younger than she is now. But I can see the wiry girl with the same fierce mouth, rubbing concealer over the bruises on her arms, shoulders, and face. 'I'm sorry,' I say. The words seem flimsy, ridiculous.

Raven clears her throat and squares her shoulders. 'It doesn't matter,' she says quickly. She breaks a long, skinny twig into quarters and feeds it, one piece at a time, into the fire. I wonder whether she has forgotten about the original course of conversation – about Blue's name – but then she starts speaking again.

'That week – the week of the rain – was one of my dad's bad times. So I went out to the site a lot. One day, I was just picking around one of the foundations. It was all cinder block and pits; hardly any of the building had actually gotten done. And then I saw this little box. A shoe box.' She sucks in a breath, and even in the dark I see her tense.

The rest of her story comes out in a rush: 'Someone must have left it there, wedged in the space underneath a part of the foundation. Except the rain was so bad it had caused a miniature mudslide. The box had rolled out into the open. I don't know why I decided to look inside. It was filthy. I thought I might find a pair of shoes, maybe some jewellery.'

I know, now, where the story is going. I am walking toward the muddy box alongside her; I am lifting the water-warped cover. The horror and disgust is a mud too: it is rising, black and choking, inside of me.

Raven's voice drops to a whisper. 'She was wrapped in a blanket. A blue blanket with yellow lambs on it. She wasn't breathing. I – I thought she was dead. She was . . . she was blue. Her skin, her nails, her lips, her fingers. Her fingers were so small.'

The mud is in my throat. I can't breathe.

'I don't know what made me try to revive her. I think I must have gone a little crazy. I was working as a junior lifeguard that summer, so I'd been certified in CPR. I'd never had to do it, though. And she was so tiny – probably a week, maybe two weeks old. But it worked. I'll never forget how I felt when she took a breath, and all that colour came rushing into her skin. It was like the whole world had split open. And everything I'd felt was missing – all that feeling and colour – all of it came to me with her first breath. I called her Blue so I would always remember that moment, and so I would never regret.'

Abruptly, Raven stops speaking. She reaches down and re-adjusts Blue's sleeping bag. The light from the fire is a low, red glow, and I can see that Blue is pale. Her forehead is beaded with sweat, and her breath comes slowly, raspingly. I am filled with a blind fury, undirected and overwhelming.

Raven isn't finished with her story. 'I didn't even go home. I just took her and ran. I knew I couldn't keep her in Yarmouth. You can't keep secrets like that for long. It was hard enough to cover up the bruises. And I knew she must be illegal – some unmatched girl, some unmatched guy. A *deliria* baby. You know what they say. *Deliria* babies are contaminated. They grow up twisted, crippled, crazy. She would probably be taken and killed. She wouldn't even be buried. They'd be worried about the spread of disease. She'd be burned, and packed up with the waste.' Raven takes another twig and throws it in the fire. It flares momentarily, a hot white tongue of flame. 'I'd heard rumours about a portion in the fence that was unfortified. We used to tell stories about the Invalids coming in and out, feasting on people's brains. Just the kind of shit you talk as a kid. I'm not sure whether I still believed it or not. But I took my chance on the fence. It took me forever to figure out a way over with Blue. In the end I had to use the blanket as a sling. And the rain was a good thing. The guards and the regulators were staying inside. I made it over without any trouble. I didn't know where I was going or what I would do once I crossed. I didn't say good-bye to either of my parents. I didn't do anything but run.' She looks at me sideways. 'But I guess that was enough. And I guess you know about that too.'

'Yeah,' I croak out. There's a shredding pain in my throat. I could cry at any second. Instead, I dig my nails, as hard as I can, into my thighs, trying to break the skin beneath the fabric of my jeans.

Blue murmurs something indecipherable and tosses in her sleep. The rasping in her throat has gotten worse. Every breath brings a horrible grating noise, and the watery echoes of fluid. Raven bends forward and brushes the sweat-damp strands of hair from Blue's forehead. 'She's burning up,' Raven says.

'I'll get some water.' I'm desperate to do something, anything, to help.

'It won't make any difference,' Raven says quietly.

But I need to move, so I go anyway. I pick my way through the frosty dark toward the stream, which is covered with a layer of thin ice, all webbed with fissures and cracks. The moon is high and full and reflects the silver surface and the dark flowing water underneath. I break through the ice with the bottom of a tin pail, gasping when the water flows over my fingers and into the bucket.

Raven and I don't sleep that night. We take turns with a towel, icing Blue's forehead, until her breathing slows and the rasping eases. Eventually she stops fidgeting and lies quiet and docile under our hands. We take turns with the towel until dawn breaks in the sky, a blush rose, liquid and pale, even though by that time, Blue has not taken a breath for hours.

now

Julian and I move through stifling darkness. We go slowly, painstakingly, even though both of us are desperate to run. But we can't risk the noise or a flashlight. Even though we're moving through what must be a vast network of tunnels, I feel just like a rat in a box. I'm not very steady on my feet. The darkness is full of whirling, swirling shapes, and I have to keep my left hand on the slick tunnel wall, which is coated with moisture and skittering insects.

And rats. Rats chittering from corners; rats scampering across the tracks, nails going *tick, tick, tick* against the stone.

I don't know how long we walk. Impossible to tell, with no change in sound or texture, no way of knowing whether we are moving east or west or going around endlessly in circles. Sometimes we move alongside old railway tracks. These must have been the tunnels for the underground trains. Despite my exhaustion and nerves, I can't help but feel amazed at the idea of all these twisting, labyrinthine spaces filled with barreling machines, and people thundering along freely in the dark.

Other times the tunnels are flowing with water – sometimes a bare trickle, sometimes a few feet of foul-smelling, litter-cluttered liquid, probably backed up from one of the sewer systems. That means we can't be too far from a city.

I'm stumbling more and more. It has been days since I've eaten anything substantial, and my neck throbs painfully, where the Scavenger broke the skin with his knife. Increasingly, Julian has to reach out and steady me. Finally he keeps a hand on my back, piloting me forward. I'm grateful for the contact. It makes the agony of walking, and silence, and straining for the sound of Scavengers through the echoes and the drips, more bearable.

We go for hours without stopping. Eventually the darkness turns milky. Then I see a bit of light, a long silver stream filtering down from above. There are grates in the ceiling, five of them. Above us, for the first time in days, I see sky: a patchy nighttime sky of clouds and stars. Unconsciously, I cry out. It is the most beautiful thing I've ever seen.

'The grates,' I say. 'Can we—?'

Julian moves ahead of me, and at last we risk the flashlight. He angles the beam upward, then shakes his head.

'Bolted tight from outside,' he says. He strains onto his tiptoes and gives a little push. 'No way to budge them.'

Disappointment burns in the back of my throat. We're so close to freedom. I can smell it – wind and space, and something else, too. Rain. It must have rained recently. The smell brings tears to my eyes. We've ended up on a raised platform. Below us, the tracks are pooled with water and a covering of leaves driven down from above. On our left is an alcove, half excavated and filled with wooden crates; a flyer, remarkably well preserved, is posted on the wall. CAUTION, it reads. CONSTRUCTION ZONE. HARD HAT AREA.

I can't stand up anymore. I break from Julian's grasp, thudding heavily to my knees.

'Hey.' He kneels next to me. 'Are you okay?'

'Tired,' I gasp out. I curl up on the ground, resting my head on my arm. It's getting harder to keep my eyes open. When I do, I see the stars above me blur into a single enormous point of light, and then fracture again.

'Go to sleep,' Julian says. He sets my backpack down and sits next to me.

'What if the Scavengers come?' I say.

'I'll stay awake,' Julian says. 'I'll listen for them.' After a minute, he lies down on his back. There's a wind sweeping down from the grates, and I shiver involuntarily.

'Are you cold?' Julian asks.

'A little,' I say. I can barely get the words out. My throat, too, is frozen.

There's a pause. Then Julian rolls over onto his side and loops his arm around me, scooting forward so our bodies are pressed together, and I am cupped in the space around him. His heart beats through my back – a strange, stuttering rhythm.

'Aren't you worried about the *deliria*?' I ask him.

'Yes,' he says shortly. 'But I'm cold, too.'

After a while his heartbeat becomes more regular, and mine slows to match his. The coldness melts out of me.

'Lena?' Julian whispers. I've had my eyes closed. The moon is now directly above us, a high white beam.

'Yeah?'

I can feel Julian's heart speed up again. 'Do you want to know how my brother died?'

'Okay,' I say, even though something in his tone of voice makes me afraid.

'My brother and my dad never really got along,' Julian says. 'My brother was stubborn. Headstrong. He had a bad temper, too. Everyone said he would be okay once he was cured.' Julian pauses. 'It just got worse and worse as he got older, though. My parents were talking about having his cure moved up. It looked bad, you know, for the DFA and all. He was wild, and he didn't listen to my father, and I'm not even sure he believed in the cure. He was six years older than me. I was – I was scared for him. Do you know what I mean?'

I can't bring myself to speak, so I just nod. Memories are crowding me, surging from the dark places where I have walled them up: the constant, buzzing anxiety I felt as a child, watching my mom laughing, dancing, singing along to strange music that piped from our speakers, a joy threaded through with terror; fear for Hana; fear for Alex; fear for all of us.

'Seven years ago, we had another big rally in New York. That's when the DFA was going national. It was the first rally I attended. I was eleven years old. My brother begged off. I don't remember what excuse he gave.'

Julian shifts. For a second his arms tighten around me, an involuntary gripping; then he relaxes again. Somehow I know he has never told this story before.

'It was a disaster. Halfway through the rally, protesters stormed city hall – that's where we were – half of them masked. The fight turned violent, and the police came to break it up, and suddenly it was just a brawl. I hid behind the podium, like a little kid. Afterward, I was so ashamed.

'One of the protesters got too close to the stage; too close to my dad. He was screaming something – I couldn't hear what. It was loud, and he was wearing a ski mask. The guard brought him down with a nightstick. Weirdly, I remember I could hear that; the crack of the wood against his knee, the thud as he collapsed. That's when my dad saw it, must have seen it: the birthmark on the back of his left hand, shaped like a big half-moon. My brother's birthmark. He jumped off the stage into the audience, tore off the mask, and . . . it was him. My brother was lying there, in agony, his knee shattered in a thousand places. But I'll never forget the look he gave my father. Totally calm, and resigned, too, like . . . like he knew what was going to happen.

'We finally made it out – had a police escort all the way home. My brother was stretched out in the back of the van, moaning. I wanted to ask him whether he was okay, but I knew my dad would kill me. He drove the whole way home without saying a word, without taking his eyes off the road. I don't know what my mom was feeling. Maybe not much. But I think she was worried. *The Book of Shhh* says that our obligations to our children are sacred, right? "And the good mother will finish discharging her duties in heaven . . ."' Julian quotes softly. 'She wanted him to see a doctor, but my dad wouldn't hear of it. My brother's knee looked bad – swollen to the size of a basketball, practically. He was sweating like crazy, in so much pain. I wanted to help. I wanted to—' A tremor passes through Julian's body. 'When we got home, my dad threw my brother into the basement and locked it. He was going to leave him there for a day, in the dark. So my brother would learn his lesson.'

I picture Thomas Fineman: the clean-pressed clothing and gold cuff links, which must give him such satisfaction; the polished watch and the neatly trimmed hair. Pure, clean, spotless, like a man who can always count on a good night's sleep.

I hate you, I think, for Julian's sake. Julian has never gotten to know those words, to feel the relief in them.

'We could hear my brother crying through the door. We could hear him from the dining room when we ate dinner. My dad made us sit through a whole meal. I'll never forgive him for that.' The last part is spoken in a whisper. I find his hand and lace my fingers in his and squeeze. He gives me a small pulse back.

For a while we lie there in silence. Then, from above, there's a soft rushing sound: then the sound separates, becomes thousands of raindrops hitting the pavement. Water drums down through the grates, pinging off the metal rails of the old tracks.

'And then the crying stopped,' Julian says simply, and I think of that day in the Wilds with Raven, taking turns mopping Blue's head while the sun broke in a wave over the trees, long after we had felt her grow cold under our hands.

Julian clears his throat. 'They said afterward it was a freak accident; a blood clot from his injury that migrated into his brain. One-in-a-million chance. My dad couldn't have known. But still, I—'

He breaks off. 'After that, you know, I was always so careful. I would do everything right. I would be the perfect son, a model for the DFA. Even once I found out the cure would probably kill me. It was more than fear,' Julian says, a sudden rush of words. 'I thought if I followed the rules, things would turn out all right. That's the thing about the cure, isn't it? It isn't just about *deliria* at all. It's about order. A path for everyone. You just have to follow it and everything will be okay. That's what the DFA is about. That's what I believed in – what I've had to believe in. Because otherwise, it's just . . . chaos.'

'Do you miss him?' I ask.

Julian doesn't answer right away, and I know, somehow, that nobody has ever asked him this before. 'I think so,' he says finally, in a low voice. 'I did for a long time. My mom – my mom told me it wouldn't be so bad after the cure. I wouldn't think about him that way anymore, she said.'

'That's even worse,' I say quietly. 'That's when they're really gone.'

I count three long seconds of silence, and in each one of them, Julian's heart drums against my back. I'm not cold anymore. If anything, I'm too hot. Our bodies are so close – skin sticking to skin, fingers entangled. His breath is on my neck.

'I don't know what's going on anymore,' Julian whispers. 'I don't understand anything. I don't know what's supposed to happen next.'

'You're not supposed to know,' I say, and it's true: the tunnels may be long, and twisted, and dark; but you are supposed to go through them.

More silence. Finally Julian says, 'I'm scared.'

He barely whispers it; but I can feel his lips moving against my neck, as though the words are being spelled there.

'I know,' I say. 'Me too.'

I can't stay awake any longer. I'm carried back and forth through time and memory, between this rain and rains before it, as though climbing up and down a spiral staircase. Julian has his arm around me, and then Alex does; then Raven is holding my head in her lap, and then my mother is singing to me.

'I'm less scared with you,' Julian says. Or maybe it is Alex who speaks, or maybe I've only dreamed the words. I open my mouth to respond but find I can't speak. I'm drinking water, and then I'm floating, and then there is nothing but sleep, liquid and deep.

then

We bury Blue by the river. It takes us hours to break through the frozen ground and make a hole big enough to accommodate her. We have to remove her jacket before we bury her. We can't afford to lose it. She feels so light as we lower her into the ground, just like a baby bird, hollow-boned and fragile.

At the last second, as we're about to cover her with dirt, Raven pushes forward, suddenly hysterical. 'She'll be cold,' she says. 'She'll freeze like that.' Nobody wants to stop her. She strips off her sweater and slides into the makeshift grave, taking Blue in her arms and wrapping her in it. She's crying. Most of us turn away, embarrassed. Only Lu steps forward.

'Blue will be okay, Raven,' she says softly. 'The snow will keep her warm.'

Raven looks up, her face wild, tear-streaked. She scans our faces once as though struggling to remember who we are. Then she jerks, suddenly, to her feet, and climbs up out of the lip of the grave.

Bram steps forward and starts to shovel the dirt over Blue's body again, but Raven stops him.

'Leave her,' Raven says. Her voice is loud and unnaturally high-pitched. 'Lu's right. It's going to snow any minute.'

It does start to snow as we're packing up camp. It continues to snow all day, as we make our way silently through the woods in a long, ragged line. The cold is a constant pain now, a fierce ache in my chest and fingers and toes, and the snow is mostly driving ice, and burns like hot ash. But I imagine that for Blue it falls more gently, and covers her like a blanket, where it will keep her safely until spring.

now

It's still raining in the morning.

I sit up slowly. I have a wicked headache, and I'm dizzy. Julian is no longer next to me. The rain is pouring through the grates, long, twisting grey ribbons of it, and he is standing underneath them.

His back is turned to me, and he has stripped down to a pair of faded cotton shorts he must have found when we scavenged for clothing and supplies. My breath catches in my throat. I know I should look away, but I can't. I'm transfixed by the sight of the rain coursing over his back – broad and muscled and strong, just like Alex's was – the rolling landscapes of his arms and shoulders; his hair, now dark with water; the way he tips his head back and lets the rain run into his open mouth.

In the Wilds, I finally got used to seeing men naked or half naked. I got used to the strangeness of their bodies, the bits of curling hair on their chests, and sometimes on their backs and shoulders, to the broad, flat panes of their stomachs and wings of their hipbones, arcing over the waistband of their pants. But this is different. There is a perfect stillness to him, and in the pallid grey light he seems to glow slightly, like a statue carved out of white rock.

He is beautiful.

He shakes his head a bit and water pinwheels from his hair, a glittering semicircle: happy and unaware, he starts to hum quietly. All of a sudden I am horribly embarrassed: I'm trespassing on a private moment. I clear my throat loudly. He whips around. When he sees me awake, he jumps out of the stream of water and scoops his clothes up off the platform lip, covering himself with them.

'I didn't know you were awake,' he says, fighting to get his T-shirt on, even though he's soaking wet. He accidentally gets his head caught in an armhole and has to try again. I would laugh if he didn't look so desperate.

Now that he has cleaned away the blood, I can see his face clearly. His eyes are no longer swollen, but they are ringed with deep purple bruises. The cuts on his lip and forehead are scabbing over. That's a good sign.

'I just woke up,' I say as he finally gets his shirt on. 'Did you sleep at all?'

Now he's wrestling with his jeans. His hair makes a pattern of water spots around the neck of his T-shirt.

'A little,' he says guiltily. 'I didn't mean to. I must have dropped off around five. It was already getting light.' His jeans are on. He hauls himself up onto the platform, surprisingly graceful. 'Ready to move on?'

'In a bit,' I say. 'I'd like – I'd like to get clean, like you did. Under the grates.'

'Okay.' Julian nods, but doesn't move. I can feel myself

blushing again. It has been a long time since I've felt this way, so open and exposed. I'm losing the thread of the new Lena, the hard one, the warrior made in the Wilds. I can't seem to pull myself back into her body.

'I'll need to get undressed,' I blurt out, since Julian doesn't seem to be taking the hint.

'Oh – oh, right,' he stammers, backing away. 'Of course. I'll just – I'll go scout ahead.'

'I'll be quick,' I say. 'We should get moving again.'

I wait until Julian's footsteps are a faint echo in the cavernous space before stepping out of my clothes. For a minute it's possible to forget that the Scavengers are somewhere out there in the dark, looking for us. For a minute it's possible to forget what I've done – what I've had to do – to escape, to forget the pattern of blood seeping across the storeroom floor, the Scavenger's eyes, surprised, accusatory. I stand naked on the lip of the platform, reaching my arms up toward the sky, as ribbons of water continue twisting through the grates: liquid grey, as though the sky has begun to melt. The cold air raises goose bumps on my skin. I lower myself to a crouch and ease myself off the platform, splashing into the tracks, feeling the bite of metal and wood on my bare feet. I slosh my way over to the grates. Then I tip my head back so the rain hits me square in the face and courses down my hair, my back, my aching shoulders and chest.

I have never felt anything so amazing in my life. I want to cry out for joy, or sing. The water is icy cold, and smells fresh, as though it has carried some of the scents of its spiralling journey past stripped branches and tiny, new March buds.

When I've let the water drive over my face and pool in my eyes and mouth, I lean forward and feel it beat a rhythm on my back, like the drumming of a thousand tiny feet. I haven't realized until right now how sore I am all over: everything hurts. My legs and arms are covered with dark bruises.

I know I'm as clean as I'm going to get, but I can't bring myself to move out of the stream of water, even though the cold makes me shiver. It's a good cold, purifying.

Finally I wade back to the platform. It takes me two tries to heave myself up off the tracks – that's how weak I am – and I'm dripping water everywhere, leaving a person-sized splatter pattern on the dark concrete. I wrap the long coil of my hair around one hand and squeeze, and even this brings me joy; the normalcy of the action, routine and familiar.

I step into the jeans I took from the Scavengers, rolling them once at the waist to keep them from falling off; even so, they hang loose from my hipbones.

Then: footsteps behind me. I whip around, covering my breasts with my arms.

Julian steps out of the shadows.

Keeping one arm wrapped around my chest, I grab for my shirt.

'Wait,' he calls out, and something about the tone of his voice – a note of command, and also of urgency – stops me. 'Wait,' he repeats, more softly.

We're separated by twenty feet of space, but the way he's looking at me makes me feel as though we're chest to chest. I can feel his eyes on my skin like a prickling touch. I know I should put on my shirt, but I can't move. I can hardly even breathe.

'I've never been able to look before,' Julian says simply, and takes one more step toward me. The light falls differently across his face, and now I can see a softness in his eyes, a blur, and it makes the roaring heat in my body melt away into warmth, a steady, wonderful feeling. At the same time, a tiny voice in the back of my head pipes up: *Danger, danger, danger.* Beneath it, a fainter echo: *Alex, Alex, Alex.*

Alex used to look at me like that.

'Your waist is so small.' That's all Julian says: in a voice so quiet I barely hear him.

I force myself to turn away from him. My hands are shaking as I wrestle the sports bra, and then my shirt, over my head. When I turn around again, I feel afraid of him for some reason. He has come even closer. He smells like rain.

He saw me topless, exposed.

He looked at me like I was beautiful.

'Feeling better?' he asks.

'Yeah,' I say, dropping my eyes. I finger the cut along my neck carefully. It is about a half-inch long, and clotted with dried blood.

'Let me see.' Julian reaches out and then hesitates, his fingers an inch from my face. I look up at him. He seems to be asking permission. I nod, and he slips his hand, gently, under my chin, tipping it up so he can look at my neck. 'We should bandage it.'

We. We are on the same side now. He is refusing to say anything more about the fact that I lied to him, and the fact that I'm uncured. I wonder how long it will last.

Julian moves over to the backpack. He rummages for the first-aid materials we stole, and returns to me with a large bandage, a bottle of peroxide, some antibacterial ointment, and several cotton puffs.

'I can do it,' I say, but Julian shakes his head.

'Let me,' he says. First he dips the cotton balls in the peroxide and dabs the cut carefully. It stings and I jerk back, yelping. He raises his eyebrows. 'Come on,' he says, hitching his mouth into a smile. 'It doesn't hurt that badly.'

'It does,' I insist.

'Yesterday you went head-to-head with two homicidal maniacs. Now you can't take a little burn?'

'That's different,' I say, glaring at him. I can tell he's making fun of me, and I don't like it. 'That was a question of survival.'

Julian raises his eyebrows but doesn't say anything. He blots my cut one more time with the cotton ball, and this time I grit my teeth and bear it. Then he squeezes a thin line of ointment onto the bandage and affixes it carefully to my neck. Alex fixed me once, just like this. It was on raid night, and we were hiding in a tiny tool shed, and a dog had just taken a chunk out of my leg. I haven't thought about that night in a long time, and as Julian's hands skate over my skin, I feel suddenly breathless.

I wonder if this is how people always get close: they heal each other's wounds; they repair the broken skin.

'There. As good as new.' His eyes have taken on the grey of the sky above the grates. 'You okay to move on?'

I nod, even though I'm still weak, and pretty dizzy.

Julian reaches out and squeezes my shoulder. I wonder what he thinks when he touches me, whether he feels the electric pulse that runs through my body. He is unused to having contact with girls, but he doesn't seem bothered by it. He has crossed a boundary. I wonder what he'll do when we finally get out of here. He'll no doubt go back to his old life – to his father, to the DFA.

Maybe he'll have me arrested.

I feel a surge of nausea and close my eyes, swaying a little on my feet.

'Are you sure you're okay to move?'

Julian's voice is so gentle, it makes my chest break up into a thousand fluttering pieces. This was not part of the plan. This was not supposed to happen.

I think about what I told him last night: *You're not supposed to know.* The hard, unbearable, beautiful truth.

'Julian' – I open my eyes, wishing my voice sounded less shaky – 'we're not the same. We're on different sides. You know that, right?'

His eyes get a little harder, more intense: even in the half-light, a blazing blue. But when he speaks, his voice is still soft and quiet. 'I don't know what side I'm on anymore,' he says.

He takes another step toward me.

'Julian—' I can barely squeeze out his name.

That's when we hear it: a muffled shout from one of the tunnels, the sound of drumming feet. Julian stiffens and in that second, when we look at each other, there's no need to speak at all.

The Scavengers are here.

The terror is a sudden jolt. The voices are coming from one of the tunnels we came through last night. Julian scoops up the backpack, and I stuff my feet quickly into my sneakers, not even bothering with socks. I grab the knife from the ground; Julian reaches for my other hand and pulls me forward, past the wooden crates and to the far end of the platform. Even fifty feet away from the grates, it's almost impossible to see. We are swallowed again in murk and darkness. It feels like stepping into a mouth, and I try to beat back the feeling of terror winging through me. I know I should be grateful for the darkness and all the chances to hide, but I can't help thinking of what the darkness could be hiding: stealthy, silent steppers; bodies swinging from the pipes.

At the far end of the platform there's a tunnel, so low Julian and I have to stoop to enter. After ten feet, we reach a narrow metal ladder, which takes us down into a broader tunnel, this one studded with old train tracks but free, thankfully, of running water. Every few feet Julian pauses, listening for the Scavengers.

Then we hear it, unmistakably, and closer now: a voice grunting, 'This way.' Those two words knock the breath out of me, exactly as if I'd been punched. It's Albino. I mentally curse myself for putting the handgun in the backpack – stupid, stupid, and no way of getting it now, in the dark, while Julian and I are pushing forward. I squeeze the handle of the knife, taking some reassurance from the smooth grain of its wood, from its weight. But I'm still weak, dizzy, and hungry, too; I know I won't do well in a fight. I say a silent prayer that we can lose them in the darkness.

'Down here!'

But the voices grow louder, closer. We hear feet ringing against the metal ladder, a sound that makes my blood sing with terror. Just then I see it: light zigzagging against the walls, flashing yellow tentacles. They're using flashlights, of course. No wonder they're coming so fast. They don't have to worry about being seen or heard. They are the predators.

And we are the prey.

Hide. It's our only hope. We need to hide.

There's an archway on our right – a cutout of even blacker darkness – and I squeeze Julian's hand, pulling him back, directing him through it, into another tunnel, a foot or so lower than the one we've been travelling, and this one dotted with puddles of stagnant, stinking water. We grope our way through the dark. The walls on both sides of us are smooth – no alcoves, no piled wooden crates, nothing to conceal us – and the panic is building. Julian must be feeling it too, because he loses his footing, stumbles, and splashes heavily into one of the narrow beds of still water.

Both of us freeze.

The Scavengers, too, freeze. Their footsteps stop; their voices fall silent.

And then the light seeps through the archway: a creeping, sniffing animal, roving the ground, ravenous. Julian and I don't move. He pulses my hand, once, then releases it. I hear him shift the backpack from his shoulder and know that he must be fumbling for a weapon. There's no longer any point in running. There's no point in fighting, either – not really – but at least we can take a Scavenger or two down with us.

My vision goes suddenly blurry and I'm startled. Tears sting my eyes, and I have to wipe them away with the inside of my wrist. All I can think is – *Not here, not like this, not underground, not with the rats.*

The light widens and expands; a second beam joins it. The Scavengers are moving silently now, but I can feel them taking their time, and enjoying it, the way a hunter draws his bow back the last few inches before releasing an arrow – those final moments of quiet and stillness before the kill. I can feel the albino. Even in the dark, I know he is smiling. My palms are wet on the knife. Next to me, Julian is breathing heavily.

Not like this. Not like this. My head is full of echoes now, fragments and distortions: the heady smell of honeysuckle in the summer; fat, droning bees; trees bowed low under the weight of heavy snowfall; Hana running ahead of me, laughing, her blonde hair swinging in an arc.

And strangely, what strikes me then – in that exact second, as I know with solid certainty that I am going to die – is that all the kisses I have ever had are behind me. The *deliria*, the pain, all the trouble it has caused, everything we have been fighting for: for me it is done, washed away on the tide of my life.

And then, just as the beams of light grow to headlights – huge, blinding, bearing down on us, and the shadows behind them unfold and become people – I am filled with desperate rage. I can't see; the light has dazzled me, and the darkness has melted into explosions of colour, spots of floating brightness, and dimly, as I leap forward, thrusting blindly with my knife, I hear shouting and roaring and a scream that bursts through my chest, whines through my teeth like the reverberation of a metal blade.

Everything is chaos: hot bodies and panting. There's an elbow in my chest and thick arms encircling me, choking out my breath. I get a mouthful of greasy hair, a blade of pain in my side; foul breath in my face, and guttural shouts. I can't tell how many Scavengers there are – three? four? – and don't know where Julian is. I am striking without looking, struggling to breathe, and everything is bodies – hardness and enclosure, no way to run, no way to break free – and the slashing of my knife. I hit flesh, and flesh, and then the knife gets wrenched from my hand, wrist twisted until I cry out.

Enormous hands find my neck and squeeze, and the air goes out of the tunnel, and shrivels to the point of a pen in my lungs. I open my mouth to gasp and find that I can't. In the darkness above me I see a tiny bubble of light, of air, floating high above me – I am reaching for it, fighting my way out of a thick, consuming murk – but there is nothing but mud in my lungs and I am drowning.

Drowning. Dying.

Faintly I hear a tiny drumming, a constant pitter-patter, and think that it must once again be raining. Then there are lights blazing again on either side of me: dancing, mobile light, twisting and live. Fire.

Suddenly the circle around my neck breaks. The air is like cold water washing into me, making me gasp and splutter. I sink to my hands and knees, and for one confused second I think I must be dreaming – I fall into a stream of fur, a blur of tiny bodies.

Then my head begins to clear and the world returns from the fog and I realize the tunnel is filled with rats. Hundreds and hundreds of them: rats leaping over one another, wriggling and writhing, colliding with my wrists and nipping at my knees. Two gunshots explode; someone cries out in pain. Above me there are shapes, people, grappling with the Scavengers; they have enormous, smouldering torches, stinking like dirty oil, and they scythe through the air with their fire like farmers cutting through fields of wheat. Various images are frozen, briefly illuminated: Julian doubled over, one hand on the tunnel wall; one of the Scavengers, face contorted, screaming, her hair lit up with fire like one of the torches.

This is a new kind of terror. I'm frozen on my knees as the rats rush around me, drumming me with their bodies, squeaking and slithering and whipping my skin with their tails. I'm sickened and paralyzed with fear.

This is a nightmare. It must be.

A rat crawls up onto my lap. I shout and swat it away, nausea rising in my throat. It hits the wall with a sickening thud, squeaking; then it scrabbles back to its feet and joins the stream again, blurring past me. I'm so disgusted I can't even move. A whimper works its way out of my throat. Maybe I've died and gone to hell, to be punished for *deliria* and all the terrible things I've done – to live in squalor and chaos, just like *The Book of Shhh* predicts for the disobedient.

'Stand up.'

I raise my head. Two monsters stand above me, holding torches. That's what they look like: beasts from the underground, only half-human. One of them is enormous, practically a giant. One of his eyes is milky white, blinded; the other is as darkly glittering as an animal's.

The other figure is hunched over, back as crookedly swollen as the warped hull of a boat. I can't tell if it's a man or a woman. Long, greasy hair mostly conceals the person's face. She – or he – has twisted Julian's hands behind his back and bound them with a cord. The Scavengers are gone.

I stand. The bandage on my neck has come loose, and my skin feels slick and wet.

'Walk.' The rat-man gestures with his torch toward the darkness behind me. I see that he is slightly doubled over and is clutching his right side with the hand not holding the torch. I think of the gunshots and hearing someone shout. I wonder if he was hit.

'Listen.' My voice is shaking. I hold up both hands, a gesture of peace. 'I don't know who you are, or what you want, but we're just trying to get out of here. We don't have much, but you can take whatever you want. Just – just let us go. Please, okay?' My voice breaks a little. 'Please let us go.'

'Walk,' the rat-man repeats, and this time jabs so close to me with his torch I can feel the heat from the flames.

I look at Julian. He gives a minute shake of his head. The expression in his eyes is clear. *What can we do?*

I turn, and walk. The rat-man goes behind me with his torch, and in front of us, hundreds of rats disappear into the darkness.

then

No one knows what to expect at the third encampment, or whether there will even be a third encampment. Since Tack and Hunter never made it home, we can't know whether they successfully buried supplies just outside of Hartford, Connecticut, roughly 180 miles south of Rochester, or whether something happened to them along the way. The cold has buried its claws in the landscape now: it is relentless, and will not let go until spring. We are tired, hungry, and defeated. Even Raven can't maintain the appearance of strength. She walks slowly, head bowed, not speaking.

I don't know what we'll do if there is no food at the third encampment. I know Raven is worried too, although she won't talk about it. None of us talk about it. We just push blindly, obstinately forward.

But the fear is there. As we approach Hartford – threading through the ruins of old towns, bombed-out shells of houses, like dry insect husks – there is no sense of celebration. Instead there is anxiety: a hum of it, running through all of us, making the woods feel ominous. The dusk is full of malice; the shadows are long, pointed fingers, a forest of dark hands. Tomorrow we will reach the third encampment, if it is there. If not, some of us will starve before we make it farther south.

And if it is not there, we can stop wondering about Tack and Hunter: it will mean that in all probability they are dead.

The morning dawns weakly and is full of strange electricity, like the waiting feeling that usually precedes a storm. Other than the crunching of our shoes in the snow, we move in silence.

Finally we reach it: the place where the third encampment should be. There is no sign that Tack and Hunter have been here: no gouges in the trees, no tattered pieces of fabric looped over tree branches, none of the symbols we've been using to communicate, and no indication that any goods or supplies have been buried here. This is what we've all feared, but still the disappointment is almost physical.

Raven lets out a short exclamation of pain, as though she's been slapped; Sarah collapses, right there in the snow, and says, 'No-no-no-no-no!' until Lu tells her to shut up. I feel as though my chest has caved in.

'There must be a mistake,' I say. My voice sounds too loud in the clearing. 'We must be in the wrong place.'

'There's no mistake,' Bram says in a low voice. 'This is it.'

'No,' I insist. 'We took a wrong turn somewhere. Or Tack found a better place for the supplies.'

'Be quiet, Lena,' Raven says. She's rubbing her temples, hard. Her fingernails are ringed with purple. 'I need to think.'

'We need to find Tack.' I know I'm not helping; I know I'm half hysterical. But the cold and the hunger have turned my thoughts dull too, and this is the only one that stands out. 'Tack has our food. We need to find him. We need to—'

I break off as Bram says, 'Shhh.' Sarah scrambles to her feet again. Suddenly we are all tense, alert. We all heard it – the crack of a twig in the woods, sharp as a rifle report. As I look around at us – all of our faces still and listening, anxious – I'm reminded of the deer we saw two days ago in the woods, the way it froze, and tensed, just before bounding away.

The woods are stark-still, brushstrokes of straight black leafless trees, expanses of white, collapsed logs and rotten tree trunks hunched in the snow.

Then, as I am watching, one of the logs – from a distance, just a mass of grey and brown – twitches.

And I know that something is very, very wrong. I open my mouth to say so, but in that exact second everything explodes: Scavengers appear from all around us, shaking off their cloaks and furs – trees becoming people becoming arms and knives and spears – and we are scattering, running, screaming in all directions.

This is, of course, how they want us: panicked, weak, and separated.

We are easier to kill that way.

now

The tunnel we are following slopes downward. For a minute I imagine that we are tunnelling toward the centre of the earth.

From up ahead, there is light and movement: a fiery glow, and sounds of banging and babbling. My neck is wet with sweat, and the dizziness is worse than ever. I am having trouble staying on my feet. I trip and barely manage to right myself. Rat-man steps forward and seizes one of my arms. I try to wrench away from his grasp, but he keeps one hand firmly on my elbow, walking beside me now. He smells terrible.

The light breaks, expands, and becomes a cavernous room filled with fire and people. The ceiling above us is vaulted, and we emerge from the darkness into a space with tall platforms on either side of us; on them, more monsters – tattered, ragged, dirty people, all of them bloodless and pale, squinting and hobbled – move among metal trash cans where several fires are burning, so the air is clotted with smoke and an old,

oily smell. The walls are tiled, and papered with faded adver-
tisements and graffiti.

As we advance along the tracks, people turn and stare. They
are all withered or damaged in some way. Many of them are
missing limbs, or have other kinds of defects: shrivelled infant-
hands, strange tumour-growths on their faces, curved spines
or crippled knees.

'Up,' the rat-man says, jerking his chin toward the platform.
It is impossibly high.

Julian's hands are still tied behind his back. Two of the larger
men on the platform come forward and grab him under the
armpits, help haul him up out of the tracks. The hunchback
moves with surprising grace. I get a glimpse of strong arms
and delicate, tapered wrists. A woman, then.

'I – I can't,' I say. The people on the platforms have stopped
now. They are staring at Julian and me. 'It's too high.'

'Up,' Rat-man repeats. I wonder if these are the only words
he knows – *stand*, *walk*, *up*, *down*.

The platform is at eye level. I place my hands flat on the
concrete and try to heave myself up, but I'm far too weak. I
collapse backward.

'She's hurt!' Julian cries out. 'Can't you see that? For God's
sake – we need to get out of here.'

It's the first time he has spoken since the Scavengers tracked
us down, and his voice is full of pain and fear.

The rat-man is piloting me back toward the platform, but
this time, as though by silent agreement, some of the observers
move simultaneously forward toward us. They crouch at the
platform lip; they reach out their arms. I try and twist away,
but the rat-man is behind me. He grabs me firmly by the waist.

'Stop it!' Now Julian is trying to break free of his captors.

The two men who helped him onto the platform are still holding him firmly. 'Let her go!'

Hands are grabbing me from all directions. Monstrous faces loom above me, floating in the flickering light.

Julian is still screaming. 'Do you hear me? Get off her! Let her go!'

A woman comes through the crowd toward me. She seems to be missing part of her face; her mouth is twisted into a horrible grin.

No. I want to scream. Hands are gripping me, lifting me onto the platform. I kick out; there is a release. I land hard on my side, rolling onto my back. The woman with the half-face looms over me. She reaches for me with both hands.

She is going to strangle me.

'Get away from me!' I scream out, flailing, trying to push her away. My head smacks back against the platform, and for a second my vision explodes with colour.

'Be still,' she is saying, in a soothing voice – a lullaby voice, surprisingly gentle – as the pain stops, and the screaming stops, and I drift away into a fog.

then

We scatter, panicked and blind. We've had no time to load our weapons, and we have no strength to fight. My knife is in my pack – useless to me now. No time to stop and retrieve it. The Scavengers are fast and strong: bigger, I think, than any normal people should be, bigger than anybody should be who makes a home in the Wilds.

'This way! This way!' Raven runs ahead of me, dragging Sarah by the hand. Sarah is too scared to cry. She can barely keep up with Raven. She is stumbling in the snow.

Terror is a heartbeat drumming in my chest. There are three Scavengers behind us. One of them has an axe. I can hear the blade whistling in the air. My throat is burning, and with each step I sink six inches, have to wrench my legs forward. My thighs are shaking from the effort.

We come over a hill and suddenly, looming ahead of us, there is an outcropping of rock, large boulders shouldering together at angles like people crowding together for warmth.

The rocks are slick with ice and form a series of interlinking caves, dark mouths where the snow has not penetrated. There is no way to go around them, or climb over them. We will be caught there, pinioned, like animals in a corral.

Raven freezes for just a second, and I can see the terror in her whole body. A Scavenger lunges for her, and I cry out. She unfreezes, dragging Sarah forward again, running straight for the rock because there is nowhere else to run. I see her fumbling at her belt for her long knife. Her fingers are clumsy, frozen solid. She can't work it out of its pouch, and I realize, heart sinking, that she intends to make a stand. That is her only plan; we will die out here, and our blood will seep into the snow.

My throat is grating, aching; bare branches whip my face, stinging my eyes with tears. A Scavenger is close to me now, so close I can hear his heavy panting and see his shadow running in tandem with mine – to our left, twin figures cast long on the snow – and in that moment, just before he catches up to me, I think of Hana. Two shadows on the Portland streets; sun hot and high; legs beating in tandem.

Then there is no place left to run.

'Go!' Raven is screaming, as she pushes Sarah forward into a dark space, one of the caves made by the rocks. Sarah is small enough to fit. Hopefully the Scavengers will not be able to get to her. Then there is a hand on my back, and I am tumbling roughly to my knees, teeth ringing as I bite down on ice. I roll onto my back, six inches from the wall of sheer rock.

He is above me: a giant, a leering monster. He raises his axe, and its blade glitters in the sun. I'm too scared to move, to breathe, to cry.

He tenses, ready to swing.

I close my eyes.

A rifle shot explodes in the silence, then two more. I open my eyes and see the Scavenger above me collapse to one side, like a puppet whose strings have been suddenly cut. His axe falls blade-first in the snow. Two other Scavengers have fallen too, pierced cleanly with bullets: their blood is spreading against the whiteness.

Then I see them: Tack and Hunter jogging toward us, rifles in hand, thin and pale and haggard and alive.

now

When I come to, I'm lying on my back on a dingy sheet. Julian is kneeling next to me, his hands unbound.

'How are you feeling?'

All of a sudden I remember – the rats, the monsters, the woman with the half-face. I struggle to sit up. Little fireworks of pain go off in my head.

'Easy, easy.' Julian puts his arm under my shoulders and helps move me into a seated position. 'You cracked your head pretty badly.'

'What happened?' We are sitting in an area that has been partially blocked off by dismantled cardboard boxes. All along the platform, flowered sheets are strung up between broken slats of plywood, offering some privacy to the squatters inside; mattresses have been placed inside enormous, sagging cardboard structures; walls and blockades have been made by interlocking broken chairs and three-legged tables. The air is still hot, stinking of ash and oil. I watch the smoke trace a line along the ceiling, before getting sucked up and out through a tiny vent.

'They cleaned you up,' Julian says quietly, in a tone of disbelief. 'At first I thought they were going to—' He breaks off, shaking his head. 'But then a woman came, with bandages and everything. She wrapped up your neck. It was bleeding again.'

I touch my neck: it has been taped up with thick gauze. They've taken care of Julian, too; the cut on his lip has been cleaned, and the bruises on his eyes are less swollen.

'Who are these people?' I say. 'What is this place?'

Julian shakes his head again. 'Invalids.' Seeing me flinch, he adds, 'I don't know any other word for them. For you.'

'We're not the same,' I say, watching the bent and crippled figures moving beyond the smoky fire. Something is cooking; I can smell it. I don't want to think about what kind of food they eat down here – what kind of animals they manage to trap. I think of the rats, and my stomach lurches. 'Don't you get that yet? We're all different. We want different things. We live different ways. That's the whole point.'

Julian opens his mouth to respond, but at that moment the monster woman appears, the one I tried to fight off at the edge of the platform. She pushes aside the cardboard barricade, and it strikes me that they must have arranged it that way so Julian and I would have some privacy.

'You're awake,' the woman says. Now that I'm not so terrified, I see that she's not missing part of her face, as I imagined; the right side of her face is just much smaller than the left, collapsed inward, as though her face is composed of two different masks, imperfectly joined. *Birth defect,* I think, even though I've seen only a few defectives in my life, and all of them were in textbooks. In school we were always taught that kids born from the uncured would end up like this, crippled and mangled in some way. The priests told us this was the *deliria* manifesting in their bodies.

Children born of the healthy and the whole are healthy and whole; children born of the disease will have sickness in their bones and blood.

All these people, born crippled or bent or misshapen, have been driven underground. I wonder what would have happened to them as babies, as children, if they had stayed aboveground. I remember, then, what Raven told me about finding Blue. *You know what they say about* deliria *babies . . . She would probably be taken and killed. She wouldn't even be buried . . . She'd be burned, and packed up with the waste.*

The woman doesn't wait for me to answer before kneeling in front of me. Julian and I are both silent. I want to say something to her, but I don't have the words. I want to look away from her face, but I can't.

'Thank you,' I finally manage. Her eyes flick to mine. They are brown and webbed with fine lines. She has a permanent squint, probably from existing in this strange, twilight world.

'How many were they?' she asks. I would have expected her voice to be mangled and broken, a reflection of her face, but it is high and clear. Pretty. When I don't immediately respond, she says, 'The Intruders. How many?'

I know immediately that she is referring to the Scavengers, though she uses a different word to describe them. I can tell from the way she says it: the mixture of anger, fear, and disgust.

'I'm not sure,' I say. 'Seven, at least. Maybe more.'

The woman says, 'They came three seasons ago. Maybe four.' I must look surprised by her way of speaking, because she adds, 'It isn't easy to keep track of time in the tunnels. Days, weeks – unless we go above, it's hard to know.'

'How long have you been down here?' I ask, almost afraid to know the answer.

She squints at me with those small, sludge-coloured eyes. I do my best not to look at her mouth and chin: there, the deformity is at its worst, as though her face is curling up into itself, a wilting flower. 'I've been here always,' she says. 'Or almost always.'

'How—?' The question gets caught in my throat.

She smiles. I think it's a smile, at least. One corner of her mouth corkscrews upward. 'There is nothing for us on the surface,' she says. 'Nothing but death, anyway.'

So it's like I thought. I wonder if that's what always happens to the babies who don't find their way underground, or to a homestead in the Wilds. Maybe they get locked in prisons and mental institutions. Maybe they are simply killed.

'For all my life, the tunnels have belonged to us,' she says. I'm still having a hard time reconciling the melody of her voice with the look of her face. I focus on her eyes: even in the dim, smoky light, I can see that they are full of warmth. 'People find their way to us with babies. This is a safe place for them.' Her eyes flick to Julian, and I notice her scan his unblemished neck; then she's back to me. 'You've been cured,' she says. 'That's what they call it aboveground, right?'

I nod. I open my mouth to try and explain – *I'm okay, I'm on your side* – but to my surprise, Julian speaks up. 'We're not with the Intruders,' he says. 'We're not with anyone else. We're – we're on our own.'

We're not with anyone else. I know he's just saying it to appease her, but the words still buoy me up, help break apart the knot of fear that has been lodged in my chest since we've been underground.

Then I think of Alex, and I feel nauseous all over again. I wish that we had never left the Wilds. I wish that I had never agreed to join the resistance.

'How did you come here?' the woman says. She pours from a jug next to me, and offers me a plastic cup: a child's cup, with faded patterns of deer prancing around its rim. This, like everything else down here, must have floated in from above – discarded, unwanted, drifting through the cracks of the earth like a melting snow.

'We were taken.' Julian's voice gets stronger now. 'Kidnapped by the Intruders.' He hesitates, and I know that he's thinking about the DFA badges we found, the tattoo I saw. He doesn't understand yet, and I don't either; but I know this was not merely the effort of Scavengers. They were paid or were supposed to be paid for their trouble. 'We don't know why,' he says.

'We're trying to find our way out,' I say, and then something that the woman said earlier strikes me, and I feel a sudden surge of hope. 'Wait – you said you have trouble keeping track of time unless you go aboveground, right? So . . . there's a way out? A way up?'

'I don't go aboveground,' she says. The way she says *above* makes it sound like a dirty word.

'But somebody does,' I persist. 'Somebody must.' They must have ways of getting supplies: sheets and cups and fuel and all the piles of half-used, broken-down furniture heaped around us on the platform.

'Yes,' she says evenly. 'Of course.'

'Will you take us?' I ask. My throat is dry. Just thinking about the sun, and the space, and the surface, makes me want to cry. I don't know what will happen once we're above again, but I push away the thought.

'You're still very weak,' she says. 'You need to eat and rest.'

'I'm okay,' I insist. 'I can walk.' I try to stand up, and find my vision clouding with black. I thud back down.

'Lena.' Julian puts a hand on my arm. Something flickers in his eyes – *Trust me, it's okay, a little longer won't kill us.* I don't know what's happening, or how we've begun to communicate in silence, or why I like it so much.

He turns to the woman. 'We'll rest for a bit. Then will someone show us the way to the surface?'

The woman once again looks from Julian to me and back again. Then she nods. 'You don't belong down here,' she says. She climbs to her feet.

I feel suddenly humbled. All these people make a life from trash and broken things, living in darkness, breathing in smoke. And yet, they helped us. They helped us without knowing us, and for no reason at all other than the fact that they knew how. I wonder whether I would do the same, if I were in their position. I'm not sure.

Alex would have, I think. And then: Julian would too.

'Wait!' Julian calls her back. 'We – we didn't get your name.'

A look of surprise crosses her face: then she smiles again, the little corkscrew lips. 'I was named down here,' she says. 'They call me Coin.'

Julian wrinkles his forehead, but I get it right away. It's an Invalid name: descriptive, easy to remember, funny, kind of sick. Coin, as in two-sided.

Coin was right: time is hard to measure in the tunnels, even harder than it was to measure in the cell. At least there we had the electric light to guide us – on during day, off at night. Every minute down here becomes an hour.

Julian and I eat three granola bars each, and some more of the jerky we stole from the Scavengers' stash. It feels like a feast, and before I'm even finished, my stomach is cramping badly. Still, after eating, and drinking the whole jug of water, I feel better than I have in days. We doze for a bit – lying so close I can feel Julian's breath stirring my hair, our legs almost touching – and we both wake at the same time.

Coin is standing above us again. She has refilled the jug of water. Julian utters a little cry as he is shaking himself into awareness. Then he sits up quickly, embarrassed. He runs his hands through his hair so it sticks up at crazy angles, every which way; I have an overwhelming urge to reach out and smooth it down.

'Can you walk?' Coin asks me. I nod. 'I'll have someone take you to the surface, then.' Again, she says *surface* as though it's a dirty word, or a curse.

'Thank you.' The words seem thin and insufficient. 'You didn't need to – I mean, we really appreciate it. We'd probably be dead if it weren't for you and . . . your friends.' I almost say *your people*, but I catch myself at the last minute. I remember how angry I've been with Julian for saying the same thing.

She stares at me for a moment without smiling, and I wonder if, somehow, I've offended her. 'Like I said, you don't belong down here,' she says. And then, her voice swelling, rising to a high pitch: 'There's a place for everything and everyone, you know. That is the mistake they make above. They think that only certain people have a place. Only certain kinds of people belong. The rest is waste. But even waste must have a place. Otherwise it will clog and clot, and rot and fester.'

A small tremor passes through her body; her right hand tugs convulsively at the folds of her dirty dress.

'I'll find someone to guide you,' she says abruptly, as though ashamed of her outburst, and turns away from us.

Rat-man is the one who comes for us, and seeing him brings back a sense of vertigo and nausea, even though this time he is alone. The rats have gone back to their holes and hiding places.

'Coin said you want to go up,' he says, the longest sentence I have heard from him yet. Julian and I are already standing. Julian has taken the backpack, and though I've told him I'm okay to stand, he insists on keeping a hand on my arm. *Just in case*, he said, and I think of how different he is from the boy I saw onstage in the Javits Centre, the cool floating screen image – unimaginable that they should be the same person. I wonder whether that boy is the real Julian, or this boy is the real one, or whether it's even possible to know.

Then it hits me: I'm not even sure who the real Lena is anymore.

'We're ready,' Julian says.

We pick our way around the piles of junk and the makeshift shelters that clutter the platform. Everywhere we go, we are watched. Figures crouch in the shadows. They've been forced down here, the way we have been forced into the Wilds: all for a society of order and regularity.

For a society to be healthy, not a single one of its members can be sick. The DFA's philosophy runs deeper – much deeper – than I'd believed. The dangerous are not just the uncured: they are also the different, the deformed, the abnormal. They must also be eradicated. I wonder if Julian realizes this, or whether he's known it all along.

Irregularity must be regulated; dirt must be cleansed; the laws of physics teach us that systems tend increasingly toward chaos, and so the chaos must be constantly pushed back. The rules of expurgation are even written into *The Book of Shhh*.

At the end of the platform, the rat-man swings down into the tracks. He is walking well now. If he was injured during the scuffle with the Scavengers, he, too, has been mended and bandaged. Julian follows, and then helps me down, reaching up and putting his hands around my waist as I manoeuvre clumsily off the platform. Even though I feel better than I did earlier, I'm still not moving very well. I've been too long without enough food and water, and my head still throbs. My left ankle wobbles as I hit the ground, and for a minute I stumble against Julian, bumping my chin on his chest, and his arms tighten around me.

'You okay?' he says. I'm ultra-conscious of the closeness of our bodies, and the encircling warmth of his arms.

I step away from him, my heart climbing into my mouth. 'I'm fine,' I say.

Then it's time to go into the darkness again. I hang back, and Rat-man must think I'm scared. He turns and says, 'The Intruders don't come this far. Don't worry.' He's without a flashlight or a torch. I wonder if the fire was just meant to intimidate the Scavengers. The mouth of the tunnel is pitch-black, but he seems perfectly able to see.

'Let's go,' Julian says, and I turn with him and follow the rat-man, and the dim beam of Julian's flashlight, into the dark.

We walk in silence, although the rat-man occasionally stops, making clicking motions with his tongue, like a man calling a dog. Once he crouches, and pulls bits of crushed crackers from the pockets of his coat, scattering them on the ground between the wooden slats of the tracks. From the corners of the tunnel the rats emerge, sniffing his fingers, fighting over the crumbs, hopping up into his cupped palms and running up over his arms and shoulders. It is terrible to watch, but I can't look away.

'How long have you been here?' Julian asks, after the rat-man has straightened up again. Now all around us we hear the chittering of tiny teeth and nails, and the flashlight lights up quick-moving, writhing shadows. I have a sudden terror that the rats are all around me, even on the ceilings.

'Don't know,' the rat-man says. 'Lost count.'

Unlike the other people who have made their home on the platform, he has no noticeable physical deformities except for his single milk-white eye. I can't help but blurt out, 'Why?'

He turns abruptly back to me. For a minute Rat-man doesn't say anything, and the three of us stand there in the stifling dark. My breath is coming quickly, rasping in my throat.

'I didn't want to be cured,' he says at last, and the words are so normal – a vocabulary from my world, a debate from above – that relief breaks in my chest. He's not crazy after all.

'Why not?' That's Julian.

Another pause. 'I was already sick,' the rat-man says, and although I can't see his face, I can hear that he is smiling just a little bit. I wonder if Julian is as surprised as I am.

It occurs to me, then, that people themselves are full of tunnels: winding, dark spaces and caverns; impossible to know all the places inside of them. Impossible even to imagine.

'What happened?' Julian persists.

'She was cured,' the rat-man says shortly, and turns his back to us, resuming the walk. 'And I chose . . . this. Here.'

'Wait, wait.' Julian tugs me along – we have to jog a little to catch up. 'I don't understand. You were infected together, and then she was cured?'

'Yes.'

'And you chose this instead?' Julian shakes his head. 'You must have seen . . . I mean, it would have taken away the pain.' There's a question in Julian's words, and I know then that he is struggling, still clinging to his old beliefs, the ideas that have comforted him for so long.

'I didn't see.' The rat-man has increased his pace. He must have the tunnel's twists and dips memorized. Julian and I can barely keep up. 'I didn't see her at all after that.'

'I don't understand,' Julian says, and for a second my heart aches for him. He is my age, but there is so much he doesn't know.

The rat-man stops. He doesn't look at us, but I see his shoulders rise and fall: an inaudible sigh. 'They'd already taken her from me once,' he says quietly. 'I didn't want to lose her again.'

I have the urge to lay my hand on his shoulder and say, *I understand*. But the words seem stupid. We can never understand. We can only try, fumbling our way through the tunneled places, reaching for light.

But then he says, 'We're here,' and steps to the side, so the flashlight's beam falls on a rusted metal ladder; and before I can think of anything else to say, he has hopped onto its lowest rung and started climbing toward the surface.

Soon the rat-man is fiddling with a metal cover in the ceiling. As he slides it open, the light is so dazzling and unexpected I cry out for a second, and have to turn away, blinking, while spots of colour revolve in my vision.

The rat-man heaves himself up and out through the hole, then reaches down to help me. Julian follows last.

We've emerged onto a large, open-air platform. There is a train track below us, torn up, a thicket of mangled iron and wood. At some point, it must descend into the underground tunnels. The platform is streaked with bird shit. Pigeons are roosting everywhere, on the peeled-paint benches, in the old trash bins, between the tracks. A sun-faded and wind-battered sign must at one point have listed the station name; it is illegible now, but for a few letters: H, O, B, K. Old tags stain the walls: MY LIFE, MY CHOICE, says one. Another reads, KEEP AMERICA SAFE. Old slogans, old signs of the fight between the believers and the nonbelievers.

'What is this place?' I say to Rat-man. He's crouching by the black mouth of the hole that leads below. He has flipped his hood up to shield his eyes from the sun, and he seems desperate to leap back into the darkness. This is the first time I've had a chance to really look at him, and I see now he is much younger than I'd imagined. Other than faint, criss-crossed lines at the corners of his eyes, his face is smooth and unlined. His skin is so pale it has the blue tint of milk, and his eyes are fuzzy and unfocused, unused to so much light.

'This is the landfill,' he says, pointing. About a hundred yards off, in the direction he indicates, is a tall chain-link fence, beyond which we can see a mound of glittering trash and metal. 'Manhattan is across the river.'

'The landfill,' I repeat slowly. Of course: the underground people must have a way to gather supplies. The landfill would be perfect: heaps and heaps of discarded food, supplies, wiring, and furniture. I feel a jolt of recognition. I scramble to my feet. 'I know where we are,' I say. 'There's a homestead nearby.'

'A what?' Julian squints up at me, but I'm too excited. I jog down the platform, my breath steaming in front of me, lifting my arm to shield my eyes from the sun. The landfill is enormous – several miles square, Tack told me, to service all of Manhattan and its sister cities – but we must be at its northern end. There's a gravel road that winds away from its gates, through the ruins of old, bombed-out buildings. This trash pit was once a city itself. And less than a mile away is a homestead. Raven, Tack, and I lived here for a month while we were waiting for papers and our final instructions from the resistance about relocation and reabsorption. At the homestead there will be food, and water, and clothing. There will be a way to contact Raven and Tack, too. When we lived there we used radio signals, and, when those got too dangerous, different-coloured cloths, which we raised on the flagpole just outside of a burned-out local school.

'This is where I leave you,' Rat-man says. He has swung his lower body back into the hole. I can tell he's desperate to get out of the sun and go back to safety.

'Thank you,' I say. The words seem stupidly insufficient, but I can't think of any others.

The rat-man nods and is about to swing himself down the ladder when Julian stops him.

'We didn't get your name,' Julian says.

The rat-man's lips twitch into a smile. 'I don't have one,' he says.

Julian looks startled. 'Everyone has a name,' he says.

'Not anymore,' the rat-man says with that twitchy smile. 'Names don't mean a thing anymore. The past is dead.'

The past is dead. Raven's refrain. It makes my throat go dry. I am not so different from these underground people after all.

'Be careful,' the rat-man says, and his eyes go unfocused again. 'They're always watching.'

Then he drops down into the hole. A second later the iron cover slides into place.

For a moment, Julian and I stand in silence, staring at each other.

'We did it,' Julian says finally, smiling at me. He is standing a little ways down the platform, the sun streaking his hair with white and gold. A bird darts across the sky behind him, a fast-moving shadow against the blue. There are small white flowers pushing up between the cracks in the platform.

Suddenly I find that I am crying. I am sobbing with gratitude and relief. We made it out, and the sun is still shining, and the world still exists.

'Hey.' Julian comes over to me. He hesitates for a second, then reaches out and rubs my back, moving his hand in slow circles. 'Hey, it's okay. It's okay, Lena.'

I shake my head. I want to tell him that I know, and that's why I'm crying, but I can't speak. He pulls me into him and I cry into his T-shirt and we stand there like that, in the sun, in the outside world, where these things are illegal. And all around us there is silence, except for the occasional twittering of birds, and the rustle of pigeons around the empty platform.

Finally I pull away. For a second I think I see movement behind him, in the shadows beyond one of the station's old stairwells, but then I'm sure I've only imagined it. The light is unrelenting. I can't imagine what I must look like right now. Despite the fact that the underground people have cleaned and treated Julian's wounds, his face is still patterned with bruises, a multicoloured patchwork. I'm sure I look just as bad, if not worse.

Belowground, we've been allies; friends. Aboveground, I'm not sure what we are, and I feel uneasy.

Thankfully, he breaks the tension. 'So you know where we are?' he says.

I nod. 'I know where we can get help from – from my people.'

To his credit, he doesn't flinch. 'Let's go, then,' he says.

He follows me down into the tracks. We startle the pigeons from their roost, and they whirl up around us, a blurry, feathered hurricane. We pick our way over the train tracks and onto the high grass beyond it, bleached pale from the sun and still sheathed in frost. The ground is hard and webbed with ice, although here, too, there is evidence of spring growth: small, curled buds of green, a few early flowers scattered among the dirt.

The sun is warm on our necks, but the wind is icy. I wish I had something warmer than a sweatshirt. The cold reaches right through the cotton, grabs on to my insides, and pulls.

Finally the landscape becomes familiar. The sun draws stark shadows on the ground – towering, splintered shapes of bombed-out buildings. We pass an old street sign, doubled over, that once pointed the way to Columbia Avenue. Columbia Avenue is now nothing more than broken slabs of concrete, and frozen grass, and a carpet of minuscule shards of glass, shattered into a reflective dust.

'Here it is,' I say. 'Right up here.' I start jogging. The entrance to the homestead is no more than twenty yards away, beyond a twist in the road.

And yet, there's another feeling drilling through me: some inner alarm sounding quietly. Convenient. That's the word that keeps floating through my mind. Convenient that we ended up so close to the homestead; convenient that the tunnels led us here. Too convenient to be a coincidence.

I push away the thought.

We turn the corner and there it is. Just like that, all my concerns get whipped away on a surge of joy. Julian stops, but I go straight up to the door, recharged, full of energy. Most homesteads – at least the ones I've seen – have been built out of hidden places: basements and cellars and bomb shelters and bank vaults that remained intact during the blitz. We have populated them like insects reclaiming the land.

But this homestead was built long after the blitz was over. Raven told me it was one of the very first homesteads, and the headquarters of the first ragtag group of resisters, who scavenged for materials and built a quasi-house, a weird patch-work structure made from timber, concrete, stone, and metal. The whole place has a junky look, a Frankenstein facade, like it shouldn't possibly be standing.

But stand it does.

'So?' I say, turning back to Julian. 'You coming or what?'

'I've never . . . It's not possible.' Julian shakes his head, as though trying to rouse himself from a dream. 'This isn't at all what I used to imagine.'

'We can build something out of almost anything – out of scrap,' I say, and I remember, then, when Raven said almost the exact same thing to me after my escape, when I was sick and weak and unsure whether I wanted to live or die. That was a half a year and a lifetime ago. For a second I feel a rush of sadness: for the horizons that vanish behind us, for the people we leave behind, the tiny-doll selves that get stored away and ultimately buried.

Julian's eyes are electric now, a mirror of the sky, and he

turns to me. 'Up until two years ago, I thought it was all a fairy tale. The Wilds, the Invalids.' He takes two steps and suddenly we are standing very close. 'You. I – I never would have believed it.'

We are still separated by several inches, but I feel as though we are touching. There is an electricity between us that collapses the space between our bodies.

'I'm real,' I say, and the electricity is an itch, a nervous jumping under my skin. I feel too exposed. It is too bright, and too quiet.

Julian says, 'I don't think – I'm not sure I can go back.' His eyes are full of watery depth. I want to look away, but I can't. I feel as though I am falling.

'I don't know what you're saying.' I force the words out.

'I mean, I—'

There is a loud bang from our right, as though someone has kicked something over. Julian breaks off, and I see his body tense. Instinctively, I push him behind me, toward the door, and wrestle the handgun from my backpack. I scan the area: all shrapnel and stone, dips and depressions, plenty of places to hide. The hair is standing up on my neck, and my whole body is an alarm now. They are always watching.

We stand in agonizing silence. The wind lifts a plastic bag across the brittle ground. It makes three slow revolutions, then settles at the base of a long-disabled streetlamp.

Suddenly there is a flicker of movement to my left. I turn around with a cry, gripping the gun, as a cat darts out from behind a mound of cinder block. Julian exhales, and I loosen my hold on the gun, letting the tension flow out of my body. The cat – skinny and wide-eyed – pauses, turning its head in our direction. It meows piteously.

Julian touches my shoulders lightly, with both hands, and I jerk away quickly, instinctively.

'Come on,' I say. I can tell I've hurt his feelings.

'I was about to say something,' Julian says. I can feel him searching for my eyes, willing me to look at him, but I am already at the door, fiddling with the rusty handle.

'You can tell me later,' I say as I lean in against the door. It gives, finally, and Julian has no choice but to follow me inside.

I am scared about what Julian has to say, and what he will choose, and where he will go. But I am terrified by what I want: for him, and worst of all, from him.

Because I do want. I'm not even sure what, exactly, but the want is there, just like the hate and anger were there before. But this is not a tower. It is an endless, tunnelling pit; it drives deep, and opens a hole inside me.

then

Tack and Hunter weren't able to salvage many supplies from the Rochester homestead. The bombs and ensuing fires did their job. But they did find a few things miraculously preserved among the smoking rubble: cans of beans, some additional weapons, traps, and, weirdly, one whole, entirely unmelted chocolate bar. Tack insists that it remain uneaten. He straps it to his backpack, like a good luck charm. Sarah eyes it as we walk.

It does seem like the chocolate brings good luck – or maybe it's just having Tack and Hunter back, and the way it changes Raven's mood. The weather holds. It's still cold, but we're all grateful for the sun.

The beans are enough to give us energy to move on, and only a half-day after we've left the last encampment we stumble upon a single house, entirely preserved, in the middle of the woods. It must have been miles from any major road when it was built, and it looks like a mushroom sprouting up from the ground: its walls are covered in brown ivy, thick as fur, and its roof is low and round, pulled down like a hat. This would have been a hermit's house, back before the blitz – far away from everyone else. No wonder it survived intact. The bombers would have missed it, and even the fires might not have spread this far.

Four Invalids have made it their home. They invite us to camp on their grounds. There are two men and two women, as well as five children, none of whom seems to belong to either couple in particular. They all act as one family, they tell us over dinner, and have inhabited the house for a decade. They are nice enough to share what they have: canned eggplant and summer squash, bitingly sour with garlic and vinegar; strips of dried venison from earlier in the fall; and various other kinds of smoked meat and fowl: rabbit, pheasant, squirrel.

Hunter and Tack spend the evening retracing our steps and slicing patterns in the trees, so next year when we migrate – if we migrate again – we will be able to locate the mushroom house.

In the morning, one of the children runs out as we are getting ready to leave. He is barefoot, despite the snow.

'Here,' he says, and presses a kitchen towel into my hand. Inside are hard, flat loaves of bread – made, I overheard one of the women say, from acorns and not flour – and more dried meat.

'Thank you,' I say, but he is already running back, bounding toward the house, laughing. For a moment I am jealous: he has grown up here, fearless, happy. Perhaps he will never even know about the world on the other side of the fence, the real world. For him there will be no such thing.

But there will also be no medicine for him when he is sick, and never enough food to go around, and winters so cold the mornings are like a punch to the gut. And someday – unless the resistance succeeds and takes the country back – the planes and the fires will find him. Someday the eye will turn in this direction, like a laser beam, consuming everything in its path. Someday all the Wilds will be razed, and we will be left with a concrete landscape, a land of pretty houses and trim gardens and planned parks and forests, and a world that works as smoothly as a clock, neatly wound: a world of metal and gears, and people going *tick-tick-tick* to their deaths.

We ration carefully, and at last, after another three days' walking, we come to the bridge that marks the final thirty miles. It is enormous and narrow, made of vast ropes of steel, all slicked with ice and blackened by weather. It looks to me like a gigantic insect, straddling the river, plunging its jointed legs into the water. Barricaded years ago, it has been so long out of use, except as a passage for travelling Invalids, that the clumsily erected wooden boards at its entrance have all but rotted away.

A large green sign, detached from its metal supports on one side, now hangs so that its words run vertically. I read as we pass: TAPPAN ZEE BRIDGE. It sways in the wind – a brutal wind; exposed as we are, it drives right through us, bringing tears to our eyes – and fills the air with ghostly moaning.

Below us, the water is the colour of concrete, and capped with waves. The height is dizzying. I read once that jumping into water from this height would feel just like a plunge into stone. I remember the news story of the uncured who killed herself by jumping from the roof of the labs on the day of her procedure, and the memory brings with it a feeling of guilt.

But this is what Alex would have wanted for me: the scar on my neck, miraculously well-healed, just like a real procedural scar; the ropy muscles, the sense of purpose. He believed in the resistance, and now I will believe in it for him.

And maybe someday I will see him again. Maybe there really is a heaven after death. And maybe it's open to everyone, not just the cured.

But for now, the future, like the past, means nothing. For now, there is only a homestead built of trash and scraps, at the edge of a broken city, just beyond a towering city dump; and our arrival – hungry, and half frozen, to a place of food and water, and walls that keep out the brutal winds. This, for us, is heaven.

now

Heaven is hot water. Heaven is soap.

Salvage – which is what we always called this home-stead – consists of four rooms. There is a kitchen; a large storage space, almost the size of the whole rest of the house; and a cramped sleeping room (filled with rickety and clumsily constructed bunk beds).

The last room is for bathing. Various metal tubs are sitting on a raised platform fitted with a large grate; beneath it, there is an area of flat stone, and bits of charred wood, remnants of the fires we kept burning through the winter, to heat the room and the water at once.

After I've fumbled through the darkness and found a battery-operated lantern, I light a fire, using the wood piled high in one corner of the storage shed, while Julian wanders with a glass lantern through the other parts of the house, exploring. Then I crank water from the well. I'm weak, and I can only fill half of one tub before my arms are shaking. But it's enough.

I take a bar of soap from storage, and I even find a real

towel. My skin is itching, crawling with dirt. I can feel it everywhere, in my eyelids, even.

Before I begin undressing, I call out, 'Julian?'

'Yes?' His voice is muffled. From the sound of it, he is in the sleeping space.

'Stay where you are, okay?'

There is no door on the bathing room. It is unnecessary, and things that are unnecessary in the Wilds do not get built, made, or used.

There is a slight pause. 'Okay,' he says. I wonder what he is thinking. His voice sounds high, strained, although that might be the effect of distortion through the tin and plywood walls.

I place the gun on the floor, then strip out of my clothes, enjoying the heavy thud of my jeans on the ground. For a moment my body looks alien, even to myself. There was a time when I was a little bit round everywhere, despite the muscles in my thighs and calves from running. My stomach had swell to it, my breasts were full and heavy.

Now I am all carved inward – wire and rope. My breasts are two small, hard peaks; my skin is criss-crossed with bruises. I wonder if Alex would still find me beautiful. I wonder if Julian thinks I am ugly.

I push away both thoughts. Unnecessary; irrelevant.

I scrub every last inch of my body: under my fingernails, behind my ears, inside my ears – between my toes, and between my legs. I lather my hair and let soap run into my eyes, burning. When I finally stand up, still slippery with soap, like a fish, the tub is ringed with dirt. I'm once again grateful that we have no mirrors here; my reflection is darkly indistinct on the surface of the water, a shadow-self. I don't want to see more clearly what I look like.

I dry myself and put on clean clothes: sweatpants, heavy socks, and a large sweatshirt. My bath has rejuvenated me, and I feel strong enough to draw more water from the well and fill another tub for Julian.

I find him in the storage room. He is squatting in front of a low shelf. Someone has left a dozen books, all of them banned long ago. He is leafing through one of them.

'Your turn,' I say, and he jerks, slamming the book shut. He straightens up, and when he turns to me his face is guilty. Then his eyes shift, an expression I can't identify.

'It's okay,' I tell him. 'You can read what you like here.'

'I—' He starts to speak, then breaks off, shaking his head. He is still watching me with that strange look on his face. My skin feels hot. The bath must have been too warm. 'I remember this book,' he says finally, but I get the sense that is not what he was going to say originally. 'It was in my father's study. His second study. The one I told you about.'

I nod. He holds up the book. It's a copy of *Great Expectations* by Charles Dickens.

'I haven't read it yet,' I confess. 'Tack always said it was one of his favourites—' I suck in a quick breath. I shouldn't have said Tack's name. I've been trusting Julian, letting him in. But he is still Julian Fineman, and the resistance's strength depends on its secrets.

Fortunately, he doesn't comment on it. 'My brother—' He coughs and begins again. 'I found this book with his things. After he died. I don't know why; I don't know what I was looking for.'

A way back, I think, but I don't say it.

'I kept it.' Julian twists one side of his mouth into a smile. 'I cut a slit in my mattress; I used to store it in there, so my dad wouldn't find it. I started reading it that day.'

'Is it good?' I ask him.

'It's full of illegal things,' Julian says slowly, as though he's reevaluating the meaning of the words. His eyes slide away from mine, and for a moment there's a heavy pause. Then his eyes click back to mine, and this time when he smiles, it's full of light. 'But yes. It's good. It's great, I think.'

For some reason I laugh; just that, the way he says it, breaks up the tension in the room, makes everything seem easy and manageable. We were kidnapped; we were beaten and chased; we have no way to get home. We come from two different worlds, and we belonged to two different sides. But everything will be okay.

'I filled a bath for you,' I say. 'It should be hot by now. You can take clean clothes.' I gesture to the shelves, neatly stacked and labelled: MEN'S SHIRTS, WOMEN'S PANTS, CHILDREN'S SHOES. Raven's work, of course.

'Thanks.' Julian grabs a new shirt and pants from the shelves, and, after a moment of hesitation, replaces *Great Expectations* among the books. Then he straightens up, hugging the clothes to his chest. 'It's not so bad here, you know?'

I shrug. 'We do what we can,' I say, but I'm secretly pleased.

He starts to move around me, toward the bathing room. When we're side by side he stops abruptly. His whole body stiffens. I see a tremor run through him, and for a terrifying second I think, *Oh my God, he's having an attack.*

Then he says simply, 'Your hair . . .'

'What?' I'm so surprised I can barely croak out the word.

Julian's not looking at me, but I can feel an alertness in his whole body, an absorption, and it makes me feel even more exposed than if he were staring.

'Your hair smells like roses,' he says, and before I can respond, he wrenches away from me and into the hall, and I am left alone, with a fluttering in my chest.

While Julian bathes, I set out dinner for us. I'm too tired to light up the old woodstove, so I set out crackers, and open up two cans of beans, and one each of mushrooms and tomatoes; whatever doesn't need to be cooked. There's salted beef, too. I take only a small tin of it, even though I'm so hungry I could probably eat a whole cow myself. But we have to save for others. That is a rule.

There are no windows in Salvage and it is dark. I turn off the lantern; I don't want to waste battery power. Instead I find a few thick candles – already burned down almost to stubs – and set those out on the floor. There is no table in Salvage. When I lived here with Raven and Tack, after Hunter had gone with the others even farther south, to Delaware, we ate like this every night, bent over a communal plate, knees bumping, shadows flickering on the walls. I think it was the happiest I'd been since leaving Portland.

From the bathing room I hear watery, sloshing sounds, and humming. Julian, too, is finding heaven in small things. I go to the front door and crack it. The sun is already setting. The sky is pale blue and threaded with pink and gold clouds. The metal detritus around Salvage – the junk and the shrapnel – smoulders red. I think I see a flicker of movement to my left. It must be the cat again, picking its way through the junk.

'What are you looking at?'

I whirl around, slamming the door accidentally. I didn't hear Julian come up behind me. He is standing very close. I can smell his skin, soapy and yet somehow still boy. His hair curls wetly around his jawline.

'Nothing,' I say, and then because he just stands there, staring at me, I say, 'You look almost human.'

'I feel almost human,' he says, and runs a hand through his hair. He has found a plain white T-shirt and jeans that fit.

I'm glad Julian doesn't ask too many questions about this homestead, and who stays here, and when it was built. I know he must be dying to. I light the candles and we sit cross-legged on the ground, and for a while we're too busy eating to talk about much of anything. But afterward we do talk: Julian tells me about growing up in New York and asks me questions about Portland. He tells me about wanting to study mathematics in college, and I tell him about running cross-country.

We don't talk about the cure, or the resistance, or the DFA, or what happens tomorrow, and for that hour while we're sitting across from each other on the floor, I feel as though I have a real friend. He laughs easily, like Hana did. He's a good talker, and an even better listener. I feel weirdly comfortable around him – more comfortable, even, than I did with Alex.

I don't mean to think the comparison, but I do, and it's there, and I stand up abruptly, while Julian is in the middle of a story, and carry the plates to the sink. Julian breaks off, and watches me clatter the dishes into the basin.

'Are you okay?' Julian asks.

'Fine,' I say too sharply. I hate myself in that moment, and I hate Julian, too, without knowing why. 'Just tired.'

That, at least, is true. I am suddenly more tired than I have ever been in my life. I could sleep forever; I could let sleep fall over me like snow.

'I'll find us some blankets,' Julian says, and stands up. I feel him hesitating behind me, and I pretend to be busy at the sink. I can't bear to look at him right now.

'Hey,' he says. 'I never got to thank you.' He coughs. 'You saved my life down there – in the tunnels.'

I shrug, keeping my back toward him. I am gripping the edges of the sink so tightly my knuckles are white. 'You saved my life too,' I say. 'I almost got stuck by a Scavenger.'

When he speaks again, I can tell that he's smiling. 'So I guess we saved each other.'

I do turn around then; but Julian has already taken up a candle and disappeared with it into the hall, so I am left with the shadows.

Julian has selected two lower bunks, and made them up as best he can, with sheets that don't quite fit and thin woollen blankets. He has placed my backpack at the foot of my bed. There are a dozen beds in the room, and yet he has chosen two right next to each other. I try not to think about what this means. He is sitting on his bunk, head ducked, wrestling off his socks. When I enter with the candle, he looks up at me, his face so full of open happiness that I almost drop the candle, and the flame sputters out. Now we are left in darkness.

'Can you find your way?' he says.

'Yes.' I feel my way toward his voice, using the other bunks to guide me.

'Easy.' His hand skates across my back, briefly, as I pass him and find my own bunk. I lie down beneath the sheet and the woollen blanket. Both of them smell like mildew and, very faintly, like mouse shit, but I'm grateful for the warmth. The heat from the fire in the bathing room didn't penetrate this far. When I exhale, small clouds of breath crystallize in the darkness. It will be hard to sleep. The exhaustion that hit after dinner has evaporated just as quickly as it came. My body is on high alert, full of a twinkling frost. I am incredibly aware of Julian's breathing, his long body almost next to mine in the pitch dark. I can feel that he is awake too.

After a while he speaks. His voice is low, a little bit hoarse. 'Lena?'

'Yeah?' My heart is beating high and fast in my throat and chest. I hear Julian roll over to face me. We are only a few feet apart – that is how close the beds have been built together.

'Do you ever think about him? About the boy who infected you?'

Images flash in the darkness: a crown of auburn hair, like autumn leaves burning; the blur of a body, a shape running next to me; a dream-figure. 'I try not to,' I say.

'Why not?' Julian's voice is quiet.

I say, 'Because it hurts.'

Julian's breath is rhythmic, reassuring.

I ask, 'Do you ever think of your brother?'

There is a pause. 'All the time,' Julian says. Then, 'They told me it would be better after I was cured.' There are a few more moments of silence. Then Julian speaks again. 'Can I tell you another secret?'

'Yes.' I pull my blanket tighter around my shoulders. My hair is still wet.

'I knew it wouldn't work. The cure, I mean. I knew it would kill me. I – I wanted it to.' The words come out in a low rush. 'I've never told anyone that before.'

Suddenly I could cry. I want to reach over and grab his hand. I want to tell him it's okay, and feel the softness of his seashell ear against my lips. I want to curl up against him, as I would have done with Alex, and let myself breathe in his warm skin.

He is not Alex. You don't want Julian. You want Alex. And Alex is dead.

But that's not quite true. I want Julian, too. My body is filled with aching. I want Julian's lips on mine, full and soft; and his warm hands on my back and in my hair. I want to lose myself in him, dissipate into his body, feel our skin melting together.

I squeeze my eyes shut, willing away the thought. But with my eyes closed, Julian and Alex melt together. Their faces merge and then separate, then collapse again, like images reflected in a stream, passing over each other until I am no longer sure which of them I am reaching for – in the dark, in my head.

'Lena?' Julian asks again, this time even more quietly. He makes my name sound like music. He has moved closer to me. I can feel him, the long lines of his body, a place where the darkness has been displaced. I have shifted too, without meaning to. I am on the very edge of my bed, as close to him as possible. But I won't roll over to face him. I will myself still. I freeze my arms and legs, and try to freeze my heart, too.

'Yes, Julian?'

'What does it feel like?'

I know what he is talking about, but still I ask, 'What does what feel like?'

'The *deliria*.' He pauses. Then I hear him slide slowly out of bed. He is kneeling in the space between our bunks. I cannot move or breathe. If I turn my head, our lips will be six inches apart. Less. 'What does it feel like to be infected?'

'I – I can't describe it.' I force the words out. Can't breathe, can't breathe, can't breathe. His skin smells like smoke from a wood fire, like soap, like heaven. I imagine tasting his skin; I imagine biting his lips.

'I want to know.' His words are a whisper, barely audible. 'I want to know with you.'

Then his fingers are tracing my forehead, ever so gently – his touch, too, is a whisper, the lightest breath, and I am still paralyzed, frozen. Over the bridge of my nose, and over my lips – the slightest bit of pressure here, so I taste the saltiness of his skin, feel the ridges and swirls of his thumb on my lower lip – and then over my chin, and around my jaw, and up to my hair, and I am full of a roaring hot whiteness that roots me to the bed, holds me in place.

'I told you' – Julian swallows; his voice is full, throaty now – 'I told you I once saw two people kissing. Will you . . . ?'

Julian doesn't finish his question. He doesn't have to. All at once my whole body unfreezes; the whiteness, the heat, breaks in my chest and loosens my lips and all I have to do is turn my head, just a little, and his lips are there.

Then we are kissing: slowly, at first, because he doesn't know how and it has been so long for me. I taste salt and sugar and soap; I run my tongue along his lower lip and he freezes for a second. His lips are warm and full and wonderful. His tongue traces my lips and then suddenly we both let go; and we are breathing into each other, and he is holding my face with his hands, and I am riding a wave of pure joy – I could almost cry, I'm so happy. His chest is solid, pressed against mine. I have drawn him up into the bed without meaning to, and I don't ever want it to end. I could kiss him and feel his fingers in my hair, listen to him say my name, forever.

For the first time since Alex died, I have found my way to a truly free space: a space unbounded by walls and uninhibited by fear. This is flying.

And then, suddenly, Julian breaks off and pulls away. 'Lena,' he gasps hoarsely, as if he has just been running a long distance.

'Don't say it.' I still feel like I could cry. There is so much fragility in kissing, in other people: it is all glass. 'Don't ruin it.'

But he says it anyway. 'What's going to happen tomorrow?'

'I don't know.' I draw his head down toward the pillow next to mine. For a second I think I sense a presence next to us in the dark, a moving figure, and I whip my head to the left. Nothing. I am imagining ghosts beside us. I am thinking of Alex. 'Don't worry about that now,' I say, as much to myself as to Julian.

The bed is very narrow. I turn onto my side, away from Julian, but when he puts his arm around me I relax backward into him, cupped in the long curve of his body as though I have been shaped for it. I want to run away and cry. I want to beg Alex – wherever he is, whatever otherworld now holds him – for forgiveness. I want to kiss Julian again.

But I do not do any of those things. I lie still, and feel Julian's steady heartbeat through my back until my heart calms in response, and I let him hold me, and just before I fall asleep, I say a brief prayer that the morning never comes.

But the morning does come. It finds its way in through the cracks in the plywood, the fissures in the roof: a murky greyness, a slight ebbing of the dark. My first moments of awareness are confused: I believe I am with Alex. No. Julian. His arm is around me, his breath hot on my neck. I have kicked the sheets to the bottom of the bed in the night. I see a flicker of movement from the hall; the cat has gotten into the house somehow.

Then suddenly, a driving certainty – no, I closed the door last night, I locked it – and terror squeezing my chest.

I sit up, say, 'Julian—'

And then everything explodes: they are streaming through the door, bursting through the walls, yelling, screaming – police and regulators in gas masks and matching grey uniforms. One of them grabs me and another one pulls Julian off the bed – he is awake now, calling to me, but I can't hear over the tumult of sound, over the screaming that must be coming from me. I grab the backpack, still balled at the foot of my bed, and swing at the regulator but there are three more, flanking me in the narrow space between beds, and it's hopeless. I remember the gun: still in the bathing room, and useless to me now. Someone pulls me by the collar and I choke. Another regulator wrenches my arms behind my back and cuffs me, then pushes me forward, so I am half dragged, half marched through Salvage and out into the bright, streaming sunshine, where more police are gathered, more members of the SWAT team carrying guns and gas masks – frozen, silent, waiting.

Setup. Those are the words drilling through me, through my panic. Setup. Has to be.

'Got 'em,' someone announces into a walkie-talkie, and all of a sudden the air comes to life, vibrates with sound: people are shouting to one another, gesturing. Two police officers gun the engines of their motorcycles, and the stink of exhaust is everywhere. Walkie-talkies cackle around us – buzzing, a cacophony.

'Ten-four, ten-four. We got 'em.'

'Twenty miles outside of regulated land . . . looked like some kind of hideout.'

'Unit 508 to HQ . . .'

Julian is behind me, surrounded by four regulators; he has been cuffed too.

'Lena! Lena!' I hear him calling my name. I try to turn around and am shoved forward by the regulator behind me.

'Keep moving,' the regulator says, and I'm surprised to hear a woman's voice, distorted through the gas mask.

A caravan of vehicles is parked on the road Julian and I walked, and there are more police officers here, and more members of the SWAT team. Some of them are in full gear, but others are leaning casually against their cars, dressed in civilian clothing, chatting and blowing on Styrofoam mugs of coffee. They barely glance at me as I am hauled, struggling, down the line of cars. I'm full of blind rage, a fury that makes me want to spit. This is routine for them. They will go home at the end of the day, to their orderly houses and their orderly families, and they will give no thought to the girl they saw screaming and kicking and dragged away, probably to her death.

I see a black town car; Thomas Fineman's white, narrow face watches me impassively as I go by. If I could shake a fist loose I would plunge it through the window. I'd watch all the glass explode into his face, see how calm he would stay then.

'Hey, hey, hey!' A policeman is waving to us from up ahead, gesturing with his walkie-talkie toward a police van. Black words stand out vividly against its sparkling white paint: CITY OF NEW YORK, DEPARTMENT OF CORRECTION, REFORM, AND PURIFICATION. In Portland, we had a single prison, the Crypts. It housed all the criminals and resisters, plus the resident loonies, many of them driven crazy by botched or early cures. In New York and its sister cities there is a web of interrelated jails, a network stretching all across the sister cities, with a name almost as bad as the one Portland gave its prison: the Craps.

'Over here, this way!' Now another policeman is waving us over to a different van, and there is a momentary pause. The whole scene is a mass of confusion, more chaotic than the raids I've seen. There are too many people. There are too many cars choking the air with exhaust, too many radios buzzing at once, people talking and shouting over one another. A regulator and a member of the SWAT team are arguing about jurisdiction.

My head hurts; the sun is burning my eyes. All I see is glittering, glaring sunshine; a metal river of cars and motorcycles, exhaust turning the air to mirage, to thickness and smoke.

Suddenly panic crests inside of me. I don't know what happened to Julian. He isn't behind me anymore, and I can't see him in the crowd. 'Julian!' I scream out, and get no answer, although one policeman turns at the sound of my voice and then, shaking his head, hocks a brown glob of saliva onto the ground by my feet. I'm fighting against the woman behind me again, trying to tear myself out of her grasp, but her hands are a vice around my wrists and the more I struggle, the tighter she holds.

'Julian! Julian!'

No response. The panic has turned to a solid lump, and it is clotting my throat. *No, no, no, no. Not again.*

'All right, keep going.' The woman's distorted gas-mask voice urges me forward. She pushes me past the line of waiting cars. The regulator who has been leading the procession is speaking rapidly into his walkie-talkie, some argument with Command about who is to take me in, and he barely glances at us as we thread through the crowd. I'm still fighting the woman behind me with every bit of strength I have, even though the way she is holding my arms sends a fiery pain from my wrists to my shoulders, and even if I did break free, I'm still handcuffed and wouldn't get more than a few feet without getting tackled.

But the rock in my throat is there, and the panic, and the certainty. I need to find Julian. I need to save him.

Beneath that, older words, more urgent words, continue to surge through me: *Not again, not again, not again.*

'Julian!' I strike backward with my foot and connect with the woman's shins. I hear her curse, and for just a second her grip loosens. But then she is once again restraining me, jerking my wrists so sharply that I gasp.

And then, as I tipped backward to give relief to my arms, trying to catch my breath, trying not to cry, she bends forward a little so the mouth of her mask bumps once against my ears.

'Lena,' she says, low. 'Please. I don't want to hurt you. I'm a freedom fighter.'

That word freezes me: that's a secret code sympathizers and Invalids use to indicate their allegiances. I stop trying to fight her off, and her grip relaxes. But she continues to propel me forward, past the caravan of cars. She walks quickly, and with such purpose that nobody stops her or interferes.

Up ahead I see a white van straddling the gutter that runs next to the dirt road. It is also stenciled with the CRAP sign, but the markings seem slightly off – they are a tiny bit too small, I realize, although you'd have to be staring to notice it. We've rounded a bend in the road and are concealed from the rest of the security detail by an enormous pile of twisted metal and shattered concrete.

Suddenly the woman releases my arms. She springs forward to the van and produces a set of keys from one of her pockets. She swings open the back doors; the interior of the van is dark, empty, and smells faintly sour.

'In,' she says.

'Where are you taking me?' I'm sick of this helplessness; for days I've been left with a swirling confusion, a sense of secret allegiances and complex plots.

'Somewhere safe,' she says, and even through the mask I can hear the urgency in her voice. I have no choice but to believe her. She helps me into the van and instructs me to turn around while she unlocks my handcuffs. Then she tosses in my backpack and slams the doors shut. My heart flips a little as I hear her slide a lock into place. I'm trapped now. But it can't be worse than what I would have faced outside the van, and my stomach bottoms as I think of Julian. I wonder what will happen to him. Maybe – I feel a brief flicker of hope – they'll go easy on him, because of his dad. Maybe they'll decide it was all just a mistake.

And it was a mistake: the kissing, the way we touched.

Wasn't it?

The van lurches forward, sending me tumbling onto an elbow. The van floor rattles and shakes as we bump along the pitted road. I try to mentally chart our progress: we must be near the dump now, headed past the old train station and toward the tunnel that goes into New York. After ten minutes we roll to a stop. I crawl to the front of the truck bed and press my ear against the pane of glass – painted black, completely opaque – that separates me from the driver's seat. The woman's voice filters back to me. I can make out a second voice, too: a man's voice. She must be talking to Border Control.

The waiting is an agony. They'll be running her SVS card, I think. But the seconds tick away, and stretch into minutes. The woman is silent. Maybe SVS is backed up. Even though it's cold in the cab, my underarms are damp with sweat.

Then the second voice is back, barking a command. The engine cuts off, and the silence is sudden and extreme. The driver's door opens and slams shut. The van sways a little.

Why is she getting out? My mind is racing: if she is a part of the resistance, she may have been caught, recognized. They're sure to find me next. Or – and I'm not sure which is worse – they won't find me. I'll be trapped here; I'll starve to death, or suffocate. Suddenly I'm having trouble breathing. The air is thick and full of pressure. More sweat trickles down my neck and beads on my scalp.

Then the driver's door opens, the engine guns to life, and the van sails forward. I exhale, almost a sob. I can somehow feel it as we enter the Holland Tunnel: the long, dark throat around the van, a watery, echoey place. I imagine the river above us, flecked with grey. I think of Julian's eyes, the way they change like water reflecting different kinds of light.

The van hits a pothole, and my stomach lurches as I rocket into the air and down onto the floor again. Then a climb, and through the metal walls I can hear sporadic sounds of traffic: the distant whirring of a siren, a horn bleating nearby. We must be in New York. I'm expecting the van to stop at any minute – every time we do stop, I half expect the doors to slide open and for the woman in the mask to haul me into the Craps, even though she told me she was on my side – but another twenty minutes passes. I have stopped trying to keep track of where we are. Instead I curl up in a ball on the dirty floor, which vibrates under my cheek. I am still nauseous. The air smells like body odour and old food.

Finally the van slows, and then stops altogether. I sit up, heart pounding in my chest. I hear a brief exchange – the woman says something I can't make out, and somebody else says, 'All clear.' Then there is a tremendous creaking, as of old doors scraping back on their hinges. The van advances forward another ten or twenty feet, then stops again. The engine goes silent. I hear the driver climb out of the van and I tense, gripping my backpack in one hand, preparing to fight or run.

The doors swing open, and as I slide cautiously out of the back, disappointment is a fist in my throat. I was hoping for some clues, some answer to why I've been taken and by whom. Instead I am in a featureless room, all concrete and exposed steel beams. There is an enormous double door, wide enough to accommodate the van, in one wall; in another wall is a second single door, this one made of metal and painted the same dull grey as everything else. At least there are electric lights. That means we are in an approved city, or close to one.

The driver has removed her gas mask but is still wearing a tight-fitting nylon cloth over her head, with cut-away holes for her mouth, nose, and eyes.

'What is this place?' I ask as I straighten up and swing the backpack onto one shoulder. 'Who are you?'

She doesn't answer me. She is watching me intently. Her eyes are grey, a stormy colour. Suddenly she reaches out, as though to touch my face. I jerk backward, bumping against the van. She, too, takes a step backward, balling up her fist.

'Wait here,' she says. She turns to leave through the double doors, the ones that admitted us, but I grab her wrist.

'I want to know what this is about,' I say. I am tired of plain walls and closed rooms and masks and games. I want answers. 'I want to know how you found me, and who sent you to get me.'

'I'm not the one who can give you the answers you need,' she says, and tries to shake me off.

'Take off your mask,' I say. For a second, I think I see a flash of fear in her eyes. Then it passes.

'Let go of me.' Her voice is quiet, but firm.

'Fine,' I say. 'I'll take it off myself.'

I reach for her mask. She swats me away but not quickly enough. I manage to lift a corner of the fabric back, peeling it away from her neck, where a small tattooed number runs vertically from her ear toward her shoulder: 5996. But before I can wrangle the mask any higher, she gets hold of my wrist and pushes me away.

'Please, Lena,' she says, and again I hear the urgency in her voice.

'Stop saying my name.' *You don't have a right to say my name.* Anger surges in my chest, and I swing at her with my backpack, but she ducks. Before I can go at her again, the door opens behind me and I spin around as Raven strides into the room.

'Raven!' I cry out, running to her. I throw my arms around her impulsively. We've never hugged before, but she allows me to squeeze her tightly for several seconds before she pulls away. She's grinning.

'Hey, kid.' She runs a finger lightly along the cut on my neck, and scans my face for other injuries. 'You look like shit.'

Tack is behind her, leaning in the doorway. He's also smiling, and I can barely keep myself from flying at him, too. I settle for reaching forward and squeezing the hand he offers me.

'Welcome back, Lena,' he says. His eyes are warm.

'I don't understand.' I'm overwhelmingly happy; relief makes waves in my chest. 'How did you find me? How did you know where I would be? She wouldn't tell me anything, I—' I turn around, gesturing to the masked woman, but she is gone. She must have ducked out the double doors.

'Easy, easy.' Raven laughs, and slings an arm around my shoulders. 'Let's get you something to eat, okay? You're probably tired, too. Are you tired?' She's piloting me past Tack, through the open door. We must be in some kind of a converted warehouse. I hear other voices, talking and laughing, through the flimsy dividing walls.

'I was kidnapped,' I say, and now the words bubble out of me. I need to tell Tack and Raven; they'll understand, they'll be able to explain and make sense of everything. 'After the demonstration I followed Julian into the old tunnels. And there were Scavengers, and they attacked me – only I think the Scavengers must have been working with the DFA, and—'

Raven and Tack exchange a glance. Tack speaks up soothingly. 'Listen, Lena. We know you've been through a lot. Just relax, okay? You're safe now. Eat up, and rest up.' They've led me into a room dominated by a large metal folding table. On it are foods I haven't had in forever: fresh fruit and vegetables, bread, cheese. It's the most beautiful thing I've ever seen. The air smells like coffee, good and strong.

But I can't sit and eat yet. First, I need to know. And I need them to know – about the Scavengers, and the people who live underground, and the raid this morning, and about Julian.

They can help me rescue Julian: the thought comes to me suddenly, a deliverance. 'But—,' I start to protest. Raven cuts me off, laying a hand on my shoulder.

'Tack's right, Lena. You need to get your strength up. And we'll have plenty of time to talk on the road.'

'On the road?' I repeat, looking from Raven to Tack. They are both smiling at me, still, and it makes a nervous prickling feeling in my chest. It is a form of indulgence, the smile doctors give children when they administer painful shots. *Now I promise, this will only pinch for a second . . .*

'We're heading north,' Raven says in a too-cheerful voice. 'Back to the homestead. Well, not the original homestead – we'll spend the summer outside of Waterbury. Hunter has been in touch. He heard about a big homestead by the perimeter of the city, lots of sympathizers on the other side, and—'

My mind has gone blank. 'We're leaving?' I say dumbly, and Raven and Tack exchange another look. 'We can't leave now.'

'We have no other choice,' Raven says, and I start to feel anger rising in my chest. She's using her singsong voice, like she's speaking to a baby.

'No.' I shake my head, ball my fists against my thighs. 'No. Don't you get it? I think the Scavengers are working with the DFA. I was kidnapped with Julian Fineman. They locked us underground for days.'

'We know,' Tack says, but I barrel on, coasting on the fury now, letting it build.

'We had to fight our way out. They almost – they almost killed me. Julian saved me.' The rock in my stomach is migrating up into my throat. 'And now they've taken Julian, and who knows what they'll do. Probably drag him straight to the labs, or maybe throw him in prison, and—'

'Lena.' Raven puts her hands on my shoulders. 'Calm down.'

But I can't. I'm shaking from panic and rage. Tack and Raven must understand; they need to. 'We have to do something. We have to help him. We have to—'

'Lena.' Raven's voice turns sharper, and she gives me a shake. 'We know about the Scavengers, okay? We know they've been working with the DFA. We know all about Julian, and everything that happened underground. We've been scouting for you around all the tunnel exits. We were hoping you would make it out days ago.'

This, at last, makes me shut up. Raven and Tack have finally stopped smiling. Instead they are looking at me with twin expressions of pity.

'What do you mean?' I pull away from Raven's touch and stumble a bit; when Tack draws a chair out from the table, I thud into it. Neither of them answers right away, so I say, 'I don't understand.'

Tack takes a chair across from me. He examines his hands, then says slowly, 'The resistance has known for a while that the Scavengers were being paid off by the DFA. They were hired to pull off that stunt you saw at the demonstration.'

'That doesn't make any sense.' I feel like my brain is covered in thick paste; my thoughts flounder, come to nothing. I remember the screaming, the shooting, the Scavengers' glittering blades.

'It makes perfect sense.' Raven speaks up. She is still standing, keeping her arms wrapped around her chest. 'Nobody in Zombieland knows the difference between the Scavengers and the rest of us – the other Invalids. We're all the same to them. So the Scavengers come and act like animals, and the DFA shows the whole country how terrible we are without the cure, how important it is to get everyone treated for *deliria* immediately. Otherwise the world goes to hell. The Scavengers are the proof.'

'But—' I think of the Scavengers swarming into the crowd; faces monstrous with screaming. 'But people died.'

'Two hundred,' Tack says quietly. He still won't look at me. 'Two dozen officers. The rest citizens. They didn't bother to tally the Scavengers who were killed.' He shrugs his shoulders, a quick convulsion. 'Sometimes it is necessary that individuals are sacrificed for the health of the whole.' That's straight out of a DFA pamphlet.

'Okay,' I say. My hands are shaking, and I grip the sides of my chair. I'm still having trouble thinking straight. 'Okay. So what are we going to do about it?'

Raven's eyes flick to Tack, but he keeps his head bowed. 'We've already done something about it, Lena,' she says, still in that baby-voice, and once again I get a weird prickling in my chest. There is something they aren't telling me – something bad.

'I don't understand.' My voice sounds hollow.

There are a few seconds of heavy silence. Then Tack sighs, and says over his shoulder to Raven, 'I told you, we should have clued her in from the start. I told you we should have trusted her.'

Raven says nothing. A muscle twitches in her jaw. And suddenly I remember coming downstairs a few weeks before the rally and hearing Tack and Raven fighting.

I just don't understand why we can't be honest with each other. We're supposed to be on the same side.

You know that's unrealistic, Tack. It's for the best. You have to trust me.

You're the one who isn't trusting . . .

They were fighting about me.

'Clued me in to what?' The prickling is becoming a heavy thud, painful and sharp.

'Go ahead,' Raven says to Tack. 'If you want to tell her so badly, be my guest.' Her voice is biting, but I can tell, under-neath that, she's afraid. She's afraid of me and how I will react.

'Tell me what?' I can't stand this anymore – the cryptic glances, the impenetrable web of half-phrases.

Tack passes a hand over his forehead. 'Okay, look,' he says, speaking quickly now, as though eager to end the conversation. 'It wasn't a mistake that you and Julian were taken by the Scavengers, okay? It wasn't an error. It was planned.'

Heat creeps up my neck. I lick my lips. 'Who planned it?' I say, though I know: it must have been the DFA. I answer my own question, saying, 'The DFA,' just as Tack grimaces and says, 'We did.'

Ticking silence. One, two, three, four. I count off the seconds, take a deep breath, close my eyes, and reopen them. 'What?'

Tack actually flushes. 'We did. The resistance planned it.'

More silence. My throat and mouth have gone to dust. 'I— I don't understand.'

Tack is avoiding my eyes again. He walks his fingers across the edge of the table, back and forth, back and forth. 'We paid the Scavengers to take Julian. Well, the resistance did. One of the higher-ups in the movement has been posing as a DFA agent – not that it matters. The Scavengers will do anything for a price, and just because they've been in the DFA's pocket for a while now doesn't mean their loyalties aren't for sale.'

'Julian,' I repeat. Numbness is creeping through my body. 'And what about me?'

Tack hesitates for just a fraction of a second. 'They were paid to hold you, too. They were told that Julian was being tailed by a girl. They were told to hold both of you together.'

'And they thought they'd get a ransom for us,' I say. Tack nods. My voice sounds foreign, as though it's coming from far away. I can hardly breathe. I manage to gasp out, 'Why?'

Raven has been standing still, staring at the ground. Suddenly she bursts out, 'You were never in any danger. Not really. The Scavengers knew they wouldn't get paid if they touched you.'

I think back to the argument I overheard in the tunnels, the wheedling voice urging Albino to stick with the original plan, the way they tried to pump Julian for information about his security codes. The Scavengers were obviously getting impatient. They wanted their payday sooner.

'Never in any danger?' I repeat. Raven won't look at me either. 'I – I almost died.' Anger is spreading hot tentacles through my chest. 'We were starved. We were jumped. Julian was beaten half to death. We had to fight—'

'And you did.' Finally Raven looks at me, and to my horror her eyes are shining; she looks happy. 'You escaped, and you got Julian out safely too.'

For several seconds I can't speak. I am burning, burning, burning, as the true meaning of everything that happened slams into me. 'This . . . this was all a test?'

'No,' Tack says firmly. 'No, Lena. You have to understand. That was part of it, but—'

I push back from the table, turn away from the sound of his voice. I want to curl into a ball. I want to scream, or hit something.

'It was bigger than that, what you did. What you helped us do. And we would have made sure you were safe. We have our own people underground. They'd been told to look out for you.'

The rat-man and Coin. No wonder they helped us. They were paid to.

I can't speak anymore. I am having trouble swallowing. It takes all my energy just to stay on my feet. The containment, the fear, the bodyguards who were killed in the subway – the resistance's fault. Our fault. A test.

Raven speaks up again, her voice filled with quiet urgency: a salesman trying to convince you to buy, buy, buy. 'You did a great thing for us, Lena. You've helped the resistance in more ways than you know.'

'I did nothing,' I spit out.

'You did everything. Julian was tremendously important to the DFA. A symbol of everything the DFA stands for. Head of the youth group. That's six hundred thousand people alone, young people, uncured. Unconvinced.'

My blood goes all at once to ice. I turn around slowly. Tack and Raven are both looking at me hopefully, as though they expect me to be pleased. 'What does Julian have to do with this?' I say.

Once again Raven and Tack exchange a glance. This time I can read what they are thinking: I am being difficult, obtuse. I should understand this by now.

'Julian has everything to do with it, Lena,' Raven says. She sits down at the table, next to Tack. They are the patient parents; I am the troublemaking teen. We could be discussing a flunked test. 'If Julian's out of the DFA, if he's cast out—'

'Even better, if he chooses out,' Tack interjects, and Raven spreads her hands as if to say, *Obviously*.

She continues, 'If he's cast out or he wants out, either way, it sends a powerful message to all the uncureds who have followed him and seen him as a leader. They might rethink their loyalties – some of them will, at least. We have a chance to bring them over to our side. Think about that, Lena. That's enough to make a real difference. That's enough to turn the tide in our favour.'

My mind is moving slowly, as though it has been encased in ice. This morning's raids – planned. I thought it was a setup, and I was right. The resistance was behind it: they must have tipped off the police and the regulators. they gave up the location of one of their own homesteads just to ensnare Julian.

And I helped ensnare him. I think of his father's face, floating in the window of the black town car: tight, grim, determined. I think of the story Julian told me about his older brother – how his father locked him in a basement, injured, to die alone and in the dark. And that was just for participating in a demonstration.

Julian was in bed with me. Who knows what they'll do to him as punishment.

Blackness surges inside of me. I close my eyes and see Alex and Julian's faces, merging together and then separating, like they did in my dream. It's happening again. It's happening again, and again it's my fault.

'Lena?' I hear a chair scrape away from the table and suddenly Raven is next to me, slipping an arm around my shoulders. 'Are you okay?'

'Can we get you something?' Tack asks.

I shake out of Raven's grasp. 'Get off of me.'

'Lena,' Raven croons. 'Come on. Have a seat.' She is reaching for me again.

'I said, get off of me.' I pull away from her, stumble backward, bump against a chair.

'I'm going to get some water,' Tack says. He pushes away from the table and heads into a hall that must lead to the rest of the warehouse. For a moment I hear a surge in conversation, raucous, welcoming; then silence.

My hands are shaking so badly I can't even squeeze them into fists. Otherwise I might hit Raven in the face.

She sighs. 'I understand why you're mad. Maybe Tack was right. Maybe we should have told you the plan from the beginning.' She sounds tired.

'You – you used me,' I spit out.

'You said you wanted to help,' Raven says simply.

'No. Not like that.'

'You don't get to choose.' Raven takes a seat again and lays her hands flat on the table. 'That isn't how it works.'

I can feel her willing me to yield, to sit, to understand. But I can't, and I won't.

'What about Julian?' I force myself to meet her eyes, and I think I see her flinch just slightly.

'He's not your problem.' Raven's voice turns slightly harder.

'Yeah?' I think of Julian's fingers running through my hair, the encircling warmth of his arms, how he whispered, *I want to know. I want to know with you.* 'What if I want to make him my problem?'

Raven and I stare at each other. Her patience is running out. Her mouth is set in a line, angry and tight. 'There's nothing you can do,' she says shortly. 'Don't you get it? Lena Morgan Jones doesn't exist anymore. Poof – she's gone. There's no way back in for her. There's no way in for you. Your job is done.'

'So we leave Julian to be killed? Or thrown in prison?'

Once again Raven sighs, as though I'm a spoiled child throwing a tantrum. 'Julian Fineman is the head of the youth division of the DFA—,' she begins again.

'I know all that,' I snap. 'You made me memorize it, remember? So, what? He gets sacrificed for the cause?'

Raven looks at me in silence: an assent.

'You're just as bad as they are,' I squeeze out, through the tightness of the fury in my throat, the heavy stone of disgust. That is the DFA's motto too: Some will die for the health of the whole. We have become like them.

Raven stands again and moves toward the hallway. 'You can't feel guilty, Lena,' she says. 'This is war, you know.'

'Don't you get it?' I fire back at her the very words she used on me a long time ago, back at the burrow, after Miyako died. 'You can't tell me what to feel.'

Raven shakes her head. I see a flash of pity on her face. 'You – you really liked him, then? Julian?'

I can't answer. I can only nod.

Raven rubs her forehead tiredly and sighs again. For a moment I think she is going to relent. She'll agree to help me. I feel a surge of hope.

But when she looks at me again, her face is composed, emotionless. 'We leave tomorrow to go north,' she says simply, and just like that the conversation is ended. Julian will go to the gallows for us, and we will smile, and dream of victory – hazy-red, soon to come, a blood-coloured dawn.

The rest of the day is a fog. I drift from room to room. Faces turn to me, expectant, smiling, and turn away again when I do not acknowledge them. These must be other members of the resistance. I recognize only one of them, a guy Tack's age who came once to Salvage to bring us our new identity cards. I look for the woman who brought me here but see no one who resembles her, hear no one who speaks the way she did.

I drift and I listen. I gather we are twenty miles north of New York, and just south of a city named White Plains. We must be skimming our electricity from them: we have lights, a radio, even an electric coffeemaker. One of the rooms is piled with tents and rolled-up sleeping bags. Tack and Raven have prepared us for the move. I have no idea how many of the other resisters will be joining us; presumably, at least some of them will stay. Other than the folding table and chairs, and a room full of sleeping cots, there is no furniture. The radio and the coffeemaker sit directly on the cement floor, nested in a tangle of wires. The radio stays on for most of the day, piping thinly through the walls, and no matter where I go, I can't escape it.

'Julian Fineman . . . head of the youth division of Deliria-Free America and son of the group's president . . .'

'. . . himself a victim of the disease . . .'

Every radio station is the same. They all tell an identical story.

'. . . discovered today . . .'

'. . . currently under house arrest . . .'

'Julian . . . resigned his position and has refused the cure . . .'

A year ago, the story would not have been reported at all. It would have been suppressed, the way the very existence of Julian's brother was no doubt slowly and systematically expunged from public records after his death. But things have changed since the Incidents. Raven is right about one thing: it is war now, and armies need symbols.

'. . . emergency convention of the Regulatory Committee of New York . . . swift judgment . . . scheduled for execution by lethal injection at ten a.m. tomorrow . . .'

'. . . some are calling the measures unnecessarily harsh . . . public outcry against the DFA and the RCNY . . .'

I sink into a dullness, a place of suspension: I can no longer feel anything. The anger has ebbed away, and so has the guilt.

I am completely numb. Julian will die tomorrow. I helped him die.

This was the plan all along. It is no comfort to think that had he been cured, he would have in all probability died as well. My body is chilled, frozen to ice. At some point someone must have handed me a sweatshirt, because I am wearing one. But still I can't get warm.

'. . . *Thomas Fineman's official statement . . .*

'*The DFA stands behind the Regulatory Committee's decision . . . They say: "The United States is at a critical juncture, and we can no longer tolerate those who want to do us harm . . . we must set a precedent . . ."*'

The DFA and the United States of America can no longer afford to be lenient. The resistance is too strong. It is growing – underground, in tunnels and burrows, in the dark, damp places they cannot reach.

So they will make a bloody example for us in public, in the light.

At dinner, I manage to eat something, and even though I still can't bring myself to look at Raven and Tack, I can tell they take this as a sign that I have relented. They are forced-cheerful, too loud, telling jokes and stories to the four or five other resisters who have assembled around the table. Still, the radio-voice infiltrates, seeps through the walls, like the sibilant hiss of a snake.

'. . . *No other statement from either Julian or Thomas Fineman . . .*'

After dinner, I go to the outhouse: a tiny shed fifty feet from the main building, across a short expanse of cracked pavement. It is the first time I've been outside all day, and the first chance I've had to look around. We are in some kind of old warehouse. It sits at the end of a long, winding concrete drive surrounded by woods on both sides. To the north I can make out the twinkling glow of city lights: this must be White Plains. And to the south, against the blush-pink evening sky, I can just detect a hazy, halo glow, the artificial crown of lights that indicates New York City. It must be around seven o'clock, still too early for curfew or mandatory blackout. Julian is somewhere among those lights, in that blur of people and buildings. I wonder whether he's scared. I wonder whether he's thinking of me.

The wind is cold but carries with it the smell of thawing earth and new growth: a spring smell. I think of our apartment in Brooklyn – packed up now, or perhaps ransacked by regulators and police. Lena Morgan Jones is dead, like Raven said, and now there will be a new Lena, just like every spring the trees bring forth new growth on top of the old, on top of the dead and the rot. I wonder who she will be.

I feel a sharp stab of sadness. I have had to give up so much, so many selves and lives already. I have grown up and out of the rubble of my old lives, of the things and people I have cared for: My mom. Grace. Hana. Alex.

And now Julian.

This is not who I wanted to be.

An owl hoots somewhere, sharply, in the gathering darkness, like a faint alarm. That's when it really hits me, the certainty like a concrete wall going up inside of me. This is not what I wanted. This is not why I came to the Wilds, why Alex wanted me to come: not to turn my back and bury the people I care about, and build myself hard and careless on top of their bodies, as Raven does. That is what the Zombies do.

But not me. I have let too many things decay. I have given up on enough.

The owl hoots again, and now its cry sounds sharper, clearer. Everything seems clearer: the creaking of the dry trees; the smells in the air, layered and deep; a distant rumbling, which swells on the air, then fades again.

Truck. I've been listening without thinking, but now the word, the idea, clarifies: we can't be far from a highway. We must have driven from New York City, which means there must be a way back in.

I don't need Raven, and I don't need Tack. And even if Raven was right about Lena Morgan Jones – she doesn't exist anymore, after all – fortunately, I don't need her, either.

I go back into the warehouse. Raven is sitting at the folding table, packing food into cloth bundles. We will strap them to our packs, and hang them from tree branches when we camp at night, so the animals won't get at them.

At least, that is what she will do.

'Hey.' She smiles at me, over-friendly, as she has been all evening. 'Did you get enough to eat?'

I nod. 'More than I've had in a while,' I say, and she winces slightly. It's a dig, but I can't help it. I lean up against the table, where small, sharp knives have been laid out to dry on a kitchen towel.

Raven draws one knee to her chest. 'Listen, Lena. I'm sorry we didn't tell you earlier. I thought it would be – well, I just thought it would be better this way.'

'It was a purer test, too,' I say, and Raven looks up quickly. I lean forward, place my palm over the handle of a knife, feel its contours pressing into my flesh.

Raven sighs, and looks away again. 'I know you must hate us right now,' she starts to say, but I cut her off.

'I don't hate you.' I straighten up again, bringing the knife with me, slipping it into my back pocket.

'Really?' For a moment Raven looks much younger than her age.

'Really,' I say, and she smiles at me – small, tight, relieved. It's an honest smile. I add, 'But I don't want to be like you either.'

Her smile falters. As I'm standing there, looking at her, it occurs to me that this may be the last time I ever see her. A sharp pain runs through me, a blade in the centre of my chest. I am not sure that I ever loved Raven, but she gave birth to me here, in the Wilds. She has been a mother and a sister, both. She is yet another person I will have to bury.

'Someday you'll understand,' she says, and I know that she really believes it. She is staring at me wide-eyed, willing me to understand: that people should be sacrificed to causes, that beauty can be built on the backs of the dead.

But it isn't her fault. Not really. Raven has lost deeply, again and again, and she, too, has buried herself. There are pieces of her scattered all over. Her heart is nestled next to a small set of bones buried beside a frozen river, which will emerge with the spring thaw, a skeleton ship rising out of the water.

'I hope not,' I say, as gently as I can, and that is how I say good-bye to her.

I tuck the knife into my backpack, feeling to make sure I still have the small bundle of ID cards I stole from the Scavengers. They will come in handy. I take a wind breaker from next to one of the cots, and, from a small nylon backpack, already packed up for tomorrow, I steal granola bars and a half-dozen bottles of water. My backpack is heavy, even after I've removed

The Book of Shhh – I won't need that anymore, not ever – but I don't dare take out any supplies. If I do manage to spring Julian, we will need to run fast and far, and I have no idea how long it will be before we stumble on a homestead.

I move quietly back through the warehouse, toward the side door that opens onto the parking lot and the outhouse. I pass only one person – a tall, lanky guy with fire-red hair who looks me over once and then lets his gaze slide off me. That is one skill I learned in Portland that I have never forgotten: how to shrink into myself, and turn invisible. I scoot quickly past the room in which most of the resisters, including Tack, are lounging around the radio, laughing and talking. Someone is smoking a hand-rolled cigarette. Someone is shuffling a deck of cards. I see the back of Tack's head and think a good-bye in his direction.

Then I'm once again slipping out into the night, and I am free.

New York is still casting its halo glow into the sky south of us – probably a good hour from curfew, and blackout for most of the city. Only the very richest people, the government officials and scientists and people like Thomas Fineman, have unlimited access to light.

I start jogging in the general direction of the highway, pausing every so often to listen for the sound of trucks. Mostly there is silence, punctuated by hooting owls and small animals scurrying in the darkness. Traffic is sporadic. It is no doubt a road used almost exclusively for supply trucks.

But all of a sudden it is there, a long, thick river of concrete, lit silver by the rising moon. I turn south and slow to a walk, my breath steaming in front of me. The air is fresh, thin, and cold, slicing my lungs every time I take a breath. But it's a good feeling.

I keep the highway on my right, careful not to venture too close. There may be checkpoints along the way, and the last thing I need is to be caught by a patrol.

It is roughly twenty miles to the northern boundary of Manhattan. It's hard to keep track of time, but I think it has been at least six hours before I see, in the distance, the high concrete wall that marks the city's border. The going was slow. I have no flashlight, and the moon was often lost beyond the thick tangle of tree branches above me, all interlocked, skeletal fingers clasped together tightly. At times I was practically feeling my way. Thankfully the highway to my right reflected some light, and served to orient me. Otherwise I'm sure I would have gotten lost.

Portland was enclosed entirely in a cheap chain-link fence, rumoured to be electrified. In New York, portions of the boundary are built of concrete and loops of barbed wire, with high watchtowers interspersed at intervals along the wall, beaming floodlights into the dark, lighting up the silhouettes of the trees on the other side, in the Wilds. I am still several hundred feet from the border – its lights are just visible, winking through the trees – but I drop into a crouch and move toward the highway slowly, listening for any sounds of movement. I doubt that there are patrols on this side of the border. But then again, things are changing now.

You can never be too careful.

There's a long, shallow gully fifteen feet from the highway, coated in a thin covering of rotting leaves, and still patchy with puddles from rain and melting snow. I manoeuvre down into the gully and press myself flat on my stomach. This should make me pretty much invisible from the highway, even if someone is patrolling. Dampness seeps through my sweatpants, and I realize I'll need to find a place to change and something to change into when I make it into Manhattan. There's no way I can walk the city streets like this without arousing suspicion. But I'll have to deal with that later.

It's a long time before I hear the rumble of a truck engine in the distance. Then headlights bloom from the dark, lighting up swirling mist. The truck rattles by me – enormous, white, and stamped with the logo of a grocery chain – slowing as it approaches the border. I prop myself onto my elbows. There is a gap in the border wall, through which the highway extends like a silver tongue; it is barred by a heavy iron gate. As the truck comes to a stop, two dark figures emerge from a guardhouse. Backlit by the floodlights, they are nothing but etched shadows and the black shape of rifles. I'm too far away to make out what they are saying, but I imagine they are checking the driver's papers. One of the guards circles the truck, inspecting it. He does not open the truck bed, though, and check the interior. Sloppy. Sloppiness is good.

Over the next few hours, I watch an additional five trucks pass. In each case, the ritual is repeated, although one truck, marked EXXON, is opened and thoroughly searched. As I wait, I plan. I move closer to the border, keeping low to the ground, moving only when the highway is empty and the moon has skated behind one of the heavy, massed clouds in the sky. When I am no farther than forty feet from the wall, I once again hunker down to wait. I am so close, I can make out individual features of the guards – both men – as they emerge periodically from the guard hut to circle the approaching trucks. I can hear snatches of conversation, too: they ask for ID, they verify license and registration. The ritual lasts no longer than three or four minutes. I will have to act quickly.

I should have worn something warmer than a wind breaker. At least the cold keeps me awake.

By the time I see an opportunity to move, the sun is already rising behind a thin covering of fleecy dark clouds. The flood-lights are still illumined, but their power is diminished in the murky dawn, and they're not nearly so blinding.

A garbage truck, with a ladder that extends up one of its sides and onto its metal roof, shudders to a halt in front of the metal gate. I move into a crouch and wrap my fingers around the rock I selected earlier from the ditch. I have to flex my fingers a few times just to get the blood flowing. My limbs are stiff, and aching with cold.

One guard circles the vehicle, completing his inspection, cradling his rifle. The other stands at the driver's window, blowing air onto his hands, asking the usual questions. *Where are you coming from? Where are you headed?*

I stand up, cupping the rock in my right hand, and thread quickly through the trees, careful to step only where the leaves have been trampled to wet mulch – a good muffler for my footsteps. My heart is drumming so hard in my throat I can hardly breathe. The guards are twenty feet to my right, maybe less. I have only one chance.

When I'm close enough to the wall to be sure of my aim, I wind up and rocket the stone toward one of the floodlights. There's a miniature explosion when it hits, and the sound of falling glass. Instantly I'm retracing my steps, circling backward as both guards whip around.

'What the hell?' one of them says, and starts jogging toward the damaged floodlight, shouldering his rifle. I'm praying that the second guard follows. He hesitates, shifting his gun from his left hand to his right. He spits.

Go, go, go.

'Wait here,' he says to the driver, and then he, too, moves away from the garbage truck.

This is it: this is my chance, while the guards are distracted, examining the shattered light forty feet down the wall. I have to approach the truck at an angle, from the passenger's side. I double over and try to make myself as small as I can. I can't risk letting the driver get a look at me in his side mirror. For twenty terrifying seconds I'm on the road, totally exposed, free of the trees and gnarled brown bushes that have been serving as cover, and just then I have a memory of the first time Alex took me to the Wilds – how scared I was sneaking over the fence, how exposed I felt – raw and terrified, as though I'd been cut open.

Ten feet, five feet, two feet. And then I'm swinging myself up onto the ladder, the metal freezing, biting my fingers. When I get up to the roof I press myself perfectly flat, belly-down on a coating of bird shit and rust. Even the metal smells sick and sweet, like rotten garbage, a smell that must have seeped over the years into the truck frame. I turn my face toward the cuff of my wind breaker to keep from coughing. The roof is slightly concave, and ringed by a two-inch metal rail, which means at least I won't be in danger of slipping off when the truck begins to move. I hope.

'Hey!' the driver is calling out to the guards. 'Can you let me through or what? I'm on a schedule.'

There's no immediate response. It feels like an eternity before I hear footsteps returning to the truck, and one of the guards says, 'All right, go ahead.'

The iron gate clanks open, and the truck begins to move. I slide backward as the truck picks up speed, but manage to wedge my hands and feet against the metal railing; I must look like a giant starfish from above, suctioned to the roof. The wind whips by me, stinging my eyes: a biting cold that carries with it the smells of the Hudson River, which I know must be close. On our left, just off the highway, is the city: billboards and dismantled streetlights and ugly apartment buildings with purple-grey faces, bruised complexions turned toward the horizon.

The truck rattles down the highway, and I strain just to hang on, to keep myself from getting bounced off and onto the road. The cold is an agony now, a thousand needles on my face and my hands, and I have to squeeze my eyes shut because they're watering so badly. The day comes dark and slow. The red glow at the horizon quickly smoulders and burns out, getting sucked up behind the woollen clouds. It begins to drizzle. Each drop of rain is a tiny shard of glass on my skin, and the roof of the truck becomes slick and difficult to hold on to.

Soon, thankfully, we are slowing and bumping off the highway. It is still very early, and the streets are mostly silent. Above me, apartment buildings loom, enormous fingers pointing toward the sky. Now I can smell food scents carried out onto the street through open windows: gasoline and wood smoke; the closeness of millions and millions of people.

This is my stop.

As soon as the truck slows at a light, I retreat down the ladder – scanning the street to make sure no one is watching – and jump lightly onto the pavement. The garbage truck continues its lumbering journey as I try to stamp some feeling into my toes and blow hot air onto my fingers. Seventy-second Street. Julian lives on Charles Street, he told me, which is all the way downtown. Judging from the quality of the light, it must be a little before seven – maybe a little later, since the thick cloud cover makes it hard to tell time accurately. I can't risk being seen on a bus looking the way I look – water-spotted, covered with mud.

I double back toward the West Side Highway, and the footpath that cuts north to south through the long, well-tended park that runs parallel to the Hudson. It will be easier to avoid people here. No one will be strolling on a rainy day this early in the morning. At this point exhaustion is burning the back of my eyes, and my feet feel leaden.

But every step brings me closer to Julian, and to the girl I pledged to become.

I've seen pictures of the Finemans' house on the news, and once I reach the tangle of narrow streets in the West Village – so different from the ordered grid that defines the rest of Manhattan, and in some ways a surprising choice for Thomas Fineman – it does not take me long to find it. The rain is still coming down, moisture squelching in my sneakers. The Finemans' townhouse is impossible to mistake: it is the largest house on the block, and the only one that is encircled by a high stone wall. An iron gate, hung with brown nests of ivy, gives a partial view of the front path and a tiny brown yard, churned mostly to mud. I walk the street once, checking the house for signs of activity, but all the windows are dark, and if there are guards watching Julian, they must be inside. I get a surge of pleasure from the graffiti someone has scrawled on the Finemans' stone wall: MURDERER. Raven was right: every day, the resistance is growing.

One more turn around the block, and this time I'm scanning the whole street, keeping my eyes up, looking for witnesses, nosy neighbours, problems, escape routes. Even though I'm soaked through, I'm grateful for the rain. It will make things easier. At least it keeps people off the streets.

I step up to the Finemans' iron gate, trying to ignore the anxiety buzzing through me. There's an electronic keypad, just like Julian said: a tiny LCD screen requests that I type in a PIN. For a moment, despite the rain and the desperate scrabbling of my heart in my chest, I can't help but stand there, amazed by the elegance of it: a world of beautiful, buzzing things, humming electricity, and remote controls, while half the country flounders in dark and closeness, heat and cold, sucking up shreds of power like dogs picking gristle from a bone.

For the first time it occurs to me that this, really, might have been the point of the walls and borders, the procedure and the lies: a fist squeezing tighter and tighter. It is a beautiful world for the people who get to play the fist.

I let hatred tighten inside of me. This, too, will help.

Julian said that his family kept clues embedded in or around the gate – reminders of the code.

It doesn't take me long to figure out the first three numbers. At the top of the gate, someone has tacked a small metal plate engraved with a quotation from *The Book of Shhh*: HAPPY ARE THEY WHO HAVE A PLACE; WISE ARE THEY WHO FOLLOW THE PATH; BLESSED ARE THEY WHO OBEY THE WORD.

It's a famous proverb – one that comes, incidentally, from the Book of Magdalena, a passage of the Book I know well. Magdalena is my namesake. I used to scour those pages, looking for traces of my mother, for her reasons and her message to me.

Book 9, Proverb 17. I type 917 into the keypad: if I'm right, I have only one number to go. I'm about to try final digits at random, when something within the yard flutters, catches my eye. Four white paper lanterns, stamped with the DFA logo, have been strung up above the porch. They are flapping in the wind, and one has been stripped almost loose of the string; it dangles awkwardly, like a semi-severed head, tapping a rhythm against the front door. Except for the DFA logo, the lanterns look like decorations you might find at a child's birthday party. They look strangely incongruous above the massive stone porch, swaying high above the bleak yard.

A sign. Has to be.

9174. The gate clicks as the locks retract, and I'm in.

I slip into the front yard quickly, closing the gate behind me, taking in as much as I can. Five floors, including a sunken basement level; curtains all drawn, everything dark. I don't even bother with the front door. It will be locked, and if there are guards anywhere, they are no doubt waiting in the hall. Instead I slip around the side of the house and find the concrete stairs that lead to a warped wooden door: the basement entrance. A small window set in the brick should allow me to see inside, but a set of heavy wooden window slats obscures the view completely. I will have to go in blind, and pray that there are no guards at this entrance.

This door is also locked, but the doorknob is old and loose, and should be relatively easy to pick. I drop to my knees and take out my knife. Tack showed me how to pick locks once with the narrow tip of a razor, not knowing that Hana and I had perfected the skill years ago. Her parents used to keep all the cookies and sweets locked in a pantry. I wedge the knife tip in the narrow space between the door and its frame. It takes just a few moments of twisting and jiggling before I feel the lock release. I tuck the knife into the pocket of my wind breaker – I'll need it close now – take a breath, and push through the door and into the house.

It is very dark. The first thing I notice is the smell: a laundry smell, of lemon-scented towels and dryer sheets. The second thing I notice is the quiet. I lean against the door, letting my eyes adjust to the dark. Shapes begin to assert themselves: a washer and dryer in the corner, a room criss-crossed with laundry lines.

I wonder whether it was here that Julian's brother was kept; whether he died here, alone, curled on the cement floor, under dripping sheets with the smell of moisture clotting his nostrils. I push the image quickly from my mind. Anger is useful only to a certain point. After that, it becomes rage, and rage will make you careless.

I exhale a little bit. There is no one with me down here – I can feel it.

I move through the laundry room, ducking under several pairs of men's briefs, which are clipped to a line. The thought flashes through my mind that one of them might be Julian's.

Stupid how the mind will try to distract itself.

Beyond the laundry room is a small pantry stacked with household cleaning supplies, and beyond that, a set of narrow wooden stairs that leads to the first floor. I ease my way onto the stairs, moving at a crawl. The stairs are warped and look like they will be loud.

At the top is a door. I pause, listening. The house is silent, and a feeling of creeping anxiety starts snaking over my skin. This is not right. It's too easy. There should be guards, and regulators. There should be footsteps, muffled conversation – something other than this deadweight silence, hanging heavy like a thick blanket.

The moment I ease open the door and step out into the hallway, the realization hits me: everyone has gone already. I'm too late. They must have moved Julian early this morning, and now the house is empty.

Still, I feel compelled to check every room. A panicked feeling is building inside of me – I'm too late, he's gone, it's over – and the only thing I can do to suppress it is to keep moving, keep slipping soundlessly across the carpeted floors and searching every closet, as though Julian might appear within one.

I check the living room, which smells of furniture polish. The heavy curtains are pulled shut, keeping out a view of the street. There is a pristine kitchen and a formal dining room that looks unused; a bathroom, which smells cloyingly of lavender; a small den dominated by the largest television screen I have ever seen in my life. There is a study, stacked with DFA pamphlets and other pro-cure propaganda. Farther down the hall, I come across a locked door. I remember what Julian told me about Mr. Fineman's second study. This must be the room of forbidden books.

Upstairs, there are three bedrooms. The first one is unused, sterile, and filled with the smell of must. I feel, instinctively, that this was Julian's brother's room, and that it has remained shut up since his death.

I inhale sharply when I reach Julian's room. I know it is his. It smells like him. Even though he was a prisoner here, there are no signs of struggle. Even the bed is made, the soft-looking blue covers pulled haphazardly over green-and-white-striped sheets.

For a second I have the urge to climb into his bed and cry, to wrap his blankets around me the way I let him wrap his arms around my waist at Salvage. His closet door is open a crack; I see shelves filled with faded denim jeans, and swinging button-down shirts. The normalcy of it almost kills me. Even in a world turned upside down, a world of war and insanity, people hang their clothing; they fold their pants; they make their beds.

It is the only way.

The next room is much larger, dominated by two double beds, separated by several feet of space: the master bedroom. I catch a glimpse of myself in a large mirror hanging over the bed and recoil. I haven't seen my reflection in days. My face is pale, my skin stretched tight over my cheekbones. My chin is smeared with dirt, and my clothing is covered with it too. My hair is frizzing from the rain. I look like I belong in a mental institution.

I rummage through Mrs. Fineman's clothing and find a soft cashmere sweater and a pair of clean, black denim jeans. They're too big around the waist, but once I belt the pants I look almost normal. I remove my knife from my backpack and wrap the blade in a T-shirt so I can safely carry it in the pocket of my wind breaker. I ball up the rest of my clothes and stuff them into the very back of the closet, behind the shoe rack. I check the clock on the bedside table. Eight thirty a.m.

On my way downstairs, I spot a bookshelf in a hallway alcove, and the small statue of a rooster perched on the highest shelf. I can't explain what overcomes me, or why it matters, but all of a sudden I need to know whether Thomas Fineman has been keeping the key to the second study there all these years. He's the kind of man who would do that, even after the hiding place had been discovered by his son. He would trust that the beating had served as a sufficient deterrent. He would do it as a test and a tease, so that every time Julian saw the stupid thing, he would remember, and regret.

The bookshelf isn't particularly big, and the last shelf isn't very high – I'm sure Julian could easily reach it now – but I have to stand on a footstool to get at the rooster. As soon as I pull the porcelain animal toward me, something rattles in its belly. The head of the rooster unscrews, and I tip a metal key into my palm.

Just then I hear the muffled sound of footsteps, and someone saying, 'Yes, yes, exactly.' My heart stops: Thomas Fineman's voice. At the far end of the hallway, I see the handle on the front door begin to rattle as he works a key in the lock.

Instinctively, I jump off the footstool, still clutching the key in my palm, and whirl around to the locked door. It takes me a few seconds of fumbling before I can make the key fit, and in that time I hear the front door locks slide open, two of them, and I am frozen in the hallway, terrified, as the door opens a crack.

Then Fineman says, 'Damn it.' Pause. 'No, Mitch, not you. I dropped something.'

He must be on the phone. In the time it takes him to pause and scoop up whatever he has dropped, I manage to get the key in the lock, and I slip quickly into the forbidden study, closing the door a split second before the front door closes as well, a double-heartbeat rhythm.

Then the footsteps are coming down the hall. I back away from the door, as though Fineman will be able to smell me. The room is very dim – the heavy velvet curtains at the window are imperfectly closed, allowing a bare ribbon of grey light to penetrate. Towers of books and artwork spiral toward the ceiling like twisted totems. I bump into a table and have to spin around, catching a heavy, leather-bound volume at the last second, before it thuds to the floor.

Fineman pauses outside the study door, and I could faint. My hands are shaking.

I do not remember whether I put the head back on the rooster.

Please, please, please, keep moving.

'Uh-huh,' he is saying into the phone. His voice is flinty, clipped: not at all the upbeat drawl he uses when he speaks on radio interviews and at DFA meetings. 'Yes, exactly. Ten a.m. It's been decided.'

Another pause, and then he says, 'Well, there really is no choice, is there? How would it look if I tried to appeal?'

His footsteps retreat up the stairs and I exhale a little, although I'm still too afraid to move. I'm terrified I'll bump into something again and disrupt one of the piles of books. Instead I wait, frozen, until Fineman's footsteps once again pound down the stairs.

'I got it,' he is saying, as his voice grows fainter: he is leaving. 'Eighteenth and Sixth. Northeastern Medical.'

Then, faintly, I hear the front door open and shut, and I am once again left in silence.

I wait another few minutes before moving, just to be absolutely sure that I'm alone, that Fineman won't be coming back. My palms are so sweaty I can barely return the book to its place. It is an oversized volume, stamped with gold lettering, perched on a table next to a dozen identical books. I think it must be a kind of encyclopedia until I see the words EASTERN SEABOARD, NEW YORK – TERRORISTS, ANARCHISTS, DISSENTERS etched on one of the spines.

I feel, suddenly, as though I've been punched in the stomach.

I squat down, peering at the spines more closely. They are not books, but records: an enumerated list of all the most dangerous incarcerated criminals in the United States, divided by area and prison system.

I should leave. Time is running out, and I need to find Julian, even if I'm too late to help him. But the compulsion is there, equally strong, to find her – to see her name. It's a compulsion to see whether she has made it onto the list, even though I know she must have. My mother was kept for twelve years inside Ward Six, a place of solitary confinement reserved exclusively for the most dangerous resisters and political agitators.

I don't know why I care. My mother escaped. She scratched through the walls, over years, over a decade – she tunneled out like an animal. And now she is free somewhere. I have seen her in my dreams, running through a portion of the Wilds that is always sunny and green, where food is always abundant.

Still, I have to see her name.

It doesn't take me long to find *Eastern Seaboard, Maine–Connecticut*. The list of political prisoners who have been incarcerated in the Crypts in the past twenty years spans fifty pages. The names are not listed alphabetically, but by date. The pages are handwritten, in chicken scrawls of varying legibility; this book has obviously passed through many hands. I have to move closer to the window, to the thin fissure of light, to read. My hands are shaking, and I steady the book on the corner of a desk – which is, itself, almost completely concealed with other books, forbidden titles from the days before the cure. I'm too focused on the list of names – each one a person, each one a life, sucked away by stone walls – to care or look closer. It gives me only marginal comfort to know that some of these people must have escaped after the bombing of the Crypts.

I easily find the year my mother was taken – the year I turned six, when she was supposed to have died. It is a section of five or six pages, and probably two hundred names.

I track my finger down the page, feeling dizzy for no reason. I know she will be in the book. And I know, now, that she is safe. But still, I must see it; there is a piece of her that exists in the faded ink traces of her name. Her life was taken by those pen-strokes – and my life was taken too.

Then I see it. My breath catches in my throat. Her name is written neatly, in large, elegant cursive, as though whoever was in possession of the log at the time enjoyed the looping curls of all the *l*'s and *a*'s: *Annabel Gilles Haloway. The Crypts. Ward Six, Solitary Confinement. Level 8 Agitator.*

Next to these words is the prisoner's intake number. It is printed carefully, neatly: 5996.

My vision tunnels, and in that moment the number seems lit up by an enormous beam. Everything else is blackness, fog.

5996. The faded green number tattooed on the woman who rescued me from Salvage, the woman with the mask.

My mother.

Now my impressions of her are shuffling back, but disjointed, like pieces of a puzzle that don't quite interconnect: her voice, low and desperate and something else. Pleading, maybe? Sad? The way she reached out, as though to touch my face, before I swatted her away. The way she kept using my name. Her height – I remember her being so tall, but she is short, like me, probably no more than five-four. The last time I saw her, I was six years old. Of course she seemed tall to me then.

Two words are blazing through me, each one a hot hand, wrenching my insides: *impossible* and *mother*.

Guilt and twisting disbelief: shredding me, turning my stomach loose. I didn't recognize her. I always thought that I would. I imagined she would be just like the mother in my memories, in my dreams – hazy, red-haired, laughing. I imagined she would smell like soap and lemons, that her hands would be soft, smoothed with lotion.

Now, of course, I realize how stupid that is. She spent more than a decade in the Crypts, in a cell. She has changed, hardened.

I slam the book closed, quickly, as though it might help – as though her name is a scurrying insect between the pages, and I can stamp it back into the past. *Mother. Impossible.* After all that, my hoping and wishing and searching, we were so close. We were touching.

And still she chose not to reveal herself. Still, she chose to walk away.

I am going to be sick. I stumble blindly down the hall, out into the drizzle. I am not thinking, can hardly breathe. It is not until I've made it to Sixth Avenue, several blocks away, that the cold begins to clear the fog from my mind. At that point I realize I'm still clutching the key to the forbidden study in one hand. I forgot to lock it again. I'm not even sure I closed the front door behind me – for all I know I have left it swinging open.

It doesn't matter now. Nothing matters. I am too late to help Julian. I am too late to do anything but watch him die.

My feet carry me toward 18th Street, where Thomas Fineman will be attending his son's execution. As I walk, head down, I grip the handle of the knife in my wind breaker pocket.

Perhaps it is not too late for revenge.

*   *   *

Northeastern Medical is one of the nicer lab complexes I've seen, with a stone facade and scrolled balconies, and only a discreet brass sign above the heavy wooden door indicating that it is a medical facility. It was probably once a bank or a post office, from the days when spending wasn't regulated; from the days when people communicated freely across unbounded cities. It has that look of stateliness and importance. But of course Julian Fineman would not be put to death among commoners, in one of the city wards or hospital wings of the Craps. Only the best for the Finemans, until the very end.

The drizzle is finally letting up, and I pause on the corner, ducking into the alcoved doorway of a neighbouring building, and shuffle quickly through the stack of ID cards I stole from the Scavengers. I select Sarah Beth Miller, a girl who resembles me pretty closely in age and looks, and use my knife to put a deep gouge in her height – five-eight – so you can't read it clearly. Then I whittle away at the identification number below her picture. I have no doubt that the number has been invalidated. In all probability, Sarah Beth Miller is dead.

I smooth down my hair, praying that I look at least halfway decent, and push through the front door of the lab.

Inside is a waiting room decorated tastefully, with a plush green carpet and mahogany furniture. An enormous clock, ostentatiously antique or made to look like it, ticks quietly on the wall, pendulum swinging rhythmically. A nurse is sitting at a large desk. Behind her is a small office: a series of metal filing cabinets, a second desk, and a coffee machine, half filled. But the clock, the expensive furniture, and even the scent of freshly brewed coffee can't conceal the normal lab smell of chemical disinfectant.

At the right-hand side of the room are double doors with

curved brass handles; these must lead to the procedural rooms.

'Can I help you?' the nurse asks me.

I walk directly to her, laying both hands on the counter, willing myself to seem confident, calm. 'I need to speak with someone,' I say. 'It's very urgent.'

'Is this regarding a medical issue?' she asks. She has long fingernails, perfectly filed into rounds, and a face that reminds me of a bulldog – heavy, low-hanging jowls.

'Yes. Well, no. Kind of.' I'm making it up as I go; she frowns, and I try again. 'It's not my medical issue. I need to make a report.' I drop my voice to a whisper. 'Unauthorized activity. I think – I think my neighbours have been infected.'

She drums her fingernails, once, against the counter. 'The best thing to do is make an official report at the police station. You can also go to any of the municipal regulatory stations—'

'No.' I cut her off. Sign-in sheets, clipped together, are stacked next to me, and I straighten them, scanning the list of doctors, patients, problems – *poor sleep/dreaming!*, *deregulated moods*, *flu* – and pick a name at random.

'I insist that I speak to Dr. Branshaw.'

'Are you a patient of the doctor's?' She drums her nails again. She is bored.

'Dr. Branshaw will know what to do. I'm extremely upset. You have to understand. I'm living underneath these people. And my sister – she's uncured. I'm thinking about her, too, you know. Isn't there some kind of – I don't know – vaccination Dr. Branshaw might give her?'

She sighs. She turns her attention to the computer monitor, makes a few quick keystrokes. 'Dr. Branshaw is completely booked up today. All of our medical specialists are booked. An exceptional event has made it necessary—'

'Yeah, I know. Julian Fineman. I know all about it.' I wave my hand.

She frowns at me. Her eyes are guarded. 'How did you know—'

'It's all over the news,' I interrupt her. I'm getting into my role now: the rich, spoiled daughter of a politician, maybe a senior member of the DFA. A girl used to getting her way. 'Of course, I guess you wanted to keep the whole thing hush-hush. Don't want the press charging in. Don't worry, they're not saying where. But I have friends who have friends and . . . well, you know how these things get around.' I lean forward, placing both hands on the desk, like she's my best friend and I'm about to tell her a secret. 'Personally, I think it's a little bit silly, isn't it? If Dr. Branshaw had just given him the cure early, when he was already in there – a little cut, a little snip, that's how it works, isn't it? – this whole thing could have been avoided.' I lean back. 'I'm going to tell him I think so, too, when I see him.' I say a silent prayer that Dr. Branshaw is, in fact, male. It's a decently safe bet. Medical training is long and rigorous, and many intelligent women are expected to spend their time fulfilling their procreative and child-rearing duties instead.

'It isn't Dr. Branshaw's case,' the nurse says quickly. 'He can't be blamed.'

I roll my eyes the way that Hana used to when Andrea Grengol said something especially stupid in class. 'Of course it is. Everyone knows Dr. Branshaw is Julian's primary.'

'Dr. Hillebrand is Julian's primary,' she corrects me.

I feel a quick pulse of excitement, but I hide it with another eye roll. 'Whatever. Are you going to page Dr. Branshaw or not?' I fold my arms and add, 'I won't go until I've seen him.'

She gives me the look of an injured animal – reproachful,

as though I've reached out and pinched her nose. I'm disrupting her morning, the routine stillness of her hours. 'ID, please,' she says.

I fish Sarah Beth Miller's ID from my pocket and pass it to her. The sound of the clock seems to have amplified: the ticking is overloud, and the air in the room vibrates with it. All I can focus on are the seconds, ticking away, ticking Julian closer to death. I force myself not to fidget as she looks it over, frowning again.

'I can't read this number,' she says.

'It went through the dryer last year.' I wave the issue away. 'Look, I'd appreciate it if you could just speak to Dr. Branshaw for me – if you could tell him I'm here.'

'I'll have to call you into SVS,' she says. Now the expression of unhappiness is deepened. She casts a doleful look behind her at the coffeepot, and I notice a magazine half-hidden underneath a stack of files. She is no doubt thinking about the evaporation of her peaceful morning. She hauls herself to her feet. She is a heavy woman. The buttons on her technician's uniform seem to be hanging on for dear life, barely keeping the fabric closed over her breasts and stomach. 'Have a seat. This will take a few minutes.'

I incline my head once, and she waddles through the rows of filing cabinets and disappears. A door opens, and for a moment I hear the sound of a telephone, and the swelling of voices. Then the door shuts, and everything is quiet except for the ticking of the clock.

Instantly, I push through the double doors.

The look of money does not extend this far. Here, at last, are the same dull linoleum tiling, the same dingy beige walls, of so many labs and hospitals. Immediately to my left is another set of double doors, marked EMERGENCY EXIT; through a small glass panel, I see a narrow stairwell.

I move quickly down the hall, my sneakers squeaking on the floor, scanning the doors on either side of me – most of them closed, some of them gaping open, empty, dark.

A female doctor with a stethoscope looped around her neck is walking toward me, consulting a file. She looks up at me curiously as I pass. I keep my eyes locked on the ground. Fortunately, she doesn't stop me. I palm the back of my pants. My hands are sweating.

The lab is small, and when I reach the end of the hall, I see that it is laid out simply: only a single corridor runs the length of the building, and an elevator bank in the back gives access to the remaining six floors. I have no plan except to find Julian, to see him. I'm not sure what I'm hoping to achieve, but the weight of the knife is reassuring, pressed against my stomach, a hard-edged secret.

I take an elevator to the second floor. Here there is more activity: sounds of beeping and murmured conversation, doctors hurrying in and out of examination rooms. I duck quickly into the first door on my right, which turns out to be a bathroom. I take a deep breath, try to focus, try to calm down. There is a tray on the back of the toilet, and a stack of plastic cups meant for urine samples. I grab one and fill it partially with water, then head back into the hall.

Two lab techs, both women, are standing outside one of the examination rooms. They fall silent as I approach, and even though I am deliberately avoiding eye contact, I can feel them staring at me.

'Can I help you?' one of them asks, as I am passing. Both women look identical, and for a moment I think they are twins.

But it is just the influence of the scraped-back hair, the spot-less uniforms, the identical look of clinical detachment.

I flash the plastic cup at them. 'Just need to get my sample to Dr. Hillebrand,' I say.

She withdraws a fraction of an inch. 'Dr. Hillebrand's attendant is on six,' she says. 'You can leave it with her.'

'Thanks,' I say. I can feel their eyes trailing me as I continue down the hall. The air is dry, overheated, and my throat hurts every time I try to swallow. At the end of the hall, I pass a doorway panelled in glass. Beyond it, I see several patients sitting in armchairs, watching television in white paper gowns. Their arms and legs are strapped to the furniture.

At the end of the hall, I push through the doors into the stairwell. In all probability, Dr. Hillebrand will be presiding over Julian's death, and if his attendant is on the sixth floor, there's a good chance that is where he conducts the majority of his work. My legs are shaking by the time I get to six, and I'm not sure whether it's nerves, or lack of sleep, or a combination of both. I ditch the plastic cup, then pause for a second to catch my breath. Sweat is tracing its way down my back.

Please, I think, to nobody in particular. I'm not sure what I'm asking for, exactly. A chance to save him. A chance, even, to see him. I need him to know that I came for him.

I need him to know that somehow, at some point in the tunnels, I began to love him.

Please.

The moment I emerge from the stairwell, I know that I have found it: fifty feet down the hall, Thomas Fineman is standing outside the door to an examination room, arms crossed, with several bodyguards, speaking in low tones to a doctor and three lab techs.

Two, three seconds. I have only a few seconds until they'll turn, until they'll spot me and ask me what I'm doing here.

Their conversation is indecipherable from this distance – they are speaking practically in whispers – and for a second my heart bottoms out and I know that it's too late, and it has already happened, and Julian is dead.

Then the doctor – Dr. Hillebrand? – consults his watch. The next words he speaks are louder – impossibly loud, in the space and the silence, as though he is shouting them.

'It's time,' he says, and as the group starts to unknot, my three seconds are up. I rocket into the first door I see. It's a small examination room, thankfully empty.

I don't know what to do next. Panic is building in my chest. Julian is here, so close, and totally unreachable. There were at least three bodyguards with Thomas Fineman, and I have no doubt there are more inside. I'll never make it past them.

I lean against the door, willing myself to focus, to think. I've ended up in a small antechamber. In one wall is a door that I know must lead to a larger procedural room, where complex surgeries and the procedure to cure *deliria* take place.

A paper-draped table dominates the small space: on it are folded gowns, and a tray of surgical instruments. The room smells like bleach and looks identical to the room in which I undressed for my evaluation, almost a year ago, on the day that started it all, that rocketed me forward and landed me here, in this new body, in this new future. For a second I feel dizzy and have to close my eyes. When I open them, I have the feeling of looking at two mirrors that have been placed face-to-face, of being pushed from the past to the now and back again. Memories begin budding, welling up – the walk to the labs in the sticky Portland air, the wheeling seagulls, the first time I saw Alex, the dark cavern of his mouth as he looked at me from the observation deck, laughing . . .

It hits me: the observation deck. Alex was watching me from an observation deck that ran the length of the procedural room. If this lab is laid out like the one in Portland, I might be able to access Julian's room from the seventh floor.

I move cautiously into the hall again. Thomas Fineman is gone, and only a single bodyguard remains. For a moment I debate whether I should take my chances on him – the knife is there, heavy, waiting, like an urge – but then he turns his eyes in my direction. They are colourless, hard, like two stones; they make me draw back, as though he has reached down the length of the hall and hit me.

Before he can say anything, before he has time to register my face, I slip around the corner and into the stairwell.

The seventh floor is darker and dingier than any of the others. It is perfectly silent: no conversations humming behind closed doors, no steady beep of medical machinery or lab techs squeaking down the halls in white sneakers. Everything is still, as though the air up here is not often disturbed. A series of doorways extends down the hall on my right. My heart leaps when I see the first one is labelled OBSERVATION DECK A.

I ease down the hall on tiptoe. There's obviously no one up here, but the quiet makes me nervous. There is something ominous about all the closed doors, the air heavy and hot like a blanket; I get the creeping feeling that someone is watching me, that all the doors are mouths, ready to open and scream out my presence.

The last door in the hall is marked OBSERVATION DECK D. My palms are sweating so badly, I can barely twist open the door handle. At the last second I remove my knife from the front pocket of my wind breaker, just in case, and uncoil Mrs. Fineman's T-shirt from around the blade. Then I drop into a crouch and scuttle through the door onto the observation deck. I'm gripping the knife so tightly, my knuckles ache.

The deck is big, dark, and empty, and shaped like an L, extending along two whole walls of the procedural room below. It is completely enclosed in glass and contains four tiered rows of chairs, all of which look down over the main floor. It smells like a movie theatre, like damp upholstery and gum.

I ease down the stairs of the deck, keeping close to the ground, grateful that the lights in the observation deck are off – and grateful, too, that the low plaster wall that encircles the deck, underneath the heavy panels of glass, should conceal me at least partially from the view of anyone below me. I ease off my backpack and place it carefully next to me. My shoulders are aching.

I have no idea what to do next.

The lights in the procedural room are dazzling. There is a metal table in the centre of the room, and a couple of lab techs circulating, adjusting equipment, moving things out of the way. Thomas Fineman and a few other men – the men from the hall – have been moved into an adjacent room; it, too, is enclosed in glass, and although chairs have been set up for them, they are all standing. I wonder what Fineman is thinking. I think, briefly, of Julian's mother. I wonder where she is.

I don't see Julian anywhere.

A flash of light. I think *explosion* – I think *run* – and everything in me knots up, tight and panicked, until I notice that in one corner is a man with a camera and a media badge clipped to his tie. He is taking pictures of the setup, and the glare of the flash bounces off all the polished metal surfaces, zigzagging up the walls.

Of course. I should have known that the media would be invited to take pictures. They must record it, and broadcast it, in order for it to have any meaning.

The hatred surges, and with it, a cresting, swelling wave of fury. All of them can burn.

There is motion from the corner, from the part of the room concealed underneath the deck. I see Thomas Fineman and the other men swivel in that direction. Behind the glass, Thomas wipes his forehead with a handkerchief, the first sign of discomfort he has shown. The cameraman swivels too: flash, flash. Two moments of blinding white light.

Then Julian enters the room. He is flanked by two regulators, although he is walking on his own, without prompting. They are tailed by a man wearing the high white collar of a priest; he holds a gold-bound copy of *The Book of Shhh* in front of his chest, like a talisman to protect him from everything dirty and terrible in the world.

The hatred is a cord, tightening around my throat.

Julian's hands have been handcuffed in front of him, and he is wearing a dark blue blazer and neatly pressed jeans. I wonder if that was his choice, or whether they made him dress up for his own execution. He is facing away from me and I will him, silently, to turn around, to look up. I need him to know that I'm here. I need him to know he's not alone. I reach my hand out unthinkingly, grope along the glass. I want to smash it to pieces, to jump down and swoop Julian away. But it would never work. I could not get more than a few feet, and then it would be a double execution.

Maybe it no longer matters. I have nothing left, nothing to return to.

The regulators have stopped at the table. There is a swelling of conversation – I hear Julian say, 'I'd rather not lie down.' His voice is muffled and indistinct – from the glass, from the height – but the sound of it makes me want to scream. Now my whole body is a heartbeat, a throbbing urge to do something. But I'm frozen, heavy as stone.

One of the regulators steps forward and unchains Julian's hands. Julian pivots so I can see his face. He circles his wrists, forward and back, wincing a bit. Almost immediately, the regulator clips his right wrist to one of the legs of the metal table, pushing down on Julian's shoulder so he is forced to sit. He has not once looked at his father.

In the corner of the room, the doctor is washing his hands in a large sink. The water drumming against the metal is over-loud. It is too quiet. Surely executions can't happen here, like this, in the bright and the silence. The doctor dries his hands, works his fingers into a pair of latex surgical gloves.

The priest steps forward and begins to read. His voice is a low drone, a monotone, muffled through the glass.

'And so Isaac grew and was the pride of his aged father, and for a time a perfect reflection of Abraham's will . . .'

He is reading from the Book of Abraham. Of course. In it, God commands Abraham to kill his only son, Isaac, after Isaac becomes sick with the *deliria*. And so he does. He takes his son to a mountain and plunges a knife straight through his chest. I wonder whether Mr. Fineman requested that this passage be read. Obedience to God, to safety, to the natural order: that is what the Book of Abraham teaches us.

'But when Abraham saw that Isaac had become unclean, he asked in his heart for guidance . . .'

I am swallowing back Julian's name. *Look at me.*

The doctor and two lab techs step forward. The doctor has

a syringe. He is testing it, flicking its barrel with a finger, as a lab tech rolls Julian's shirt to his elbow.

Just then there is a disturbance from below. It ripples through the room at once. Julian looks up sharply; the doctor steps away from him and replaces the syringe on the metal tray one of the lab techs carries. Thomas Fineman leans over, frowning, and whispers something to a bodyguard, as another lab tech bursts into the room. I can't make out what she's saying – I can tell it's a she, even though she's wearing a paper mask and a bulky, too-big lab coat, because of the braid swinging down her back – but she is gesturing agitatedly.

Something is wrong.

I inch closer to the glass, straining to hear what she is saying. A thought is fluttering in the back of my mind, an idea I can't quite hold on to. There's something familiar about the lab tech, about the way she keeps using her hands, gesturing emphatically as she points the doctor out into the hall. He shakes his head, removes his gloves, and balls them up into his pocket. He barks a short command before striding out of the procedural room. One of the lab techs scurries after him.

Thomas Fineman is pushing his way to the door that gives entry to the lab. Julian is pale, and even from here I can tell that he is sweating. His voice is higher than normal, strained.

'What's going on?' His voice floats up to me. 'Someone tell me what's happening.'

The lab tech with the braid has moved across the room and is opening the door for Thomas Fineman. She reaches into her lab coat as he bursts into the room, red-faced.

And just when the idea breaks, washes over me – the braid, the hands, Raven – there is a single explosion, a cracking noise, and Thomas Fineman's mouth falls open, and he teeters backward and slumps to the ground as red petals of blood bloom outward across his shirt front.

For a moment, everything seems to freeze: Thomas Fineman, splayed on the ground like a rag doll; Julian, white-faced on the table; the journalist with the camera still raised to his eye; the priest in the corner; the regulators next to Julian, weapons still strapped to their belts; Raven holding a gun.

Flash.

The lab tech, the real one, screams.

And everything is chaos.

More gunshots, ricocheting around the room. The regulators are screaming, 'Down! Get down!'

Crack. A bullet lodges in the thick glass directly above my head, and from it a web of fissures begins to grow. That's all I need. I grab a chair from behind me and swing it, hard, in an arc, praying that Julian has his head down.

The sound is tremendous, and for a split second everything is silent again except for the cascade of glass, a sharp-pointed rain. Then I vault over the concrete wall and drop to the floor below me. Glass crunches under my sneakers as I land, off balance, tipping down onto one hand to steady myself, which comes up smeared with blood.

Raven is a blur of motion. She twists her body out of reach of a regulator, doubles back, cracks down hard on his knee with the butt of her gun. As he bends forward, she plants a foot in his back and pushes: a *crack* as his head collides with the metal sink. And she is already turning toward the room that contains Fineman's bodyguards, shoving a small metal scalpel into the keyhole of the door, jamming it. She wedges a metal rolling tray in front of the door for good measure.

Medical instruments scatter everywhere as they push, shouting, tilting the table several inches. But the door won't open, at least not just yet.

I'm ten feet from Julian – shouting, gunshots, and now an alarm is wailing, shrieking – then five feet, then next to him, grabbing his arms, his shoulders, wanting simply to feel him, to make sure he's real.

'Lena!' He has been struggling with the handcuff that keeps one of his wrists clipped to the table, trying to pry it off. Now he looks up, eyes bright, shining, blue as sky. 'What are you—'

'No time,' I tell him. 'Stay low.'

I sprint toward the regulator still slumped by the sinks. Dimly, I am aware of shouting, and Raven still turning, spinning, ducking – from a distance, she might be dancing – and muffled explosions. The journalist is gone; he must have run.

The regulator is barely conscious. I kneel down and slice off his belt, quick, then grab the keys and sprint back toward the table. My right palm is wet with blood, but I can barely feel the pain. It takes me two tries to fit the key in the lock on the handcuffs; then I do, and Julian pulls his wrist free of the table, and draws me toward him.

'You came,' he says.

'Of course,' I say.

Then Raven is next to us. 'Time to move.'

A minute, maybe less, and Thomas Fineman is dead, and the room is chaos, and we are free.

We sprint through the antechamber just as there is a shuddering, tinny crash, a clattering of metal, and a crescendo of shouts – the bodyguards must have gotten out. Then we duck into the hall, where the alarms are blaring and already we can hear pounding feet from the stairwell.

Raven jerks her head to the right, toward a door marked ROOFTOP ACCESS, EMERGENCIES ONLY. We move quickly, in silence, wound up – through the door and onto the fire escape. Then we pound down the metal stairs, single file, toward the street level. Raven wrestles out of her oversized lab coat and slips off the paper mask, discarding them in a Dumpster just underneath the stairs. I wonder where she got them, and I flash to the heavy woman at the front desk, her breasts nearly exploding out of her lab coat.

'This way,' Raven says shortly, as soon as we're on the ground. When she turns her head, I see that she has several small cuts on her cheek and neck; the glass must have skimmed her.

We've ended up in a small, dingy courtyard, dominated by a set of rusted patio furniture and a patch of wiry brown grass. It is enclosed in a low chain-link fence, which Raven climbs easily. It is a little harder for me, and Julian, who is following, puts a hand up to steady me. My hand has started throbbing, and the chain-link is slick. It's raining harder now.

On the other side of the fence is another tiny courtyard, nearly identical to the first, and another bleak brown building. Raven charges right through the door, which has been propped open with a cinder block, and we pass into a dark hall, and more closed doors affixed with gold placards. For a second I panic that we've ended up back in the labs. But then we emerge into a large lobby, also dark, and outfitted with several fake potted plants and various signs that point the way to EDWARD WU, ESQ. and METROPOLITAN VISION ASSOCIATES. A set of glass revolving doors gives us a blurry view of the street outside: people streaming by, carrying umbrellas, jostling one another.

Raven heads right for the doors, pausing just long enough to scoop up a backpack she must have stashed earlier behind one of the plants. She turns around and tosses Julian and me an umbrella each. She slips on a yellow rain slicker and pulls the hood up over her head, cinching it tight so the cuts on her face are concealed.

Then we are flowing out into the street, moving into the blur of people on their way to or from somewhere – a faceless crowd, a mass of moving bodies. Never have I been more grateful for the hugeness of Manhattan, for its appetite; we are swallowed in it and by it, we become no one and anyone: a woman in a yellow poncho; a short girl in a red wind breaker; a boy with his face concealed by an enormous umbrella.

We make a right on Eighth Avenue, then a left on 24th Street. By now we have escaped the crowd: the streets are empty, the buildings blind, curtains drawn and shutters closed against the rain. Light smoulders behind tissue-thin curtains above us; rooms turned inward, with their backs up against the street. We go undetected, unobserved, through the grey and watery world. The gutters are gushing, swirling with trash, bits of paper and cigarette butts. I have dropped Julian's hand, but he walks close to me, adjusting his stride to the rhythm of my walk, so we are almost touching.

We come to a parking lot, empty except for a white van I recognize: the van outfitted like a CRAP cruiser. I think once again of my mother, but this is no time to ask Raven about her. Raven unlocks the double doors at the back of the van and flips off her hood.

'In,' she says.

Julian hesitates for a second. I see his eyes skating over the words: CITY OF NEW YORK, DEPARTMENT OF CORRECTION, REFORM, AND PURIFICATION.

'It's okay,' I say, and climb into the back, sitting cross-legged on the dirty floor. He follows me in. Raven nods at me and shuts the door behind us. I hear her climb into the passenger seat. Then there is silence except for the drumming rain on the thin tin ceiling. Its rhythm sends a humming vibration through my whole body. It's cold.

'What—,' Julian asks, but I shush him. We are not out of danger, not yet, and I will not relax until we are safely out of the city. I use the wind breaker to wipe the blood off my palm, ball up its hem, and squeeze.

We hear pounding footsteps, the driver's door opening, and Tack's voice, a grunt. 'Got 'em?'

Raven's reply: 'Would I be here if I hadn't?'

'You're bleeding.'

'Just a scratch.'

'Let's roll, then.'

The engine shudders to life, and all of a sudden I could shout for joy. Raven and Tack are back – snapping at each other, as they have always done and will always do. They came for me, and now we will go north: we are on the same side again. We will return to the Wilds, and I'll see Hunter again, and Sarah, and Lu.

We will curl back into ourselves, like a fern folding up against the frost, and leave the resistance to its guns and its plans, and the Scavengers to their tunnels, and the DFA to their cures, and the whole world to its sickness and blindness. We will let it fall to ruin. We will be safe, shielded under the trees, nesting like birds.

And I have Julian. I found him, and he followed me. I reach out in the half-dark, wordlessly, and find his hands. We interlace our fingers, and though he doesn't say anything either, I can feel the warmth and energy passing between us, a soundless dialogue. *Thank you*, he is saying, and I am saying, *I am so happy, I am so happy, I needed you to be safe.*

I hope he understands.

I have not slept in twenty-four hours, and despite the jerking motion of the van, and the thunderous sound of the rain, at some point, I fall asleep. When I wake, it is because Julian is speaking my name quietly. I am resting on his lap, inhaling the smell of his jeans. I sit up quickly, embarrassed, rubbing my eyes.

'We've stopped,' he says, although it's obvious. The rain has faded to a gentle patter. The van doors slam; Raven and Tack are hooting, exuberant and loud. We must have made it well past the border.

The double doors swing open and there Raven is, beaming, and Tack behind her, arms crossed, looking pleased with himself. I recognize the old warehouse from the cracked surface of the parking lot, and the peaked outhouse behind Tack.

Raven offers me her hand, helping me scoot out of the van. Her grip is strong.

'What's the magic phrase?' she says, as soon as my feet hit the pavement. She is relaxed now, smiling and easy.

'How did you find me?' I ask. She wants me to say thank you, but I don't. I don't have to. She gives my hand a squeeze before pulling away, and I know she knows how grateful I am.

'There was only one place you would be,' she says, and her eyes flick behind me, to Julian, and then back to me. And I know that is her way of making peace with me, and admitting she was wrong.

Julian has climbed out of the van too, and he is staring around him, wide-eyed, mouth hanging open. His hair is still wet, and has started to curl just a little at the ends.

'It's okay,' I say to him. I reach back and take his hand. The joy surges through me again. Here it is okay to hold hands, to huddle together for warmth, to mould ourselves together at night, like statues designed to fit side by side.

'Come on!' Tack is walking backward, half skipping, toward the warehouse. 'We're packing up and moving out. We've lost a day already. Hunter will be waiting with the others in Connecticut.'

Raven hitches her backpack a little higher and winks. 'You know how Hunter gets when he's cranky,' she says. 'We better get moving.'

I can sense Julian's confusion. The patter of dialogue and strange names, the closeness of the trees, untrimmed and untended, must be overwhelming. But I will teach him, and he will love it. He will learn and love, and love to learn. The words stream through me – calming, beautiful. There is time for absolutely everything now.

'Wait!' I jog after Raven as she starts to follow Tack into the warehouse. Julian hangs back. I keep my voice low so Julian can't hear.

'Did – did you know?' I say, swallowing hard. I feel out of breath, though I've run less than twenty feet. 'About my mom, I mean.'

Raven looks at me, confused. 'Your mom?'

'Shhh.' For some reason I don't want Julian to overhear – it is too much, too deep, too soon.

Raven shakes her head.

'The woman who came for me at Salvage,' I say, persisting despite Raven's look of total confusion. 'She has a tattoo on her neck – 5996. That's my mother's intake number, from the Crypts.' I swallow. 'That's my mother.'

Raven reaches out two fingers as though to touch my shoulder, then thinks better of it and drops her hand. 'I'm sorry, Lena. I had no idea.' Her voice is uncharacteristically gentle.

'I have to talk to her before we go,' I say. 'There are – there are things I need to say.' Really, there is only one thing I want to say, and just thinking of it makes my heart speed up: *Why, why, why? Why did you let them take you? Why did you let me think you were dead? Why didn't you come for me?*

Why didn't you love me more?

Once you let in the word, once you allow it to take root, it will spread like a mould through all of your corners and dark spaces – and with it, the questions, the shivery, splintered fears, enough to keep you permanently awake. The DFA is right about that, at least.

Raven draws her eyebrows together. 'She's gone, Lena.'

My mouth goes dry. 'What do you mean?'

Raven shrugs. 'She left this morning with some of the others. They're higher-level than I am. I don't know where they were headed. I'm not supposed to ask.'

'She's . . . she's part of the resistance, then?' I ask, even though it's obvious.

Raven nods. 'Top-top,' she says gently, as though that makes up for anything. She spreads her hands. 'That's all I know.'

I look away, biting my lip. To the south, the clouds are breaking up, like wool slowly unravelling, revealing patches of bare blue sky. 'For most of my life, I thought she was dead,' I say. I don't know why I tell her, or what difference it will make.

She does touch me then, skimming my elbow. 'Someone arrived from Portland last night – a fugitive. Escaped the Crypts after the bombing. He hasn't said much, hasn't even given his name. I'm not sure what they did to him up there, but—' Raven breaks off. 'Anyway, he might know something about your mom. About her time there, at least.'

'Okay,' I say. Disappointment makes me feel heavy, dull. I don't bother telling Raven that my mom was kept in solitary the whole time she was in prison – and besides, I don't need to know what she was like then. I want to know her now.

'I'm sorry,' Raven repeats, and I can tell she means it. 'But at least you know she's free, right? She's free and she's safe.' Raven smiles briefly. 'Like you.'

'Yeah.' She's right, of course. The disappointment breaks apart a little. Free and safe – me, Julian, Raven, Tack, my mom. We're all going to be okay.

'I'm going to see if Tack needs help,' Raven says, turning businesslike again. 'We leave tonight.'

I nod. Despite everything that has happened, it feels good to talk to Raven, and to see her like this – in go mode. That's how it should be. She pushes into the warehouse, and I stand for a moment, closing my eyes, inhaling the cold air: smells of damp earth and wet bark; a moist, wet smell of renewal. We'll be okay. And someday, I'll find my mom again.

'Lena?' Julian's voice pipes up quietly, behind me. I turn. He's standing near the van, arms hanging heavily at his sides, as though he's afraid to move in this new world. 'Are you okay?'

Seeing him there – with the trees spread out darkly on all sides of us, and the clouds retreating – joy wells up in me again. Suddenly I am closing the space between us, not thinking, and barrelling into his arms with so much force he almost topples backward. 'Yes,' I say. 'I'm okay. We're okay.' I laugh. 'Everything's going to be fine now.'

'You saved me,' he whispers. I can feel his mouth moving against my forehead. The touch of his lips makes heat dance through me. 'I couldn't believe – I never thought you would come.'

'I had to.' I pull away so that I can look up at him, keeping my arms looped around his waist. He rests his hands on my back. Even though I have spent a long time in the Wilds, it strikes me again that it is a miracle to stand this way with someone. No one can tell us no. No one can make us stop. We have picked each other, and the rest of the world can go to hell.

Julian reaches up and brushes a piece of hair out of my eyes. 'What happens now?' he asks.

'Anything we want,' I say. The joy is a surge: I could soar away on it, ride it all the way to the sky.

'Anything?' Julian's smile spreads slowly from his lips to his eyes.

'Anything and everything,' I say, and Julian and I move at the same time, and find each other's lips. At first, it's clumsy: his nose bumps my lips, and then my chin bumps his chin. But he's smiling, and we take our time, and find each other's rhythm. I run my lips lightly over his, explore his tongue, softly, with mine. He puts his fingers in my hair. I inhale the smell of his skin, fresh and also woodsy, like soap and evergreen trees, mixed. We kiss slowly, gently, because now we have all the time in the world – nothing but time, and the space to get to know each other freely, and to kiss as much as we want. My life is beginning again.

Julian pulls away to look at me. He traces my jaw with one finger. 'I think – I think you've given it to me,' he says, slightly out of breath. 'The *deliria*.'

'Love,' I say, and squeeze his waist. 'Say it.'

He hesitates for just a second. 'Love,' he says, testing the word. Then he smiles. 'I think I like it.'

'You'll grow to love it. Trust me.' I raise myself on my tiptoes and Julian kisses my nose, then skims his lips over my cheekbones, brushing against my ear, planting tiny kisses across the crown of my head.

'Promise me we'll stay together, okay?' His eyes are once again the clear blue of a perfectly transparent pool. They are eyes to swim in, to float in, forever. 'You and me.'

'I promise,' I say.

Behind us the door creaks open, and I turn around, expecting Raven, just as a voice cuts through the air: 'Don't believe her.'

The whole world closes around me, like an eyelid: for a moment, everything goes dark.

I am falling. My ears are full of rushing; I have been sucked into a tunnel, a place of pressure and chaos. My head is about to explode.

He looks different. He is much thinner, and a scar runs from his eyebrow all the way down to his jaw. On his neck, just behind his left ear, a small tattooed number curves around the three-pronged scar that fooled me, for so long, into believing he was cured. His eyes – once a sweet, melted brown, like syrup – have hardened. Now they are stony, impenetrable.

Only his hair is the same: that auburn crown, like leaves in autumn.

Impossible. I close my eyes and reopen them: the boy from a dream, from a different lifetime. A boy brought back from the dead.

Alex.